NEW STORIES
FROM THE SOUTH

The Year's Best, 1997

The editor wishes to thank Memsy Price,
whose taste, skill, and tact are essential
to this anthology.

Edited by
Shannon Ravenel

with a preface by Robert Olen Butler

NEW STORIES
FROM THE SOUTH

The Year's Best, 1997

Algonquin Books of Chapel Hill

Published by
ALGONQUIN BOOKS OF CHAPEL HILL
Post Office Box 2225
Chapel Hill, North Carolina 27515-2225

a division of
WORKMAN PUBLISHING
708 Broadway
New York, New York 10003

ISSN 0897-9073
ISBN 1-56512-175-9

CONTENTS

Editor's Note: *After writing eleven prefaces to this annual anthology, I have come to realize that a single preface writer has a limited store of fresh arguments for reading, relishing, and celebrating the yearly crop of outstanding short fiction being written in and about the American South. There are, of course, many more arguments than mine to be made. And who better to make them than those who believe in them most? Thus we turn to the short story writers themselves—from this edition on, one of each year's contributors will be invited to introduce the collection. As Robert Olen Butler's inaugural guest preface proves, there is indeed more to say and more to learn about the short story, Southern or otherwise.* —Shannon Ravenel

PREFACE

I'm here to declare a truce. For eleven years Shannon Ravenel has offered us remarkable annual collections of short stories from a region she knows and loves. In her prefaces to these volumes, she has frequently strived, with a splendid articulateness, to identify what "Southern" is, sometimes in response to reviewer challenges that have ranged from befuddled to whiny to hostile.

But I remember as a kid reading those wonderful Viking Portable and Modern Library story anthologies—*The Irish Reader* and *The Russian Reader* and *Great German Short Novels and Stories* and *An Anthology of Famous British Stories*—and I doubt if anyone ever dreamed of fussing at these collections over what "Irish" might really be, or "Russian" or "German" or "British." There were works in these volumes by writers who shared something legitimate—a place—but this something faded well into the background as soon as the books were opened. For these were stories spoken into existence by dream-driven personal visions of the way the world works, or fails to, at its deepest levels. Which is to say, these were works of art.

And, ultimately, art does not spring from geography or sociology or anthropology or politics. The writers themselves understand that. For more than a decade, because of some obvious elements in many of my books, I was often referred to as a "Vietnam writer." Then, after I'd settled into Louisana and begun to draw on that rich locale in my work, I was perceived in many places as a "Southern writer." These were two expressions of the same phenomenon. Some years ago I appeared on a panel in Washington, D.C., with Tim O'Brien, Larry Heinemann, and Phil Caputo, where a reporter asked us to speak of our roles as "Vietnam novelists." Just that morning I'd been wandering around the National Gallery, and it occurred to me to answer in these terms: if a writer aspires to art, then to call him a "Vietnam novelist" is like calling Monet a "lily-pad painter." The same is true of the label "Southern novelist." For the artist, her cultural history or her settings are simply the surface, sensual ways into her true matter—be it, for the visual artist, the deepest nature of color and light and form or, for the literary artist . . . what?

What, if not Southernness, is this collection of stories about? What is the essential matter of a piece of fiction? It seems to me that fiction has a very few absolutely inescapable characteristics from which flow, inevitably, the essence of the art form. Fiction is about human beings, certainly, and, more precisely, human feelings. But there is another, often overlooked, characteristic of fiction that beats at the heart of the best works and is silent in the center of works that fail.

Fiction is a temporal art form. When a writer lets the length of the written line run on and turns the page, that writer is "upon a time." And one can learn from any Buddhist how difficult— indeed, impossible—it is to exist in time as a human being on the planet Earth without desiring something. Without *yearning* for something. This is not the same, by the way, as having problems, which is a passive, static thing. Yearning is the dynamic of our lives. And so fiction is, at its heart, the art form of human yearning.

James Joyce identified the experience of a short story by appropriating the notion of "epiphany" from the Catholic Church. The word, from the Greek, literally means a "showing forth" or a "shining forth." The church applies it to the manifestation of Christ's divinity to the Gentiles in the persons of the Magi. Joyce applied it to the moment at the end of a story when a character or a situation shines forth in its essence. And this is a true and crucial understanding of the art form. But I think there are two epiphanies in the best stories: the one that Joyce describes and one that occurs very near the beginning of a story. In this prior epiphany, the central character's yearning shines forth. And from this, everything else follows.

This year's *New Stories from the South* is full of this essence of the fictional art, from Dale Ray Phillips's narrator in "Corporal Love," striving to find the way to transubstantiate carnal delight into spiritual love, to Charles East's central character in "Pavane for a Dead Princess," aching for the company of the angelic as she faces death alone. And there is yearning in all the stories in between, whether they be set in a "two-story, caved-in, paint-peeling dump" in Ramone, Texas, on the deck of a yacht off the coast of Miami, or in a house in New Orleans "a mere two well-placed sticks of dynamite away from oblivion."

These are, in the sublimely simple premise of this collection, all places in the South, brought to life by writers with a feel for the rich and varied sensual particularities of each. But I say to those who read this volume, let there be peace now about what the South was or is or isn't. Here, a lily pad is never just a lily pad. Here, the "South" is just a great excuse to bring some wonderful artists together to peer deep into the yearnings of the human heart.

—Robert Olen Butler
Lake Charles, Louisiana
1997

Publisher's Note

The stories reprinted in *New Stories from the South: The Year's Best, 1997* were selected from American short stories published in magazines issued between January and December 1996. Shannon Ravenel annually consults a list of ninety-five nationally distributed American periodicals and makes her choices for this anthology based on criteria that include original publication first-serially in magazine form and publication as short stories. Direct submissions are not considered.

NEW STORIES
FROM THE SOUTH

The Year's Best, 1997

Dale Ray Phillips

CORPORAL LOVE

(from *Story*)

I first heard about the types of love in the seventh grade, when pursed-lipped teachers herded the girls into the library and corralled the boys in the gymnasium so that experts could explain sex. The lecturer—a man about my age now—was the local Army recruiter who made extra money terrorizing adolescent audiences with the consequences of Onan's sin (hairy palms and a deterioration of the thought processes) and premarital sex (venereal diseases and Eternal Damnation). His military uniform included a hat neatly tucked and folded along his beltline. He resembled a cross between a scoutmaster and an officer—a lower level ambassador in the hierarchy of passion.

"Hey, Corporal Love," someone yelled. The name stuck—he didn't seem decorated enough to be a real officer. "Get to the good stuff. Tell us about poontang."

His lecture was supplemented with slides depicting the male and female reproductive organs and a film about the horrors of gonorrhea and syphilis. The diseases didn't scare anyone; penicillin could cure anything, and besides, it took twenty or so years for the spirochetes to crawl up the urinary tract and infect the brain or spinal column. Corporal Love showed the facade of Dix's Hill— the mental asylum for our region of North Carolina—and of the hundred-plus windows, fifteen or so were X-ed over because they housed syphilitically insane patients. At age thirteen, a bed in a room where you were crazy seemed a fair price to pay for twenty years of unmitigated fornication.

After the disappointing slide show (just diagrams, not real genitals) and the film ("Where are the *tits*?" Skeeter Rainy kept yelling. "My dad has films with women who show their tits.") an open discussion followed. Corporal Love invited us to bellow out every name we knew for genitalia. He chuckled and smoked a cigarette thoughtfully. In our junior high, teachers hid in the lounge to smoke, and this unabashed violation of etiquette was exotic. He bet our arsenal of nouns and verbs for sex would be exhausted before he finished his cigarette. He was right.

Then he stormed into a discourse on love. He named the four types: for God and country; between parents and children; the intellectual kind between friends; and the combustible feeling that exists between men and women. Of these, God and country was highest, and he quoted Latin to prove it—*dulce et decorum est pro patria mori*. This was during Vietnam, when men were saying no to that particular commitment. Would we give our bodies for freedom, our blood to staunch the red tide of communism? We all knew he would not unveil door number four until he received a correct answer.

"Yes, Corporal Love," we shouted.

"I can't *hear* you."

"Yes, Sir," we thundered.

We had pleased Corporal Love, and he smiled. He explained carnal love was lowly but necessary. Its function was to build a populace, a nation. He shook his head sadly and prophesied that many of us would become slaves to sexual desire. His message was simple: We should save ourselves for the right woman to marry, but we should be prepared in this holy quest to stumble a time or two. We must pick ourselves up and persevere. God, America, and our future wives required a pure heart. He then spoke of girls who did it, whom we should avoid. Our mission in life was to win the affections of a girl who was of a pure essence. We should marry and worship her. It was spiritual love versus carnal delights, and he made the flesh irresistible.

Three weeks later, on a hunting trip with my father and uncle, my father made a joke about my having found my Willie. I reddened because he knew why I stayed in the shower long after the hot water ran cold. A doe was strapped to the car's hood; we would eat hunter's fare—backstrap meat with biscuits and gravy—that night. My uncle had recently returned from Vietnam in one piece with stories of communist prostitutes with razors hidden in their vaginas and anecdotes of the pleasures a pack of Winstons would fetch. My father countered with escapades involving Korean women. Then they remembered I was in the backseat and stopped their reminiscing. My uncle decided to pull over and urinate before the old logging road fed into the hard-topped highway. He asked for the time, pulled a pill from his pocket, and washed the capsule down with a Blue Ribbon. My father said he was tired of me snitching beer from the refrigerator and handed me one. My uncle braced both hands on either side of the deer and grunted when the stream finally shot forth.

My father explained his brother had come home with an Asian malady difficult to cure. I explained what Corporal Love had told us about penicillin. My father nodded—not really listening—and contemplated the doe with its little lopsided tongue. He had been distant since my mother left a month before to "visit" a friend. He tossed back another beer and warned me to watch out for the stuff. I didn't know if he meant booze or his and my mother's misfortune or what my uncle had contracted in southeast Asia. I repeated the Corporal's words, *Love's Diseases*, in a silent litany. I reasoned I was immune to them because I wasn't allergic to the cure.

My first love knocked out my front incisor so I could buy her a charm bracelet with the tooth fairy money. She climbed the dogwood which straddled our yards, perched on a limb so that her foot was level with my mouth, and punted. She took out several other baby teeth in the process; we were rich for a week, and she treated me like a wounded hero. I was eight or nine and couldn't understand why her bald biscuit excited such a stiffening when we played doctor. My penis made a little tent of feelings in my shorts. Her eighth-grade sister dated boys with cars. Big sister had explained the mechanics of coupling to Holly, who relayed them to me. These dispatches got garbled in the translation; Holly explained we were supposed to pee on each other. Inside a double-wide playhouse built of refrigerator boxes her brothers had taped together, Holly and I fumbled with the adult concept of union. If I swept the dirt floors and brought bologna sandwiches from home, I got a glimpse of what I would later learn to call her mound of Venus. For a timed minute on her Cinderella watch, Holly allowed me to stroke and kiss something as foreign as the moonscape. *You're so nasty,* she'd say. *Go home now before anyone knows.* When I rounded the corner of her house, her other boyfriend Monty Sox ambushed me. If I curled up like an armadillo, he couldn't kick my stomach. Often, Holly would hear us and come watch. Sometimes she'd throw a rock at him or threaten to call her brothers, who smoked cigarettes in front of their parents and threatened the life of a mailman trying to deliver a draft notice.

"You took that beating for me, didn't you?" Holly said. She called me her champion. "He said dirty things about what we do, so you stood up for my honor." I agreed. All the notions I had about happiness and America would get entangled with this girl-next-door. When they teach you that our country is a woman whose virtue must be protected, what else is a fellow to think?

Certain weekends when I was seventeen, while Walter Cronkite recapped the Watergate hearings, my father announced it was time for a barbeque and dragged out the grill. Senator Sam's soothing drawl seemed better dining music than the previous years' body counts or race riots. Looking back, my people always took their meals to a backdrop of broadcast misfortune, but of all the woes we broke bread over, none seemed sadder than the lonesomeness of supper in a house love had abandoned. My father sensed this, and if my mother was between boyfriends, he'd phone and coax her over for a family reunion though their divorce was finalized. If she were melancholy and needed propping up, she'd arrive around five. Holly's parents, the Locklears, were invited; my father had started an electrical wiring company with Holly's father Lamar. Holly's mother Wanda and my mother had been high school homecoming queens; they sipped Tab laced with gin and complimented each other on their girlish figures. Glasses clinked as toasts were made to happy times in rented seaside bungalows where we had vacationed together. When the gin was gone some whiskey got opened; the first fire went to ashes and I laid another. Those afternoons, whatever conspiracy my parents had enjoyed somehow surfaced. My father and Lamar raced the car's engine and peeled tires like teenagers as they went to buy steaks.

"He's still in love with me," my mother said once, as the LaSabre fishtailed away. "That's probably the most flattering thing in the world."

"Why don't you love him back?" I asked.

"Oh, Richard," she said, "I do. I'm just not *in* love with him. I hope you never have to know the difference."

Holly and I were engaged by then, and our parents always insisted we drive to the VFW and have a drink. My father commandeered the Harley and drove my mother while I chauffeured the Locklears. Post 349 had a cement dance floor and a brown bag license. People formed couples and danced to "Blue Moon Over Kentucky." When our parents wobbled huffing back to the table, Holly and I made our excuses and our exit. Sometimes, whole groups of couples would gather in the gravel parking lot to admire the Harley's grumbling and talk motorcycle talk before we roared off. Once, someone threw wedding rice from a reception held a few days earlier. Our parents waved as we left, and I could never tell if they were acknowledging what they remembered or what they still believed in.

Holly and I drove through the countryside to a deserted mill village that resembled a ghost town. The houses were gutted shells of themselves missing panes and sinks and copper tubing. Anything of worth had been confiscated and sold for salvage. It was difficult to imagine people laughing and playing checkers and giving birth in these barren rooms. The deserted village had sidewalks sprouting grass and a church with a condemned sign that resembled a bigger mill house with a steeple. For some superstitious reason, the pews and part of the altar were intact.

I lost my virginity on the splintery floor of that church. Holly simply grinned, sat astraddle me, wriggled, and I exploded. After that my catechumenical instruction began. Holly showed me where to touch, what force to use, when to hold back, and when to un-rein. Nothing was forbidden: We tried fellatio in the pulpit, cunnilingus in the choir box, dorsal commingling before the altar. Our moans and gasps congregated in the empty corners and came back at us as the oldest of cantatas. The roof had a hole from wind damage, and lying beside Holly after love, looking up into the evening's first stars, I'd physically shudder. Holly would make the joke about someone walking over my grave and we'd make love again and have our laugh at time. Then we'd talk about our future after I went to college, the house we'd buy, and the names we would give our children.

This was in 1973.

My next engagement was ten years later to Felice. I was nearly thirty and had spent my twenties on relationships with a string of dancers. The first graduate school I quit boasted a dance department with a building of mirrored rooms where women in tights fought gravity to hang suspended in space. My forays were more earthbound. I jumped from a first-story bedroom window when Sharon's boyfriend surprised us on Halloween, got dumped by Vanessa for a female potter whose hands knew shapes. Once, I woke up bound to a bed while a woman in a merry widow painted my toenails. The soaring love I promised each of these women crashed. The casualties mounted, and I became a veteran of such skirmishes.

Watch the evening news—disasters must be reported calmly. I slugged Felice once, during a lover's argument, as she was beating on me and screaming that I would *not* ignore her. When I hit her, it seemed like slow motion. She ran into the bedroom and called 911. Our apartment was in a converted Victorian house, and though she had locked the bedroom door, the phone jack was in the hall. When I unplugged it, her threats became serious. I wondered, would our neighbors ignore us as we did them when they fought? Prostrate before the locked door, I begged forgiveness. I was the essence of a batterer.

We sought help from a therapist who specialized in domestic disharmony. She smoked more than I did, and she openly flirted with me. This therapist lit my cigarettes and asked for details of my sex habits and fantasies. When Felice piped up, she'd cut her short.

"It's probably just part of the counseling process," I told Felice as she complained on the way home from our third and last visit. We both had been accepted to graduate schools in different states, and were plotting escapes.

In addition to the couples therapist, Felice visited a psychiatrist weekly and an abortionist once. I had wanted the baby, but there were careers to consider. Back home in bed after the abortion, I held Felice, feeling guilty for wanting to make love yet wondering when we could. The act of physical commingling might carry us past the truth that our life together was ending.

I never hit a woman again, though I plotted ways to kill a man to protect the woman I would marry, Lisa.

The guy she dated before me was a stalker. When Lisa first moved into my apartment, he'd call and claim he was watching us both, then hang up. He added a desperado quality to our love. On his crazier days, he made threats from my parking lot on one of the first car phones in Arkansas. He seemed to want phone warfare, so I retaliated. I called the utility companies, pretending to be him and said I was moving to Alaska. His services were stopped. We switched to an unlisted number when his phone was reconnected.

Lisa and I were finishing graduate school together, and he began prowling the halls like an echo, bouncing back and startling us. He frequented the pool hall where I drank beer, sat on a stool next to me, and smiled as he twiddled his thumbs. I had friends in the pool hall who would, if I asked, rough him up. The owner slipped me a napkin with the number of a man who remedied such problems for fifty bucks, and I seriously considered protecting my love for Lisa in this fashion.

"Piece of advice, pal," I said to the stalker once. I waved to the bartender that things were all right. "You and Lisa just weren't meant to be. Besides, you can't lose what you never had. You better remember that."

Then he said he would kill us.

When Lisa and I got married, he changed tactics. He'd appear in parking lots—a grinning face behind a windshield. His bumper followed a foot from my thigh as we lugged groceries to our car. Evenings when we walked in the deserted stillness of an old graveyard, he'd rocket through and laugh as we scattered into the headstones. We moved to an old hunting cottage on top of a mountain, reasoning you had to be lost to find your way there. The district attorney with whom we filed twenty-nine complaints of harassment explained bodily injury had to occur.

By then Lisa was pregnant, *sacred*, full of figure and of what our love had begat. The stalker never found us on that mountain; I heard he threw a log through another girlfriend's window when they broke up.

It's strange, but as the due date neared, I became convinced this guy was biding his time like some pestilence. Surely, he was waiting to kill us in our sleep. Nights after making love, while Lisa slept, I sat on the front porch protecting my family from him and other uncertainties. Sipping whiskey, I formulated what I'd do if he were luckless enough to stumble upon our house and cross the threshold I had carried Lisa over. Twice I got out an old double-barreled sixteen-gauge shotgun issued by the Army in WWI. I set a box of buckshot by my feet and jumped when box turtles or deer rustled the leaves in our garden. Who knows what I would have done if he had showed up. I'd like to think I could have talked him into leaving, or that my aim would have guided the buckshot whistling past his ear, frightening him into running. Then again, there's the part of me that *wanted* him to cross over the mark separating loved ones and invited guests from burglars and thieves. That part of me wanted to lay waste to his heart.

My marriage to Lisa lasted four years and relocation into as many states. I hauled us to one-year lectureship appointments at community colleges. We had our daughter in Arkansas, held screaming matches in Oklahoma, and spoke openly of divorce in Mississippi. We tried to rekindle our relationship in Texas, the state which stamped its seal on our divorce decree. We loved each other—often noisily—and for that I am grateful. Those four years were so much like other people's attempts at love that it's easy to chart an image of them. One essay I now teach, written by a famous psychologist, insists we each carry around a love map—a sketchy cartography formed in childhood which outlines the topography of the people to whom we will surrender our hearts. I told this to Lisa once, when she had strewn my clothes like police body outlines across the front lawn.

"If that's the case," she said, "your love map looks like a battlefield."

This was during the divide and conquer stage of our divorce. Our strife has given way to seasonal reunions much like my parents', when the weather along the White River in Arkansas is accommodating or at least forgiving. Lisa and I live three states apart, and we rendezvous at a campsite miles upstream from the real estate scandal. The last time we spent the night, Lisa was en route from Little Rock, where she teaches, to Missouri, where her significant other lived. Our daughter and I would head back to South Carolina for a few weeks.

While Lisa was on the car phone explaining this spur of the moment camping trip to the man who would take my place, I pitched the tent. The guy had none of my unreasonable qualities and asked would I send him some trout if we caught enough. We pitched camp and Lisa claimed first rights to the hammock.

I took our daughter wade fishing. A few hundred yards downriver from the campsite, I imagined us a family on one of the world's earliest evenings. We seemed exiles from the little disturbances that rule mankind. I hooked a fat rainbow and steadied my daughter in the current as I gave her the rod to fight the fish. She asked me where did the fish's colors go after I had gutted and gilled it. I didn't know what to say, so I named what I knew of the appearing stars and hoisted her on my back with supper in tow. Fathers don't like to be ignorant of things, especially the heavens, so I manufactured names for the configurations I didn't know. I *did* get Venus right, though my daughter remarked the evening star looked like a beacon that warns planes of the earth's proximity. I thought of all the names she would know love by—from her mother's to mine to the stranger she would marry to the sounds by which they would know their children.

That night we ate the first trout my daughter ever battled. Though it was July, we built a fire, and I told her stories of the first time I had ever seen her mother. I put in all the true clichés about my knees going akimbo and my crazy habit of going into a room Lisa had left to inhale the perfume of where she had been. Our daughter fell asleep as if I were telling her a fairy tale.

"If I didn't know you any better, I'd think you believed in that stuff." Lisa had returned from carrying our daughter inside the tent, and she stood at the firelight's edge, part shadow, part real. When she came over to grab a cigarette from my pocket, she shrugged—she was trying to quit—and lit it with a smoldering stick. I poured us bourbon as she smoked thoughtfully. I knew her well enough not to speak and to guess what she was deciding. When she said we should go into the tent but be *quiet* about it, I followed.

"That's the last time we'll do that," she said when we finished.

Lying beside her in our aftermath, I lifted up my hand to test its strength in the tent's shadowy light. I wished for all of us whatever solace a hand raised in salutation could offer. This hand had admired breasts and traced iliac crests and caught a daughter and cut her umbilical cord. It had hit, and it had shut my father's eyes on his deathbed. It had pointed fingers in accusation and shushed away fears; it had worn rings and flung them away. This hand was no stranger to love's hierarchy of feelings. I remembered Corporal Love waving good-bye that day, admonishing us to be good soldiers with pure hearts, and my father's laugh when he admitted that in his service days he had fallen victim to love's diseases. Then Lisa's hand rose up to meet mine—she didn't know what I was thinking, but she knew it was time for a laying on of hands. We did that children's trick and chanted *here's the church, here's the steeple, open the doors, and there's all the people.* When our daughter whimpered in her sleep, we brought her between us and stroked her hair. When I touched Lisa's face and neck—not in a sexual way this time because we had gone past where the body matters— her features felt like my own and yet someone else's. Then Lisa curled around our daughter and slept, and like a foot soldier, I held watch over their sleeping beauty. I knew that to doze would break the spell of what I was feeling. The chittering of birds outside finally reminded me I had promised Lisa and our daughter a breakfast of hashbrowns and trout prepared Scottish style. I would have to muster my stiff bones soon, but for a while longer I lingered, adoring them, in love with these women, and the grace of this borrowed moment, and the imperfection of things which pass.

———

Dale Ray Phillips's short stories have appeared in *The Atlantic, GQ, Story, New Stories from the South,* and *The Best American Short Stories*. He teaches at Clemson University, where he is completing a book of stories.

I wrote "Corporal Love" to form a bridge between certain stories in my book. Memory and invention are so muddled for me that I don't know where the idea came from. Writing a story is a strange act of discovery; generally, I find that what I have uncovered is nothing more than what I have always known. Also—and I'm embarrassed to admit this—I love to lie, and fiction offers an acceptable channel for this compulsion.

Judy Troy

RAMONE

(from *The New Yorker*)

At the beginning of August, a week after my fourteenth birthday, my stepfather, McKinley, my mother, and I left Houston for Ramone, Texas. McKinley's dying father was our reason for going. He was eighty-three years old and sick with lung cancer and had only a few months left to live, and McKinley wanted us to care for him. He said that he and my mother could get jobs in Lubbock.

We left on a humid Friday morning before the sun came up. In the pale sky we could see Venus and a half moon. McKinley turned on the inside light to show me how Texas took up five pages in the road atlas. "We're driving six hundred miles without crossing a state line, Roberta," he said.

I was in the back seat, and my mother was driving. She was afraid that McKinley, talking about his father, or his sister, who also lived in Ramone, would start to cry. He hadn't been home in nine years—he'd been in the Army, and had married the wrong person before he married my mother—and he was an emotional person, just as my real father had been. My father, who my mother never talked about except sometimes after church, had died of a heart attack five years before.

The sun came up, and as we left refineries and oil wells behind we came upon empty flat fields, nowhere towns, and more historical markers than probably exist in any normal-sized state.

"Let's stop," McKinley said, each time we passed one. My mother stopped twice; each time, the marker was for a man who'd come from Alabama and tried to grow cotton.

"Isn't this interesting?" McKinley said to us.

"To be truthful, no," my mother said.

"I'd rather just get there," I said. "The sooner you start a new life the sooner it becomes an old life."

"What's your hurry to make it old?" McKinley asked.

"I don't know," I said. But I felt my heart speed up, which told me that the answer had to do with being afraid. My father had told me once that I was hooked up inside to a kind of lie detector.

"I like the travelling part," my mother said. "I'd just as soon never get anywhere."

"That's weird," I said.

"It's not," my mother said.

"You two argue because you're so much alike," McKinley told us.

It took us all day to get there, even though we'd left so early—loading the car and U-Haul the night before, in darkness, because my mother was worried that we'd be robbed by somebody watching. The only person I saw was Roy Lee Hollis, standing under a stairway at our apartment complex, trying to apologize. He was my best friend—the only person I'd bothered to tell I would miss—and he had refused to kiss me. He proved for me something that my mother had always said—that it was foolish to like a boy more than he liked you. But it made moving away easier. I'd be in a tiny town in West Texas with a dying person I'd never met, but at least I would never again have to see Roy Lee Hollis.

I didn't expect him to show up at the last minute. I hardly let him speak. I walked away—in the stiff-legged way I'd seen high-heeled women in soap operas do—just as McKinley came down the stairs with a suitcase. "Why wouldn't you say goodbye to that boy?" he asked me later.

That question and Roy Lee's sad expression were on my mind as we drove into Ramone. The sky was darkening over a one-block street of one-story buildings. At the end of the block the pavement ended and the street became dirt. That's where our neighborhood began.

McKinley drove past three shabby houses, raising behind us a storm of dust, then stopped in front of a two-story, caved-in, paint-peeling dump.

"Jesus Christ," he said. He didn't move to get out. My mother put her hand over her mouth.

The door opened, and an ancient, smaller, yellow version of McKinley stepped onto the broken porch. He slowly lifted one hand in a wave.

"I guess that's Grandpa," I said.

My mother laughed.

"That's not funny," McKinley said to us.

McKinley's father had emphysema and liver disease in addition to cancer; he'd been sent home from the hospital to die.

"At least they came straight out and told him," my mother said later that night. "At least they didn't sugarcoat it."

'You wouldn't want any sympathy creeping in," McKinley said.

It was after ten. McKinley's father, Emerson, had gone to bed, and we'd investigated the house and the neighborhood and walked the short distance into town. We'd had dinner at Luigi's Lone Star Pizza, which was a convenience store and gas station as well as a restaurant. Now we were settled outside, in back, on the weedy lawn. We couldn't see each other in the hot darkness. Behind us in an empty field cicadas were buzzing. My mother and I were too depressed to talk, but for some reason, sick as Emerson was, McKinley had gotten happier being around his father. McKinley said he hoped his daddy would live long enough to see the house repaired.

"Repaired by who?" my mother said meanly. It was doubly mean, because both my mother and McKinley had been construction workers before they married. It was how they'd met.

"I know you're disappointed," he said, "but sniping at me won't make it better."

"What will, then?" she asked.

"Cheering up. Seeing the good things. Finding a little brightness in the dark corners."

My mother scratched her leg. "I'll tell you what's in this corner," she said. "Chiggers." She stood up and walked off toward the house. Overhead you couldn't see a single star.

"I think we'll end up liking it here," McKinley said.

I slept in a tiny room upstairs. McKinley and my mother were next door, in the double bed McKinley's father had been born in. Sometime in the night I heard McKinley cry out in his sleep.

"It's no wonder you're having a nightmare," I heard my mother say.

I fell back to sleep and dreamed that my father wasn't dead but only in a room that I couldn't find the door to. Then I dreamed that Roy Lee chose me as his partner in biology class but couldn't remember my name.

McKinley woke me at seven.

"Your Aunt Mavis Jean used to sleep in that bed," he told me. "Wait till you meet her."

"She's not my aunt," I said.

"I forget that," McKinley said. "It seems to me you've always been mine."

"I've never been yours," I told him.

"Don't you get tired of being so tough?" he asked me.

Then he disappeared. A moment later I heard him downstairs, saying to Emerson, "Just hold on to me, Pop. I won't let you go."

Across the narrow hall, in the bathroom, I could hear my mother trying to get clean water out of the bathtub faucet. I'd tried the night before.

"I think it's sewage," I shouted through the wall.

"Goddam shit," my mother said. It was such a shock to hear her say those words that I went in and looked at her sitting on the floor in McKinley's boxer shorts and undershirt.

"Why are you wearing that?" I asked.

"Why shouldn't I wear it?"

"Well, it's not exactly attractive."

"Pardon me," my mother said. "Let me get on a negligee."

"Don't do it for my sake. I'm not married to you."

"So those are the words you choose to start the day with," she said. "Fine."

We stared at each other stubbornly. As usual, I looked away first.

When my mother and I came downstairs, McKinley said, "Daddy was just asking about you two."

It was hard to tell if that was true. Emerson was partly deaf and looked confused. McKinley had fed him and got him into a lop-sided chair on the broken porch. McKinley sat down next to him. I thought that the two of them, side by side, were like a before-and-after "Don't Smoke" advertisement.

"Hello," Emerson said.

"Hi," I said.

"Step out here into the yard," McKinley said.

My mother and I went to stand in the dandelion grass. Last night's clouds had blown off; the sky was bluer and wider than it had ever seemed in Houston. Wind was moving through the branches of the cottonwood trees and rippling the wheat field across the road.

"I told you it was pretty, didn't I?" McKinley said.

"Where did you get that thing on your head?" my mother asked. He was wearing a cowboy hat.

"Hello!" Emerson said again. He needed to shout.

"Hello!" I shouted back.

"I knew you two would have a lot to talk about!" McKinley said.

I was afraid he'd gone crazy. But he hadn't. He was just happy and sad at the same time.

A few minutes later, McKinley's sister, Mavis Jean, drove up with her husband in a boat-size Chevy. They were both large people. Mavis Jean was as tall as McKinley but not as skinny, and had reddish hair like his. She walked right over and hugged me; my mother moved herself out of range. Mavis Jean's husband was big and bald, and a tobacco chewer. I thought he might not know how to talk until I heard him say "Thank you" very quietly, in the dilapidated kitchen, when Mavis handed him a doughnut. She'd brought two boxes of them, plus a thermos of coffee. She'd brought orange juice for me.

"I have pictures of the both of you in my living room," she said, beaming down at my mother and me, where we stood side by side in front of the rusty refrigerator. "You're already family."

"Neither one of us takes a good picture," my mother said.

At the cluttered table, Mavis's husband and McKinley were writing up a list of tools and supplies they'd need to fix the house. After they left to get them, Mavis sat down with us and showed us Emerson's pills—which ones he needed to take when.

"He gets the pain pills whenever he wants them," she said. "Sometimes I give him one just when he looks real bad." Her eyes got wet, and she let tears run down her face. "I've seen Daddy almost every day for the past thirty years," she said. "It's like seeing the sun. You don't expect it to disappear."

My mother looked out the window. She tapped her nails on the table. "Is there a Presbyterian church around here?" she asked.

"The minister's already got your name," Mavis Jean said. "McKinley said you were religious."

"I don't like that word," my mother said. "I prefer 'churchgoing.'"

"I don't go myself," Mavis told her. "Maybe I should. But I feel I have God in my heart."

When my mother didn't respond, Mavis said gently, "Not everybody makes it personal like I do."

In the afternoon, my mother and I shopped for supper groceries at the convenience store. The temperature was up to a hundred and six degrees, we heard on the radio, and on top of that there was a drought. We were both having trouble with our hair, which turned limp with no humidity.

"We look like dogs," my mother said as we got out of the car. "If we're lucky they'll put us in the pound."

Inside, she got a cold, quart-size beer and drank most of it as we walked around the store. On the way home, she pulled the car over and stepped out into an overgrown field and threw up.

"Don't mention that when we get home," she warned me.

"Why would I?"

We didn't talk after that, not even when we pulled up to the house and saw Mavis Jean in the yard, swinging a rug beater at the moldy gray living-room carpet she'd hung from a tree.

McKinley, on the porch, was carefully holding up a stained pea-colored plate. "Mama's china," he said reverently to my mother.

Inside, Emerson, positioned next to the window air-conditioner, was wheezing out some sort of song.

Just then my mother snapped. "Get the groceries in, Roberta!" she yelled at me.

She tore at the loose, rotten upholstery on the couch and the chair; ripped up a corner of the kitchen linoleum, which had half risen and curled; yanked down the bathroom wallpaper, which had a kind of yellow dampness seeping through.

We all got out of her way, including Emerson: Mavis Jean's husband came in and lifted up him and his chair and deposited them both in the back bedroom.

McKinley stood in the doorway and watched. He'd never seen my mother exercised like that, although I'd told him once how right after my father's funeral she went into their bedroom and boxed up all his things. "Helen, let that go for now," my grandmother had said. She and I had stood in the doorway—just as McKinley was now—watching my mother sort through mismatched socks. She'd wanted to pair them up, even though she was putting his clothes in boxes to give to the charity-drive ladies at our church.

It was almost dark by the time my mother stopped. We had all—except for Emerson—tried to stay on the outskirts but still help.

"Just think of us as worker bees," Mavis Jean had said light-heartedly to my mother, when Mavis got in her way for a second. My mother had been holding a putty knife, though, and for a moment none of us were sure what she might do next.

Finally, she collapsed on the front porch, where she'd been prying up boards. Her sweaty hair was sticking to the back of her neck. Her sleeveless shirt was so wet you could tell where her bra was held together with pins.

"Honey, you need some new underwear," Mavis Jean said quietly.

We had supper in the cramped kitchen and then sat in the cool dimness of the living room. I fell asleep and dreamed again about Roy Lee—he was kissing and touching me—and I woke afraid that I'd been making noises. But the noises I'd heard must have been Emerson's breathing. He'd seemed all right earlier, although he hadn't eaten any dinner. "Sometimes the only food you want is sweets," I'd told him—that was how my father used to tempt me to eat when I was sick. But Emerson hadn't wanted so much as a cookie.

"Daddy?" Mavis Jean said. "What's wrong? What do you need?" She was sitting close to him, holding a pair of his trousers in her lap; she was sewing up a ripped hem.

He opened his mouth to speak but all he did was take in air. McKinley got up and went to his side; my mother went into the kitchen and came back with a glass of water. We all, except my mother, crowded around him, watching his chest rise and fall, and the look in his eye, and the way his hands were clutching the arms of his chair.

"Give him some room!" my mother shouted in a high-pitched voice.

Mavis Jean was taking his pulse, her head bent down, her eyes on her watch. Her husband put his hand on her shoulder. McKinley was all but holding his daddy in his arms. I stood right next to McKinley, leaning against him even, although I hadn't meant to. I heard him tell his father he loved him.

Then it was over. Emerson's breathing grew regular; he looked less scared; and he didn't die—not for another six months, and it was in his bed, during the night, while he was asleep.

It was an hour before we trusted that he was O.K. During that time only my mother left the house; she went out to the porch and sat on the steps.

"Come help me get coffee and cake," Mavis Jean said to me.

I followed her into the kitchen, and when she picked up the coffeepot I saw that her hands were shaking.

"I can do that," I said.

She went over to the sloping counter under the window, looking off into the dark back yard. Then she turned around and looked at me.

"What was it like," she asked softly, "having your daddy die?"

"I only know what it was like afterward," I told her. "I wasn't there when it happened."

"Oh, no," she said. "You didn't get to say goodbye."

She came close and pushed back my straggly hair, and I saw that her own hair was more gray than red. I'd forgotten that she was older than McKinley.

"'Cross at the light, Roberta,'" I said. "That was the last thing he said to me."

"That has some sweetness in it," she said. "Sweetness and good advice."

In the living room, Mavis Jean set the coffeepot down and put a blanket over Emerson's shoulders.

"You don't need a chill on top of everything else," she told him.

"It's ninety-seven degrees outside," my mother said, her voice still strange. She stood in the doorway, ignoring that she was letting in hot air and letting out cool.

"He seems most comfortable at a hundred and two," Mavis Jean said.

"Close the door, honey," McKinley said to my mother. "Come sit here by me.

My mother went outside instead. She left the door open, and her work boots were noisy on the broken boards and the cracked sidewalk. After a few minutes McKinley went out after her. Through the window I could see them standing in the road, my mother facing the empty field on the other side, and suddenly I knew how afraid she was—not of Emerson's dying but of how it made her feel, to feel too much. It was like loving a boy more than he loved you, I thought; you couldn't help it, and you couldn't stop it, and you made him love you in your dreams.

They stayed outside a long time. I sat down finally and ate a piece of cake, watching the way Mavis Jean double-rolled the hem of the pants leg before she sewed it.

Behind her, Emerson was eying me. He leaned forward to speak.

"Does that little girl belong to me?" he asked Mavis Jean.

She told him yes.

Judy Troy was born in Indiana. She has worked as a waitress, a salesclerk, a bartender, and a professor. She is now Alumni-Writer-in-Residence at Auburn University. In 1993 her story collection, *Mourning Doves*, was nominated for a *Los Angeles Times* Book Award, and in 1996 she received a Whiting Writers' Award. Her first novel, *West of Venus*, was published in May of 1997 by Random House. She lives in Auburn, Alabama, with her husband, Miller Solomon, and her dog, Hardy.

"*Ramone*" took shape in my mind as my husband and I drove back roads through Texas, visiting his relatives in Marshall and my aunt and uncle in Austin. It was late August, the temperature over a hundred, and we drove through the small, flat towns with historical markers you had to look hard for. We found one half-hidden by tangled weeds in front of a dilapidated house. It was—they all were—about a man from Alabama trying to grow cotton.

On the way home we drove through sprawling, industrial Houston. I *was thinking about something my uncle—my mother's brother—had said to me the night before about my father. I realized then that until that visit, my uncle and I hadn't seen each other since my father's funeral, five years earlier. I'd lived in Missouri that year and hadn't gone home when my father got sick. He died the day before he was supposed to be released from the hospital.*

I started writing "Ramone" as soon as my husband and I got back to Alabama. I invented the characters and situation, but the emotions fueling them were my own, including the conflict between the empathetic side of me and the cold, fearful side. I think it's a conflict a lot of people have. "Ramone" was one of those stories that you write and then say: So that's how I've been feeling all these years. And because of that, "Ramone" means a lot to me.

Robert Olen Butler

HELP ME FIND MY SPACEMAN LOVER

(from *The Paris Review*)

I never thought I could fall for a spaceman. I mean, you see them in the newspaper and they kind of give you the willies, all skinny and hairless and wiggly-looking, and if you touched one, even to shake hands, you just know it would be like when you were about fifteen and you were with an earth boy and you were sweet on him but there was this thing he wanted, and you finally said okay, but only rub-a-dub, which is what we called it around these parts when I was younger, and it was the first time ever that you touched . . . well, you know what I'm talking about. Anyway, that's what it's always seemed like to me with spacemen, and most everybody around here feels about the same way, I'm sure. Folks in Bovary, Alabama, and environs—by which I mean the KOA camp off the interstate and the new trailer park out past the quarry—everybody in Bovary is used to people being a certain way, to look at and to talk to and so forth. Take my daddy. When I showed him a few years ago in the newspaper how a spaceman had endorsed Bill Clinton for president and they had a picture of a spaceman standing there next to Bill Clinton—without any visible clothes on, by the way—the spaceman, that is, not Bill Clinton, though I wouldn't put it past him, to tell the truth, and I'm not surprised at anything they might do over in Little Rock. But

I showed my daddy the newspaper and he took a look at the space-man and he snorted and said that he wasn't surprised people like that was supporting the Democrats, people like that don't even look American, and I said no, Daddy, he's a spaceman, and he said people like that don't even look human, and I said no, Daddy, he's not human, and my daddy said, that's what I'm saying, make him get a job.

But I did fall for a spaceman, as it turned out, fell pretty hard. I met him in the parking lot at the twenty-four-hour Wal-Mart. We used to have a regular old Wal-Mart that would close at nine o'clock and when they turned it into a Super Center a lot of people in Bovary thought that no good would come of it, encouraging people to stay up all night. Americans go to bed early and get up early, my daddy said. But I have trouble sleeping sometimes. I live in the old trailer park out the state highway and it's not too far from the Wal-Mart and I live there with my yellow cat Eddie. I am forty years old and I was married once, to a telephone installer who fell in love with cable TV. There's no cable TV in Bovary yet, though with a twenty-four-hour Wal-Mart, it's probably not too far behind. It won't come soon enough to save my marriage, however. Not that I wanted it to. He told me he just *had* to install cable TV, telephones wasn't fulfilling him, and he was going away for good to Mobile and he didn't want me to go with him, this was the end for us, and I was understanding the parts about it being the end but he was going on about fiber optics and things that I didn't really follow. So I said fine and he went away, and even if he'd wanted me to go with him, I wouldn't have done it. I've only been to Mobile a couple of times and I didn't take to it. Bovary is just right for me. At least that's what I thought when it had to do with my ex-husband, and that kind of thinking just stayed with me, like a grape-juice stain on your housedress, and I am full of regrets, I can tell you, for not rethinking that whole thing before this. But I got a job at a hairdresser's in town and Daddy bought me the trailer free and clear and me and Eddie moved in and I just kept all those old ideas.

So I met Desi in the parking lot. I called him that because he talked with a funny accent but I liked him. I had my insomnia and it was about three in the morning and I went to the twenty-four-hour Wal-Mart and I was glad it was there and it was open— I'd tell that right to the face of anybody in this town—I was glad for a place to go when I couldn't sleep. So I was coming out of the store with a bag that had a little fuzzy mouse toy for Eddie, made of rabbit fur, I'm afraid, and that strikes me as pretty odd to kill all those cute little rabbits, which some people have as pets and love a lot, so that somebody else's pet of a different type can have something to play with, and it's that kind of odd thing that makes you shake your head about the way life is lived on planet Earth— Desi has helped me see things in the larger perspective—though, to be honest, it didn't stop me from buying the furry cat toy, because Eddie does love those things. Maybe today I wouldn't do the same, but I wasn't so enlightened that night when I came out of the Wal-Mart and I had that toy and some bread and baloney and a refrigerator magnet, which I collect, of a zebra head.

He was standing out in the middle of the parking lot and he wasn't moving. He was just standing still as a cow and there wasn't any car within a hundred feet of him, and, of course, his spaceship wasn't anywhere in sight, though I wasn't looking for that right away because at first glance I didn't know he was a spaceman. He was wearing a long black trench coat with the belt cinched tight and he had a black felt hat with a wide brim. Those were the things I saw first and he seemed odd, certainly, dressed like that in Bovary, but I took him for a human being, at least.

I was opening my car door and he was still standing out there and I called out to him, "Are you lost?"

His head turns my way and I still can't see him much at all except as a hat and a coat.

"Did you forget where you parked your car?" I say, and then right away I realize there isn't but about four cars total in the parking lot at that hour. So I put the bag with my things in the seat and I come around the back of the car and go a few steps toward him. I feel bad.

So I call to him, kind of loud because I'm still pretty far away from him and also because I already have a feeling he might be a foreigner. I say, "I wasn't meaning to be snippy, because that's something that happens to me a lot and I can look just like you look sometimes, I'm sure, standing in the lot wondering where I am, exactly."

While I'm saying all this I'm moving kind of slow in his direction. He isn't saying anything back and he isn't moving. But already I'm noticing that his belt is cinched *very* tight, like he's got maybe an eighteen-inch waist. And as I get near, he sort of pulls his hat down to hide his face, but already I'm starting to think he's a spaceman.

I stop. I haven't seen a spaceman before except in the newspaper and I take another quick look around, just in case I missed something, like there might be four cars *and* a flying saucer. But there's nothing unusual. Then I think, oh my, there's one place I haven't looked, and so I lift my eyes, very slow because this is something I don't want to see all the sudden, and finally I'm staring into the sky. It's a dark night and there are a bunch of stars up there and I get goose bumps because I'm pretty sure that this man standing just a few feet away is from somewhere out there. But at least there's no spaceship as big as the Wal-Mart hanging over my head with lights blinking and transporter beams ready to shine down on me. It's only stars.

So I bring my eyes down—just about as slow—to look at this man. He's still there. And in the shadow of his hat brim, with the orangey light of the parking lot all around, I can see these eyes looking at me now and they are each of them about as big as Eddie's whole head and shaped kind of like Eddie's eyes.

"Are you a spaceman?" I just say this right out.

"Yes, ma'am," he says and his courtesy puts me at ease right away. Americans are courteous, my daddy says, not like your Eastern liberal New York taxi drivers.

"They haven't gone and abandoned you, have they, your friends or whoever?" I say.

"No, ma'am," he says and his voice is kind of high-pitched and he has this accent, but it's more in the tone of the voice than how he says his words, like he's talking with a mouth full of grits or something.

"You looked kind of lost, is all."

"I am waiting," he says.

"That's nice. They'll be along soon, probably," I say, and I feel my feet starting to slide back in the direction of the car. There's only so far that courtesy can go in calming you down. The return of the spaceship is something I figure I can do without.

Then he says, "I am waiting for you, Edna Bradshaw."

"Oh. Good. Sure, honey. That's me. I'm Edna. Yes. Waiting for me." I'm starting to babble and I'm hearing myself like I was hovering in the air over me and I'm wanting my feet to go even faster but they seem to have stopped altogether. I wonder if it's because of some tractor beam or something. Then I wonder if they have tractor beam pulling contests in outer space that they show on TV back in these other solar systems. I figure I'm starting to get hysterical, thinking things like that in a situation like this, but there's not much I can do about it.

He seems to know I'm struggling. He takes a tiny little step forward and his hand goes up to his hat, like he's going to take it off and hold it in front of him as he talks to me, another courtesy that even my daddy would appreciate. But his hand stops. I think he's not ready to show me his whole spaceman head. He knows it would just make things worse. His hand is bad enough, hanging there over his hat. It's got little round pads at the end of the fingers, like a gecko, and I don't stop to count them, but at first glance there just seems to be too many of them.

His hand comes back down. "I do not hurt you, Edna Bradshaw, I am a friendly guy."

"Good," I say. "Good. I figured that was so when I first saw you. Of course, you can just figure somebody around here is going to be friendly. That's a good thing about Bovary, Alabama—that's where you are, you know, though you probably do know that, though maybe not. Do you know that?"

He doesn't say anything for a moment. I'm rattling on again, and it's true I'm a little bit scared and that's why, but it's also true that I'm suddenly very sad about sounding like this to him, I'm getting some perspective on myself through his big old eyes, and I'm sad I'm making a bad impression because I want him to like me. He's sweet, really. Very courteous. Kind of boyish. And he's been waiting for me.

"Excuse me," he says. "I have been translating. You speak many words, Edna Bradshaw. Yes, I know the name of this place."

"I'm sorry. I just do that sometimes, talk a lot. Like when I get scared, which I am a little bit right now. And call me Edna."

"Please," he says, "I am calling you Edna already. And in conclusion, you have no reason to be afraid."

"I mean call me *just* Edna. You don't have to say Bradshaw every time, though my granddaddy would do that with people. He was a fountain pen salesman and he would say to people, I'm William D. Bradshaw. Call me William D. Bradshaw. And he meant it. He wanted you to say the whole name every time. But you can just call me Edna."

So the spaceman takes a step forward and my heart starts to pound something fierce, and it's not from fright, I realize, though it's some of that. "Edna," he says. "You are still afraid."

"Telling you about my granddaddy, you mean? How that's not really the point here? Well, yes, I guess so. Sometimes, if he knew you for awhile, he'd let you call him W. D. Bradshaw."

Now his hand comes up and it clutches the hat and the hat comes off and there he stands in the orange lights of the parking lot at three in the morning in my little old hometown and he doesn't have a hair on his head, though I've always liked bald men and I've read they're bald because they have so much male hormone in them, which makes them the best lovers, which would make this spaceman quite a guy, I think, and his head is pointy, kind of, and his cheeks are sunken and his cheekbones are real clear and I'm thinking already I'd like to bake some cookies for him or something, just last week I got a prize-winning recipe off a can of cooking spray that looks like it'd put flesh on a fence post. And, of course, there are these big eyes of his and he blinks once, real slow, and I think it's because he's got a strong feeling in him, and he says, "Edna, my name is hard for you to say."

And I think of Desi right away, and I try it on him, and his mouth, which hasn't got anything that look like lips exactly, moves up at the edges and he makes this pretty smile.

"I have heard that name," he says. "Call me Desi. And I am waiting for you, Edna, because I study this planet and I hear you speak many words to your friends and to your subspecies companion and I detect some bright-colored aura around you and I want to meet you."

"That's good," I say, and I can feel a blush starting in my chest, where it always starts, and it's spreading up my throat and into my cheeks.

"I would like to call on you tomorrow evening, if I have your permission," he says.

"Boy," I say. "Do a lot of people have the wrong idea about spacemen. I thought you just grabbed somebody and beamed them up and that was it." It was a stupid thing to say, I realize right away. I think Desi looks a little sad to hear this. The corners of his mouth sink. "I'm sorry," I say.

"No," he says. "This is how we are perceived, it is true. You speak only the truth. This is one reason I want to meet you, Edna. You seem always to say what is inside your head without any attempt to alter it."

Now it's my turn to look a little sad, I think. But that's okay, because it gives me a chance to find out that Desi is more than courteous. His hands come out toward me at once, the little suckers on them primed to latch onto me, and I'm not even scared because I know it means he cares about me. And he's too refined to touch me this quick. His hands just hang there between us and he says, "I speak this not as a researcher but as a male creature of a parallel species."

"You mean as a man?"

His eyes blink again, real slow. "Yes. As a man. As a man I try to say that I like the way you speak."

So I give him permission to call on me and he thanks me and he turns and glides away. I know his legs are moving but he glides, real smooth, across the parking lot and I can see now that poor Desi didn't even find a pair of pants and some shoes to go with his trench coat. His legs and ankles are skinny like a frog's and his feet look a lot like his hands. But all that is unclear on the first night. He has disappeared out into the darkness and I drive on home to my subspecies companion and I tell him all about what happened while he purrs in my lap and I have two thoughts.

First, if you've never seen a cat in your entire life or anything like one and then meet a cat in a Wal-Mart parking lot in the middle of the night all covered with fur and making this rumbling noise and maybe even smelling of mouse meat, you'd have to make some serious adjustments to what you think is pretty and sweet and something you can call your own. Second—and this hits me with a little shock—Desi says he's been hearing how I talk to my friends and even to Eddie, and that sure wasn't by hanging around in his trench coat and blending in with the furniture. Of course, if you've got a spaceship that can carry you to Earth from a distant galaxy, it's not so surprising you've got some kind of radio or something that lets you listen to what everybody's saying without being there.

And when I think of this, I start to sing for Desi. I just sit for a long while where I am, with Eddie in my lap, this odd little creature that doesn't look like me at all but who I find cute as can be and who I love a lot, and I sing, because when I was a teenager I had a pretty good voice and I even thought I might be a singer of some kind, though there wasn't much call for that in Bovary except in the church choir, which is where I sang mostly, but I loved to sing other kinds of songs too. And so I say real loud, "This is for you, Desi." And then I sing every song I can think of. I sing "The Long and Winding Road" and "Lucy in the Sky with Diamonds" and "Everything is Beautiful" and a bunch of others, some twice, like "The First Time Ever I Saw Your Face." Then I do a Reba McEntire medley and I start with "Is There Life Out There" and then I do "Love Will Find Its Way to You" and "Up to Heaven"

and "Long Distance Lover." I sing my heart out to Desi and I have
to say this surprises me a little but maybe it shouldn't because
already I'm hearing myself through his ears—though at that
moment I can't even say for sure if he had ears—and I realize that
a lot of what I say, I say because it keeps me from feeling so lonely.

The next night there's a knock on my door and I'm wearing my
best dress, with a scoop neck and it shows my cleavage pretty good
and on the way to the door I suddenly doubt myself. I don't know
if spacemen are like earthmen in that way or not. Maybe they don't
appreciate a good set of knockers, especially if their women are as
skinny as Desi. But I am who I am. So I put all that out of my
mind and I open the door and there he is. He's got his black felt
hat on, pulled down low in case any of my neighbors are watching, I figure, and he's wearing a gray pinstripe suit that's way too
big for him and a white shirt and a tie with a design that's dozens
of little Tabasco bottles floating around.

"Oh," I say. "You like hot food?"

This makes him stop and try to translate.

"Your tie," I say. "Don't you know about your tie?"

He looks down and lifts the end of the tie and looks at it for a
little while and he is so cute doing that and so innocentlike that my
heart is doing flips and I kind of wiggle in my dress a bit to make
him look at who it is he's going out with. If the women on his
planet are skinny, then he could be real real ready for a woman like
me. That's how I figure it as I'm waiting there for him to check out
his tie and be done with it, though I know it's my own fault for
getting him off on that track, and me doing that is just another
example of something or other.

Then Desi looks up at me, and he takes off his hat with one
hand and I see that he doesn't have anything that looks like ears,
really, just sort of a little dip on each side where ears might be. But
that doesn't make him so odd. What's an ear mean, really? Having
an ear or not having an ear won't get you to heaven, it seems to
me. I look into Desi's big dark eyes and he blinks slow and then
his other hand comes out from behind his back and he's got a
flower for me that's got a bloom on it the color of I don't know

what, a blue kind of, a red kind of, and I know this is a spaceflower of some sort and I take it from him and it weighs about as much as my Sunbeam Steam Iron, just this one flower.

He says, "I heard you sing for me," and he holds out his hand. If you want to know an exact count, there's eight fingers on each hand, I will end up counting them carefully later on our date, but for now there's still just a lot of fingers and I realize I'm not afraid of them anymore and I reach out to him and the little suckers latch on all over my hand, top and bottom, and it's like he's kissing me in eight different places there, over and over, they hold on to me and they pulse in each spot they touch, maybe with the beat of his heart. It's like that. And my eyes fill up with tears because this man's very fingertips are in love with me, I know.

And then he leads me to his flying saucer, which is pretty big but not as big as I imagined, not as big as all of Wal-Mart, certainly, maybe just the pharmacy and housewares departments put together. It's parked out in the empty field back of my trailer where they kept saying they'd put in a miniature golf course and they never did and you don't even see the saucer till you're right up against it, it blends in with the night, and you'd think if they can make this machine, they could get him a better suit. Then he says, "You are safe with me, Edna Bradshaw daughter of Joseph R. Bradshaw and granddaughter of William D. Bradshaw."

It later turns out these family things are important where he's from but I say to him, "William D. is dead, I only have his favorite fountain pen in a drawer somewhere, it's very beautiful, it's gold and it looks like that Chrysler Building in New York, and you should forget about Joseph R. for the time being because I'm afraid you and my daddy aren't going to hit it off real well and I just as soon not think about that till I have to."

Then Desi smiles at me and it's because of all those words, and especially me talking so blunt about my daddy, and I guess also about my taking time to tell him about the beautiful fountain pen my granddaddy left for me, but there's reasons I talk like this, I guess, and Desi says he came to like me from hearing me talk.

Listen to me even now. I'm trying to tell this story of Desi and me and I can't help myself going on about every little thing. But the reasons are always the same, and it's true I'm lonely again. And it's true I'm scared again because I've been a fool.

Desi took me off in his spaceship and we went out past the moon and I barely had time to turn around and look back and I wanted to try to figure out where Bovary was but I hadn't even found the USA when everything got blurry and before you know it we were way out in the middle of nowhere, out in space, and I couldn't see the sun or the moon or anything close up, except all the stars were very bright, and I'm not sure whether we were moving or not because there was nothing close enough by to tell, but I think we were parked, like this was the spaceman's version of the dead-end road to the rock quarry, where I kissed my first boy. I turned to Desi and he turned to me and I should've been scared but I wasn't. Desi's little suckers were kissing away at my hand and then we were kissing on the lips except he didn't have any but it didn't make any difference because his mouth was soft and warm and smelled sweet, like Binaca breath spray, and I wondered if he got that on earth or if it was something just like Binaca that they have on his planet as well.

Then he took me back to his little room on the spaceship and we sat on things like beanbag chairs and we talked a long time about what life in Bovary is like and what life on his planet is like. Desi is a research scientist, you see. He thinks that the only way for our two peoples to learn about each other is to meet and to talk and so forth. There are others where he lives that think it's best just to use their machines to listen in and do their research like that, on the sly. There are even a bunch of guys back there who say forget the whole thing, leave them to hell alone. Let everybody stick to their own place. And I told Desi that my daddy would certainly agree with the leave-them-the-hell-alone guys from his planet, but I agreed with him.

It was all very interesting and very nice, but I was starting to get a little sad. Finally I said to Desi, "So is this thing we're doing here like research? You asked me out as part of a scientific study? I was called by the Gallup Poll people once and I don't remember what it was about but I answered 'none of the above' and 'other' to every question."

For all the honesty Desi said he admired in me, I sure know it wasn't anything to do with my answers to a Gallup Poll that was bothering me, but there I was, bogged down in all of that, and that's a kind of dishonesty, it seems to me now.

But he knew what I was worried about. "No, Edna," he says. "There are many on my planet who would be critical of me. They would say this is why we should have no contact at all with your world. Things like this might happen."

He pauses right there and as far as I know he doesn't have anything to translate and I swallow hard at the knot in my throat and I say, "Things like what?"

Then both his hands take both my hands and when you've got sixteen cute little suckers going at you, it's hard to make any real tough self-denying kind of decisions and that's when I end up with a bona fide spaceman lover. And enough said, as we like to end touchy conversations around the hairdressing parlor, except I will tell you that he was bald all over and it's true what they say about bald men.

Then he takes me to the place where he picked the flower. A moon of some planet or other and there's only these flowers growing as far as the eye can see in all directions and there are clouds in the sky and they are the color of Eddie's turds after a can of Nine Lives Crab and Tuna, which just goes to show that even in some far place in another solar system you can't have everything. But maybe Desi likes those clouds and maybe I'd see it that way too sometime, except I may not have that chance now, though I could've, it's my own damn fault, and if I've been sounding a little bit hit and miss and here and there in the way I've been telling all this, it's now you find out why.

Desi and I stand in that field of flowers for a long while, his little suckers going up and down my arm and all over my throat and chest, too, because I can tell you that a spaceman does too appreciate a woman who has some flesh on her, especially in the right places, but he also appreciates a woman who will speak her mind.

And I was standing there wondering if I should tell him about those clouds or if I should just keep my eyes on the flowers and my mouth shut. Then he says, "Edna, it is time to go."

So he takes my hand and we go back into his spaceship and he's real quiet all the sudden and so am I because I know the night is coming to an end. Then before you know it, there's the earth right in front of me and it's looking, even out there, pretty good, pretty much like where I should be, like my own flower box and my own propane tank and my own front Dutch door look when I drive home at night from work.

Then we are in the field behind the house and it seems awful early in the evening for as much as we've done, and later on I discover it's like two weeks later and Desi had some other spaceman come and feed Eddie while we were gone, though he should have told me because I might've been in trouble at the hairdressing salon, except they believed me pretty quick when I said a spaceman had taken me off, because that's what they'd sort of come around to thinking themselves after my being gone without a trace for two weeks and they wanted me to tell the newspaper about it because I might get some money for it, though I'm not into anything for the money, though my daddy says it's only American to make money any way you can, but I'm not that American, it seems to me, especially if my daddy is right about what American is, which I suspect he's not.

What I'm trying to say is that Desi stopped in this other field with me, this planet-Earth field with plowed-up ground and witchgrass all around and the smell of early summer in Alabama, which is pretty nice, and the sound of cicadas sawing away in the trees and something like a kind of hum out on the horizon, a nighttime sound I listen to once in a while and it makes me feel like a train whistle in the distance makes me feel, which I also listen for, especially when I'm lying awake with my insomnia and Eddie is sleeping near me, and that hum out there in the distance is all the wide world going about its business and that's good but it makes me glad I'm in my little trailer in Bovary, Alabama, and I know every face I'll see on the street the next morning.

And in the middle of a field full of all that, what was I to say when Desi took my hand and asked me to go away with him? He said, "I have to return to my home planet now and after that go off to other worlds. I am being transferred and I will not be back here. But Edna, we feel love on my planet just like you do here. That is why I know it is right that we learn to speak to each other, your people and mine. And in conclusion, I love you, Edna Bradshaw. I want you to come away with me and be with me forever."

How many chances do you have to be happy? I didn't even want to go to Mobile, though I wasn't asked, that's true enough, and I wouldn't have been happy there anyway. So that doesn't count as a blown chance. But this one was different. How could I love a spaceman? How could I be happy in a distant galaxy? These were questions that I had to answer right away, out in the smell of an Alabama summer with my cat waiting for me, though I'm sure he could've gone with us, that wasn't the issue, and with my daddy living just on the other side of town, though, to tell the truth, I wouldn't miss him much, the good Lord forgive me for that sentiment, and I did love my spaceman, I knew that, and I still do, I love his wiggly hairless shy courteous smart-as-a-whip self. But there's only so many new things a person can take in at once and I'd about reached my limit on that night.

So I heard myself say, "I love you too, Desi. But I can't leave the planet Earth. I can't even leave Bovary."

That's about all I could say. And Desi didn't put up a fuss about it, didn't try to talk me out of it, though now I wish to God he'd tried, at least tried, and maybe he could've done it, 'cause I could hear myself saying these words like it wasn't me speaking, like I was standing off a ways just listening in. But my spaceman was shy from the first time I saw him. And I guess he just didn't have it in him to argue with me, once he felt I'd rejected him.

That's the way the girls at the hairdressing salon see it.

I guess they're right. I guess they're right, too, about telling the newspaper my story. Maybe some other spaceman would read it, somebody from Desi's planet, and maybe Desi's been talking about me and maybe he'll hear about how miserable I am now and maybe I can find him or he can find me.

Because I am miserable. I haven't even gone near my daddy for a few months now. I look around at the people in the streets of Bovary and I get real angry at them, for some reason. Still, I stay right where I am. I guess now it's because it's the only place he could ever find me, if he wanted to. I go out into the field back of my trailer at night and I walk all around it, over and over, each night, I walk around and around under the stars because a space-ship only comes in the night and you can't even see it until you get right up next to it.

Robert Olen Butler has published nine books since 1981: seven novels and two volumes of short fiction—*Tabloid Dreams,* which is being developed into a series for Home Box Office, and *A Good Scent from a Strange Mountain,* which won the 1993 Pulitzer Prize for Fiction. His new novel, *The Deep Green Sea,* will debut this fall. His stories have appeared widely and have been chosen for inclusion in four annual editions of *The Best American Short Stories* and six annual editions of *New Stories from the South.* He teaches creative writing at McNeese State University in Lake Charles, Louisana.

Formally, this story began, as did many of the stories in my recent collection, Tabloid Dreams, *with a headline from a supermarket tabloid. But certainly there must also be a long-forgotten moment from my adolescence in Granite City, Illinois—a steel mill town just across the Mississippi River from St. Louis—that deeply informs this piece. I must have stood some late night looking across a dark field of horseradish to a trailer park, where a single light burned in a window, with the sky red from the blast furnace and the air full of the smell of naphtha and the sound of a train whistle out on the horizon. Surely Edna Bradshaw was yearning out there in the spill of that lamp. And there is, as well, a clear literary influence for Edna's voice. My wife, Elizabeth Dewberry, writes first-person voices of Southern women in her two novels. I could never have heard Edna if I hadn't read Betsy.*

Patricia Elam Ruff

THE TAXI RIDE

(from *Epoch*)

Jimmy went over to the dialysis clinic at Howard Hospital three times a week. He had to sit for four hours at a time hooked up to a machine with all them needles in his arm. One of the boys would take us over there in the morning and I'd stay until it was time for him to go on the machine. I'd go to the cafeteria, get my tea, and drink it with him while we waited. Sometimes Jimmy wanted me to read Maya Angelou out loud and I'd do that, too. His eyes was startin to go bad from sugar diabetes, but he said he liked the way wrote-down words sounded when I said them. While he was on the machine all he did was watch TV.

When Jimmy first started goin to the clinic I used to stay all day with him, but the boys could see it was wearin me down (my pressure kept goin up and I couldn't rest much as I needed). They decided I should go on home stead of waitin there; one of them would bring Jimmy back after they got off work.

After the nurses came to hook Jimmy up, I'd leave and walk to the bus stop. Weather had got real cold and I'd have to take the scarf from my neck and wrap it round my hat to keep the wind from biting my ears. I'd get my coat buttoned almost to the top but then I could feel that arthritis kickin up again, making my fingers act like they wasn't mine. Bus took me down Florida Avenue to West Virginia Avenue. Sometimes I'd get lucky and somebody'd take pity on me, I guess, and give me a seat. (It ain't like it was when I was growin up—my mama woulda beat my hindpots if I didn't jump up and give my seat to an elderly person.) When I did get a seat, my feet'd be so tired from standin, they'd like to cry when I finally sat down.

I was standin out there waitin for the bus on one of them real cold days when I could see my breath. I started thinkin bout Jimmy to take my mind off the cold. I wondered if Jimmy was ever gonna be hisself again. Seem like so much of the old Jimmy was already gone that it'd be a mighty far ways for him to come back. The old Jimmy used to stay up late talkin to me, bout his dreams for us and the world. He used to say come retirement we was gonna travel all around, go back to places he'd been when he was in the war. Like Paris, France, and a village in Italy where he said they got streets so small only two people can walk down them at a time. He described the places so good I felt like I'd be able to find my way around once I got there.

Before retirement had a good chance to impress us, though, Jimmy started gettin sick. The sick Jimmy didn't do much talkin, seemed to take too much effort. Them legs of his that liked to dance on the weekends became full of pain and slow-movin; his skin that used to shine from smilin withered up and turned the color of ashes. I knew he was getting close to dyin. It would be specially on my mind when I was watchin him sleep. He used to sleep hard as a rock and snore somethin awful with his eyes shut tight. But them sick days, seem like he was half-expectin to die every time he went to sleep—the way he kept his eyes open a crack. Only the white part showed and it made him look like he was on the way to see his Maker.

I'd touch his arms or his chest gentle-like, just to let him know I loved him, and he'd try to wink at me the way he used to but instead, it just looked like he was blinkin. Then he'd usually start talkin some mess bout gettin with the boys so he could get his papers straight. That way I wouldn't have no burdens when he was gone. And I'd tell him it didn't matter bout all that, I just didn't want him to leave me. Then he'd get quiet again and sad lookin and go on to sleep.

One of my days was twin to the next. I don't care much for the mess they got on television—too much cussin and killin and people half-naked so I'd read my books and my newspaper until Oprah came on—most of the time I can stomach her show. Then I'd cook dinner. By that time Latrice would be home from school and soon, Edward or Lance would bring Jimmy home. After dinner Jimmy'd sit in front of the television and fall asleep there most likely. I'd help him get in bed. Most nights I'd fall asleep after I started readin again, but sometimes I'd need to make myself a hot toddy. Them days, I got real acquainted with lonely.

A young girl with two babies came and stood next to me at the bus stop. It was all I could do not to tell her to cover the baby's face up from the cold and wipe the other one's nose. Snot looked like it'd been there since the days of Methuselah. My boys, Lance and Edward, keep tellin me not to say nothing to strangers nowadays—specially the young ones. And they right. I don't know what's got into some of them teenagers but they just plain crazy. Read in the paper the other day bout a poor seventy-five-year-old woman (same age as me) who told one of them young girls she should stop slappin her child around. Next thing you know the girl done punched the old woman. Well, you don't have to tell me twice. When I saw this young girl at the bus stop I just held my tongue and told myself: it ain't that bad. Just a young girl who don't know what she doin.

The girl, tired of waitin I guess, started tryin to flag down a taxi. There was one taxi man who was always around drivin folk to and from the hospital and he used to ask me all the time did I need a ride. Sometimes he'd say, "Ain't gonna charge you today, ma'am," but I never took him up on it. I was thinkin, I wish he woulda asked me today, that's how cold it was. Anyway, he drove up when the young girl put her hand in the air. He musta read my mind, too, cause he rolled down the window and said, "Mighty chilly out, ma'am." I looked around every side of me to make sure he wasn't talkin to somebody else. When I seen he was talkin to me, I thought about how I only had enough money for the bus and I didn't want to be nobody's charity case. I just wrapped my arms around myself and said, 'No, sir, thanks for askin, though."

Well, next thing you know that man got out the taxi and came over to me. Now he ain't a young man, mind you. I don't think a young man would give a damn. This was a well-seasoned man (the way Jimmy was fore he got sick) wearin a raggedy but respectable sportscoat and tippin his hat to me. "The hawk's out here today, ma'am. I don't want it to get you so I'll take you where you got to go. No charge."

My cold feet overtook my pride and I sat up front next to him cause the young girl was in the back with her two squealin babies. We dropped her downtown at the paternity and child support place on G Street. I thought bout changin to the back seat when the girl got out but that's all I did was think bout it. He had some of them beaded seat covers up front. Them things feel like a miracle on your back; leave the imprint on your clothes, though.

He took one hand off the steerin wheel and extended it to me. "Name's Alonzo Murphy, ma'am. D.C. born and bred." And he gave an uphill laugh along with his name.

I took his hand in my glove without looking at him cause I didn't want him to take his eyes off the road. "Helen Jones," I said. "You any relation to the Murphys belong to Israel Baptist up on the hill?" I held my purse on my lap, gave me somethin to do with my hands.

"Could be," he said. "Most of my people gone from here, though and I don't do much church-goin. But could be. Had a white lady in here the other day, looked at my hacker's license and said her father-in-law name Murphy, too. I told her same thing—never know, could be some relation." He let out that rich laugh again.

"What the white woman say to that?"

"Well, she didn't have too much to say. She was just tryin to make conversation at first, I guess, and when I said we might be related it got a little uncomfortable for her."

I told him where I was goin when I realized he hadn't asked.

"You in a hurry?" he said, slow as beans cookin in a crockpot.

I thought for a minute. I looked at his hands, brown as a paper bag, restin on the steerin wheel while we was stopped at a red light. His fingers were thick and knotted; hard-workin hands but with a kindness to them. His hands reminded me of my daddy who picked tobacco for most of his life. I noticed he wasn't wearin no weddin ring. I twisted mine around and around, rubbin my finger back and forth cross the small diamond Jimmy had saved so long to get.

I looked at Murphy's eyes, too, when he asked the question. Tired eyes, with specks of red in them. Truthful eyes that don't try to hurt nobody.

Murphy had one of them green air fresheners in the shape of a tree hangin off the cigarette lighter and it smelled just like a pine cone. You could hear the heat hummin along with the soft music station on the radio. It was a nice change from the rap songs the kids play on the bus that set your head to poundin. Somethin told me wasn't no call to be scared, Alonzo Murphy wasn't no serial killer or rapist. For one thing, he was too old to be one. I glanced at him again from the corner of my eye. He was singin along with the radio tune, his hat tilted to the front of his head like Frank Sinatra. The way his beard seemed to smile along with his mouth set my mind at ease.

"I ain't in no hurry," I said, unbuttonin my overcoat. I surprised myself but there wasn't nobody or nothin home waitin for me, that's for sure, so I was only tellin the truth.

Murphy drove around, pickin up passengers and pointin out sites in between, even though I told him I had lived in D.C. for most of my life, too. We talked bout things I hadn't thought bout in a long time, from black people tryin to bleach their skin to Adam Clayton Powell, Jr. "Folk couldn't understand why he married that Hazel woman. Thought she was just too dark for him.

But that woman was a looker, I'll tell you. She was a real looker."
Then I felt him lookin at me. "I hope you don't mind me sayin so,
but you could almost pass for her twin."

My face felt feverish and my eyes were jumpy. I didn't know
what to say. The only men I talked to, other than Jimmy, was Mr.
Washington cross the street, Preacher Wilkins, the deacons at
church, and my boys, who sometimes pass for men.

But I let Murphy drive me around for a couple of hours and
didn't think nothin more bout it. Acted just like I was sposed to
be there when he picked up and dropped off passengers. I noticed
how Murphy could conversate with anybody. He joked with some
of the businessmen bout the stock market and which football
teams did what over the weekend, he discussed the President's
European trip with somebody from the Russian Embassy, and he
talked numbers with two ladies we picked up near Rhode Island
and Brentwood, coming from a church meeting. The next people
he picked up was a man and woman couldn't hardly keep they
hands off each other, just kept gigglin, smoochin, and gettin on
my last nerve.

Murphy drove through Northeast, tellin me he had lived for
awhile in the parkside projects, which use to be off Benning Road,
but don't exist no more. He had a buddy who lived in some other
projects and they was always arguin bout which had the most broken windows and the worst reputation. We was laughin and then
Murphy got serious, makin creases come in his forehead. "We was
poor as dirt back then," he said, 'but we wasn't comin apart at the
seams the way we is now. As a people, you know what I mean? We
wasn't killin each other, that's for damn sure."

I felt an excitement growin in me because the way the conversation was headin reminded me of how Jimmy and I used to talk
about things. It had been so long since somebody was interested
in my opinion (all Lance and Edward wanted to do was tell *me*
what to do, like they the parent). I told Murphy bout my seven-
teen-year-old granddaughter Latrice (Edward's chile Jimmy and
me raised) who been to more funerals in one year than I been most

of my life (cept for now when my friends is dyin off like flies). "What you think gonna make all this violence stop?" I asked him.

"More whuppins," he said just like that. "Young people nowadays don't whup they kids way they did when we was comin up. My mama would beat us for what we was thinkin about and damn near kill us for what we did. If these kids got more beatins at home, they wouldn't be actin like they do out here on the street. I wish I had me one big long hose to whup all of them."

"Ain't that simple," I said. "You can't just beat kids. You gotta talk to them. I'm tellin you what I know. I wish I'd talk to my own more and beat them less. Kids today got more things to face than we did. I believe they scared and they got a lot to be scared of."

"Like what?" Murphy seemed impatient.

"Like this crack cocaine, this AIDS, all these guns and killin. I read in the paper the other day bout eleven-year-old kids plannin they own funeral. They ain't got no business thinkin bout stuff like that."

The lovebirds in the back of the cab interrupted us to say we was approachin they destination. Murphy slowed down near a three-story building, collected his fare, and let them out. "I don't know," he said when he started to drive again. "Sometimes I think there's too much thinkin and figurin out bout problems. We didn't waste a whole bunch of time on thinkin. I know my mama and daddy didn't. You did wrong, you got beat, you learned your lesson. That was that."

We kept on talkin and Murphy kept on drivin and pickin up "fares" as he called them. I was wonderin bout why he wanted to give me a ride in the first place but I figured maybe underneath his smilin, he was just lonely like me. He had a smooth way of drivin so I didn't even feel all the bumps in the street, way I do when I'm ridin with my boys. He said he been drivin a taxicab since he dropped out of high school. "Same one?" I asked. He caught on that I was tryin to be smart and let out a short laugh. Somethin told me to check my watch and sure enough it was time for one of the boys to be bringin Jimmy back home. "Mr. Murphy," I said. "I gotta be goin home now. My husband be comin home from the clinic any minute." Murphy looked at me good, studyin me.

"What's the matter with him?"

"Oh, his liver and his kidneys ailin him. He goes over to the hospital to get hooked up to the dialysis machine. Plus he got sugar diabetes and high blood pressure. Been that way for awhile now. Doctors givin him another year they said." I started buttonin my overcoat back up.

"Doctors get on my nerves with that talk. Don't nobody got the right to say how long somebody else got in this world, I don't care who they is. If they ain't God." What he said impressed me and I nodded my head. "Where'd you say you live at?" he asked.

I told him I lived on Trinidad off West Virginia Avenue and started tryin to give directions. He waved me off with his hand and drove straight to my house by a route I never woulda thought of. My house needed paint and roof work, the walk was crumblin, and the yard was crowded with tools, broken furniture, and old appliances Jimmy meant to do something with one day. I felt kinda shamed bout it when we pulled up. "Been thinkin of sellin, getting somethin less tiresome," I said quickly. "Can't take care of it all myself."

"I thought you mentioned some boys back aways? Why can't they do it?"

"They grown. They got they own places and I'm just lucky they take they daddy to and from the hospital I guess."

Murphy nodded. "Well don't worry bout it. It looks just fine. Who said everybody got to have a picture perfect house, huh? Yours here got . . . character."

I extended my hand to say goodbye and offered to pay him. Silly, cause I didn't have no money and had already told him so. He didn't say nothing, though, just waved me off again. I started to let myself out but he touched my arm to stop me and came around to open the door like a gentleman's sposed to. When I took his hand to balance myself climbin out I looked up and saw

Edward at the window. Murphy was sayin somethin about me takin a ride again. "When you got sick folks life ain't always easy and you might need a break sometime." I didn't answer cause the look on Edward's face was worryin me; just thanked him and went on in the house.

Jimmy was propped up in his chair watchin a game show. I kissed his cheek before takin off my coat and scarf. Edward stood next to the hall closet with his arms folded, watchin me. "Mama, where you been?"

I stepped into my bedroom slippers which I keep near the radiator so they'll be nice and warm. I ignored that chile cause I didn't like what I heard in his voice.

Edward has always been my most difficult chile. He has somethin called dyslexia but we didn't know it back then and he was frustrated somethin awful in school and played hooky a lot. Seem like Jimmy was always beatin him but it didn't do no good. That's why I ain't for all that beatin no more. Anyway, Edward dropped out of high school and got a job baggin groceries. He messed around with drinkin and drugs and all that goes with it; had to go to court a couple of times but I prayed hard over that boy. He took some night classes and we found out about the dyslexia. That helped him a lot. Gave him some hope. Boy got a steady job now at a parkin lot downtown and got his own place. Course in the meantime he had Latrice by a gal who was on that stuff and me and Jimmy had to raise her. Edward spends time with her, though, gives us money sometimes and he buys her school clothes and whatnot so I ain't complainin.

He took Jimmy's sickness hard though, I guess cause he and Jimmy was mad at each other for so long. When Jimmy got sick they didn't have time to be mad no more but it didn't seem like they had enough time to make up neither. Edward started up drinkin again as a result. That's why I wished he hadn't seen me with Murphy that day.

I fixed me a cup of hot tea and sat at the kitchen table just thinkin about my day, goin back over it again and again, tryin to taste it. Edward followed me in there. "You late, Mama. You wasn't even here when Daddy got home. How you think he feel?"

"I'm sorry, Edward."

"Well, where you been? Shoppin? Visitin? Huh? Mama, I'm talkin to you!" He was shoutin at me, with his hands stretched in front of me on the table, twitchin. I smelt the liquor every time he opened his mouth. "And what was that taxi man doin talkin to you so long?"

"Nothin, Edward. There ain't no reason for you to be so upset. I had some errands to do and the man gave me a ride home. That's all."

"Ain't no dinner cooked or nothin. You always got catfish on Friday, Mama. Somethin ain't right." Edward shook his head, still wearin that troublesome expression, but there was somethin sad mixed in with the mad.

Latrice came downstairs and asked her father bout all that yellin. He don't like her to know he been drinkin so he had to get himself together and he left me alone. I went out to the living room and sat down with Jimmy. "I ain't fixed nothin to eat yet," I said. "You hungry?" I knew he hated the food in the hospital cafeteria and was always glad to be home for dinner. His drooping eyes were almost closed when he nodded. I noticed the bones in his face seemed to be right at the edge of his skin. It gave him a helpless, pleading look. A look I didn't like seein in him. I would have given half the days the Lord has left for me to get my old Jimmy back.

The picture of me and Jimmy when we got married was on the mantel in the living room and I focused on it, amazed that I had been in the company of another man even for a few hours. In the picture Jimmy had on his army uniform and I was wearin the dress my mama created from scraps of material left over from the dresses she made for white women. I was holdin a bouquet of wildflowers. I stared at the picture, trying to remember that Jimmy. He was standing so straight, makin him seem taller than the 5'8" he was. In the photograph I was gazin into his eyes, under a spell from that powerful grin he had. I remembered the way he used to dance with me on the tops of his shoes, tryin to teach me to jitter-bug, his legs bendin every which way, too quick for me to catch on.

When I got up, Edward came and sat down with Jimmy to watch the news. Latrice was on the phone—her favorite spot. I cooked up what I had in the refrigerator and tried not to think bout my ride with Alonzo Murphy.

Jimmy slept through most of the weekend. He woke up a few times, ate and went to the bathroom but he said he wanted to stay in the bed. On Sunday when I came back from church he was still sleepin. I called Lance to come over cause I couldn't wake him and I got scared. Lance shook him hard. "I ain't dead?" was the first thing Jimmy said when he finally woke. That night he sat down and went over his papers with the boys like he'd been talkin bout so that told me somethin.

Lance acted like wasn't nothin different in his life. He always been that way. Mr. Cool and Calm. Even as a little chile, when he got beat he wouldn't never cry. Edward be screamin so loud I used to think the neighbors gonna call the social workers on Jimmy. Ain't it somethin how children born from the same parents and so close in age (eleven months apart) could turn out different as night and day? Lance married, got a nice stable home life, good gov-ernment office job, no kids, and don't raise his voice to his parents. But he trouble me in other ways, cause I know when you keep so much in you can get ulcers and such. I ask him questions all the time. He say, "Don't worry, Mama. I'm all right."

After the weekend was over, Jimmy went back to the clinic like regular. He asked me to read something to pass the time. I read him some of Miss Maya Angelou; I keeps her in my purse. I think she's a mighty fine writer cause she makes me feel as if me and her been places together. I put my readin glasses on and started in with Miss Maya's *All God's Children Need Traveling Shoes*. Jimmy smiled every once and again and said, "Ummhmm" a couple of times so I know he liked what I was readin him.

One of the nurses came in and said the doctor would like to speak to me. They had three or four different doctors that used to tend to him. They nice enough but they all seem to act like I couldn't comprehend what was goin on with Jimmy, so they didn't have no need to try to explain it. That riled me something else. Anyway, one of the lady doctors was in the waitin room when I got there. She sat me down and spoke gentle and soft in a slow whisper voice, like she was sharin a secret with a chile.

One thing I find with white people is no matter how many times you seen them or talked to them, they always act like it the first time. Somethin bout the way they look straight through you like you transparent; their words don't stick, just touch you lightly, then gone. She wasn't no different. "I'm sorry to have to tell you this. But we think that . . . your husband doesn't have much time left. We would like to hospitalize him from here on so that we can monitor him much better and do everything we can to make him comfortable." Her jump-around eyes got wide while she waited for me to answer.

I told her no. I could take care of Jimmy fine at home and besides, Jimmy didn't want to die cooped up in no hospital. Who would? She asked me wasn't it a burden to bring him back and forth three times a week. I told her sure, it was a pain in the rear, but that comes with life. She too young and white to know that yet, I guess, but I watched my mouth, I didn't tell her so. She talked a little more, askin me if I wanted her to discuss it with my sons. I didn't even answer that. Then she finally said it was my decision. Which, course, I already knew. Mine and Jimmy's.

When I left there that mornin, my stomach wasn't settin right. I guess havin the doctor tell me Jimmy's time was gettin closer rattled my nerves. For her to tell me face to face meant it was more than just my thinkin or feelin. I took my time walkin to the bus stop, hopin I could get my stomach to act right before I had to mix it with all them smells be on the bus.

Well, lo, and behold, Murphy's taxi was waitin at the bus stop. Lord, he just don't know, I thought. He was wavin at me and smilin. I got in the front even though wasn't nobody in the back. "Good afternoon. What you doin here?"

He turned the radio down. "Thought I'd see if you needed a ride today. I remembered this was bout the time I picked up you Friday. But I wasn't sure if you'd be back today or later in the week." He looked at me, liftin one eyebrow. "You look a little perturbed. Did I do the wrong thing?"

"No, no," I said settlin in the seat. "It's just . . . Jimmy's doctor told me today that it won't be long and I guess it gettin to me."

"Well, sure. Course it would. I'm sorry. That's got to be some kind of somethin to hear. Look, I'm givin you my number in case you need anythin. Never know." He started writin and then handed me a piece of note paper folded in half.

I wanted to ride around with him again but thought better of it. "I think it'd be best if I waited for the bus. Thank you anyhow, Mr. Murphy." I unfolded the paper and looked at his scratchy hand-writin. I put my hand on the door and started to get out.

"Call me Alonzo, please. Is it all right if I call you Helen?"

I nodded without lookin up.

"Tell you what. I'll take you straight home. You already in here, no sense in you goin back out in the cold. How often you up at the hospital, anyway?"

"I come Monday, Wednesday, and Friday."

"Well, I'll make you a promise. Monday, Wednesday, Friday, I'll be right here waitin on you. I'll take you straight home or you can ride around with me till it's time. Whichever, whatever. How's that?" He hadn't even pulled off or nothin. We was just sittin there. I wasn't sure what to think about this offer. My first reaction was to say yes, thank you Jesus. No more freezin my toes off, besides the fact I liked conversatin with the man. But it was a scary feelin. Been so long since I thought about any man other than my Jimmy, to tell you the truth, I really didn't know how to act. Murphy seemed to understand what my hesitation was about cause he turned to me and said, "I ain't tryin to upset you or nothin. I just see you got a situation that could be better and I got a way of makin it a little better. That's all there is to it."

"I don't know," I said.

Before he took me home, we drove over to the wharf cause he said he wanted some catfish. "You ain't tasted no catfish till you tasted mine," he said. "Used to fish myself till I got arthritis in my arm." I told him I know all bout arthritis. Murphy gave me some of the catfish, sayin he only had himself to feed. When he dropped me off I thanked him for everything: the conversation, the catfish, and most of all—for takin my mind off my sadness.

He got out, of course, and came around to let me out. Fore I had a chance to take stock of anything, Edward came up on us, like a storm, and started pushin on Murphy. "What you think you doin with my mama, you ol' joker?" Murphy looked startled and almost fell over on top of me. He backed up and stood up straight, brushin his hands over his jacket. I got out by leanin on the door handle. I could see Edward's liquor-stoked eyes heatin up. "Ain't you got no decency, Mama? Your husband's on his deathbed and you out there gallivantin with this ol' . . ." Edward raised his hand again.

I reached out and tried to stop him. "Edward, calm down. You don't know what you're sayin. Mr. Murphy is just tryin—."

Edward cut me off. "Tryin to what? Tryin to figure out if you got any money comin once Daddy dies! And you fallin for it, you should be ashamed. I'm ashamed for you. Ashamed to call you my mother!" He glared at me, veins threatin to press through his forehead. He shoulda been cold cause he wasn't wearing no coat.

"Watch how you talkin to your mama, young man," Murphy said in a gentle tone.

Edward looked like he was gonna push him again or hit him but just then Lance's car pulled up behind Murphy's taxi. I said, thank you, Lord, to myself. "Lance!" I yelled. When I realized I was shakin all over, I started cryin.

Lance rushed over to us and asked what was goin on. Edward

was talkin loud and glarin at Murphy. "Brought Daddy home early today cause they called me and said he was feelin weak. Get home—she ain't even here. Your mother been runnin around all day with this . . . bum while Daddy sittin up there dyin!" He pointed toward the house. We all turned and Jimmy, lookin small as a chile, was in his wheelchair watchin us through the storm door.

Lance glanced at me. "Mama?" I shook my head and wiped my eyes with my gloves. Lance put his hand on Edward's shoulder. "Edward, go on inside with Mama. You handled it fine, man. I'll take it from here." He took Murphy's elbow, saying, "Maybe you should leave now," and they moved away from us. Edward, poutin, went ahead of me, through the gate and up the walk.

I could hear Murphy sayin, "I didn't mean no harm at all." I looked back at them. It seemed like Lance and Murphy was talkin peaceful, and so some of the tightness went out of my chest.

Jimmy said he was having shortness of breath and the doctors wanted to keep him but Jimmy didn't want to stay. He told me he was sleepy and didn't even want no dinner; just a bath. I ran the water and Edward helped get him in the tub. Edward wasn't talkin but at least he wasn't yellin no more. I put some of my bubble bath in the water, sat on a low stool, and started bathin Jimmy. Edward went on out. "Do it feel nice?" I asked Jimmy. He nodded but he was lookin awful weary. "What's wrong, sweetness?" I said. "Somethin paining?"

"Nothin new," he said, real slow and his voice sounded gravelly, like he had marbles in his mouth. "I sure wish Edward would stop drinkin. I don't want to have to worry bout none of y'all after I'm gone."

"Watch you talkin bout? Where you goin?" That's what I always said when he talked like that. Lance poked his head in the door ancl asked if we needed help. I told him no. But he didn't go away; I could feel him listenin at the door.

"I'm roundin the corner, Helen," Jimmy said. "We got to face it. It's right up on me now and I guess I'm ready. My mind and my body is sure tired." He lifted his brown, wrinkled hands out of the water and stared at them, turning them over. "Wonder what it'll be like not to reach cross and touch you no more or wake up to the sun in my eyes. Ain't nobody alive who can tell me bout it, though, is there?" He talked more that night than he had in a month. "I ain't scared no more, Helen. Just the other day I got a comfortable feelin that it's gonna be okay. I know it ain't bad what's about to happen to me. Even left me with the impression it might be good." We both laughed till he started coughin up blood.

"Listen, Helen," he went on after I wiped around his mouth. "I don't know if I told you lately how much you mean to me." I began washin his back cause I didn't know what to say. He brought my hand down and clasped it inside his. "Of all the joys in my life, over these years, you the most important one. I just wish I coulda taken you to France and Italy like we always talked bout. I just wish I had a little more time." I moved closer and put my arms around his neck and just laid my head next to his. We stayed that way for a few minutes.

I let the drain plug out. He put one tremblin hand on my shoulder and the other on the pole the boys put around the tub. Lance came into the bathroom and helped me get Jimmy out. I heard Lance sniffle and I looked up at him, catchin sight of bold tears on his face. Shocked me so, I almost let go of Jimmy. I ain't seen Lance cry since he was a baby and I'm his mama.

While we were takin Jimmy to the bedroom, he muttered to Lance, "Ain't no call for tears now. Don't want to spoil a perfect record, do ya?" (Jimmy musta been thinkin same way as me.) Lance cracked a smile and he and Jimmy hugged for the first time in a good while. I sat on the bed next to Jimmy, puttin lotion on him, rubbin it good into all his creases. I gave him a massage at the same time until my finger bones began achin. He sighed cause of how good it felt I guess. "It ain't but six o'clock," I said to him while I fluffed the pillow behind his neck.

"That's all right," he said and turned out the lamp next to the bed. I went out and cooked up Murphy's catfish for me, Latrice, and the boys.

Jimmy died later that night in his sleep. Boys was long gone by then. I sat in the rockin chair beside him till the sun came up.

The rest of that week I felt like somebody's robot; people just told me what to do and I did it. Food and folk came and went. Preacher Wilkins gave a powerful sermon at Jimmy's funeral on Saturday. He called Jimmy a "champion of life." Said he always did his best and never complained. That was mostly true. I sat up front—Edward on one side of me, Lance on the other. Next to Lance was his wife, Geraldine, and then Latrice, lookin like a grown woman in one of Geraldine's black dresses.

After the scripture readin Latrice recited a poem she wrote about Jimmy back in eighth grade. I cried a lot. It came from way deep inside me, a place I didn't even know about, and shook my whole body. Everyone kept lookin at me and handin me tissues.

We walked out of the church behind the casket holdin Jimmy. Edward held onto my arm as if he were keepin me in check. All the faces I passed were blurs of dark color. By the time I got in the family car I had stopped cryin but I felt a big empty space spreadin, like a stain, inside my chest. A space I was scared might never get filled up again.

The cemetery was the hardest part. Preacher Wilkins was mercifully short-winded, though. People took flowers out the funeral wreaths brought from the church and placed them on top of Jimmy's casket. Someone handed me a rose. I laid it where I thought his heart would be. I promised myself I would leave him with a smile. It was hard but I did.

We all started walkin back toward to the roadway where the family car was parked. That's when I saw Alonzo Murphy standin near an evergreen tree. He nodded at me and tipped the hat he held in his hand. It dawned on me that I hadn't gone to the clinic on Wednesday or Friday like I said and he had probably been there waitin. I wanted to go over and thank him for comin but I just went ahead and got in the limousine. I looked out the window and saw Lance walkin toward Murphy. They shook hands and Murphy gave Lance one of his slow, easy smiles.

"Who's that man?" Latrice wanted to know.

"Nobody special," I said. "Just an old friend." Lance came soon after and joined the rest of us in the family car.

Patricia Elam Ruff has written for *Essence, Emerge,* and *The Washington Post* and provided commentary for National Public Radio and CNN. She lives in Washington, D.C., where she is at work on a novel.

I rarely take taxis, but one day my car was in the shop, my feet hurt, and I hailed one. The driver was an older gentleman and he was accompanied by an older woman who sat up front with him. I immediately noticed that there was something very comfortable and caring about their relationship. Whether they were talking or silent, they were constantly communicating. During the brief time I was in their presence, I became aware of the romance and love they shared even though there was no physical touching between them. The experience was quite magical and I had no choice but to go home and try to write a story about it.

Tim Gautreaux

LITTLE FROGS IN A DITCH

(from *GQ*)

O ld man Fontenot watched his grandson draw hard on a slim cigarette and then flick ashes on the fresh gray enamel of the front porch. The boy had been fired, this time from the laundry down the street.

"The guy who let me go didn't have half the brains I got," Lenny Fontenot said.

The old man nodded, then took a swallow from a can of warm beer. "The owner, he didn't like you double-creasing the slacks." He wouldn't look at the boy. Instead he watched a luminous cloud drifting up from the Gulf.

"Let me tell you," Lenny said with a snarl, his head following a dusk-drawn pigeon floating past the screen, "there's some dumb people in this world."

"Give it a rest," the old man said, looking down the street to the drizzle-washed iron roof of the laundry. His grandson was living with him again, eating his food, using all the hot water in the mornings. "If you work on your attitude a little bit, you could keep a job."

Lenny stood up and put his nose to the screen. "I didn't need a laundry job anyway. I'm a salesman."

"You couldn't sell cow cakes to a rosebush."

Lenny threw down his cigarette and mashed it with the toe of a scuffed loafer. "Hey, I could sell a pigeon."

His grandfather picked up his cap and looked at him. "Who the hell would buy a pigeon?"

"I could find him."

"Lenny, if someone wanted a pigeon, all he'd have to do is catch him one."

"A dumb man will buy a pigeon from me." He clopped down the steps to the side yard. At the rear of the lot was a broad, unused carport, swaybacked over broken lawn mowers and wheelbarrows. He looked up into the eaves to the ragged nests dripping dung down the side of a beam. With a quick grab he had a slate blue pigeon in his hands, the bird blinking its onyx eyes stupidly. He turned to his grandfather, who was walking up. "Look. You can pluck them like berries under here."

Old man Fontenot gave him a disgusted look. "Nobody'll eat a pigeon."

Lenny ducked his head. "Eat? I ain't said nothing about eat." He smiled down at the bird. "This is a homing pigeon."

"Come on. That thing's got fleas like a politician. Put it down." The old man pulled at his elbow.

Lenny's eyes came up red and filmy. "Your Ford's got a crack in the head and you can't afford to get it fixed. I'm gonna make some money for you."

His grandfather knew Lenny wanted the car for his own but said nothing. He looked at the bird in his grandson's hands, which was pedaling the air, blinking its drop of dark eye. "I told your parents I wouldn't let you get in any more trouble." He watched Lenny make a face. The grandfather remembered the boy's big room in his parents' air-conditioned brick rancher, the house they sold from under Lenny to buy a Winnebago and tour the country. One day the boy had come home from a long weekend and everything he owned was stacked under the carport, a Sold sign out front.

Two days later, the old man watched Lenny fold back the classified section to his ad, which read "Homing pigeons $10 each. Training instructions included." His grandfather read it over his shoulder, then went into the kitchen to cook breakfast. Lenny came in and looked down at the stove.

"You gonna cook some eggs? Annie likes eggs."

"She coming over again?" He tried to sound miffed, but in truth he liked Annie. She was a big-boned, denim-clad blonde who worked in a machine shop. He felt sorry for the girl because Lenny made her pay for their dates.

Lenny rumbled down the steps, and the grandfather watched him through the kitchen window. From behind the carport he pulled a long-legged rabbit cage. He shook out the ancient pellets and set it next to the steps. With his cigarette-stained fingers, he snatched from the carport eaves a granite-colored pigeon and clapped him into the cage. Most of the other birds lit out in a rat-tat-tat of wings, but he managed to snag a pink-and-gray. The old man clucked his tongue and turned up the fire under the peppery boudin.

Annie came up the rear steps lugging a toolbox. At the stove, she took a helping then sat at the kitchen table, spooning grits and eggs into herself.

"Annie, baby." Lenny plopped down across from her with a plate of smoking sausage. After they finished eating, she asked him why he was going into the pigeon business. He told her he was doing it for her, so they could use the car. Then the doorbell jittered, and everyone got up to see who it was.

On the front porch, they found a white-haired gentleman staring at a torn swatch of newsprint. He was wearing nubby brown slacks and a green checkered cowboy shirt.

"I'm Perry Lejeune from over by Broussard Street. About five blocks. I saw your ad."

Mr. Fontenot gave his grandson a scowl and pulled off his cap as if he would toss it.

Lenny straightened out of his slouch and smiled, showing his small teeth. "Mr. Lejeune, you know anything about homing pigeons?"

The other man shook his head. "Nah. My little nephew Alvin's living at my house and I want to get him something to occupy his time. His momma left him with me and I got to keep him busy, you know?" Mr. Lejeune raised his shoulders. "I'm too old to play ball with a kid."

"Don't worry, I'll fill you in," he said, motioning for everyone to follow him back to the carport. He put his hand on the rickety rabbit cage and made eye contact with Mr. Lejeune. "I've got just two left. This slate," he nodded toward the plain bird, "is good in the rain. And I got that pink fella if you want something flashy."

Mr. Lejeune put up a hand like a stop signal. "I can't afford nothing too racy."

"The slate's a good bird. Of course, at this price, you got to train him, you know."

"Yeah, I want to ask you about that." Mr. Lejeune made a pliers of his right forefinger and thumb and clamped them on his chin. Annie came around close, and the grandfather looked at the bottom of his back steps and shook his head.

Lenny put his hands in the cage and caught the pigeon. "You got to build a cage out of hardware cloth with a one-way door."

"Yeah, for when he comes back, you mean."

Lenny gave Mr. Lejeune a look. "That's right. Now to start training you got to hold him like a football, with your thumbs on top of him and your fingers underneath. You see?"

Mr. Lejeune put on his glasses and bent to look under the pigeon. "Uh-hun."

"Stand exactly where your property line is. Then you catch his little legs between your forefingers and your middle fingers. One leg in each set of fingers, you see?" Lenny got down on his knees, wincing at the rough pavement. "You put his little legs on the ground, like this. You see?"

"Yeah, I got you."

"Then you walk the bird along your property line, moving his legs and coming along behind him like this. You got to go around all four sides of your lot with him so he can memorize what your place looks like."

"Yeah, yeah, I got you. Give him the grand tour, kinda."

Annie frowned and hid her mouth under a bright hand. His grandfather sat on the steps and looked away.

Lenny waggled the bird along the ground as the animal pumped its head, blinked, and tried to peck him. "Now it takes commitment to train a bird. It takes a special person. Not everybody's got the character it takes to handle a homing pigeon."

Mr. Lejeune nodded. "Hey, you talking to someone's been married forty-three years. How long you got to train 'em?"

Lenny stood and replaced the bird in the cage. "Every day for two weeks, you got to do this."

"Rain or shine?" Mr Lejeune's snowy eyebrows went up.

"That's right. And then after two weeks, you take him in a box out to Bayou Park and set his little butt loose. He might even beat you home, you know?"

The man bobbed his head. "Little Alvin's gonna love this." He reached for his wallet. "Any tax?"

"A dollar."

Mr. Lejeune handed him a ten and dug for a one. "Ain't the tax rate 8 percent in the city?"

"Two percent wildlife tax," Lenny told him, reaching under the cage for a shoe box blasted with ice-pick holes.

That day Lenny sold pigeons to Mankatos Djan, a recent African immigrant, and to two children who showed up on rusty BMX bikes. By the twelfth day, he had sold twenty-six pigeons and had enough to fix the leaf-covered sedan. Lenny counted his money and walked up to the front porch, where his grandfather was finishing a mug of coffee in the heat. He looked at the cash in Lenny's outstretched hand. "What's that?"

"It's enough money to fix the car."

His grandfather looked away toward the laundry. "I saw you take $20 from some children for a lousy pair of flea baits. You got no morals."

"Hey. It's for your car, dammit."

"That poor colored guy who couldn't hardly speak a word of English. Black as a briquette and he believed every damned thing you told him. My grandson sticks him for eleven bucks that'd feed one of his relatives living in a grass shack back in Bogoslavia for a year." He looked up at Lenny, his veiny brown eyes wavering from the heat. "What's wrong with you?"

"What's wrong with me?" he yelled, stepping back. "Everybody's getting money but me. I ain't even got a job, and I start a business, just like everybody else does."

"You don't know shit about business. You're a crook."

"All right." He banged the money against his thigh. "So I'm a crook. What's the difference between me and the guy that sells a Mercedes?"

The grandfather grabbed the arms of his rocker as his voice rose. "A Mercedes won't fly off toward the clouds, crap in your eye, and not come back after you paid good money for it."

Lenny jerked his head toward the street. "It's all how you look at it," he growled.

"There's only one way to look at it, dammit. The right way." His grandfather stood up. "You get out of my house. Your parents got rid of you and now I know why. Maybe a few nights sleeping in the car will straighten you out."

Lenny backed up another step, the money still in his outstretched hand. "They didn't get rid of me. They moved out west."

"Get out." The old man brought his thin brows down low and beads of sweat glimmered on his bald head. "Don't come back until you get a job."

"I can't live out on the street," Lenny said, his voice softening, his face trying a thin smile.

"Crooks wind up on the street and later they burn in hell," the old man said.

Lenny kicked the bottom of the screen, and his grandfather yelled. Five minutes later, he was standing next to the sagging Ford, listening to the feathery pop of wings as the old man pulled pigeons out of the rabbit cage and tossed them toward the roof-tops.

That night the grandfather couldn't sleep and rolled up the shade at the tall window next to his bed, looking into the moonlit side yard at his car parked against the fence. He knelt on the floor and folded his arms on the window sill, thinking how Lenny should be back at the cleaner's, smiling through the steam of his pressing machine. Down in the yard, the Ford bobbled, and he imagined that Lenny was slapping mosquitoes off his face, that the boy was turning over, putting his nose into the crack at the bottom of the seat back, smelling the dust balls and old pennies and cigarette filters. The grandfather thought of Annie, her Pet milk skin, her big curves. Lenny talked with longing of her paychecks, nearly $2,400 a month, clear. Lenny had never made above minimum wage and complained often about how undervalued he was. His grandfather wondered if some dim sense of the real world of work would ever settle on him. The old man climbed into bed but couldn't sleep because he began to see people Lenny had sold birds to, the dumb children, the African, and wondered how the boy could sell his soul for $11.

At six o'clock, he went down into the yard and opened the driver's door to the car. The boy lay back against the seat and put an arm over his eyes. "Aw, man."

His grandfather pushed on his shoulder. "You get a job yet?"

Lenny cocked up a red eye. "How'm I gonna get a job smelling bad with no shave and mosquito bites all over me?"

The old man considered this a moment, looking his grandson in his sticky eyes. He remembered the inert feel of him as a baby. "OK. I'll give you a temporary reprieve on one condition."

"What's that?" Lenny hung his head way back over the seat.

"St. Lucy has confessions before seven o'clock daily Mass. I want you to think about going to confession and telling the priest what you done."

Lenny straightened up and eyed the house. The old man knew he was considering its old deep bathtub and its oversized water heater. "Where in the catechism does it say selling pigeons is a mortal sin?"

"You going, or you staying outside in your stink?"

"What am I supposed to tell the priest?" He turned his hands up in his lap.

His grandfather squatted down next to him. "Remember what Sister Florita told you one time in catechism class? If you close your eyes before you go to confession, your sins will make a noise."

Lenny closed his eyes. "A noise."

"They'll cry out like little frogs in a ditch at sundown."

"Sure," Lenny said with a laugh, his eyeballs shifting under the closed lids. "Well, I don't hear nothing." He opened his eyes and looked at the old man. "What's the point of me confessing if I don't hear nothing?"

His grandfather stood up with a groan.

"Keep listening," he said.

After Lenny cleaned up, they ate breakfast at a café on River Street, and later, walking home, they spotted Annie coming up the street carrying her toolbox, her blonde hair splashed like gold on the shoulders of her denim shirt.

Lenny gave her a bump with his hip. "Annie, you're out early, babe."

She lifted her chin. "I came to see you. Somebody told me you were sleeping in the car like a bum." She emphasized the last word.

"The old man didn't like my last business."

"It wasn't business," she snapped. Annie looked at the grandfather, then at Lenny's eyes, searching for something. "You just don't get it, do you?"

"Get what?" When he saw her expression, he lost his smile.

She sighed and looked at her watch. "Ya'll come on." She picked up her toolbox and started down the root-buckled sidewalk toward Broussard Street. After five blocks, they crossed a wide boulevard, went one more block, and stopped behind a holly bush growing next to the curb. Across the street was a peeling weatherboard house.

"This is about the time I saw him yesterday," Annie said.

"Who?" the grandfather asked.

"The old guy Lenny sold the pigeon to."

Lenny ducked behind the bush. "Jeez, you want him to see me?"

Across the street, there was movement at the side of the house, and Mr. Lejeune came around his porch slow, shuffling on his knees like a locomotive. The grandfather stood on his toes and saw that the old man was red in the face, and the pigeon itself looked tired and drunk.

"Man," Lenny whispered, "he's got rags tied around his knee-caps."

"Yesterday I saw he wore the tips off his shoes. Look at that." Behind Mr. Lejeune walked a thin boy, perhaps 9 years old, awkward and pale. "Didn't he say he had a nephew?" The boy was smiling and talking down to his uncle. "The kid looks excited about something."

"Two weeks," Lenny said.

"Huh?" The grandfather cupped a hand behind an ear.

"Today's two weeks. They'll probably go to Bayou Park this afternoon and turn it loose."

Mr. Lejeune looked up and across toward where they were standing. He bent to the side a bit and then lurched to his feet, waving like a windshield wiper. "Hey, what ya'll doing on this side the boulevard?"

The three of them crossed the street and stood on the walk. "We was just out and about," Lenny told him. "How's the bird doin'?" The pigeon seemed to look up at him angrily, blinking, struggling. Someone had painted its claws with red fingernail polish.

"This here's Amelia," Mr. Lejeune said. "That's what Alvin named him. Or her. We never could figure how to tell, you know." He looked at his nephew. The grandfather saw that the boy was trembling in spite of his smile. His feet were pointed inward, and his left hand was shriveled and pink.

"How you doing, bud?" The grandfather asked, patting his head.

"All right," the boy said. "We going to the park at four o'clock and turn Amelia loose."

Lenny forced a smile. "You and your uncle been having a good time training old Amelia, huh?"

The boy looked over to where his uncle had gone to sit on the front steps. He was rubbing his knees. "Yeah. It's been great. The first day, we got caught out in a thunderstorm and I got a chest cold, but the medicine made me feel better."

"You had to go to the doctor?" Annie asked, touching his neck.

"Him too," the boy volunteered in a reedy voice. "Shots in the legs." He looked up at Lenny. "It'll be worth it when Amelia comes back from across town."

"Why's it so important?" Lenny asked.

The boy shrugged. "It's just great that this bird way up in the sky knows which house I live in."

The old man struggled to his feet, untying the pads from his knees. "Come in the backyard and look at the cage." He shook out his pants and tugged the boy toward the rear of the house to a close-clipped yard with an orange tree in the middle. Against the rear of the house was a long-legged cage, shiny with new galvanized hardware cloth.

"That took a lot of work to build, I bet," the grandfather said out of the side of his mouth to Lenny, who shrugged and said that he'd told him how to do it. The comers of the cage were finished like furniture, mortised and tenoned. In the center was a ramp leading up to a swinging door. The pigeon squirted out of the old man's hand into the cage, crazy for the steel-mesh freedom.

"We'll let him rest up for the big flight," Mr. Lejeune said.

Lenny glanced over at Annie's serious face. She looked long at the pigeon, then over at where the boy slumped against the orange tree. "You know," Lenny began, "if you decide you ain't happy with the bird, you can have your money back."

Mr. Lejeune looked at him quickly. "No way. He's trained now. I bet he could find this house from the North Pole."

The grandfather told Mr. Lejeune how much he liked the cage, then touched Annie's shoulder, and they said their goodbyes. On the walk home, she was silent. When they got to the grandfather's, she stopped, rattled her little toolbox, glanced back down the street and asked, "Lenny, what's gonna happen if that bird doesn't come back to the kid?"

He shook his head. "If he heads for the river and spots them grain elevators, he'll never see Broussard Street again, that's for sure."

"Two weeks ago, you knew he was buying Amelia as a pet for a kid."

Lenny turned his palms out. "Am I responsible for everything those birds do until they die?"

The grandfather rolled his eyes at the girl. She wasn't stupid, but when she looked at Lenny there was too much hope in her eyes.

Annie clenched and unclenched her big pale hands. "If I was a bad sort, I'd hit you with a crescent wrench." She looked at him the way she studied a gadget whirling in her lathe, maybe wondering if he would come out all right.

Lenny lit up a cigarette and let the smoke come out as he talked. "I'm sorry. I'll try to think of something to tell the kid if the bird don't come back."

She considered this for a moment, then leaned over and kissed him quickly on the side of his mouth. As the grandfather watched her stride down the sidewalk, he listened to the Williams sockets rattling in her toolbox, and then he saw Lenny wipe off the hot wetness of her lips.

That night, a half hour after dark, Annie, Lenny, and his grandfather were watching a John Wayne movie in the den when there was a knock at the back screen door. It was Mr. Lejeune, and he was worried about Amelia.

"I turned her loose about 4:30, and she ain't come back yet," the old man told Lenny. "You got any hints?"

Lenny looked at a shoe. "You want a refund?"

"Nah." He pushed back his white hair with his fingers. "That ain't the point. The boy's gonna get a lift from seeing the bird come back." Alvin's pale face tilted out from behind his uncle's waist.

Annie, who was wearing shorts, peeled herself off the plastic couch, and the grandfather put a spotted hand over his eyes. Lenny turned a serious face toward the boy. "Sometimes those birds get in fights with other birds. Sometimes they get hurt and don't make it back. What can I tell you? You want your money?" He put a hand in his pocket but left it there.

The old man sidestepped out onto the porch. "Me and Alvin will go and wait. If that bird'd just come back once it'd be worth all the crawlin' around, you see?" He held the boy's twisted hand and went down ahead of him, one step at a time. Annie moved into the kitchen and broke a glass in the sink. The grandfather tried not to listen to what happened next.

Lenny went to see what caused the noise, and there was a rattle of accusations from Annie. Then Lenny began to shout. "Why are you bitching at me like this?"

"Because you gypped that old man and the crippled kid. I've never seen you do nothing like that."

"Well you better get used to it."

"Get used to what?" She used a big, contrary voice better than most women, the grandfather thought.

"Get used to doing things the way I like."

"What, like stealing from old people and kids? Acting like a freakin' slug? Now I know why your parents left your ass in the street."

Lenny's voice came through the kitchen door thready and high-pitched. "Hey, nobody left me. They're on vacation, you cow."

"People don't sell their houses, leave the time zone and never write or call because they're on vacation, you retard. They left because they found out what it took me a long time to just now realize."

"What's that?"

And here a sob came into her voice, and the grandfather put his head down.

"That there's a big piece of you missing that'll never turn up."

"You can't talk to me like that," Lenny snarled, "and I'll show you why." The popping noise of a slap came from the kitchen, and the grandfather thought, Oh no, and struggled to rise from the sofa, but before he could stand and steady himself, a sound like a piano tipping over shook the entire house, and Lenny cried out in deep pain.

After the grandfather prepared an ice pack, he went to bed that night but couldn't sleep. He thought of the handprint on Annie's face and the formal numbness of the walk back to her house as he escorted her home. Now he imagined Mr. Lejeune checking Amelia's cage into the night, his nephew asking him questions in a resigned voice. He even formed a picture of the pigeon hunkered down on a roof vent above the St. Mary Feed Company elevator, trying with its little bird brain to remember where Broussard Street was. About one o'clock, he smacked himself on the forehead with an open palm, put on his clothes, and went down to the old carport with a flashlight. In the eaves, he saw a number of round heads pop into his light's beam, and when he checked the section from which Lenny had plucked Amelia, he thought he saw her. Turning off the light for a moment, he reached into the straw and pulled out a bird that barely struggled. Its claws were painted red, and the grandfather eased down into a wheelbarrow to think, the bird in both hands, where it pecked him resignedly. He debated whether he should just let the animal go and forget the Lejeunes, but then he imagined how the boy would have to face the empty cage. It would be like an abandoned house, and every day the boy would look at it and wonder why Amelia had forgotten where he lived.

* * *

At 2:15 the grandfather walked down the side of Mr. Lejeune's house, staying close to the wall and out of the glow of the streetlight. When he turned the corner into the backyard, he was in total darkness and had to feel for the cage, and then for its little swinging gate. His heart jumped as he felt a feathery movement in the palms, and the bird leaped for the enclosure. At that instant, a backyard floodlight came on, and the back door rattled open, showing Mr. Lejeune standing in a pair of mustard-colored pajama bottoms and a sleeveless undershirt.

"Hey, what'cha doing?" He came down into the yard, moving carefully.

The grandfather couldn't think of a lie to save his soul, but stood there looking between the cage and the back door. "I just wanted to see about the bird," he said at last.

The other man walked up and looked into the cage. "What? How'd you get ahold of the dumb cluck? I thought she'd be in Texas by now." He reached back and scratched a hip.

The grandfather's mouth slowly fell open. "You knew?"

"Yeah," Mr. Lejeune growled. "I may be dumb, but I ain't stupid. And no offense, Mr. Fontenot, but that grandson of yours got used-car salesman writ all over him."

"Why'd you come by the house asking about the bird if you knew it'd never come back?"

"That was for Alvin, you know? I wanted him to think I was worried." Mr. Lejeune grabbed the grandfather by the elbow and led him into his kitchen, where the two men sat down at a little porcelain-topped table. The old man opened the refrigerator and retrieved two frosty cans of Schlitz. "It's like this," Mr. Lejeune said, wincing against the spray from the pull tabs, "Little Alvin's never had a daddy, and his momma's a crackhead that run off with some biker to Alaska." He pushed a can to the grandfather, who picked it up and drew hard, for he was sweating. Mr. Lejeune spoke low and leaned close. "Little Alvin's still in fairy-tale land, you know. Thinks his momma is coming back when school starts up in the fall. But he's got to toughen up and face facts. That's why

I bought that roof rat from your grandson." He sat back and began rubbing his knees. "He'll be disappointed about the little thing, that bird, and maybe it'll teach him to deal with the big thing. That boy's got to live a long time, you know what I mean, Mr. Fontenot?"

The grandfather put his cap on the table. "Ain't that kind of a tough lesson, though?"

"Hey. We'll watch the sky for a couple days and I'll let him see how I take it. We'll be disappointed together." Mr. Lejeune looked down at his purple feet. "He's crippled, but he's strong and he's smart."

The grandfather lifted his beer and drank until his eyes stung. He remembered Lenny, asleep in the front bedroom with a big knot on the back of his head and a black eye. He listened to Mr. Lejeune until he was drowsy. "I got to get back home," he said, standing up and moving toward the door. "Thanks for the beer."

"Hey. Don't worry about nothing. Just do me a favor and put that bird back in its nest." They went out, and Mr. Lejeune reached into the cage and retrieved Amelia, dropping her into a heavy grocery bag.

"You sure you doing the right thing, now?" the grandfather asked. "You got time to change your mind." He helped fold the top of the bag shut. "You could be kind." He imagined what the boy's face would look like if he would see that the bird had returned to the cage.

Mr. Lejeune slowly handed him the bag. For a moment, they held it together and listened. Inside, the bird walked the crackling bottom back and forth on its painted toes, looking for home.

———

Tim Gautreaux was raised in Morgan City, Louisiana. He earned a doctorate in English at the University of South Carolina and now lives in Hammond, Louisiana, with his wife and two sons. His fiction has appeared in *The Atlantic, Harper's, GQ, Story,* and *Best American Short*

Stories, among other places. He is the recipient of a NEA fellowship as well as the National Magazine Award for fiction. For many years he has directed the creative writing program at Southeastern Louisiana University. St. Martin's Press has recently published his book of short stories, *Same Place, Same Things*, and will publish his novel early next year.

I overheard two grown men talking about mean tricks they'd played on people when they were children. One fellow bragged about selling common roof pigeons by putting an ad in the paper claiming they were untrained homing pigeons. Training directions would be provided with each bird.

The men went on their way, but I was left to think about the type of person who would sell common birds to folks who would waste a couple of weeks of their lives following asinine training directions. I wondered what it must be like to have such a person for a relative or a friend. So I made up Lenny and set him in motion. Sometimes a character is like that for a writer; he's a wind-up toy the author puts on the floor to see where he'll wobble off to. Lenny makes his girlfriend pay for dates, eats his grandfather's food, and takes money from children and old men for worthless pigeons. His girlfriend dumps him, his grandfather throws him out of the house, and even his saddest victim, the savvy Mr. Lejeune, turns a ten-dollar pigeon into a valuable lesson for both his crippled nephew and Lenny's grandfather.

Lenny makes life a little harder for his customers. Taking advantage of people is his only talent, and everyone who comes in contact with him finds this out the hard way. He never seems to see, though, that he makes life hardest for himself.

Marc Vassallo

AFTER THE OPERA

(from *The Gettysburg Review*)

I

After *Don Giovanni* and the milling about on the Kennedy Center promenade, the swirling sea of furs and greatcoats, I drove my mother back to the suburbs, keeping as close to the river as I could. The river flowed silently in the other direction, suburb to city, its black water silver-touched in the moonlight, its moist banks growing wider as it coursed toward the bay. I would glimpse the river through the twisted oaks along the canal, lose it for a stretch, then find it again, a shimmering thread stitching pieces of night together.

At my mother's request, we had taken my father's car, a black Mercedes with a black interior that still smelled of fresh leather. I wore his best suit, also at my mother's request—the tweed blazer I'd brought simply wouldn't do—and his Italian shoes and black leather driving gloves. I wore his watch, too, the one thing of his I wore every day, a burnished silver watch with a thin gold rim, two gold hands, and nothing else: no second hand, no tick marks, no sense of time moving, no way to measure time except by approximation. It was in every way my father's watch, faulty quartz timing tempered by the ambiguity of an unblemished face; it looked better than the time it told. It was the watch of a man destined to die young.

73

I drove the way I imagined my father would drive after the opera, slowly, gloved hands lightly touching the wheel, eyes moving from the river to the road to my mother and back again, one of Don Giovanni's arias playing in my head. In less than an hour, we would be out on the river, my mother and I, for the second half of the deal we had struck: I would accompany her to the opera if she would camp out with me afterward on Tuckerman's Island.

My mother and I had struck deals like this before—she used to take me to the zoo if I would attend church with her—but I had no idea why she had agreed to camp with me; I had to assume that what she told me on the phone was true: she desperately wanted to go to the opera again, but not alone. And yet I was suspicious, since, although she co-chaired the neighborhood garden club and assiduously weeded her azalea beds, she was as foreign to the night woods as I was to the opera house. I had driven up from Charlottesville for the night, as long as I felt I could be away from Laura and the baby, prompted by the realization that in the six months since the funeral, my mother and I had never once mentioned my father, the man whose voiceless memory sat between us, the man whose body once filled the clothes I wore, the man who had purchased the car I was driving for its quiet ride. I still wondered about his final words: "Where shall we abandon our carts?" I hoped my mother knew their meaning.

She made small talk as I drove through Georgetown—about Don Giovanni's pantaloons, about the pizzelle she was making for Phyllis Caputo, about the theft of an entire rack of dresses at a boutique in Potomac Village—and I listened vaguely, thinking instead of how the hair on my father's legs once bristled against the pants I now wore, of how the hair felt when I massaged his arthritic limbs, and of how, in the bitter end, I threw out everything I knew about therapeutic massage and ran my hand gingerly over his ruined body, as much to satisfy my disbelief as to comfort him: across his chest, along the base of his distended stomach, down the sides of his legs to his twisted, jaundiced feet, swollen with the same fluid that would soon fill his lungs, weigh down his body, lighten his soul, take him away.

As we turned from the river at Glen Echo, my mother grew uncharacteristically silent, as if in deference to what I was thinking, then began to speak in a hushed voice.

"Sometimes we'd stop in Georgetown for a walk along the canal," she said, speaking of my father without naming him, looking straight ahead. "There was a cafe alongside the towpath where we'd order espresso and perhaps a pastry. If the weather was nice, we'd sit outside and listen in on the conversations of people passing by. It felt almost like Paris." She paused, and in the stillness of the car's interior, I heard her sigh. "One especially cold December night," she said, "from inside, we watched skaters spinning on the frozen canal. We thought the whitish flecks blowing around them were snow flurries, but they turned out to be ashes from a bonfire."

Her words had an unaccustomed lyricism, an amorous passion I associated more with my father than with her. Perhaps, I thought, the opera or the sight of me in my father's clothes had stirred up a long-buried wistfulness. I felt suddenly ridiculous in my father's suit, and responsible, too, for compounding my mother's melancholy. But I dared not break the spell. I slowed down and glanced at her. In the yellow light of the streetlamps, her thick, dark hair and smooth skin made her look much younger than sixty. I detected youth in her voice, as well, which sounded hopeful and unburdened.

"He was a graceful skater," she said. "He knew how to hold himself, how to position his hands, what to do with his skates." I pictured him on the big river, the one time we skated there instead of on the canal, my father cutting crisp figure eights with a single blade, his other skate high in the air, as if he were a ballet dancer, the embodiment of fluid geometry. I held out my gloved hand and my mother took it, squeezed it.

"He was a beautiful dancer, too," I said, but I spoke into a silence that was no longer electric. The moon appeared above the

trees, an orange globe, watching. We entered my old neighborhood and drove past the Englemans', the Changs', and the Stouf-
fers', then turned onto our cul-de-sac. Mr. and Mrs. Landon were
standing in their driveway, Mr. Landon hefting suitcases from the
trunk of their car, back from who knew where. Mrs. Landon
waved to us. My mother let go of my hand to wave back. Whatever spell she had been under was broken.

"Should I wear long johns?" she asked when we reached the
driveway. "The temperature is supposed to drop below freezing."

"You should at least bring them," I said.

"How far did you say the walk was?" she said. "Are animals
going to be a problem? Will we be home in time for breakfast?"
She asked half a dozen questions, one on top of the other.

"Are you sure you still want to do this?" I said.

"I'm certain," she said. She sounded too sure, too eager.

"Tell me the truth," I said. "Why did you agree to camp out?" I
stopped the car and pushed the button for the garage door opener.

"There's something I need to tell you," she said. "I thought
perhaps you would be more inclined to listen if you were in your
element."

"I'm wearing my father's clothes," I said. "I'm sitting with my
mother in front of the house I grew up in. I'm in my element. Tell
me now." The garage door was up, the bluish light from the garage
shining on us. My mother looked wan, ancient. She bit her lip.

"I," she said. "Joe. You remember Joe Palmieri."

The man who beat my father out of a top position at the
Department of Energy, a big, brazen man who used to grab hold
of my whole arm with his thick hand, rattle my bones, and say:
"Shake the hand that shook the hand of Abraham Lincoln!" He
was six-six, close to three hundred pounds, and had one arm. How
could I forget him. "Don't tell me," I said. "He had a heart attack."

"No," she said. "Actually, he invited me over to help him make
pasta a few months ago and, well, let's just say we've been making
pasta ever since."

"Joe Palmieri?" His name was all I could think to say.

"I ran into him at the annual office picnic," my mother said. "We got to talking, Joe said he . . . we both found it so difficult to be alone at suppertime . . . he's an excellent cook."

"Good God," I said. I tightened my grip on the steering wheel and concentrated on my breathing, not wanting to appear as alarmed as I felt.

"Joe's not one for the opera," my mother continued at a clip. "Phyllis had two tickets she couldn't use, she's in the hospital, you know, bad back, and I thought you and I might, I wanted to tell you, and then you proposed a campout and, well, I thought that if you were in your element, perhaps—"

"Just shut up," I said. "Please, just shut up."

I stepped on the gas pedal a tad harder than I meant to. The Mercedes lurched forward, too close to the right side of the garage door opening, tearing off the side-view mirror. "No looking back now," I thought. The pathetic humor of that thought was the only thing that kept me from stepping on the gas again and crashing through the wall and into her bedroom.

II

"You don't need a flashlight," I told my mother as we walked across a swinging wooden footbridge, some twenty feet over a thin, streamlike stretch of the Potomac, no more water than was necessary to make Tuckerman's Island an island. "Trust your eyes," I said once we were in the woods again. "Give me that." I stopped short and, as she stumbled into me, I reached behind and took the flashlight from her hand and put it in my jacket pocket.

"Christopher," she said. "Please."

I ignored her, picked up the pace. The trail beneath us was hard but not yet frozen, easy to follow even when the moon disappeared behind a cloud. For a time, I forgot about Joe Palmieri. The air was cold and moist; it felt good on my cheeks, unexpected, like basement air in summertime.

We walked for perhaps twenty minutes before we reached a

grassy clearing along the rivershore and then the campsite I knew would be waiting for us, with a rock-ringed fire pit and a patch of bare ground for our tent. We were close enough to the river to hear the water lapping against the muddy bank of the island.

My mother laid her two extra sweaters over a log and sat down by the fire pit. I built a small fire with the kindling that had been left there, gathered enough wood to last the night, and then set up the tent and arranged our sleeping gear. I worked calmly, purposefully, trying not to think beyond the task at hand. "Where shall we abandon our carts?" I said over and over to myself, like a mantra. My mother sipped at the coffee she had brought in a thermos. She dared not say a word.

Once I had the fire going, I sat on the log beside her. Then I took off my wool jacket and rolled up the sleeves of my flannel shirt. I knew my mother wanted to say, "You'll catch a cold, Christopher," but she held her tongue. As I removed my boots and socks, she looked at me suspiciously. I curled my toes inches from the flames. The crackle of the fire and the lap of river against the bank were the only sounds.

Neither of us spoke for ten or fifteen minutes. We had scarcely said a word since the driveway; my mother had not even commented on the side-view mirror. Finally she turned to me. "So, what did you think of the opera?" She had asked earlier, on the Kennedy Center promenade, and I had answered, merely, "I liked it."

Now in the woods, I said, "I cried the whole time. I guess you didn't notice. I was thinking about Dad, about all those Sunday mornings he listened to the opera, about how much music meant to him, even in the end . . . especially in the end."

"I noticed," she said. She paused a moment, then said, "Did you like the costumes?"

"I did," I said. I refused to make small talk about the opera all night. I said, "Dad told me something the week before he died, right after he got off the phone with Joe. He told me that when Joe first arrived at DOE, he didn't have a security clearance, so they made him work in a trailer next to the main building. Dad said they called Joe's trailer The Cage. He said he used to visit Joe every day at lunch. He was the only one who visited." I threw a log on the fire.

"I know about The Cage," my mother said. She poured another cup of coffee; the rich smell of it mixed with the musty aroma of the decaying log. "My relationship with Joe is about where we find ourselves now," she said, "not about Dad and Joe, not about the past."

"First he takes Dad's job," I said, "then his wife. He's diverted your attention, and now mine. We should be talking about Dad, not about Joe Palmieri."

"I can't talk about Dad," my mother said.

"You did pretty damn well in the car," I said.

"I don't know what came over me," she said. She wrapped the army jacket she had borrowed from me more tightly around her. "And I don't know what you mean about Joe having diverted my attention."

"I think I can guess what came over you," I said. "Thirty-five years of marriage came over you, Dad's spirit came over you, guilt came over you."

"That's enough," she said, sounding as if she thought I was five. "And my attention's not something to be diverted by anyone; I pay it to whomever I please."

"Well, don't forget your family."

"I'm sitting in the middle of the woods with you," she said. "I invited you to the opera."

"As a ruse," I said. "You could have called me and told me about Joe when you first started seeing him."

"I thought it best to exercise some discretion."

"You talk about discretion like it's some kind of inimitable virtue," I said. "What about frankness?"

"I've always been frank with you, Christopher."

"Like hell," I said. "Remember when you took those girlie magazines from under my dresser and replaced them with, what was it, a Catholic sex education manual?"

"Christopher, I—"

"And the time you took the bag of dope off my desk and held onto it until dinner, parading into the kitchen with it so that I would have to answer to Dad. I still don't know what you think about pot, not that it matters anymore."

"I was frank with you in the driveway," she said, "and for that you gave me the silent treatment."

"You shocked me," I said. "You spoke so beautifully about Dad on the way home, I thought—"

"I told you," my mother almost shrieked, "I don't know what came over me." She was shaking. "It's hard sometimes . . . don't think I've forgotten . . . sometimes I—" Now she was crying openly.

"For Pete's sake," I said. I sat still for an awkward, painful moment, and then I put my arm around her shoulder. She stiffened, then leaned into me, and for the first time in my life I held her longer than the length of a perfunctory hug.

"You haven't been so forthright, yourself," she said, in between sobs, "not about what you think of Joe."

I looked up at the moon. It glowed orange through the tracework of the oaks. "Mom, I—"

"I know some people find Joe a bit garish," she said over top of what I had begun to say. "I suppose he is, especially in his professional life. But he's a sweet man, and a fine—"

"All right, all right," I said. "Let me tell you something about Joe Palmieri that I bet you don't know." She pulled away from me, gently but firmly. I said, "His daughter was once in a dance marathon with a friend of mine from Churchill High, one of those contests where you ask people to pledge so much money for every hour you stay on your feet and the person who raises the most money wins. My friend danced for thirty straight hours; he raised seven hundred dollars in pledges, one quarter at a time, enough for first place if it wasn't for Rose Palmieri, who danced for only ten hours but won anyway because her father pledged three thousand bucks, flat out, whether she danced or not."

"Joe's quite generous with charities," she said.

"Give me a break," I said. I stood and walked far enough from the fire to feel the cold night air, and for the first time since the driveway, I thought about Charlottesville, about Laura and little Pete, snug in the bedroom, and then I returned to the fire and sat on the log again.

"Let me tell *you* something about Joe," my mother said. She finished wiping away her tears. "Joe and Dad were in the Korean War together."

"I know that," I interrupted. "Dad told me once." But that was all I knew. Dad never talked about the war, no matter how many times I asked. He had an aversion to wars, and more especially to guns, that went well beyond even his basic timidity and kindness, an aversion that was a mystery to me.

My mother ignored my comment. "The two of them were on patrol one night when their platoon, or whatever it's called, ran into an ambush," she began. "Joe and Dad were somehow separated from the platoon and pinned down by enemy fire." She went on about how Dad and Joe spent the night hunkered behind a rock outcropping, trying to figure out how to signal for air power to push back the enemy. I had no idea anything like this had taken place; my father had told me only that he assisted a medic at an internment camp.

"Dad favored staying put," my mother continued, "waiting until morning, hoping against hope that the situation would clear up by then. But the enemy had moved closer. Joe decided to make a break for the platoon. It was on the way back that he lost his arm. He was able to identify Dad's position so they could radio for a helicopter." My mother stopped and licked her lips. She looked straight at me. "Dad never fired a shot," she said. "Not even when Joe was making his break."

I shook my head. I had once seen my father shrink from killing a bat in our fireplace; my Uncle Sal had to come downstairs and do it. At the time, I reasoned not that my father lacked courage but that Uncle Sal lacked compassion. I had been proud of my father for not killing that bat. Now I didn't know what to think. I looked at my mother. She held her head in her hands, concealing her mouth, as though she felt she had betrayed my father.

"That doesn't change anything about the directorship," I said. "It was Dad's for the taking until Joe made a hullabaloo."

"Joe was better qualified," my mother said. She reached over and put her hand on my thigh. "He admired Joe a great deal, Christopher; he told me that on more than one occasion. He knew Joe was the man for the job; to be frank, I think he envied him."

"To be frank," I said, "I think you're spending too much time listening to Joe Palmieri."

"Well," my mother said, "he is my husband."

"What? Come on, you're joking."

"I'm perfectly serious," she said. "We had a quiet service at St. Sebastian's two weeks ago. He moves in next week."

Now I was the one shaking. "How could you?" I said.

She said nothing. When I most wanted her to say something, the woman who began talking to me probably from the moment I left her womb and had hardly paused to catch her breath since said nothing. I had a sense of myself from outside myself, as if from above: me in the woods on Tuckerman's Island, water on all sides, one hundred and twenty miles from home.

I stepped away from the light of the fire again, into the dampness. Some twenty yards away, I ducked behind an oak tree and sat down on a bed of moss. Eventually I had to relieve myself. When I was through, I stood and let the cool air waft through my open pants zipper, smelling the piquant aroma of my pee as it seeped into the moss, listening to the peepers, studying the dappled moonlight on the trees. I saw my father's face in front of me as I stood beside the tree, his face as it was in the end, as he drew his last breath on the couch in the living room: his sunken, jaundiced cheeks, his mottled, hairless scalp, thin skin draped over a skull that seemed to have grown larger, his tongue pushed against his dry lips, and his eyes, liquid green, rolling back in their sockets as he whispered, dark fluid gurgling up from his lungs: "Where shall we abandon our carts?" His piss had been the color of beef broth. I zipped up my pants and shuddered.

"Listen to me," I said as calmly as I could when I got back to the fire. "Now I want you to be honest with me, and I mean it. I want to know what Dad's final words mean. I think you know; I saw the way you started when he said them."

"Not now, Christopher," she said. "Some other time, perhaps in the morning." She still held her head in her hands.

"Be honest."

"I don't know what Dad's last words mean."

"You know something about them," I said. She took a deep, lingering breath, tapped her long fingernails on her thighs. "Mom?"

"They were the words Grandpa Malardo wrote on the note he left before he took his life."

I had been told he died of a stroke.

"He shot himself," my mother said. "Dad found him in the basement one afternoon during a vacation from college. It wasn't the first time Grandpa had tried. Another time Uncle Sal found him with his head in the oven."

That was as much as I could take. "I need to be alone," I said. I draped my sleeping bag over my shoulder and headed toward the river without looking back, stumbling barefoot over the damp earth. I heard my mother behind me, saying, "Christopher, please. Please, Christopher."

My feet landed in moist sand. The river was ten feet in front of me, surging, smelling like iron. I let my sleeping bag drop, then sat down on it and pushed my feet into the sand. In the moonlight, I saw that I was on a little beach that had formed upstream of a dead white oak whose thick trunk jutted beyond the riverbank. My body was numb. My lungs burned. I had never been so ashamed: ashamed of my mother, and of my father, and of my grandfather, and of Joe Palmieri, and mostly of myself. I massaged the cool skin on my arms, my right arm with my left hand, my left arm with my right hand, working from my fingers toward my shoulders, moving always, as I had been taught, toward the heart.

I grasped the loose skin on my left shoulder and kneaded it between my thumb and finger, and then the skin on my right shoulder, and then I kneaded the tight muscles in my lower back, applying rhythmic pressure with my thumbs along either side of my spine, moving upward, toward the heart.

When the blood and the warmth had returned to my toes, I slipped into my bag and pulled the drawstring tight around my shoulders. I refused to think about my mother. I thought instead about my father, who I saw, at that moment, as the more noble of the two, the more wronged.

I wondered what he had been thinking the night he spent pinned behind a rock by gunfire, alone in a foreign land, ten thousand miles from home. Or the afternoon he found his father in the basement, a dank, cramped, dirt-floored room that smelled a lot like the moist sand beneath me. I looked out over the river and tried to imagine the pain of a childhood my father had almost never talked about, the pain of his father's suicide, the pain of his rheumatoid arthritis, contracted while he was still in his prime, destined to take him if the cancer didn't get there first, the pain of his work, pain that drove him to lose sleep and make up for it with coffee and cigarettes, the pain of the cancer that did come and take him, the pain of knowing the cancer was coming, as he must have.

A chill wind blew off the river. I hoped my mother had gotten into her bag by now. I looked back toward the campsite. She had managed, somehow, to maintain the fire. I decided not to worry about her. She was not the only one who had ever betrayed my father; I, too, had deceived him, many times.

I still hadn't gotten over the first time, a trip with him to a variety store called Elliot's. I could not have been more than five. It was an unusual outing, just the two of us, on a weekday after he had come home from work, moments before suppertime, as the sun was going down. My mother must have needed something vital for the meal and sent him to get it. At the cash register was a carton of baseball cards. I asked my father if he would buy me a pack, and he told me I could pick four. This didn't seem right to me: four packs was too many. But I grabbed them, anyway. When we got back in the car, I opened the first pack. There were eight or ten cards inside. My father was stunned. He told me that when he was a child baseball cards came individually wrapped, one card with one stick of gum. He wanted me to have more than one card, but not dozens. It was an innocent mistake on my part. And yet I had felt ashamed of myself for taking more than one pack. And I had felt sorry for him, too, this I remembered vividly as I sat on the river, so inexplicably sorry that cards came one to the pack when he was a young boy, so terribly sorry—even then—that I had duped him.

The moon returned and I watched it, growing less sorry for my father, more sorry for myself, for my son. Pete would have Joe Palmieri in place of a grandfather, Joe Palmieri and pictures in books and the bittersweet shadow of my father in me. And then I began to worry about my mother again. I thought perhaps I should go back to the campsite. But before I had a chance to make up my mind, I heard my mother scream. She was banging something, the plastic cup against the thermos jug. "Christopher!" I heard her shout. "Christopher!" I squirmed out of my bag and ran back to the campsite, fearing that she might have burned herself.

"There's something moving in the tent," she shouted when I reached her, "an animal, I don't know." She was still banging the cup against the thermos. "I went to get in, I—"

"Calm down," I said. "Go stand behind the fire. Stop all that racket." I grabbed a stick and swatted at the tent. Something jumped around inside, scratching at the nylon floor. I went and got the flashlight from my jacket pocket, flicked on the light, and pointed it at the tent. Now I saw a dark shape, about the size of a football, pressed against the sidewall. I swatted again, this time aiming for the bulge in the tent. The moment I hit it, I knew it was a raccoon. The poor thing jumped around in the tent some more, then burst out through the unzipped flaps. It loped wide-eyed past the fire and shinnied up a poplar.

I looked over at my mother. She was shivering, her eyes wider than the raccoon's. I'll always remember her at that moment, on the log by the campfire, wearing Laura's boots, my father's jeans, and my army jacket. She seemed so frail and alone, hunched over the fire. It was possible to see who she really was when she wasn't wearing clothes from some boutique. I saw her, then, as the priest must have seen her at the funeral. He had called her Rosie in his Irish brogue, tenderly, as though she were still a little girl: Rosie—not Rose, not Mom, not Mrs. Malardo—as if my father's passing had taken away her adulthood, as in a sense it had. She had seen my father through to the end; she had earned a second chance.

"I won't get a minute's sleep," she said. "I don't know why I came. Take me home, Christopher, please."

"Easy, now," I said to her, coming up to her from behind, as if I was talking to a spooked horse. "Breathe," I said gently. My heart still raced from my run through the woods. I took a deep, centering breath. Then I lay my hands on her shoulders. She grabbed hold of my fingers, the way she had done in the car, only this time no glove came between her skin and mine. She began to cry.

"It's all right," I said. I slipped my hands from her grip and began kneading her shoulders as best I could through the jacket, feeling the thickness of them, the softness, comparing them to my father's shoulders. All those times I had massaged my father, to soothe his swollen joints, to strip away the tension, she had stood by, puttering at the sink while he lay on the couch beside the dinner table, sitting on one couch in the living room while my father lay on the other; she never asked for her turn, and I never offered. "Be easy," I said. Her shoulders began to relax.

I grabbed hold of her arms and kneaded them, working from the elbows toward her shoulder, toward the heart. After a few minutes, she said, "I have never stopped loving your father."

"You don't have to confess anything," I said. I moved my fingers up her neck. Her hair was thick and cool to the touch, damp like the night air. Don Giovanni's aria played in my head.

"I see him cutting figure eights at night sometimes," my mother said, "in his Greek fisherman's cap, the green sweater I knitted for him, and his leather gloves. When I wake up, I can still see the patterns he cut."

He was indeed a beautiful skater. As I stood behind my mother in the moonlight in the woods on Tuckerman's Island, pressing my fingers gently on the back of her neck, I wondered what my grandfather had meant when he said, "Where shall we abandon our carts?" and what my father had meant by it, and if I might be the first to live long enough to see the birth of my child's child.

Marc Vassallo holds an M.F.A. in fiction from the University of Virginia and is a magazine editor at the Taunton Press. His stories have appeared in *Ploughshares, Puerto del Sol,* and *Southern Exposure.* He lives with his wife and son in New Haven, Connecticut.

"After the Opera" is unlike other stories I have written in that I wrote it on demand. Well, not exactly, but it was, in fact, an assignment for a graduate seminar on Shakespeare. I want to thank my enlightened professor, Arthur Kirsch, who rightly and mercifully allowed the creative writing students in his Shakespeare class to write poetry or fiction rather than literary criticism. Thanks to Mr. Kirsch, I read each play with the hope that it might be the one to inspire in me a short story. In doing so, I brought myself far closer to the emotional center of each play than I had on previous academic readings, when the need to write an essay kept me tangled up in themes, characters, and plots. Having lost my father a few years before, I found myself commiserating with, of all people, Hamlet. Although my own mother in no way behaved like Gertrude, it now seemed possible to imagine the Hamlet in me if she had. "After the Opera" is based loosely on Act III, Scene iv, in which Hamlet confronts his mother in the Queen's closet and there stabs Polonius through an arras. Suffice it to say, the narrator in my story stands for Hamlet, the narrator's mother for the Queen. And that something in the tent, might it not be Polonius?

Dwight Allen

THE GREEN SUIT

(from *The Missouri Review*)

Once upon a time—September of 1976, to be exact—I went to New York. I was twenty-three. I had a diploma from a college in the hills of eastern Tennessee, a school that until my junior year had not admitted women. As I drove to New York from Kentucky, where my parents lived, I sometimes looked at myself in the rear-view mirror. I had longish hair and dismayingly round, soft cheeks that required little shaving. My small, turned-down mouth showed the effect of my wanting to be taken seriously. In my eyes I thought I saw something flashing, some twitchy eagerness I'd failed to suppress in my desire to be a person whom life wouldn't burn. When I stopped at the George Washington Bridge tollbooth and looked at myself a final time before entering Manhattan, I saw someone who had drunk seven or eight cups of coffee and smoked a pack of cigarettes between the Ohio River and the Hudson. The thrumming I felt at my temples was almost visible.

I'd made arrangements to stay at my Aunt Vi's apartment on the upper West Side. Aunt Vi was my mother's older sister, a painter, twice-divorced. She had a house out in Westchester, her primary residence, which she shared with two Airedales. I was supposed to get the keys to her apartment from a man named Elvin.

It was after eleven when I found my aunt's building, a brownstone between Central Park West and Columbus Avenue. A man was sitting out on the stoop, taking the mild September air. He wore a lizardy green suit. The trousers were flared and the jacket lapels were as big as wings. The suit brought words to mind—predatory, naive, hopeful—but none of them seemed quite right. The suit shined in the sulphurous glow of the street lights, but it would have shined in pitch dark, too.

The man, who wore a white T-shirt beneath the jacket, didn't look at me as I came up the stoop with my luggage. He was smoking a cigarette. He had thick, dark, wetted-back hair, like an otter, and a pale, bony face that was not unhandsome despite the crooked nose. Under his right eye was a purplish smudge—the remnant of a shiner, perhaps. I thought he might have been in his late twenties, older than me by several years, anyway.

Across the street two men were shouting at each other in Spanish. Their curses flew back and forth, blurring the air.

"I'm looking for somebody named Elvin," I said to the man on the stoop. I remembered that my aunt had said that Elvin was from down South—Mississippi, maybe. "He's a hick just like you, honey," she'd said, "except he's got a lot of mustard on him."

The man picked a piece of tobacco off the tip of his tongue and flicked it away. "You're looking at him, bro," he said.

"You're the building superintendent, right?"

"I guess I am," Elvin said. "I'd rather be the Sultan of Swing, but you got to deal with the cards that get dealt to you, don't you?" He was watching the two men across the street; one stalked away from the other and then turned back quickly to deliver an elaborate, gaudy curse. New York was like opera, I'd read somewhere. People in costumes discussing things at the top of their lungs.

Elvin said, "So you must be Violet's nephew. Come to get down in the big city." He smiled and brushed something visible only to himself off the sleeve of his jacket. Where, I wondered, did Elvin go in his suit and his ankle-high black boots that zipped up the side?

"Peter Smith," I said, holding out my hand.

"Pleased to meet you," he said. He clasped my hand soul-brother style. "What you got in that box there?" He pointed to the case that held my new Olivetti, a graduation gift.

"A typewriter," I said.

"Ah," he said. "Tap, tap, tap into the night, right?" He dragged on his cigarette and then launched it toward the sidewalk. "I used to know this writer who lived in New Orleans. He died of a brain tumor or something." Elvin rose from the stoop and looked skyward. He'd been sitting on a magazine to keep his trousers clean.

"Looks like we got a big, old, hairy moon on our hands," he said.

I'd seen the moon earlier, driving across New Jersey toward New York. It was a harvest moon, the dying grass moon. Seeing it had made me shiver a little. Then it had slid behind clouds. Now, when I saw it again, hanging above apartment buildings topped with water tanks, it seemed no more than an ordinary celestial body on its appointed rounds. A big, old, cratered thing shedding a little extra light on over-lit New York.

"My old man used to say 'Katy, bar the door' when the moon got full," Elvin said. "I used not to believe any of that ass-trology stuff, but I might have to change my mind. I'm feeling a tad were-wolfish tonight." He undid the middle button of his jacket.

"You're going out now?" I asked. "It's a little late, isn't it?"

"Never too late for love, bro," Elvin said. "Never too late for some of that."

A few days later, I took a typing test at a temporary employment agency. It was decided that I was a "pretty good" typist, even though I made a slew of errors while typing at a rate of thirty-five words per minute. I was thought to be presentable—a smooth-cheeked college graduate who didn't have straw in his hair or cowshit on his Desert Boots—and the agency sent me off to midtown companies in need of secretarial help. I worked for a direct-marketing firm, a bank, a company that sold gag items such as hand buzzers, an oil company, a cosmetics firm. I wore my tweed coat with the elbow patches and read Faulkner on my lunch breaks. I doused my typing mistakes with correction fluid, hoping I wouldn't be exposed as a charlatan. Late that winter the agency sent me to a publishing house on Fifth Avenue. I was put in the office of a vacationing editor and given a piece of a manuscript to retype. "Be careful you don't spill anything on the original," an editor, a woman in a black pants suit, said, tapping the top of a Thermos of coffee I'd brought with me. The manuscript pages were faded yellow second sheets; they looked as delicate as dried flower petals. After the editor went back to her desk, I held a page to my nose and sniffed it.

The section of the manuscript I typed was about an American couple travelling in the south of France. She had cut her hair short to make herself look like a boy. He wrote stories in cheap notebooks with sharp pencils. They swam naked in the cold blue sea and drank absinthe in cafes and made love. I had read most of the prescribed Hemingway in school, and I thought that what I was typing now, on an old manual Olympia, must be more of him or at least a very good imitation. I was excited. I was enthroned in an office five flights above Fifth Avenue and black New York coffee was running through my veins and sunlight was flowing in the windows—late-winter sunlight that seemed to illuminate the pleasure I felt in being where I was (however fleeting my tenancy was likely to be) and to promise more: spring, love, a life in literature. Now and then the editor put her head in the door to check on me. Once, when she came all the way into the room, I felt an urge to tell her how much I liked her black pants suit, which was Asian in style and rustled slightly when she moved. But I lost my nerve.

A few weeks later I got a permanent job at a publishing house called Church & Purviance, a sleepy, old-line company. (It was thought by some people in the publishing industry to be in a coma from which it was not likely to recover.) I worked for an elderly editor named Mr. Stawicki, who had a corner of the C & P building all to himself. He was responsible for the house's military history books. He had white hair that streamed away from his pale, speckled forehead—one could imagine him on the deck of a frigate, spyglass in hand, studying the horizon for enemy cutters—and in close quarters he gave off a sweetish scent that was a mix of talcum powder, butterscotch candy, and decrepitude. Mr. Stawicki had trouble getting my name right, for some reason that seemed only partly related to his age. He called me Son or Champ or, once, William, which was the name of a nephew of his who sold bonds on Wall Street. "Well, William," he said, " I think it's time for Mr. Powell's morning constitutional." Mr. Powell was Mr. Stawicki's thirteen-year-old Sealyham, whom I was required to walk two or three times a day.

One reason that Mr. Stawicki may have been unable to utter my name was that my predecessor's name, Petra, was close to my own. Mr. Stawicki carried a torch for Petra, who had left him to work for an editor named Marshall Hogue. On the one occasion when Mr. Stawicki and I went to lunch together, at a dark Lexington Avenue bar where both he and his dog were known, he said, following his second Rob Roy, "You know, son, you're a nice boy, but I can't forgive that man Hogue for stealing Petra from me." He pronounced her name with a soft "e" and a trilled "r." And then he alluded to the dust bin of history—he called it the "dust bed" of history—and predicted that he would soon be lying in it.

I'd gotten my job at C & P through Mr. Hogue, whom I'd met at a party at my aunt's house in Westchester. He grew up in Louisville with Aunt Vi and my mother, who sat next to him in fifth grade. He went away to boarding school, and then to college and into the service, and he returned to Louisville only for the occasional holiday. But he had acquired a certain allure while away, and when he did come back he became an object of interest to the girls of my mother's set. My mother went to dances with him. But he was just passing through. He wasn't going to stay put. Like Vi who'd gone to New York to study painting, he was bound for other places.

At my aunt's party, Mr. Hogue and I drank wassail and ate salty country ham on beaten biscuits and talked about the town where we no longer lived. His voice had been whisked clean of all but a trace of an accent. He had a tidy grayish beard and close-cropped hair and he wore wire-rimmed glasses. He was tall and thin, like a swizzle stick. He told me that I looked like my mother, a comment I'd heard before. It flustered me nonetheless, for it confirmed my fear that the softness of feature my mother had bestowed on me suggested a certain lack of personality. I swallowed some wassail, the scent of cinnamon riding up my nose, and stammered something. Then Mr. Hogue told me that I should come see him whenever I decided to give up the temporary employment racket. Spaces opened up at C & P now and then, he said. Of course, the pay was dreadful and much of the work was humdrum, but literature must be served, mustn't it? He laughed a small, refined laugh.

In the evening, after I had finished my work for Mr. Stawicki, I went home to my aunt's apartment. The building was near the Columbus Avenue end of the block, the less genteel end, across the street from an empty, paved-over lot where kids played stickball and a man once stood with a goat in the rain and read from the Book of Isaiah. Aunt Vi had moved into the building in 1959, after bouncing around the Village for more than a decade. For a number of years she used a second apartment in the brownstone as a studio. Then, around 1970, she decided to move her easels to the countryside. The apartment she left behind, the one I sublet, didn't receive much light, but the ceilings were high and the claw-footed bathtub was large and the bedroom looked down upon a kind of courtyard that the two Irish sisters who lived below me had planted with vinca and lamium. Sometimes I would see Grace and Betty down there on warm evenings, sitting in matching aluminum-tube lawn chairs, sipping Dubonnet.

Aunt Vi's apartment was sparsely furnished. There was a card table, folding chairs, a metal cot, a worn red velvet sofa that might have passed for cathouse furniture, kitchenware (including several Kentucky Derby souvenir glasses), a small pine desk, and a couple of Aunt Vi's paintings. One was a nature morte—a sea bass on a platter, its mouth agape and eye bulging. In the other, Aunt Vi stared at the viewer through big, black-framed glasses. She had a cigarette in the corner of her mouth. Her chin was uptilted, as if she were waiting for an answer to a question. Her skin she'd painted a hazy rose color, the color of smoke mixed with the tomatoey hue that years of drinking produces in some people. The painting hung above the desk where I sat most evenings, trying to write a story called "The Green Suit." After several months of looking at my aunt looking at me and failing to make much progress with "The Green Suit" or its spinoffs (I rarely got beyond an opening page, which I obsessively rewrote, with a Bic, in a narrowlined, spiral notebook), I decided to cover the painting with a dishtowel whenever I sat down at the desk. Covering the portrait seemed less radical than taking it down or moving the desk to the opposite wall, where the dead fish was hung. I imagined that if I removed that picture of my aunt scrutinizing me, I'd be upsetting a certain balance of forces in the apartment.

One reason I had trouble writing was that I had a crush on Mr. Stawicki's former assistant, Petra Saunders. I sometimes found myself thinking about Petra in the midst of trying to imagine what Elvin did when he stepped out in his green suit. (I'd learned that he sometimes went to New Jersey—"the land of opportunity," he called it—and so I thought of his suit as his going-over-to-Jersey outfit.) Or I would find myself thinking about Petra while trying to light upon the word to describe the complexions of Grace and Betty, who were both tellers at a bank in Chelsea, who both wore white gloves to work. Grace and Betty were going to be in "The Green Suit," a story in which the narrator, a boy from the provinces not unlike myself, is drawn into the peculiar New York life of a man not unlike Elvin. I foresaw the story turning violent at some point—Grace and Betty mugged? Elvin wild with anger?—though I was a long way from reaching that point. The distance between where I was and where I wanted to be seemed immense, and I often found it easier to retire to Aunt Vi's dilapidated sofa, where I could give myself up to thoughts of Petra.

Not too long after I'd been hired at Church & Purviance, Mr. Hogue took me out to lunch. Petra came along. "You don't mind, do you?" he asked. We went to an expensive Chinese restaurant. I drank two gin-and-tonics and struggled with my chopsticks and confessed to liking Faulkner and Hemingway. "Faulkner more," I added.

"The big boys," Mr. Hogue said, pinching a snow pea with his chopsticks.

Petra didn't comment on my literary tastes, though I guessed, from the way she sipped her ice water and averted her eyes, that she didn't approve. She was quiet—even, I thought at first, evasive. Some part of her face always seemed to be in shadow, eclipsed by her long, dark, wayward hair or by a hand pushing the hair back. When I asked her where she'd grown up, she said, "Oh, you know, all around. My father was in the Foreign Service." She said this as if it were common for American children to grow up in Rome, Addis Ababa, and Bethesda. When I went back to the office that afternoon, my head full of gin and tea and fish sauce, I got my diary out of my desk and wrote, *Is she supercilious or am I blind? Perhaps the latter? She doesn't drink—at least not at lunch. She's reading an obscure Japanese novelist—obscure to me, anyway—which Marshall, as she calls Mr. Hogue, recommended. She looks at Mr. Hogue fondly. When she says the words Addis Ababa, I think of all those soft "a"s tumbling around in her mouth. She has a large mole between her collarbone and left breast. She wore a scoop-necked summer dress—blue, beltless.*

One afternoon a couple of weeks later, after I'd walked Mr. Powell and returned him to his cedar-scented bed in Mr. Stawicki's office, I went downstairs to the C & P library. Mr. Stawicki had asked me to look up something about a diplomat who had attended a naval conference in London in 1930. By the time I reached the library, I'd forgotten the diplomat's name. The library, which was small and windowless, smelled of orange. Petra was sitting at the table, a handsome old oak piece on which the first Mr. Purviance (so the story went) had once been pinned by an author armed with a penknife. Petra didn't look up when I entered the library. She was reading, one hand lost in her dark hair. Then I saw that hand reach for a slice of orange—it was laid out in sections on a napkin—and

convey it to her mouth. The name of the naval conference partic-
ipant suddenly came to me, or almost came to me, but when Petra
looked up, her mouth full of orange, the name squirted away, leaving a sort of bubbly, phosphorescent trail in my brain.

"I'm doing research for the Colonel," I said, referring to Mr. Stawicki by his nickname. "For his encyclopedia of warships. The two-
volume thing. I can't remember what I was supposed to look up."

"That's a problem," Petra said. She was wearing a plain white
blouse and a dark skirt. The mole below her collarbone wasn't visible. With her book and her lunchbox, she looked like a proper
schoolgirl. Except that her lunchbox had a picture of Mickey and
Minnie on it. I took this to mean that she might have a sense of
humor.

"Are you still reading that Japanese guy?" I asked. I waited for
his name to surface. "Tanizaki?"

"I finished him," she said. She put another section of orange in
her mouth. "Marshall asked me to read this Yugoslav writer to see
if we should commission a translation." She held the book out
toward me. I came closer. Her fingers and wrists were bare, no
jewelry. On the cover of the book, crows or bats were swirling
around a man wearing a derby and a clownish cravat. "It's sort of
a surrealist satire of life under Tito. This is the Italian translation."

"Are you going to be reading that book tonight, after work, I
mean?" I put my hands in the pockets of my khakis.

"What?" she asked.

"Does Mr. Hogue—Marshall—send you home with work at
night?" Though I was up to my neck in desire and self-pity—I
could count on one finger the number of times I'd kissed anybody
during the nine months I'd lived in New York—it seemed prudent
to backpedal. Backpedaling was something I could almost do with
my eyes shut. "Is Mr. Hogue fun to work for?"

"He does interesting books," she said. She put the orange peels
and napkin in her lunchbox, which, I saw, also contained a Milky
Way candy bar. I found it comforting that she had a vice.

"And you don't have to walk a dog," I said.

"No," she said, latching her lunchbox and getting up from the table. "But I didn't mind walking Mr. Powell. I went all over town with him. I could be gone for two hours and Mr. Stawicki wouldn't say anything."

"He's sweet on you," I said.

"He's kind of lonely, don't you think?" Petra said. "Well, good luck with your research."

After work that day I walked over to Korvettes to buy a window fan. The weather had turned hot, summer having laid its heavy hand on the city before May was out. The day's heat was in the sidewalks, in the buildings I walked past, in the sweaty, pock-marked face of the blind man who stood with his tin cup and his guide dog at the corner of Fifth and Forty-eighth, rocking back and forth like a man taken over by spirits.

When I came out of Korvettes with my fan and began to walk up Fifth Avenue, I saw, a half-block ahead, Mr. Hogue and Petra. They seemed to not be walking so much as gliding—as far as that was possible on a crowded sidewalk. At several points, Mr. Hogue, who was wearing an olive-green suit (cuffed trousers, narrow lapels), touched Petra on the arm and guided her around a clot of slow-moving tourists or out of the way of some speeding local. I remembered that my mother had said of Mr. Hogue in a recent phone conversation, "He was quite a dancer in his heyday. All the girls wanted to be led by him. Little did they know!"

"Little did they know what?" I'd asked.

"That he preferred men to women," she'd said. "Haven't you figured that out yet?" She sounded perturbed.

Instead of turning left, toward Sixth Avenue, where I could catch an uptown train, I followed Petra and Mr. Hogue up Fifth Avenue. Where were they going—Petra with her lunchbox and musette bag, Mr. Hogue with his Moroccan leather satchel? Neither lived in the direction they were walking. (Petra lived way over in the east eighties; once, after going to a movie in her neighborhood, I'd walked by her building, a drab, yellow-brick sliver squeezed between brownstones.) Perhaps they were going to meet an agent or an author for a drink. Perhaps they were going to an early movie and then to supper at some Turkish or Balinese place Mr. Hogue would know about and then—my mother's assertion about Mr. Hogue's sexual preferences notwithstanding—to a mutual bed. Wasn't it possible that they were lovers, even if (to coin a phrase) Mr. Hogue was old enough to be Petra's father? There was that moment, for instance, outside the tobacconist's at Fifty-fifth, where Mr. Hogue held Petra's lunchbox while she fished around in her musette bag for money to give to a legless man who rolled himself along the sidewalk on a little furniture dolly. And then, after Mr. Hogue returned the lunchbox to Petra, there was the way, too delicate to be fatherly, he touched the small of her back, nudging her toward wherever they were going.

I followed a half-block behind, humping my three-speed fan and my briefcase, sweating through my seersucker jacket. At Grand Army Plaza, where I stopped to light a cigarette, I got caught in an autopedestrian crosswalk snarl and fell a block behind. I lost sight of my quarry for a minute, and then I spotted them disappearing under the canopy at the Hotel Pierre.

I walked across the Park, toward the West Side, secure in the knowledge that the life I wanted to possess was going to elude me. I saw a man drinking a carton of orange juice while riding a unicyle. I saw some Hare Krishnas crossing the Sheep Meadow in their saffron robes. Then, on a path near the Lake, a man wearing a floppy red-velvet beret-like hat on top of his Afro stopped me and asked for my wallet. He showed me an X-Acto knife, no more than an inch of blade sticking out of its gray metal housing. I gave him my wallet and stared at the carotid artery in his neck, which seemed to be throbbing. He went through my wallet without saying a word. I felt I should say something, and so I asked him if he wanted my fan, too.

"No, I don't want your dumb-ass fan, you dumb-ass bitch," he said. He dropped the wallet on the ground and walked off. He'd taken the cash and a ticket I'd bought for *La Bohème*.

I walked out of the Park and up Central Park West. By the time

I'd reached the Museum of Natural History, I'd stopped shaking. By the time I reached my street I felt oddly at ease, as if I could float the final half-block past the spindly young trees whose trunks were wrapped with tape, right on up the stoop, on which Grace and Betty had set a pot of geraniums. I picked a cigarette butt out of the geranium pot, flicked it away, and went up to my apartment. The door was ajar. I heard Aunt Vi's voice, and then I saw Elvin sitting on the couch, smoking.

"Hey, bro," Elvin said. "You're just in time for cocktails." Elvin was wearing a black sleeveless T-shirt and blue jeans. No shoes. The shirt was made of a shimmery material, like his green suit. He was all muscle and bone, and he gave you the impression that he'd done nothing to achieve it, except perhaps smoke to curb his appetite. At one time, he'd told me, he'd worked as a mud logger on an oil rig in the Gulf of Mexico and commuted with wads of cash between New Orleans and New York. Before that, he'd been in the Army, but had somehow avoided a tour in Vietnam. More recently he'd worked as a car jockey in a parking garage in Midtown. Now he did odd jobs for the landlord to pay off his rent. And occasionally earned beer money by modeling for Aunt Vi.

Aunt Vi came out of the kitchen with a drink in each hand. "I let myself in, Petey," she said. "I hope you don't mind." She gave Elvin his drink and surveyed me through her big black glasses. The glasses made her seem both distant and overbearing, like a bird of prey.

"No, I don't mind," I said, setting down the fan but leaving my jacket on for the moment. I didn't consider the apartment to be mine, any more than I considered myself to be a resident of New York.

"I had to come into town to see Dr. Bickel, so he can pay for the addition on his summer house in Quogue," Aunt Vi said, laughing her heavy, tobacco-crackled laugh. "The old buzzard would cap every one of my teeth if he could."

I looked around the room, as if some clue to my existence were to be found there. On the mantel above the non-working fireplace, I saw the wine bottle that I'd not quite emptied the night before while sitting at my desk, waiting for inspiration to blow through me and prickle the hairs on the back of my hand. Beside the sofa, not far from Elvin's bare feet, the pale, bony dogs which had carried him far from Mississippi, were one blue sock and a packet of newspaper clippings my mother had sent me from Kentucky. On the wall was Aunt Vi's painting of her ripe, florid self; I'd had the foresight to remove the dishtowel.

"You look like you could use a drink," Aunt Vi said.

"You've been working too hard, bro," Elvin said, hoisting his glass, grinning. "Take a load off."

"I wouldn't mind having a drink," I said to Aunt Vi. I thought I probably wouldn't tell her and Elvin about my run-in in the Park.

My aunt went back into the kitchen. Elvin said, "I'm thinking of going over to Jersey on Saturday. You want to come?"

"What do you do there?" I asked.

"Study the landscape, do a little recon," Elvin said, blowing a stream of unfiltered smoke toward the ceiling. "Go bowling sometimes. See this girl I know."

I wondered if Elvin went bowling in his green suit, or if he took a change of clothes.

"Sounds nice," I said, not wishing to offend Elvin, who was, after all, the building's super and could requisition me an extra door lock, if I should ever need one. "I'll check my social calendar."

Aunt Vi returned with my drink, a gin-and-tonic, heavy on the gin, in a Kentucky Derby glass. The gin went straight to that part of me that wished to lie down, and so I excused myself, saying I was going to change out of my work clothes.

"Sound your funky horn, man," Elvin said, snorting.

"What's that supposed to mean, Elvin?" Aunt Vi asked.

"It's just a song I used to sort of like," Elvin said, dreamily.

I went into the bedroom, undressed, polished off the gin, and lay down on the cot. I looked at the Monet poster I'd stuck on the wall — a sun-drenched beach scene, flags rippling in the breeze.

"The boy needs to get laid," I heard Elvin say. He made two syllables out of "laid."

"I'm sure he'd be touched by your concern," Aunt Vi said. "When are you going to sit for me again?" Elvin was one of my aunt's favorite subjects. She'd painted him clothed and unclothed — once in repose on a couch, in the manner of Manet's "Olympia," with a Mets cap covering his genitals. His eyes were near to being closed. "Drowsy Elvin," my aunt called the painting.

They talked about dates and fees. I started to drift off, my body tingling as I went. At one point, I heard Aunt Vi ask me if I wanted to go out for supper. No, I thought. I'll just lie here forever.

Three weeks later, a warm mid-June evening, I lay upon the same bed, absorbing the breeze generated by my fan. I was wearing basketball shorts and a University of the South T-shirt. Now and then I heard firecrackers explode. The Fourth was approaching, and every kid in the neighborhood was armed to the teeth. Below my window, in the dim courtyard, Grace and Betty sipped cocktails and discussed the events of the day: the rudeness of a young officer at the bank, the elderly Negro man whom they no longer saw on the Number 11 downtown bus, Elvin's failure to fix a dripping faucet, whether the church they went to could afford to install air-conditioning.

I'd been home since about three in the afternoon, having fled the office in the wake of Mr. Powell's death. I'd taken Mr. Powell for a lunchtime walk over in Turtle Bay, where trees provided shade and there was the occasional poodle or Boston terrier for my charge to sniff. On Second Avenue I slipped Mr. Powell's leash around the top of a fire hydrant and went into a deli to buy a sandwich. Mr. Powell, being old, wasn't frisky, and I expected him to do no more than wait patiently on the curb while I got my turkey on rye. But he stretched his leash and wandered off the curb into the gutter, where there was garbage to be inspected. I didn't witness the accident, but I was told by a pedestrian, a well-dressed man walking a Chow, that a cab turning left and cutting the corner close had struck Mr. Powell, that the driver had hit his brakes, but then had gone on, perhaps at the urging of his fare.

Mr. Powell had been killed instantly, but as I carried him back to the office, in a black garbage bag that the deli manager had given me, I kept thinking, absurdly, Maybe he's just sleeping. When I'd picked him up out of the gutter there hadn't been any blood on his thick white coat and the only certain sign of death that I could see was in his eyes, which were open but of no apparent use. However, he didn't stir as I bore him toward his master, and toward, I felt increasingly sure, my own termination. Mr. Powell grew heavier as I rode in the elevator to my floor, accompanied by silent Jimmy, the uniformed elevator operator, who was the most phlegmatic man in New York.

When Mr. Stawicki saw me with the garbage bag, he said, "Please don't tell me that's my dog." I said it was and that I was very sorry and that it had happened suddenly and that Mr. Powell hadn't seemed to suffer much, if at all.

Mr. Stawicki looked stricken. He waved me out of his office.

I sat down at my desk and wrote him a note of apology, restating my remorse at his loss, saying that I planned to look for work elsewhere but would stay on until he found a replacement. I put the note in the In box outside his door. Then I went downstairs to the main editorial floor to see Mr. Hogue and tell him about Mr. Powell and my decision to leave Church & Purviance.

But Mr. Hogue was not in his office. Nor was Petra in her adjoining nook, though the coffee in her mug was warm. So I went back upstairs, got my briefcase, and walked home, via the Park, where I encountered no muggers, only a violinist dressed up in a bear suit. At the apartment, I drank plain lemonade and listened to Mississippi John Hurt sing "Candy Man" in his gentle, rocking-chair voice. Then I lay down on the bed and napped, dreaming that I was a child sick in bed and that Grace and Betty were ministering to me, bringing me broth (in a church collection plate) and magazines and stuffed animals.

Later, awake, listening to the drone of the fan and the voices of

Grace and Betty, I considered the idea of returning home to Louisville and hooking on with my grandfather's brokerage firm and eating high-cholesterol lunches with my father at the downtown club where he played penny-a-point bridge and marrying any one of several young women I knew whose interest in literature was about the same as their interest in ethnography or limnology. This notion occupied me for several minutes—deeply enough that the sound of my door buzzer didn't immediately rouse me. When I did finally leave my cot and go downstairs, I at first saw only Elvin, shirtless, standing in the vestibule, where the mailboxes were. Then, beyond the outer door, on the stoop, I saw Petra, her musette bag over her shoulder. She was leaving. I opened the door and called her name.

Elvin, scratching his flat, naked belly, said, sotto voce, "Hey, man, if she's the reason you bugged out on me, I forgive you."

I hadn't gone bowling with Elvin in New Jersey. I'd pleaded a tight schedule.

"Thanks," I said. I was happy to be on Elvin's good side. I stepped out the door onto the stoop. Elvin remained in the vestibule.

"I was sorry to hear about Mr. Powell," Petra said. She was wearing a white, open-necked blouse and a blue jean skirt.

"Thanks," I said. The stoop felt warm on my bare feet.

"I'm coming from my dentist," she said, "down on Eighty-first. Dr. Fingerhut. He's this old guy whose only flaw is that he believes in minimal anesthesia. He plays Schubert or Mozart while he's scraping tartar off your teeth. 'Ah, my dear, you haf vut looks like a very sweet tooth. Ve must repair before it becomes a very tot tooth.' Marshall told me about him. He's cute, except for his ideas about anesthesia." She paused, as if to consider her presence on my stoop.

I didn't know what was more improbable: a suddenly chatty Petra or the fact that she was standing near me on a warm summer evening. The air—the grimy, hazy, fume-laden air of Manhattan— seemed almost fresh. There was nearly enough oxygen in it to make your head spin.

"Dr. Fingerhut told me about this Cuban-Chinese restaurant on Amsterdam somewhere," Petra said. "I thought you might be able to help me find it."

"I'll get my shoes," I said.

We found the Cuban-Chinese place, up Amsterdam, in the shadow of a new housing project, but it didn't serve liquor, which, it turned out, Petra avoided only during work hours. We walked back to a bar called the Yukon, down the block from the laundromat that I and Elvin and Grace and Betty frequented. I'd watched some baseball in the Yukon, and had even, once, tried writing there. Except for the refrigerated air, there wasn't anything in the Yukon that suggested the remote Canadian Northwest. No pictures of Jack London or sled dogs, anyway.

We sat toward the back, in a booth that had a view of the dartboard. A fat, bearded man and his petite female companion were playing.

"Tell me again how Mr. Powell got killed," Petra said. She'd been out of the office for part of the afternoon, and had heard about the incident fourthhand, from Mrs. Berlin, the receptionist.

I told Petra the story of Mr. Powell's death, and then I said that I was going to look for work elsewhere and was even thinking of moving back to Kentucky, where I could whittle sticks with my friends. I was hoping, of course, that she would try to dissuade me from the latter idea and give me room to imagine that I could displace Mr. Hogue as her lover. The notion that she was Mr. Hogue's lover had taken root and flourished in the little hothouse of my mind.

"I've never been to Kentucky," Petra said, turning the frosted glass that contained her vodka-and-tonic. "Marshall talks about spring down there, how pretty it is."

"Um," I said. I let pass the chance to ask about her relationship with Mr. Hogue. A couple more beers and I might have managed it. "What was spring in Addis Ababa like?"

"It was nice, mild. Addis Ababa is eight thousand feet above sea level, you know," Petra said. She was looking past me. She laid her hand on my free hand, the one that wasn't gripping the bottle of Rheingold, and nodded in the direction of the dart players.

"Look," she whispered. "On the floor. The bag."

I turned and leaned out of the booth and saw a gym bag under the table that held the dart players' drinks. Then I saw the man, who was wearing a billowy shirt that had a tropical theme, flick a dart toward the target. The motion his hand made was dainty and precise; it was if he were dotting an "i."

"What?" I asked Petra. She'd removed her hand from mine almost as quickly as she'd put it there. If she touched me again, I thought, that would mean something. I was a boy who required reassurance, an appalling trait to have in a place like New York.

"The bag," Petra said. "It's moving. There's something in it."

I rubbernecked again, and saw that there was indeed something moving inside the bag, flexing it this way and that.

"Maybe it's a ferret." I looked at the mole below her collarbone; I wanted to put my thumb on it.

"No," Petra said, firmly. "It's a snake. Those people look like snake owners."

I turned around once more. The woman was studying us. She did somewhat resemble a person you might see at a roadside reptile farm — the proprietor's thin-lipped wife, who keeps the books and dreams about running off with the guy who stocks the farm's Coke machine. She had a hard face that was once pretty.

"You don't like snakes?" I asked Petra.

"I don't expect to see one in a bar," she said. "It kind of takes the wind out of your sails."

"I know what you mean." As she finished her drink, I thought I could see her considering whether to take a cross-town bus home or to spring for a cab. If she was going home, that is. In any event, it seemed clear that she didn't wish to spend any more time in the Yukon.

I paid for the drinks and waited by the jukebox while Petra used the Ladies'. When she came out, she stopped to talk with the dart players. Then she came on toward me, the news that she'd been right about the contents of the bag written on her face. She was a person who took some satisfaction in being right.

"It's a python," she said. "A baby python. They have a bunch."

We walked out into the warm, jarring air. The sky was still an hour short of turning the smudgy color that was the local version of nighttime. Yellow cabs were streaking down Columbus. A man wearing beltless, crimson slacks and a shirt of several hideous colors came up the avenue, cutting a wide swath, singing, muttering, nodding violently to himself.

"I guess I'll go now," Petra said. She stepped off the curb and waved for a cab.

"O.K.," I said.

A cab cut across two lanes and came to a halt a yard or so from Petra's sandaled foot. She didn't flinch. "Don't feel too bad about Mr. Powell," she said. "And don't go home to Kentucky with your tail between your legs. Be brave." She gave me a quick kiss on the cheek. Its delicate placement reminded me of the way the fat man had thrown the dart.

"What are you reading nowadays?" I asked, as she got into the cab, a part of her leg that I'd not seen before becoming briefly visible.

The thought that I was homosexual had of course occurred to me now and again—for instance, on those occasions when I'd lain on my narrow, squeaky cot, solemnly holding myself. But if this were true, why did the sight of Petra's thigh, not to mention the touch of her mouth, move me so?

"Proust," she said, pulling the door to. "He's great. You should try him. He'll make you want to . . ." The cab shot away, like a cork flying out of a bottle, leaving me to imagine what she thought Proust would make me want to do. Learn French? Run naked down Broadway shouting "Hallelujah"? Sleep with men? Proust, I knew, had been homosexual. That was about all I knew about him. He hadn't been on the syllabus at my college in east Tennessee.

I headed back up Columbus. Standing in the doorway of the laundromat, smoking, watching the world rush by, was Elvin. He signaled to me. Over his jeans, he was wearing what looked like a pajama shirt, V-necked, with red piping. His muscle shirts must have been in the wash.

"Hey, bro," he said, "maybe we can double sometime."

"Double?" I asked, thinking this was street slang I'd failed to absorb.

"Double date," he said. "You and your chick, me and mine."

"Yeah," I said. "Maybe we could do something like that."

Elvin drove up the Henry Hudson Parkway, slaloming in and out of the thick Saturday afternoon traffic like a stunt driver—a style that made it difficult for me to concentrate on the long sentences describing the amatory practices of M. Swann. So I put my book down. But watching Elvin drive—one-handed, mostly, while he sucked on a joint—was too frightening. And looking out the window at the river, sparkling though it was in the July sun, was insufficiently distracting. So I fixed upon Connie's dark, shag-cut head. Connie, who was Elvin's girlfriend. Who was—as far as I could deduce—not much older than sixteen. She had an operator's license, anyway; she'd driven the car, her father's, over from Jersey before giving the wheel to Elvin. Connie, who had said to Elvin as he laid down rubber at the last stop we'd see until we hit the Spuyten Duyvil bridge, "My father's going to fucking kill me if you wreck it." To which Elvin had said, "Be cool."

We were going to my aunt's house in the green hills of northern Westchester. It was her fifty-fifth birthday, and she was giving herself a party. She'd invited a great flock of people—painter friends, Village friends, Grace and Betty, my parents, Mr. Hogue, other Kentuckians, her dentist. Grace and Betty declined (they were going to Mystic with a church group), and so did my parents, who, according to my mother, had a long list of conflicts. But Mr. Hogue was coming, and so was the dentist. Petra was supposed to be there, too. In any event, I'd asked her, and she'd said yes, though the yes was provisional, dependent upon whether she could resolve something in her social schedule.

I'd asked Petra to Aunt Vi's party about a week before I was to leave Church & Purviance. One effect of being nearly unemployed was that I didn't feel my usual diffident self around Petra. Anyhow, the sight of her standing next to the copy machine, a cranky, unreliable thing that wheezed and heaved before disgorging paper, had emboldened me. She'd gotten her hair cut quite short; her exposed neck was as pale as a photographic negative. And so I'd asked her for a date, and after she'd startled me with her yes (provisional though it was), I'd also asked if she were no longer seeing Mr. Hogue.

Petra looked at me with her small, bright, critical eyes for as long as it took the copy machine to cough up three pages of somebody's five-hundred-page bildungsroman.

"I like Marshall and he likes me, but we don't 'see' each other," Petra said, smiling at my foolishness, revealing her teeth, which were imperfect. She had a snaggly upper right canine. "He has other interests."

"Ah," I said, which was the sound of my mind opening slightly to receive important information. Air entering the hothouse.

"Ah," I said again, two weeks later, as I, fully unemployed, rocketed up the Saw Mill with stoned Elvin and his barely legal girlfriend, and without Petra, who would get to Aunt Vi's on her own, if a lunch date she had with Ethiopian friends of her father didn't take forever. The "Ah" this time was the sound of air being nervoudly expelled. I thought there was a good chance that Elvin would fail to negotiate one of the many curves on the narrow Saw Mill, or if we got that far, one of the many curves on the even narrower Taconic. I thought, too, that there was a good chance that I wouldn't see Petra, even if Elvin didn't wipe us out. She'd made no promises.

Connie passed me a bottle of beer and smiled. She was wearing a retainer, which made her look even younger than she was. She had a pretty mouth with a fleshy underlip, and brown eyes clouded by worry. How had Elvin acquired her, I wondered. Had he been wearing his green suit when he seduced her? I drank my beer rapidly and asked Connie, who was keeping pace, for another. We made more eye contact. Elvin, singing along with a Peter Frampton song, miraculously steered us off the Taconic and down a snaky, wooded road to my aunt's house.

It felt wonderful to have the ground under my feet, and after I'd kissed my aunt (who was wearing a huge, brocaded sombrero), and after I'd gotten a plate of food and another bottle of beer, I sat down on the grass under a large sugar maple, next to Beau Jack, one of Aunt Vi's two Airedales. Elvin took Connie to see Aunt Vi's studio, an old implements shed that she'd fixed up. Beau Jack panted and watched me eat barbecued chicken. It was a hot, breezeless afternoon. The whirligig on top of the implements shed didn't twitch. Insects crackled. A group of guests sat on the screened-in front porch, under a ceiling fan. I gave Beau Jack a chunk of chicken, and then I saw Mr. Hogue walking across the lawn toward me. He wore long, white pants (cuffed) and a blue polo shirt. The heavy July air seemed to part for him. Sweat didn't sit upon his forehead and it didn't mark his shirt. His wirerimmed glasses caught the light and scattered it.

He settled himself in the grass with his drink, something with a wedge of lime floating in it. "How do you like being retired?" he asked. There was amusement in his eyes, though the amusement was polite. He had offered to help me find a job at another publishing house, but I'd declined, saying I hadn't decided what I was going to do next.

Now I said, "Retirement is O.K. so far. I sleep in and I read Proust. Slowly. All those long sentences, you know, that drag themselves across the page like bloated serpents after a meal." I took a gulp of beer. I was high and was hoping to get higher. I hoped to see Petra soon, before I peaked.

"Petra is reading Proust, I think."

An old wood-panelled Country Squire station wagon rolled up the driveway, crunching gravel. Four men in white shirts got out. Musicians.

"I'm in love with Petra," I said, in a voice that one might use when taking an oath of office.

"I gather you're trying to say you're not queer," Mr. Hogue said evenly.

"No," I said. "I mean, yes, I'm not." I drained my beer and looked toward my aunt's studio. Elvin stood outside the shed, pouring beer down his throat. In the flat mid-afternoon light, he seemed somehow two-dimensional, tinny: Man with a Big Thirst. I didn't see Connie.

"How would you know that you aren't queer?" Mr. Hogue gazed at me in a kindly, schoolmasterly sort of way.

Was there a correct answer? "I can just feel it," I said.

Mr. Hogue rose from the grass and laid his hand on the ridged trunk of the sugar maple. There were tap holes at the tree's waist. "A young friend of mine told me about a drug he once took—MDA, I think he called it—that made him want to fuck trees. Even skinny saplings excited him. He was out in the woods, you see, trying to get in touch with his soul. And he spent hours, under the influence of this drug, dry-humping anything with a trunk. And he was perfectly happy. Don't you think it's odd that a little chemical adjustment, a jot of this or that, is enough to make you surrender to a tree?"

"You have to watch what you put in your mouth," I said smartly.

"But then a tree is always there for you, isn't it?" Mr. Hogue said. "Well, let me know if you change your mind and want to get back into the publishing business. I won't tell anybody that you killed Stawicki's dog." He smiled pleasantly and walked away.

I drank more beer and kept an eye out for Petra while playing croquet with Elvin, my aunt, and her dentist, Dr. Bickel. With a cigarette clamped between her lips and her sombrero set securely on her head, Aunt Vi drove Dr. Bickers ball thirty yards off the course, into the weeds beyond the edge of the lawn. "Oh, doctor," she shouted joyfully, "when you fetch that ball, beware the stinging nettle and the wily copperhead!"

The band, which was set up on the other side of the house,

played "Blueberry Hill." Elvin sang along and drove my ball into the nettles and fleabane. "Take a hike, bro," Elvin said, and then cruised around the course in a single turn. "It's scary how good I am," he said. "And I'm stoned out of my mind."

The band played a slow blues number and I went for a hike. I walked past Aunt Vi's studio—through the window I saw a large canvas of Elvin sitting in a high-backed rattan chair in his green suit; he looked like a small-time criminal dressed for dinner—and then I walked through a field toward a spring-fed pond that was at the back of the property. I'd had five beers, but I could still walk a fairly straight line and identify some of the plants that grew in the field: goldenrod, wild carrot, fleabane. Down in a swale, fifty yards from the pond, was a clump of purple loosestrife. The sun shone brightly and the high grass brushed against my shins, making them itch. I felt some throbbing in the neighborhood of my left eye: pain gathering for a frontal assault. I'd about given up on Petra's coming. I was looking forward to sticking my head in the water.

There was a swimmer in the pond—three, actually, if you counted Beau Jack and his mother, Cornelia, who were wading in the reedy shallows. The human swimmer was Connie. She was naked as a baby, her white bottom pointed at the pale blue sky. Her head was turned away from me. Then she dove under and when she resurfaced, her black hair sleek and shiny, she saw me. I was standing on the grassy bank, unbuttoning my shirt. She seemed unalarmed by my presence. She'd given me that lingering look in the car, after all, which I'd interpreted to mean: I wouldn't mind it if you saved me from Elvin. Though this reading of things was perhaps nothing more than vanity on my part. I had a habit of seeing sparks where there were none.

"How's the water?" I asked. I put my shirt on the ground, next to Connie's pile of clothes. The dogs came over to sniff me.

"O.K.," she said. "Cool."

She looked away as I got out of my shorts and underwear. Had she seen me trembling, my heart whanging away under my bare chest? Proust: "We do not tremble except for ourselves, or for those whom we love." I didn't love Connie, needless to say.

I waded into the pond, soft, oozy mud sucking at my feet, and then I dove out toward the middle, beneath the sunstruck surface. The cool water gripped me, held me under. I could see nothing. If I kept swimming, I thought, I could end up on the other side of the world, far from harm. But the other side of the world wasn't really where I wanted to be now.

I came up behind Connie, my mouth inches from her shoulder blade and knobby vertebrae. She turned and pushed away from me a bit. Her arms were folded across her breasts. She was wearing a cross around her neck.

"Where'd you meet Elvin?" I asked.

"The Moon Bowl," she said. "In Moonachie. Where I go bowling."

"Do you like him?" I heard the band—the boom-da-boom of the bass, an undulant melody from the saxophone. Cornelia caught the scent of something and ran into the field. Beau Jack continued to work the pond shallows.

"Yeah, sure," Connie said. "Except he's kind of crazy, you know." She smiled and I saw the retainer wire across her teeth. "He has this, like, Saturday Night Special that he bought from this guy at the bowling alley. He got it so he could protect himself from nuts and stuff."

"Would he shoot me," I asked, "if he saw us getting it on?" I moved toward Connie. The pain above my eye had increased.

"Don't," she said, backing toward the shore, her hands still covering her chest. I saw the fear on her face, the way her wet, dark hair framed her tightening features. But I said nothing. I half-closed my eyes and lunged at her. Bone knocked against bone as she fell back. Her head went under for a second. I pulled her up toward me. She'd swallowed water and was coughing. I pressed my mouth against hers and tried to insert my tongue between her teeth. She shook her head free.

I let go. "I'm sorry," I said.

"Go die," she said. She coughed and wiped her mouth against her forearm. She was sitting where the water was perhaps a foot deep. Her breasts were small and waifish.

I turned away and drifted toward the middle of the pond, where the water came up to my chest. I squatted there, in the brilliant sunshine. I heard Connie get out of the water, but I didn't move. I heard Beau Jack's collar tags jangling. I stayed in the water for a long time, watching the skin on my fingers pucker, waiting to hear Elvin's voice. Would he ask me to turn around before he shot me with his Saturday Night Special? If, for some reason, he didn't shoot me, I thought I might try to resuscitate the story I'd been writing about him.

The sun slipped down the sky and swallows made passes over the pond. I wanted a cigarette and got out of the water. My clothes weren't where I thought I'd left them, however, nor were they anywhere nearby. Connie had removed them, apparently. I walked out into the field and there, among the loosestrife, found one of my sneakers. With the sneaker in my hand, I walked back and forth across the field, stepping lightly among the milkweed and fleabane and hairy-stemmed ragweed, looking for the rest of my clothes. After a while, I sat down, using my shoe as a cushion. I was a hundred yards from my aunt's house. I could see people playing croquet, my aunt among them, with her absurd flying saucer of a hat. I could walk naked to my aunt's house now or later. Or I could simply sit here and wait for the turkey vulture, making black circles in the sky to the south, to descend upon me.

Then I saw two figures crossing the field. One was Elvin, his shimmery blue muscle shirt hanging out of his jeans. The other was a young woman wearing a dark skirt and white shirt. Petra. She trotted to keep up with Elvin, who was making tracks, despite being unable to walk straight. They were talking. I heard Elvin say, "I don't know what exactly he did. All I know is what my girl told me."

Petra stopped and held her hand up against the declining sun. Elvin came on. I rose to my feet. I held the sneaker in front of my crotch.

"You look like fucking Mr. Pitiful, bro," Elvin said, squinting, angling his head so that the sun wouldn't strike it so directly. I did not think it was to my advantage that he was wobbly drunk. "But I'm going to hit you anyway. You know why."

I didn't say anything smart or brave. I didn't say anything at all. I just stood there, hiding my privates behind my shoe, looking past Elvin at Petra, wondering where she and her Ethiopian friends had gone for lunch. Wasn't there an Ethiopian dish called *wat*? A hot, peppery dish that made your lips burn? Perhaps she'd had some of that for lunch, perhaps the taste of it was still there on her tongue.

Dwight Allen grew up in Louisville, Kentucky, and attended college and graduate school in the Midwest. He was on the editorial staff of *The New Yorker* during the 1980s and for several of those years wrote the magazine's Night Life column. His stories have appeared in *The Missouri Review*, *American Short Fiction*, *The Midwesterner*, and *Gulf Coast*. He lives in Madison, Wisconsin.

"*The Green Suit*" *is one of a group of stories I've been writing about a genteel Kentucky family that bears some resemblance to my own. In this story, the fresh-out-of-college narrator, like thousands of narrators before him, leaves home for New York City. In most respects, he fares worse than I did when I lived in New York. (I too worked at a publishing house, but my duties, while not exalted, didn't include walking an editor's dog.) He certainly fares poorly in matters of love, and his thwarted ambition leads him to commit a stupid act, for which his victim's boyfriend does not forgive him. Down the road, however, he is finally able to write a story called "The Green Suit," which could be read as both a petition for forgiveness as well as a description of a lonely Southern boy lost in New York.*

Pam Durban

GRAVITY

(from *The Georgia Review*)

Whenever she visited her mother in the last weeks of the elder woman's long, long life, Louisa knew that if the nurse's aide had turned Mother's wheelchair to face the bridges over the Cooper River, she would have to listen to the Mamie story again. On Mother's bad days, which seemed to fall at the beginning and end of the week, bracketing the lucid days, Mamie looked back at her out of every black woman's face. The nurse, the woman who brought her meals or helped her to the bathroom—if she was black, her name was Mamie.

Also, any footsteps might be hers. "Mamie?" Mother's voice would wobble out to meet Louisa as she walked down the hall toward her Mother's room. "Mamie?" When Louisa came into the room, Mother would be watching the door, her swollen hands folded in her lap, a look of pained brightness on her face, until she saw her daughter and the brightness dimmed. On the good days, Louisa's mother laid down her search for the actual Mamie (dead, now, for fourteen years), was content to tell Mamie's story again. In her last weeks, the Mamie story became, Louisa thought, like a lighthouse beam: whenever Mother sailed too far out of sight of land, she swung toward its light and traveled home.

Why Mamie? Louisa asked herself often that spring. In the small, walled garden behind their house, in the brief cool of early morning as she watered the ferns and impatiens, the question would trickle through her mind like the thin stream of water that splashed in the garden fountain. Surely it was not Mamie herself, the person, the individual human being, that Mother was trying to keep alive by telling that story. Mamie's family had been part of their family for so long that any questions about them—if there had been any to begin with—had long since been answered. Mamie's family had served the Hilliard family since time was, her mother always said, in slavery and in freedom down through the generations until the last: Mamie's granddaughter Evelyn, who at sixteen left the kitchen house apartment in their yard where her grandmother had raised her and went to live with relatives out on Yonges Island. Who came in to work at ten, then at noon, and finally, not at all.

Besides, Mother's descriptions had all been of Mamie's labor and usefulness, her place in their world. *A good pair of black hands,* Mother had called Mamie with such affection, sometimes with tears in her eyes, you'd have thought she was praising Mamie's character or remembering the light the woman's soul gave off. In Mother's more formal moods, she called Mamie *the laundress and housekeeper and cook.* Finally, when the useful part of her life was done, she became *the family retainer* who lived out her days in their old kitchen house. ("Who else would take care of her, tell me that?" Mother asked.) How old was Mamie? No one knew. No white person anyway. "They destroyed my dates" was all Mamie would say if you asked her age, then set her jaw as if she'd clamped a plug of words between her back teeth.

"Who, Mamie?" Louisa would ask.

"I be just born, time of the shake," she would say. At least that date was fixed by something other than an old colored woman's memory: the earthquake of 1886. Then would follow a long, tangled account of dates written in a family Bible, a fire.

That morning, the Friday before Palm Sunday, Louisa wondered again— why Mamie?— as she stood out of sight behind the tea olive tree and waited for the tour guide, who had stopped his carriage in front of her house, to finish his speech to the tourists he carried and move on. Just that morning she'd hung the sign on the brick gatepost beside their wrought-iron gate. "Kindly Admire the Garden from the Street," it read, green words painted on gray slate with flowering jasmine twined around them to sweeten the message: go away, no one here wants to talk to you about this house, its people, or its history.

The guide, blond and friendly, a college boy, wore a gray Confederate army cap on his head and a red, fringed sash tied around his waist. His horse, a muscular chestnut Percheron, dozed with one back hoof cocked on the pavement. The boy stood up in the front of the carriage and turned to face his passengers, the reins draped loosely over one hand. This much she could see. And what she could hear was the story she knew so well she heard mostly tone when he spoke. The Hilliard house was one of the finest examples of the typical Charleston house still standing. Set gable end to the street, with piazzas up and down and a garden tucked behind a brick wall, its architecture was West Indian. Specifically, its influences came from Barbados, from which windward isle many of the planters had made their way to the Holy City of Charleston. She flinched at the oversized and pompous strokes with which the boy painted his picture of ease and wealth, the soft movie-mush of a Southern accent that made his speech sound like a parody and himself like the Southern aristocrat in a bad melodrama.

"Please note the exceptionally ornate ironwork of the gate," he said, "and the chemin de fer, a bristle of iron spikes set along the top of the brick wall as protection against the pirates who once freely roamed and pillaged through these streets. Notice the bricks of which the house and its attendant wall were constructed," he said. "They were fired in the brickyard at Fairview, the Hilliard family's plantation, out on the Edisto River.

"Now, the Hilliard family," he said, bowing slightly, "as was the custom with wealthy rice planters of their day, owned this house in town and the plantation house at Fairview—between which residences they divided their time. In late winter, they came into the city for the balls and races of the social season, then left for the plantation in time to oversee the planting of the rice crop in the spring. During the summer, the sickly season, they lived in town, then journeyed back to the plantation for the fall harvest and stayed there through the Christmas season."

Finally, it was over. The guide clucked to the horse and the carriage moved on, leaving a drift of horse smell in the warm air. Closing the iron gate behind her, Louisa stepped carefully over the slate flagstone sidewalk in front of the house that Hilliards had built, where Hilliards had lived forever. Even though she'd been born a Marion— her father's name and fine in its own way, with Francis Marion, the Swamp Fox, back in the line—she and her mother always thought of themselves as Hilliards first. That spring Louisa was seventy-five; her body felt rickety, full of drafts and cracks. Crossing the uneven flagstone sidewalk in front of her house, she felt her frail ankle bones, her brittle spine, and rigid hips. Sometimes at night she imagined the calcium sifting out of her skeleton as though her body were dissolving, bone by bone. Soon, she would be a rounded soft lump of a woman, like a tabby foundation after a few centuries in the weather. Soon, she would be an old woman who scuttled along, humped over and studying the ground.

Still, thanks to a daily dose of estrogen and to willpower, she walked erect as she moved steadily north, a woman with a wide, quiet face, a Prince Valiant helmet of white hair, a raw-silk shirtwaist dress, teal, set off with a dramatic scarf. She carried a flowered portmanteau and walked with her head held high and quiet on a long neck, enjoying the subtle prickle of salt air on her face, the smells from the gardens she passed, the sound of trickling water, the cries of gulls. Passing the market and the wharves, she walked through the smells of fish, coffee, and incense. The door to the ship's chandler's shop stood open, and she inhaled the oily, hayfield smell of rope that drifted from the narrow door. Out in the harbor the sheer green side of a freighter rose, the red and white Danish flag flying from its bridge.

At the place where Mother lived now, a private nursing home in an old house on Society Street, Louisa walked on tiptoe up the stairs and down the hall until she came to her mother's room, poked her head in the door.

"Mamie?" her mother asked from her wheelchair which, this being Friday, faced the window and the bridges.

"It's Louisa, Mother—here we are," she said as she always said, as though they'd arrived together at some destination. Then pulled a chair close to the wheelchair and sat with her needlepoint (Pax and the paschal lamb that she was stitching on the linen Easter banner for St. Phillip's Church) through her mother's first grieving silence. While her mother huffed, whimpered, muttered, Louisa crossed her ankles, straightened her back, smoothed her face, submerged her mind in a quiet pool of patience and culti-vated charity, practiced forbearance.

Soon the bundle of pink quilted satin with a failing heart and lungs inside that was her mother began to stir. She had room in her and breath enough, but just enough, to tell her story. "The Cooper River Bridge was the bridge we had to cross, you see . . ." she said, catching the story's current and eddying into it. Louisa pushed her needle in and out of the linen, knotted the paschal lamb's woolly fur. Maybe, Louisa thought, the old soul (the words made her see something tarnished and heavy, smooth and almost round, like an old iron egg) told the story of Mamie and the bridge because it was the only story she remembered that could still carry her out and over the water, away from her present life. What amazed Louisa (and on her own bad days, literally caused her skin to itch, made her want to jump up and scream, "Get to the point, for God's sake, Mother!") was how the story never varied from telling to telling by one detail, pause, or inflection; how it seemed to be asking a question, by which construction a person might assume that the story had a point, a destination. How, though it traveled in that direction, it never seemed to arrive.

Once, browsing through old newspapers in the reading room of the Charleston Library Society in search of a mention of some nineteenth-century Hilliard, Louisa had come across this advertisement in a copy of the *Charleston City Gazette* published in the summer of 1820: "$10 Reward. Drifted from Haddrill's Point, a CANOE, painted red or a bright Spanish brown, branded with my name in several places, has row locks for 6 oars." That is how she thought of her mother's mind: a one-hundred-and-two-year-old bright Spanish-brown canoe of a mind, drifting here, drifting there, stranded on an oyster bank at low tide, lifted again and set adrift when the tide came in, drawn by tides and currents always back toward Mamie and the Cooper River Bridge.

"The Cooper River Bridge was the bridge we had to cross, you seer, to get from the Charleston peninsula over to our beach house on Sullivan's Island. We spent our summers there away from the city's heat," she confided to Louisa as if she were giving one of her famous talks on local geography and history to a stranger. As if her own daughter were a tourist.

Her mother did not say this, but the Cooper River Bridge was not always the wide concrete six-lane road of a bridge it is today, a chunk of Interstate 26 lofted over the river, with reversible lanes and concrete walls to keep you from looking down or sailing off the edges. Crossing the new bridge you might as well be flying over the river in an armchair. The old bridge, however, which still stands beside the new one and carries traffic one way into the city from the north, was once the only bridge coming or going: a narrow two-lane steel girder suspension bridge with rusty open railings (like some rickety roller coaster at a county fair) through which you could look down onto the wings of gulls and onto rusty barges, sailboats, tankers and, now and then, the periscope of a submarine heading downriver from the navy base toward the harbor and the open ocean beyond.

That was the bridge Mamie was required to cross with their family every summer on the way to the beach house where she was the one who picked the crab meat from the bushels of crabs the family hauled in. Where she peeled shrimp, cooked, walked the children to the beach, swept the sand out of the house. Where she lived in a room underneath the house and slept on a rusty iron bed and pomaded her hair in front of a mirror with most of the silver peeled off. Where she read her Bible out loud to herself every night or sang and ironed in front of the oscillating fan until long past midnight.

"Well, Old Mamie had an absolute and utter terror of that bridge," Mother said. She was launched now, Louisa saw, and there would be no turning back. Louisa pushed her needle harder through the stiff linen. "Something about being high up in the air like that, crossing water, scared her so much that when I told her it was time to get ready to go to the beach, those little bitty pig-tails she used to wear would practically stand straight out from her head, and she'd drop to her knees in the kitchen or wherever I'd spoken to her and start wringing her hands. 'Lord, Missis,' she'd wail. 'Lord God. Leave I back behind on solid earth. I too old. Be crossing that water soon enough.' I'd tell her I'd carry her petition to my husband, but I knew it wouldn't do any good. He never would put up with nonsense from the colored. 'She'll ride with us, as usual,' he always said. 'I'm not going to inconvenience my family to accommodate Mamie's superstitions.'"

Listening that day, Louisa asked herself: was this perhaps a story of injustice, historic and ongoing? Not likely. When the concept of injustice finally pushed its way into their world, her mother had been outraged. "Injustice?" Mother would say, revolted by the taste of the word. "What injustice? When we carried them all those years. Who turned on whom? Who deserted whom?" She came from that generation whose childhoods had touched the outer rim of the time in which the conclusions about race still felt like certainties. Such as: The Hilliards had been good masters, kind masters who seldom had to raise the whip to their people. So after freedom the Fairview slaves had stayed on the place: Teneh and Cuff, Binah, Scipio, Daniel and Abby and Maum Harriette, Mamie's mother. Her own mother had been born there and cared for by Mamie's mother. Such as: The Hilliards take care of their own. When King Hopkins, Mamie's husband, got drunk and cut a man at a juke joint up on Calhoun Street, who bailed him out of jail? (Hugh Marion Sr., himself.) Who went to court with him and got him off? (Mr. Marion, again.) Such as: Evelyn grew up in their yard, too, didn't she? After Mamie's daughter died, who allowed Evelyn to come live with her grandmother? They didn't have to do that, Mother insisted, or let Mamie stay in the kitchen house in their yard either, for that matter. When Evelyn graduated from South Carolina State, who drove Mamie up to her granddaughter's graduation? It was Louisa herself, that's who." Round and round the stories went, round and round, miraculous wheels that rolled through time and never warped or splintered as they rolled.

When the civil rights movement came along and the hospital workers went on strike, demonstrators had lined King Street singing and chanting, holding their signs: FREEDOM NOW. WE SHALL NOT BE MOVED. Evelyn had marched into Pierce Bros. department store, which did not serve Negroes, and asked to try on a pair of shoes. Mother had been personally hurt and affronted that blacks should have seen themselves damaged by the cordial and correct distances the races had agreed to keep from one another, the obvious and necessary ranking that kept them apart, in the separate worlds they lived in so comfortably, side by side. Once, in a bitter mood about the city's handling of the protests, after his fifth trip to the cut-glass decanter of port on the dining room sideboard, Louisa's brother Hugh had said, "Keep Mother away from the windows. She's liable to ask Martin Luther King if he's looking for yardwork." She might have, too. Mother was as invulnerable to the idea of injustice as a turtle latched in its shell.

"Well, for about two weeks before we left for the beach there were some odd comings and goings around our kitchen house. Her pastor must have visited her half a dozen times. Then there were the other characters. That old scarecrow of a man who used to run errands for us. The vegetable cart man. A one-eyed woman who sold baskets down at the market. You'd hear them knocking on the screen door of the kitchen house all hours of the day or night. 'Aunt Mamie,' they'd call. 'Aunt Mamie.' But we knew what they were doing. They were root doctors and so forth, bringing charms to her. We pretended we didn't know," she leaned forward and confided in her daughter, "but we did. On the morning of our departure, Mamie would appear with her Bible clutched in one hand, her suitcase in the other. She'd have her lucky dime on a string around her ankle, nutmeg around her neck along with a big silver cross on a red ribbon and a cloth pouch she'd sewed herself. She never would tell us what was in it. Graveyard dirt, I suppose. They were big on that. Crab claws, maybe. I'd just have to turn my back to keep from laughing at the poor old thing and hurting her feelings.

"Mamie sat in the back between you and Hugh. As soon as we started up the bridge, she'd grab the door handle with one hand and the rope across the back of the front seat with the other. Remember that big, black, sixteen-cylinder Buick we owned, your father's pride and joy? Those little ropes across the backs of the seats? Up we'd go onto the bridge, Mamie hanging onto that rope for dear life, with her eyes squeezed shut, praying. 'Sweet Jesus! Lord have mercy! Great God! Do, Jesus! Great King!' I think she used up every name they have for their God before we'd gotten over the first span. She'd start off low, grumbling and muttering to herself—she knew your father didn't want to listen to her carrying on—but before we'd reached the top of the first span, she'd practically be shouting. Of course I'd see what was coming by the way your father scowled into the rearview mirror with increasing severity, and then all of a sudden, *Mamie,*' he would say, so quietly *I* almost couldn't hear him, and I was sitting beside him in the front seat, but Mamie would jerk straight up as if he'd yanked her by a chain. 'Do I need to remind you that you are riding in my family car, you are not at some camp meeting out in the Congaree Swamp?'

" 'No suh,' she'd say, 'sure don't,' and all the while she'd be studying the floor with her old bottom lip poking out about a mile. Mamie was light skinned—*high yellow* we called those kind—much lighter than your blue-black Negro, with more refined features and a few freckles across her nose and cheeks. She had light hazel eyes. But she sure prayed like an African. Well, after your father spoke to her, she'd simmer down and mumble her prayers to herself until we were safely across the bridge and down onto Mt. Pleasant. Old Mamie. Didn't she make the best biscuits?"

And right there, her mother stopped, as she always stopped, as though the thread had all run off that spool. She nodded an emphatic period, smoothed down the skirt of her bathrobe over her knees, and stared out at the bridges until her eyes began to droop. This drowsiness was Louisa's signal that the story and the visit were over. Mother would not talk again that day. She had come to the end of the story; there was nothing more to tell. It was time for Louisa to fold up the linen banner and pack it away in her portmanteau along with her embroidery floss and the small silver scissors—the ones with handles shaped like the curved necks and out-stretched heads of flying cranes—that had once belonged to her ancestor Eliza Hilliard, another spinster seamstress. Time to help her mother out of the wheelchair and onto the bed. Time to draw the covers up around her mother's neck, kiss the pink scalp that showed through the white hair that stood out like mist around her mother's head, and tiptoe out of the room, closing the door behind her. Time to walk out into the nursing-home parking lot, into the smells of fish and oil and sun on water, and to remember how the water had looked from the top of the highest span of the old Cooper River Bridge: like a floor, hard and glittering, swept with light.

It was not her mother's drifting Spanish-brown canoe of a mind that had landed her in the nursing home; it was her body. One night earlier that spring Louisa had waked to her mother's call. Though her voice had thinned, it was sharp as a needle, and like a needle it had pierced Louisa's sleep. "Louisa, Louisa, I need to tee-tee."

Sleep-clogged, stiff, Louisa had dragged herself out of her canopied bed in the upstairs corner room. Snapping on the light

in the bedroom next to hers she'd found Mother propped on pil-
lows on the chintz-covered chaise lounge where she slept upright
in order to ease her breathing. Oxygen tubes ran up her nose, a
canister of oxygen on wheels sat at her side.

Louisa meant no disrespect when she thought of her mother as
grotesque. One hundred and two and elephantine with a face like
a pudding, she was bloated from medications and edema and from
an appetite which (until her most recent and steepest decline
soured her stomach) she had not even attempted to curb since her
husband died. No sooner had Hugh Wyman Marion gone to St.
Phillips churchyard than she began to pour half-and-half on her
breakfast cereal, to stir four thick pats of butter into every plate of
rice, to set her shrimp bubbling in two inches of melted butter and
bacon grease. Now she was hung with slabs, folds, and pouches of
fat, as if she were outfitting herself in flesh for a long trip into a
land of famine.

As Mother had ballooned, so had her stubbornness, her imper-
ial selfishness (this much resentment Louisa would allow herself—
more would be unhealthy), which kept her from listening to the
doctor ("My *God, Elizabeth, you've gained another fifteen pounds.
What are we going to do with you?*") or from agreeing to a wheelchair or allowing Louisa to hire someone to help them. Absolutely
not. No. If Mother's silver cane tip marred the floors, the floors
would be refinished. If in the middle of the night Mother required
a four-letter synonym for *decaying plant matter* or a reminder of the
precise location of the cruet stand, Louisa tried to answer. Hiring
help was out of the question—her mother's demands rested on
historical precedent. Juliana Hilliard (Elizabeth's mother) had
cared for *her* mother; now Louisa would care for hers. In that way
the generations would hold and a shining vein of loyalty and devo-
tion would run through dark and crumbling time. Sometime that
spring, watching her mother munch toast, jaws rolling, watching
her lips reach for the rim of the coffee cup and delicately suck the
hot liquid in, Louisa decided that to call her grotesque (in private,
of course, and only to herself) was simply to state a fact, something

with which Louisa had made the firmest and longest-lasting relationship of her life.

The night of the bathroom call, Louisa had knelt and forced her mother's feet into the bedroom slippers that she needed then, mustard-colored corduroy loafers from the Woolworth's on King Street, the kind that Mother had never allowed Mamie to wear around the house because they slapped against her heels with such a slovenly sound. Size twelve and still the heel had to be cut away to keep them from squeezing Mother's swollen feet. Hoisting her mother, Louisa said "Upsy-daisy," just to hear the optimistic lilt of those words in the dark. Louisa rolled the oxygen tank with one hand, kept the other arm around her mother's waist. Together they struggled and staggered toward the bathroom at the far end of the hall. Louisa felt her mother's weight bear down on her, her damp armpits and clammy neck; she heard her mother's breath whistle past her ear. It was too hot for this work, but Mother always ordered the air conditioning shut off at 8 P.M. sharp and the windows opened — even when it was still stifling outside and the air so muggy it seeped through the screens like fog through a sieve.

"She's leaning her whole weight on me," Louisa thought as they inched toward the bathroom. "We're going to fall. We're going to collapse right here in the middle of the hall." Louisa felt the beginning of a panicky tightening in her lungs.

But they didn't collapse in the hall. They had made it all the way to the bathroom and then — as she tried to ease her mother down onto the toilet seat, holding her around the waist with one arm while Mother grappled with her underpants and yanked at the oxygen tank — Louisa's feet slipped on the tile floor. To keep herself from falling she let go of her mother, who sat down hard on the floor with the high furious cry of a baby. When Louisa couldn't get her mother up, and the old woman could no longer hold back her water, Mrs. Elizabeth St. Julian Hilliard Marion had peed on the bathroom floor in the house where Hilliards had made their high or low, prolonged or shortened transits from birth to death for more than two centuries. When her mother was done, Louisa picked up the wet towels and dropped them down the laundry chute in the bathroom closet. Then she called 911 from the phone in the upstairs hall. "My mother has fallen in the bathroom," she said, "and I can't get her up."

After she'd returned from making the call, Louisa had sat on the cool tile floor and leaned against the toilet, holding her mother, who dozed with her head resting against Louisa's thin breasts and one hand splayed out on her cheek as if she were thinking something over. The thin hiss of oxygen up the tubes into her mother's nose was the only sound in the room besides the whine of a mosquito, that had discovered them helpless on the floor and attacked Louisa's ankles. As they sat and Mother dozed, her chin pillowed in the fat of her neck, and as the sound of the siren came toward them through the night, Louisa looked down and saw the slack, puckered elastic of her mother's yellowed nylon underpants. At least she, Louisa, had thought to put on her robe.

That was the night Louisa knew that she'd come to the end of something. She knew that she would date some ominous accelerating of time from the moment she'd laid three thick monogrammed towels on the floor next to her mother, then stepped out of the room and stood in the hall with her hand on the heavy glass doorknob of the bathroom door while her mother wet the towels. Before that night, age had worked on Louisa one piece at a time. In cold, rainy weather, her knuckles swelled and ached. Her hips felt stiff every morning. Some days the smell of her pillow—like gray iron—startled her. Or the smell that rose from her mouth when she flossed her teeth, that carried her back to her grandmother and what had been on her breath. How foreign and startling it had seemed then, how familiar now. There were migrating patches of numbness and constriction, fine lines that radiated out from her mouth, into which her lipstick spread. Signs of aging, true, but never overwhelming, never all at once.

On the floor of the bathroom that night, propped up against the toilet with her mother's slack weight resting against her, she'd felt old all over, as though age were something she was swamped in, as if she were curing in it, like the nineteenth-century Hilliard Madeira and peach brandy still curing in barrels down in the cellar. Both of them, herself and the liquor, steeped in time, which caused the collapse of one and deepened the flavor and value of the other. And she wept for the two old women they'd become, two old women with their stains and flows. Two old women not able to keep up with the laundry anymore, and the younger, who was herself, unable to help the older, who was her own mother, up from the bathroom floor or even to pull her nightgown out from under her body and cover the underpants and slack thighs and ugly slippers that the ambulance attendants would notice.

Later, sitting over coffee in some Waffle House up on Ashley Phosphate Road, those men would shake their heads and laugh together about the old ladies they'd hauled up off the bathroom floor of their house in the historic district. "They pee just like the rest of us," one of them would say from behind his cigarette smoke—she imagined he would have a knuckly, mournful face and a big Adam's apple, his hair so thickly oiled the drag marks of the comb stayed in place all day—and the waitress would laugh too. That night, after the vision of the Waffle House left her, Louisa had laid her cheek down on her mother's head and whispered, "Mother, don't you think it's time to move on?"

Later, she wondered if Mother had heard her that night. The week after the bathroom crisis, at their doctor's insistence, Mother had gone to the nursing home without complaint. She'd even sent Louisa a note—shaky handwriting that skated down her heavy cream notepaper—thanking her daughter for finding her such a nice place, a private care home in an old house like their own. Quiet and clean, it did not smell, and the help were the courteous, almost invisible, old-style colored you seldom found working anywhere anymore. The woman who ran the home was a woman like herself, Louisa thought, a *discreet matron* as they used to describe themselves in the *Mercury* when they advertised their music or sewing or watercolor lessons for young ladies.

Mother had been in the home for three months when the owner called in the middle of the night. "Miss Marion," she said, "I'm sorry, but I must inform you that your mother has passed away." Even while the woman went on talking (just died, she said, not half an hour ago) Louisa felt restless. Hugh needed to know that their mother had died, and she was the oldest; she must make the call. Besides, the news of her mother's death had gone into her and started growing, pushing everything else out until it was just a big, spinning hollow place inside, like the swirling cloud of wind on a hurricane tracking map, and she was in danger of dropping into this fact of death without another soul to know it with her. "I'll be right there," she said, "but first I must call my brother."

She switched on the gooseneck lamp on the telephone table in the hall and took her address book out of the drawer. She ripped through it, looking for Hugh's page, while fear rose inside her, hissing softly like Mother's oxygen. She had to find his number before the fear filled her and she was lost in it. This terrified Louisa over every other terror—to be lost in time. Not to know where you were, who you were, to look and not to recognize what you saw, to lose your bearings.

By the light of the small gooseneck lamp, she found her brother's page in the address book. HUGH, she'd printed in block letters across the top. His addresses, entered and crossed out, filled the entire page. The apartment on King Street that he'd moved into after he gave up on law school at the University of South Carolina. The house on the marsh on Isle of Palms where he'd lived one summer while he rented floats on the beach out of a little shack made of raw pine boards covered with palmetto fronds. The apartment near the Navy base in North Charleston where it was never quite clear what he did.

And the house on Station Creek in McClellanville. Hugh liked to laugh about how termites had been swarming there when the real estate agent had showed it to him, a twitching carpet of them laid over the downstairs floors, but Hugh had waded through them and rented the house anyway. So close to the creek that the full-moon spring and autumn tides had washed up under the porch. Hugh had pulled his batteau up onto the mud bank there and tied it to one of the brick pillars that held up the front porch. He spent his days fishing, crabbing, drinking, traveling in his batteau down the tidal creeks to the ocean. Sometimes he threw parties that lasted for days, cooked up kettles of shrimp that he'd pulled from a creek with his cast net. He'd call her at two in the morning, a chaos of merriment going on behind his voice, to invite her to the party, and when she'd refuse, he'd turn maudlin and insist: she was his sister, she belonged there, partying with him and his friends.

This had been in the late sixties, early seventies, and what Hugh had really been doing was unloading marijuana off the boats that slipped up the creeks near McClellanville, then running the dope down to Charleston to sell. Hugh was getting rich at it, too, for once in his life, having spent all of the money their father had left him between the year he started law school at Carolina and the time two years later when he left school for good.

When state drug agents set out to break up the smuggling along that part of the coast, they went to the real estate agencies in Charleston that sold houses in the historic district and collected the names of people who'd made large cash down payments on houses. They did the same at marinas and luxury car dealerships. Hugh's name came to them from the Mercedes-Benz dealership in North Charleston, but they never did catch up with him. He moved too fast.

Then she was fully awake and Hugh was dead, as he'd been for twenty years. She closed the address book and put it back in the drawer, turned off the lamp, and with one hand on the wall, found her way back to her room, where she sat on the edge of her bed and rocked a little, preparing herself. The dark from the hall seemed to flow into the room. It smelled of old wood and wet air, something green trailing through it. The smell of ghosts, Mamie had said. She wouldn't go into the hall at night, where the ghosts were so thick, jostling each other. "Black and white, all jam up together" was how Mamie described what happened up in the hall at night. Once, Mamie said, a witch jumped her and rode on her back all the way down the stairs and out into the yard, where she shook it off and stuffed it down the well. Louisa remembered being up there with Mamie, the feel of Mamie's fingers plucking at her sleeve. "Walk over this side the hall, Miss," she'd say, and Louisa would know that they were detouring around one of her ancestors, or Mamie's. She'd find Mamie standing on the flag-stones in front of the house, broom in hand, staring up at the chimney. "They pouring out now, Miss," Mamie would say, mean-ing, Louisa knew, the ghosts. Pouring out like smoke.

It happened quickly, the owner said, as she opened the front door and let Louisa into the entrance hall of the big house. It hap-pened in her sleep, she said, steering Louisa by the elbow toward the stairs. Louisa was grateful that the woman was dressed for work, that her hair was combed. She wore glasses, low-heeled pumps, and she carried papers in her hand as though she'd been awake for hours. Louisa appreciated the woman's efficiency. No bathrobe, no straggling hair or slack, bewildered face to show that death had surprised her.

"I'm going to let you talk to Yvonne, the nurse's aide who was on duty when your mother passed away," the woman said as she and Louisa climbed the stairs. Walking down the hall toward her mother's room, Louisa caught herself listening. *Mamie?* It was quiet except for the sound of their feet on the carpet, and the moon sent the shape of the window at the end of the hall ahead of them as they walked.

In her mother's room, the bedside lamp was turned down low. A woman sat in a rocking chair beside the bed, one hand on the spread, rocking and patting the spread and humming to herself. Then she stood up when Louisa came in, smoothing down her uniform and smiling. Louisa saw a gold front tooth, a quick, kind smile.

"This is Mrs. Marion's daughter, Yvonne," the owner said, and went out of the room closing the door with a soft click as she went.

"She was a sweet, fine lady," Yvonne said. "She didn't struggle against it. Look here, sheets smooth, face sweet." She touched the dead woman's cheek. "You blessed. Some struggle and fight. One lady try to climb out the window—had to call in two mans for to hold her back." She had checked on Mother at midnight, then gone down the hall to look in on someone else, and when she'd come back at 12:45, Mother had ceased to breathe.

"So she didn't say anything?"

"Not as I am aware of."

"Thank you for all you've done," Louisa said, anxious for the woman to leave, and when Yvonne had gone, she sat down beside her mother on the bed. Her mother lay on her side with her eyes closed, her hands tucked between her knees. They'd disconnected the oxygen tubes from her nose and rolled the canister away. On her mother's upper lip, Louisa saw the outline of the tape that had held the tubes in place. She licked her thumb and moved to scrub, then stopped. The undertaker would clean those away, she thought. He would clean all the marks of life away. Now there was only silence in the room, and the sound of her own breathing.

The expression on her mother's face was peaceful. In fact, Louisa thought, it was the same expression that she'd seen a hundred times when her mother had caught up with Mamie and her biscuits and put them back where they belonged and finished her story. It occurred to Louisa that at the moment of death her mother might have been dreaming of Mamie's biscuits. She remembered that they felt dense and heavy in your hand, then dissolved like buttery clouds when you bit into them. And she saw that it was comfort her mother had been looking for, telling that story—comfort and consolation and certainty in the memory of those biscuits and of Mamie's silly old colored-woman terrors, so much more primitive and obscure than their own.

Sitting beside her mother's body, Louisa felt she'd entered another world of silence and stillness that lapped out from the body on the bed and surrounded her. It was the stillness, the vacancy, that she could not bend her mind around. She almost said, "Mother?" the way she used to do, to wake her. But she brushed back wisps of hair from her mother's forehead and kept still. Whatever life is, she saw, it visits the body, then goes, taking nothing you could catch, store in a bottle, or press and keep under glass. Taking nothing visible and taking everything. And she remembered a darkened room stuffed with summer heat, the wooden shutters latched over the windows and herself sick with diphtheria on the canopied bed, the cool feel of her mother's fingers rubbing hand cream on her lips. The last person who knew her before she knew herself, the last one who could say, "When you were a baby . . ." and hand her a piece of her life that had existed before she even knew herself to be in it.

Looking up, Louisa saw the lights of the bridges over Cooper River and thought of how Hugh might have driven north across the new bridge to Sullivan's Island. He had let himself into the beach house, rummaged in drawers, drank half a bottle of port, sat in every chair and lay on every bed. (For weeks the imprint of his backside was left in the chair cushions and the restless twist of his body stayed in the white chenille bedspreads until someone smoothed them.) Then he had driven his dark blue Mercedes up onto the dunes in front of the house until the tires sank in the sand, cut the engine, and shot himself in the head.

Looking at the bridges, remembering Hugh, she felt afraid again. To this day, when crossing that bridge, her throat tightened, her heart beat slow and hard, and her face felt as if a bright light shone on it. She wanted only to make it safely to the other side. She remembered the scene from her mother's story: all of them in the car together, crossing the bridge high over the water, listening to Mamie's prayers and her father's outburst. Now she was the only survivor of those who had lived that story. It was her story now, and there was no comfort in it, for she also remembered how her father had grown philosophical after he'd silenced Mamie. Looking down at the water, he'd offered them the same detail every time. Water would feel like concrete if you fell into it from this height, he'd say. And just like that, how high they were became how far they could fall, how close they were to falling. Silent as one of Mamie's ghosts, the knowledge of their actual and precarious place on earth had traveled with them to the other side.

Pam Durban is the author of a book of short stories, *All Set About With Fever Trees*, and a novel, *The Laughing Place*. Her stories have appeared in numerous magazines and anthologies. A native of South Carolina, she currently lives in Atlanta and teaches at Georgia State University.

*W*riting this story is, in part, my attempt to question for myself the stories about race on which I was raised, stories that have been handed down through generations of white Southerners in my home state of South Carolina. Working on the story has served as an antidote to any self-righteousness I might feel about the superiority of my own racial attitudes, since I am reminded every day how fluent I am in the more appalling opinions, how much they are a part of me. I located the story in the South Carolina Low Country, in Charleston and the surrounding coast, because to me that place feels like the center of the slave-holding world and the seedbed of white South Carolina's idea of itself. I lived for a short time on an old rice plantation on the Edisto River where in the 1970s the outlines of an older world were still visible: the big house on the bluff, a stand of live oaks, the rice fields, a line of falling-down wooden shacks back in the pines. At the time, the significance of that place as something more than a world of ease and beauty was invisible to me and silent. Nothing in my education or upbringing had taught or encouraged me to see it otherwise. In the story, my intention is to bring that world and the world of the city of Charleston to life in order to question its assumptions and trace its influence.

One of the most meaningful rituals of the church year is to me the Palm Sunday service. In that service, the minister reads the part of Pontius Pilate trying — feebly — to save Christ's life, and the congregation takes the part of the mob, demanding his crucifixion. It's a significant ceremony, I think, because, in playing the part of the mob, you break down the belief in your own innocence, and that's a healing act.

Lee Smith

NATIVE DAUGHTER

(from *The Oxford American*)

Mama always said, "Talk real sweet and you can have whatever you want." This is true, though it does not hurt to have a nice bust either. Since I was blessed early on in both the voice and bosom departments, I got the hell out of Eastern Kentucky at the first opportunity and never looked back. That's the way Mama raised us, not to get stuck like she did. Mama grew up hard and married young and worked her fingers to the bone and wanted us to have a better life. "Be nice," she always said. "Please people. Marry rich."

After several tries, I am finally on the verge of this. But it has been a lot of work, believe me. I'm a very high-maintenance woman. It is *not easy* to look the way I do. Some surgery has been involved. But I'll tell you, what with the miracles of modern medicine available to our fingertips, I do not know why more women don't go for it. *Just go for it!* This is my motto.

Out of Mama's three daughters, I am the only one that has gotten ahead in the world. The only one that really listened to her, the only one that has gone places and done things. And everywhere I go, I always remember to send Mama a postcard. She saves them in a big old green pocketbook which she keeps right by her bed for this very purpose. She's got postcards from Las Vegas and Disney World and Los Angeles and the Indianapolis 500 in there. From the Super Bowl and New York City and Puerto Vallarte. Just this morning, I mailed her one from Miami. I've been everywhere.

As opposed to Mama herself, who still cooks in the elementary school cafeteria in Paradise, Kentucky, where she has cooked for thirty years, mostly soup beans. Soup beans! I wouldn't eat another soup bean if my life depended on it, if it was the last thing to eat on the earth. I grew up on soup beans. Give me caviar. Which I admit I did not take to at first as it is so salty, but now have acquired a taste for, like Scotch. There are some things you just have to like if you want to rise up in the world.

I myself am upwardly mobile and proud of it, and Mama is proud of me, too. No matter what kind of lies Brenda tries to tell her about me. Brenda is my oldest sister who goes to church in a mall where she plays tambourines and dances all around. This is just as bad as being one of those old Holiness people up in the hollers handling snakes, in my opinion. Brenda tells everybody I am going to Hell. One time she chased me down in a car to lay hands on me and pray out loud. I happened to have a new boyfriend with me at the time and I got so embarrassed I almost died.

My other sister, Luanne, is just as bad as Brenda but in a different way. Luanne runs a little day care center at home, which has allowed her to let herself go to a truly awful degree, despite the fact that she used to be the prettiest one of us all, with smooth, creamy skin, a natural widow's peak, and Elizabeth Taylor eyes. Now she weighs over two hundred pounds and those eyes are just little slits in her face. Furthermore she is living with a younger man who does not appear to work and does not look American at all. Luanne claims he has Cherokee blood. His name is Roscoe Ridley and he seems nice enough, otherwise I never would let Tiffany stay with them. Of course this arrangement is just temporary until I can get Billy nailed down. I feel that Billy is finally making a real commitment by bringing me along this weekend, and I have cleared the decks for action so to speak.

But speaking of decks, this yacht is not exactly like *The Love Boat* or the one on *Fantasy Island,* which is more what I had in mind. Of course I am not old enough to remember those shows, but I have seen the reruns. I never liked that weird little dwarf guy. I believe he has died now of some unusual disease. I hope so. Anyway, thank goodness there is nobody like that on *this* boat, we have three Negroes who are nice as you please. They smile and say yes ma'am and will sing calypso songs upon request, although they have not done this yet. I am looking forward to it, having been an entertainer myself. These island Negroes do not seem to have a chip on their shoulder like so many in the U.S., especially in Atlanta, where we live. My own relationship with black people has always been very good. I know how to talk to them, I know where to draw the line, and they respect me for it.

"Well, baby, whaddya think? Paradise, huh?" This is my fiancé and employer Billy Marcum who certainly deserves a little trip to paradise if anybody does. I have never known anybody to work so hard. Billy started off as a paving contractor and still thinks you can never have too much concrete. This is also true of gold, in my opinion, as well as shoes.

Now Billy is doing real well in commercial real estate and property management. In fact we are here on this yacht for the weekend thanks to his business associate Bruce Ware, one of the biggest developers in Atlanta, though you never know it by looking at him. When he met us at the dock in Barbados wearing those one hundred-year-old blue jeans, I was so surprised. I believe that in general, people should look as good as they can. Billy and I had an interesting discussion about this in which he said that from his own observation, *really* rich people like Bruce Ware will often dress down, and even drive junk cars. Billy says Bruce Ware drives an old jeep! I cannot imagine.

And I can't wait to see what his wife will have on, though I *can* imagine this, as I know plenty of women just like her—"bow-heads" is what I call them, all those Susans and Ashleys and Elizabeths, though I would never say this aloud, not even to Billy. I have made a study of these women's lives which I aspire to, not that I will ever be able to wear all those dumb little bows without embarrassment.

"Honey, this is fabulous!" I tell Billy, and it is. Turquoise blue water so clear you can see right down to the bottom where weird fish are swimming around. Strange jagged picturesque mountains popping up behind the beaches on several of the little islands we're passing.

"What's the name of these islands again?" I ask, and Billy tells me, "The Grenadines." "There is a drink called that," I say, and Billy says, "Is there?" and kisses me. He is such a hard worker that he has missed out on everything cultural.

Kissing Billy is not really great but okay.

"Honey, you need some sunscreen," I tell him when he's through. He has got that kind of redheaded complexion that will burn like crazy in spite of his stupid hat. "You need to put it every-where, all over you, on your feet and all. Here, put your foot up on the chair," I tell him, and he does, and I rub sunscreen all over his fat white feet one after the other and his ankles and his calves right up to those baggy plaid shorts. This is something I will not do after we're married.

"Hey Billy, how'd you rate that kind of service?" It's Bruce Ware, now in cut-offs, and followed not by his wife but by some younger heavier country-club-type guy. I can feel their eyes on my cleavage.

"I'm Chanel Keen, Billy's fiancée." I straighten up and shake their hands. One of the things Billy does not know about me is that my name used to be Mayruth, back in the Dark Ages. Mayruth! Can you imagine?

Bruce introduces his associate, Mack Durant, and then they both stand there grinning at me. I can tell they are surprised that Billy would have such a classy fiancée as myself.

"I thought your wife was coming," I say to Bruce Ware, looking at Billy.

"She certainly intended to, Chanel," Bruce says, "but something came up at the very last minute. I know she would have enjoyed being here with you and Billy." One thing I have noticed about very successful people is that they say your name all the time and look right at you. Bruce Ware does this.

He and Mack sit down in the deck chairs. I imagine their little bowhead wives back in Atlanta shopping or getting their legs waxed or screwing the kids' soccer coach.

Actually I am relieved that the wives stayed home. It is less competition for me, and I have never liked women much anyway. I never know what to say to them, though I am very good at drawing a man out conversationally, any man. And actually a fiancée such as myself can be a big asset to Billy on a business trip which is what this is anyway, face it, involving a huge mall and a sports complex. It's a big deal. So I make myself useful, and by the time I get Bruce and Mack all settled down with rum and Cokes and sunscreen, they're showing Billy more respect.

Bruce Ware points out interesting sights to us, such as a real volcano, as we cruise toward St. Felipe, the little island where we'll be anchoring. It takes three rum and Cokes to get there. We go into a half-moon bay which looks exactly like a postcard, with palm trees like Gilligan's Island. The Negroes anchor the yacht and then take off for the island in the dinghy, singing a calypso song. It is *really foreign* here! Birds of the sort you find in pet stores, yachts, and sailboats of every kind flying flags of every nationality, many I have never seen before. "This is just *not American* at all, is it?" I remark, and Bruce Ware says, "No, Chanel, that's the point." Then he identifies all the flags for Billy and me. Billy acts real interested in everything but I can tell he's out of his league. I bet he wishes he'd stayed in Atlanta to make this deal. Not me! I have always envisioned myself on a yacht, and am capable of learning from every experience.

For example, I am interested to hear Bruce Ware use a term I have not heard before, "Eurotrash," to describe some of the girls on the other yachts. Nobody mentions that about half the women on the beach are topless, though the men keep looking that way with the binoculars. I myself can see enough from here—and most of those women would do a lot better to keep their tops on, in my opinion. I could show them a thing or two. But going topless is not something which any self-respective fiancée such as myself would ever do.

The Negroes come back with shrimp and limes and crackers, etc. I'm so relieved to learn that there's a store someplace on this island, as I foresee running out of sunscreen before this is all over. While the Negroes are serving hors d'oeuvres, I go down to put on my suit which is a little white bikini with gold trim that shows off my tan to advantage. I can't even remember what we did before tanning salons! (But then I remember, all of a sudden, laying out in the sun on a towel with Brenda and Luanne, we had painted our boyfriends' initials in fingernail polish on our stomachs so we could get a tan all around them. CB, I had painted on my stomach for Clive Baldwin who was the cutest thing, the quarterback at the high school, he gave me a pearl ring that Christmas before the wreck but then I ran off to Nashville with Randy Rash.)

"You feel okay, honey?" Billy says when I get to the top of the little stairs where at first I can't see a thing, the sun is so bright, it's like coming out of a movie.

"Sure I do." I give Billy a little wifely peck on the cheek.

"*Damn,*" Mack Durant says. "You sure *look* okay." Mack himself looks like Burt Reynolds but fatter. I choose to ignore that remark.

"Can I get one of the Negroes to run me in to the beach?" I ask. "I need to make a few purchases."

"Why not swim in?" Bruce suggests. "That's what everybody else is doing." He motions to the other boats, and this is true. "Or you can paddle in on the kickboard."

"I can't swim," I say, which is not technically true, but I have no intention of messing up my makeup or getting my hair wet, plus also I have a basic theory that you should never do anything in front of people unless you are really good at it, this goes not just for swimming but *everything*.

Bruce claps his hands and a Negro gets the dinghy and I ride to the beach in style, then tell him to wait for me. I could get used to this! Also, I figure that my departure will give the men a chance to talk business.

There's not actually much on the island that I can see, just a little shack of a store featuring very inferior products and a bunch of pathetic-looking Negroes begging, which I ignore, and selling their tacky native crafts along the beach. These natives look very unhealthy to me, with their nappy hair all matted up and their dark skin kind of dusty looking, like they've got powder on. The ones back in Atlanta are much healthier in my opinion, though they all carry guns.

I pay for my stuff with some big green bills that I don't have a clue as to their value. I'm sure these natives are cheating me blind. Several Italian guys try to pick me up on the beach, wearing nasty little stretch briefs. I don't even bother to speak to them. I just wade out into the warm clear water to the dinghy and ride back and then Billy helps me up the ladder to the yacht where I land flat on my butt on the deck, to my total embarrassment. "It certainly is hard to keep up your image in the tropics!" I make a little joke as Billy picks me up.

"Easier to let it go," Bruce Ware says. "Go native. Let it all hang out."

In my absence, the men have been swimming. Bruce Ware's chest hair is gray and matted, like a bathmat. He stands with his feet wide apart as our boat rocks in the wake of a monster sailboat, looking perfectly comfortable, as if he grew up on a yacht. Maybe he did. Billy and I didn't, that's for sure! We are basically two of a kind, I just wish I'd run into him earlier in life. This constant rocking is making me nauseous, something I didn't notice before when we were moving. I am not about to mention it, but Bruce Ware must have noticed because he gives me some Dramamine.

Billy and I go down below to dress up a little bit for dinner but I won't let Billy fool around at all as I am sure they could hear us. Billy puts on khaki pants and a nice shirt and I put on my new white linen slacks and a blue silk blouse with a scoop neck. I am disappointed to see that Bruce and Mack do not even bother to change for dinner, simply throwing shirts on over their bathing trunks, and I am further disappointed by the restaurant which we have to walk up a long steep path through the actual real jungle to get to. It's at least a half a mile. I'm so glad I wore some flats.

"This better be worth it!" I joke, but then I am embarrassed when it's not. This restaurant is nothing but a big old house with Christmas lights strung all around the porch and three mangy yellow dogs in the yard, why I might just as well have stayed in Eastern Kentucky!

We climb up these steep steps onto the porch and sit at a table covered with oilcloth and it is a pretty view, I must admit, overlooking the little harbor. There's a nice breeze too. So I am just relaxing a little bit when a chicken runs over my foot which causes me to jump a mile. "Good Lord!" I say to Billy, who says, "Shhh." He won't look at me.

Bruce Ware slaps his hand on the table. "This is the real thing!" He goes on to say that there are two other places to eat, on the other side of the island, but this is the most authentic. He says it is run by two native women, sisters, who are famous island cooks, and most of the waitresses are their daughters. "So what do you think, Chanel?"

"Oh, I like it just fine," I say. "It's very interesting," and Billy looks relieved, but frankly I am amazed that Bruce Ware would want to come to a place like this, much less bring a lady such as myself along.

"Put it right here, honey," Bruce says to a native girl who brings a whole bottle of Mount Gay rum to our table and sets it down in front of him, along with several bottles of bitter lemon and ice and drinking glasses which I inspect carefully to choose the cleanest one. None of them look very clean, of course they can't possibly have a dishwasher back in that kitchen which we can see into, actually, every time the girls come back and forth through the bead curtain. There's two big fat women back there cooking and laughing and talking a mile a minute in that language which Bruce Ware swears is English though you can't believe it.

"Its the rhythm and the accent that makes it sound so different," Bruce claims. "Listen for a minute." Two native men are having a loud back-slapping kind of conversation at the bar right behind us. I can't understand a word of it. As soon as they walk away together, laughing, Bruce says, "Well? Did you get any of that?"

Billy and I shake our heads no, but Mack is not even paying attention to this, he's drinking rum at a terrifying rate and staring at one of the waitresses.

Bruce smiles at us like he's some guy on the Discovery Channel. "For example," he lectures, "One of those men just said, 'Me go she by,' which is really a much more efficient way of saying 'I'm going by to see her.' This is how they talk among themselves. But they are perfectly capable of using the King's English when they talk to us."

I make a little note of this phrase, the King's English. I am always trying to improve my vocabulary. "Then that gives them some privacy from the tourists, doesn't it?" I remark. "From people like us."

"Exactly, Chanel." Bruce looks pleased and I realize how much I could learn from a man like him.

"Well, this is all just so interesting, and thanks for pointing it out to me," I say, meaning every word and kicking Billy under the table, who mumbles something. Billy seems determined to match Mack drink for drink, which is not a good idea. Billy is not a good drunk.

Unfortunately I have to go to the bathroom (I can't imagine what *this* experience will be like!) so I excuse myself and make my way through the other tables which are filling up fast, I can feel all those dark native eyes burning into my skin. When I ask for the ladies' room, the bartender simply points into the jungle. I ask again and he points again. I am too desperate to argue. I stumble out there and find a portable toilet such as you would see at a construction site. Luckily, I have some Kleenex in my purse.

It is all a fairly horrifying experience made even worse by a man who's squatting on his haunches right outside the door when I exit, I almost fall over him. "Oh!" I scream and leap back, and he says something. Naturally, I can't understand a word of it. But for some reason I am rooted to the spot. He stands up slow and limber as a leopard and then we are face to face and he's looking at me like he knows me. He is much lighter-skinned and more refined-looking than the rest of them. "Pretty missy," he says. He touches my hair.

I'm proud to say I do not make an international incident out of this, I maintain my dignity while getting out of there as fast as possible, and don't even mention it to the men when I get back, as they are finally talking business, but of course I will tell Billy later.

So I just pour myself a big drink to calm down, and Billy reaches over to squeeze my hand, and there we all sit while the sun sets in the most spectacular fiery sunset I have ever seen in real life and the breeze comes up and the chickens run all over the place, which I have ceased to mind, oddly enough, maybe the rum is getting to me, it must be some really high proof. So I switch to beer though the only kind they've got is something called Hairoun which does nor even taste like beer in my opinion. The men are deep in conversation though Mack gets up occasionally and tries to sweet-talk the pretty waitress who laughs and brushes him off like he is a big fat fly. I admire her technique as well as her skin which is beautiful, rich milk chocolate. I laugh to think what Mack's little bow-head wife back in Atlanta would think if she could see him now! The strings of Christmas lights swing in the breeze and lights glow on all the boats in the harbor. Billy scoots closer and nuzzles my ear and puts his arm around me and squeezes me right under the bust which is something I wish he would not do in public. "Having fun?" he whispers in my ear, and I say "yes" which is true.

I am expanding my horizons as they say.

This restaurant does not even have a menu. The women just serve us whatever they choose, rice and beans and seafood mostly, it's hard to say. I actually prefer to eat my food separately rather than all mixed up on a plate which I'm sure is not clean anyway. The men discuss getting an 85 percent loan at 9 percent and padding the specs, while I drink another Hairoun.

The man who touched my hair starts playing guitar, some kind of island stuff, he's really good. Also, he keeps looking at me and I find myself glancing over at him from time to time just to see if he is still looking, this is just like seventh grade. Still, it gives me something to do since the men are basically ignoring me, which begins to piss me off after a while since Mack is *not* ignoring the pretty waitress. The Negro with the guitar catches me looking at him, and grins. I am completely horrified to see that his two front teeth are gold. People start dancing. "I don't know," Billy keeps saying to Bruce Ware. "I just don't know."

I have to go to the bathroom again and when I come back there's a big argument going on involving Mack who has apparently been slapped by the pretty waitress. Now she's crying and her mother is yelling at Mack who is pretty damn mad, and who can blame him? Of course he didn't mean anything by whatever he did, he certainly wasn't going to sleep with her and get some disease. "Goddamn bitch," he says, and Bruce tells Billy and me to get him out of there, which we do, while Bruce gets into some kind of fight himself over the bill. These Negroes have overcharged us. Bruce's behavior at this point is interesting to me. He has gone from his nice Marlin Perkins voice to a real J. R. Ewing obey-me voice. *Thank God there is somebody here to take charge* I'm thinking as I stand at the edge of the jungle with a drunk on each arm and watch the whole thing happening inside the house like it's on television. The ocean breeze lifts my hair up off my shoulders and blows it around and I don't even care that it's getting messed up, though of course I am somewhat mad at Billy for getting so drunk.

"You okay, honey?" Bruce Ware says to me when he gets everything taken care of to his satisfaction, and I say, "Yes." Then Bruce takes Mack by the arm and I take Billy and we walk back down to the harbor two-by-two, which seems to take forever in the loud rustling dark. I wouldn't be a bit surprised if a gorilla jumped out and grabbed me, after everything that's happened so far! Bruce goes first, with the flashlight. I love a capable man.

When we finally make it down to the beach, I am so glad to see our Negroes waiting, but even with their help it's kind of a problem getting Mack into the dinghy, in fact it's like a slapstick comedy, and I finally get tickled in spite of myself. At this point Mack turns on me. "What are you laughing at, bitch?" he says, and I say, "Billy?" but all Billy says is "Shhh."

"Never mind, Chanel," Bruce tells me. "Mack's just drunk, he won't even remember this tomorrow. Look at the stars."

By now the Negroes are rowing us out across the harbor.

"What?" I ask him.

"Look at the stars," Bruce says, "you see a lot of constellations down here that you never get to see at home, for instance that's the Southern Cross right over there to your left."

"Oh yes," I say, though actually I have never seen *any* constellations in my life, or if I did I didn't know it, and certainly did not know the names of them.

"There's Orion," Bruce says. "See those three bright stars in a row? That's his belt."

Of course I am acting as interested as possible, but by then we've reached the yacht and the Negro on board is helping us all up (they have quite a job with Mack and Billy) and then two of them put Mack to bed. "Scuse me," Billy mutters, and goes to the back of the boat to hang his head over and vomit. Some fiancé! I stand in the bow with Bruce Ware, observing the southern sky, while the Negroes say good night and go off with a guy who has come by for them in an outboard. Its motor gets louder and louder the farther they get from us, and I am privately sure that they are going around to the other side of the island to raise hell until dawn.

Bruce steps up close behind me. "Listen here, whatever your real name is," he says, "Billy's not going to marry you, you know that, don't you?"

Of course this is none of Bruce Ware's business, so it makes me furious. "He most certainly is!" I say. "Just as soon as . . ."

"He'll never leave Jean," Bruce says into my ear. "Never."

Then he sticks his tongue in my ear which sends world-class shivers down my whole body.

"Baby—" Its Billy, tumbling up beside us.

"Billy, I'm just, we're just—" now I'm trying to get away from Bruce Ware but he doesn't give an inch, pinning me against the rail. "Billy," I start again.

"Hey, baby, it's okay. Go for it. I know you like to have a good time." Billy is actually saying this, and there was a time when I would have actually had that good time, but all of a sudden I just can't do it.

Before either my ex-fiancé or his associate can stop me, I make a break for it and jump right down into the dinghy and pull the rope up over the thing and push off and grab the oars and row like crazy toward the shore. I use the rowing machine all the time at the health club, but this is the first time I have had a chance at the real thing. It's easy.

"Come back here," yells Bruce Ware. "Where the hell do you think you're going?"

"Native," I call back to them across the widening water. "I'm going native."

"Shit," one of them says, but by now I can barely hear them. What I hear is the slapping sound of my oars and the occasional bit of music or conversation from the other boats, and once somebody says, "Hey, honey," but I just keep on going straight for the beach which lies like a silver ribbon around the harbor. I look back long enough to make sure that nobody's coming after me. At least those natives can speak the King's English when they want to, and I am perfectly capable of helping out in the kitchen if need be. I'm sure I can pay one of them to take me back to Barbados in the morning. Won't that surprise my companions? Since I am never without some "mad money" and Billy's gold card, this is possible, although I do leave some brand new perfectly gorgeous shoes and several of my favorite outfits on the yacht.

A part of me can't believe I'm acting this crazy, while another part of me is saying, "Go, girl!" A little breeze comes up and ruffles my hair. I practice deep breathing from aerobics, and look all around. The water is smooth as glass. The whole damn sky is full of stars. It is just beautiful. All the stars are reflected in the water. Right overhead I see Orion and then I see his belt, as clear as can be. I'm headed for the island, sliding through stars.

———————————

A native of southwest Virginia, Lee Smith is the author of ten novels and two collections of short stories. Her latest book, a collection of novellas and short stories entitled *News of the Spirit,* will be published in the fall of 1997. Smith has lived in North Carolina for many years and teaches writing workshops at North Carolina State University.

Several years ago, my husband and I went on a vacation to the tiny Caribbean island of Mayreau. One night when we were having dinner at a restaurant exactly like the one described in this story, I became fascinated by a group at a nearby table — a striking young woman with three drunk men. I never met her, or talked to any of them, but I kept wondering how she had gotten herself in that situation, and what was going to happen next. I immediately began to make up a story about them in my mind, with this result.

Over the years, a chance encounter such as this one has often sparked a narrative.

Janice Daugharty

ALONG A WIDER RIVER

(from *The Georgia Review*)

Now that he is ninety-some-odd years old and can no longer
lumber down the banks of the Alapaha, he has to scooch
low and back like an old turtle. Down the root ladder set in packed
gray dirt to the dais of roots below—under a broad tupelo and a
cypress older than he is. Still, the cypress is sprouting tender green
needles, and the tupelo struts out over the slow water. Cypress
knees, like pagan idols, stand in the eddy along the edge, with
gray-pied moccasins braided around some of them. A buzz of
crickets and locusts join with a hawk crying over the banks of
inward-leaning birches. The felled heart cypress and pine along the
unsunned banks match the fish-roe tint of Dump Sanders who, in
his patched khaki, blends right in.

On the platform of roots he stands, cranking his backbone to
straight position—he will fish now—then reaches for his cane pole
waiting in the wattle of bamboos growing along the bank. The
pole has caught many a jack, and more mudcats than he can count.
He practically lives on fish, has raised a big family on fish caught
out of this hole—that and the corn and peas and such he grew on
halves, plus coons he trapped in the muddy slews and hammocks
of Swanoochee County. Unwinding the line of his pole, he listens
for sounds that belong—the river's rilling, a crow's sorethroated
caw—sorting them from sounds that don't belong: the clank of

wood on metal, which likely means somebody is fishing from a boat upriver.

He goes dead still, his shadow merging with the shadows of maple switches on the sun-spotted water. As he gazes upriver, his cataracted eyes pick up the blur of boat and man spiriting from the tea-tinted shallows toward the smoky drop-off of Dump's fishing hole. In a minute the boat will pass, and in another minute Dump will bait up with that worm he can't yet see on the nearby red-stemmed maple branch. In spring, you don't have to bring bait. A smart fisherman can *find* bait, a smart fisherman can also whittle cork from the driftwood. It helps when you are old and poor and on your own.

The boat trolls right into Dump's fishing space, not two feet from him but blocked from view by the wall-like tupelo. Its metal sides scrub against the curb of cypress roots, scaring off the fish. While the man fishes, Dump listens. *Phoof!* The pulled tab on a can of cola or beer. Sounds of swigging. A plastic tackle box snaps open and clacks shut. Then some cursing—the bite of a hook maybe. Hugging the tree trunk, Dump sidles north along the bank of snaky roots, careful not to trip, careful not to pry his shadow from the shadow of the tupelo now falling across the bow of the boat.

The man's fishing line sings, snaps—"Sonofabitch!"

Dump draws back as if stung by a yellow jacket. He knows that voice—that harpy, gruff boom—a voice he hates. Boss Pender. Dump fears that the voice is all in his head, since he hears it so often, waking and sleeping. Maybe he's only conjuring it from nothing now, he might be losing his mind.

When you get done turning under that back field, Pender used to say, *go on over to the old Watson place and fertilize that corn. Rain's on its way.*

But it's sundown now, Dump would say to himself, tipping the sweatsopped brim of his hat and peering west/southwest toward the Gulf. No clouds scrolling up, just a butchered sun leaking blood onto the pineline. *He never said that to Pender, never talked back to any of the men he farmed for. But of course sundown was the whole point: keeping Dump on a job that would carry over into the night and stall him from returning home—home being a small, green, dogtrot house that Dump could call his own only as long as he share-cropped for Pender—or as long as Pender could do what he had in mind to do with certain other shared property.*

Dump waits now till he hears the boat risping along with the current, then peeps through the bole of the tupelo at Boss Pender's padded back and silver head gliding in and out of the broomed willow shadows downriver. Though Dump believes he'll have to wait another hour or so before his fish will come back, he tips to the maple tree left of the tupelo, plucks a couple of worms, and deposits them in the Prince Albert can in his shirt pocket. Then he perches on the bench of tree roots and waits.

Sunday—the worst day of the week for running into others fishing the Alapaha. Seems like Dump spends the better part of his days dodging them. They don't go to church, but Dump doesn't blame them. Church is here. God is here, on this sunny morning. A breeze ruffles the treetops, then wrinkles the surface of the water like silk.

Suddenly Dump hears the boat come banging back—oar on metal, oar on metal—and then it shows in the sun-blared strip of black water off the far bank. Too late for him to get up and hide. Riding high and heavy on the jacked-up seat, Pender clanks his paddle to the bottom of the boat, grunts himself forward, and feeds up a rope tied to the bow from the mangle of tackle boxes, rods, and brown paper sacks. Dump is so still, he's barely breathing. He can feel the pain festering in his joints, but his mind never strays. Shoulders tucked, knees crossed, shrunken, he watches his shadow on the burnished bower of roots, barely thicker than the cane pole in his hand.

Pender swivels left in the elevated seat and wraps the rope around a cypress knee, swivels right and picks up a rod, rears and casts. A glittery red and blue split-tail plastic worm *ploops* into the water almost at Dump's feet. Boss Pender is squinting into the sun now, face red as a ripe tupelo berry, his silver hair shining like sun on frost.

Dump has just about decided that Boss can't see him because of the sun in his eyes, or maybe because Dump blends so well into the background. Then Pender reels in and casts again, this time downstream of the tupelo, and shades his eyes with his hand, gazing right at Dump. "Hey," he hollers, "you wouldn't happen to know a man goes by the name of Dump Sanders, would you?"

Dump clears his throat, spits—he's been dying to spit for God knows how long. "Can't say as I do," he calls back.

"Well," says Pender, shifting and bracing one hand on his bloated waist, "I'm from the IRS. Been looking for a feller owes us some *money*." His great haunches spread on the boat seat, his gut settles on his lap.

Dump tee-hees into his hand.

Boss laughs. "How you, Dump?"

"Ain't no good," says Dump, and wipes his mouth with the back of his hardened hand, then crosses his wrists on his crossed thighs.

"Come by here a second ago, didn't see you," says Pender. No mention of fishing in what everybody knows is Dump's hole.

"I been right here," says Dump.

The tip of Pender's rod dips, then bends and creaks, as he starts to reel in, watching the water dash as his fish lunges and wallows, then sulls on its side for Pender to winch it into the boat.

"Old mudfish," says Pender. "You want him?"

"Can't say as I do," says Dump. When his wife was living she would make mudfish balls—Dump loved them—fried brown.

Pender lifts the fish by its bottom lip, yanks the hook free, and drops the fish flapping to the bottom of the boat. Poles and cans ringing and knocking. "Old mammy fish like that'll eat up your bass," he says. He rifles through his tackle box until he finds his pocketknife, thumbnails a blade to open position, and rams the blade into the flouncing fish. Then he rinses the knife in the water and puts it back in his tackle box. Hardly missing a beat, he picks up his rod, checks his glittery plastic worm, and casts it upriver—

Dump's side. The line swings down into Dump's hole as if pulled by a magnet.

"Been catching much this spring?" asks Pender.

"None to speak of."

Pender's rod bends, goes straight. Silence. Then, "Sears is got a li'l ole trolling motor I been looking at. I ain't much for all this paddling and it getting hot." He squints up at the sun, then at Dump posing in the shade as if he's been planted there.

"Course my knees in the shape they in," says Pender, "won't be many more trips for me. That old gout! Can't hardly put in and take out no more."

He reels in, changes lures—this time a yellow plastic worm with a green head and bead eyes—and swings it out, watching water rings form. He has cast midriver, halfway between him and Dump. "That oughta do it," he says, and leans back till the boat seat groans. "I had to put in up there at the bridge this time. My landing washed out last winter when the river come up."

Dump knows—and he suspects Pender knows he knows—that Pender no longer owns a boat landing, no longer owns even the land the landing was on.

Pender waits, reels in a bit. "Looks like this old river's getting wider, don't it?" He rests one hand on his tree-trunk thigh, staring up and down the river.

"Yessir, it do." Dump has been watching the river widen for many years—current skiving away the sandy banks and lashing at the tiers of trees till the treeline that used to stand midbank has stepped up to the edge to meet its doom, naked roots anchoring to the riverbottom. He's been watching the river change, just as he's been watching Boss Pender change from rich man to poor man. All that farm and timberland in the seventies, dwindling to nothing. Overtaxed, undervalued, lost.

Not that Dump could gloat over Pender and the others losing their inherited farms; without them and their land, Dump was out of work, out of house, out of money—not pride, since he couldn't lose what he never had. But it had almost been worth his losses to see Pender lose it all. Watching Pender grow fat and feeble and foolish after years of being so lean and mean and proud.

Hate like the devil, Dump, to have to leave you with next to nothing, Pender used to say, *right here at the end of the year and Christmas coming. You with that big drove of younguns to buy Santy Claus for. But you know how it is—I got that fertilizer bill to pay. Seed bill and what-have-you. Looks like farming's going to nothing. Maybe next year . . .*

Pender's rod bends, his line sings, and he reels with the leisure of a satisfied fat man. A ten-pound bass shines silver beneath the umber surface, streaks left then right, flips from the churning water with its sleek body arched, then bellyflops toward the riverbottom. The line whips and the boat rocks, balancing itself like scales. Pender grins, laughs, whoops, holds his line tight and high, and trawls the big fish in. "I got you, boy!" he says and lifts the fish with its notched tail furling. He lowers it like a baby into the boat.

Both hands spread on his knees now, Pender presents his gleeful face to Dump. "Man, I'm burning up," he says. The fish writhes and drums on the boat floor, sounds vibrating across the bothered river. "Reckon I'll just mosey on in," says Pender, swiveling his seat and reaching for the rope wound around the cypress knee.

Suddenly he yelps, jerks back and jumps up, clutching his right hand with his left. The boat pitches side to side with Pender now lunging and spraddling his legs, trying to steady it. Too late. One more pitch of the stern and water pours into the boat. Dump watches Pander tilt sidelong, hollering "Snake!" in that voice that counts in Swanoochee County, then gurgling as he goes under, silver hair streaming over his red open face. Then he bobs among the scatter of tackle boxes and ice chest, empty cola cans, and sinking paper sacks now releasing cellophane-wrapped Moon Pies and saltine crackers. The bloody carcass of the mudfish, white belly up, adds its marbling to the river water. Darts from the freed bass point toward Dump's hole.

Dump, on his feet now but stiff and silent, watches as Pender dog-paddles to the other bank, downriver from the snake-wrapped

cypress knee, and drags himself up onto a toppled cypress, pant-
ing and gasping. He just hangs there over the water-polished
cypress, half-in, half-out of the water. "Old moccasin got me," he
yells, as if in explanation for looking the fool. "What you do 'bout
that?" He eyeballs his right hand like it's a fascinating rock.

"They say if you got ery knife," yells Dump, "cut it and suck the
pysin."

Still clinging to the cypress with one arm, Pender digs into his
right pocket, then gazes downstream at his tackle box floating past
a sandbar.

"You got your knife on you?" he calls.

"Yessir," says Dump, and fishes his jackknife from his pants
pocket. "Got one right here I'll loan you."

"How 'bout bringing it on over here."

"Can't swim a lick," says Dump. He can—or used to could—but
he's not going to.

"Don't know if I can make it over there," says Pender, wrench-
ing round to look at the far bank. "I'm just about whipped."

Dump's heart starts pumping hard, as if the snake venom is
pumping from Pender's bloodstream to his. "Want me to run up
to the commissary for help?"

"I reckon," says Pender, resting his head on the cypress trunk.

"Hate to leave you like that."

"I hate for you to," says Pender and checks his hand—now
swollen and stiff as a tarry work glove.

"It's a good piece there and back," Dump calls, as if to keep talking is the best medicine. "You gone be awright?"

"I don't know," says Pender with his head still on the log.

"I'll be on back," says Dump and starts his slow progress up the
bank, looking back now and then at Boss Pender.

"Man that old and fat ain't got no business," Dump says to himself, halfway up the bank.

"Hey, Dump," yells Pender, "I don't think you oughta go yet."

"How come's that?" Dump yells back.

"I don't want to die . . . to be by myself."

"What you say?"

No answer.

"You OK?" Dump is scooting down the bank again. He'll just have to try swimming, try to help.

"I ain't OK," says Pender. "Ain't OK atall. Think it's my heart."

Dump's foot slips from the rooty ledge, and he slides on his belly to the platform below. He grunts. On his knees, he crawls around till he can spot the bloated body through the warp of heat. "I done fell over here," he calls, "broke something."

No answer, no movement from the log, just water lights spiraling up the trees on the west bank.

"You ain't pulling my leg, are you?" Dump, who never saw the snake, can imagine Boss Pender and his fox-hunting buddies at the commissary teasing him later about rushing around trying to get help for Pender, who most likely is playing a prank on him. They do it all the time. Once, Dump's coon dog leaped off the tailgate of his pickup and hung himself by his leash, and Dump didn't find the dog, dragging behind the truck like a butchered hog, till he coasted in at the commissary for gas and saw them all on the porch laughing.

And then there was that other time: all of them gathered to josh and lie and laugh about Pender sending Dump out to work at night so Pender could be with Dump's oldest daughter, who by rights should have been ruined but instead went on to college—paid her own way—and became a school teacher. A good daughter. Dump can depend on her to bring him home-cooked food and take him to the doctor—been twice in his life—and she even gives him Father's Day cards which he doesn't deserve because he never said, "Stop that, Pender; don't you mess with my daughter no more." He never said that—not even to his wife, who likewise went along to the fields at night to open the fertilizer sacks and dump them into the hopper. Both of them knowing, but neither of them saying, just eyeing one another from where she stood by the truckload of fifty-pound sacks with Dump on the tractor, the *chut-chut-chut* of the engine scuttling across the emerald rows of marching corn and rising in marl and potash dust to the star-pricked sky. Dump's hand had been on the switch key, threatening to cut the sound so his wife could hear clear what he had to say, that she'd best be getting on to the house—"Stay there where you belong, Woman, and see to the younguns." But he never said that either.

"You better say something," Dump calls to Pender. "I'm long gone if you don't."

The slow water rills. The hawk lifts over the river, crying.

Janice Daugharty is writer-in-residence at Valdosta State University and the author of four books, including *Going Through the Change*. Her new novel, *When You Whistle the Wind Will Blow*, will be published in the spring of 1998.

I always knew I would write about the Alapaha River—blood of my homeland, Echols County. But to make it into fiction, I needed a story with characters and conflict. Then one sunny spring morning while fishing from a boat on the Alapaha, I saw an old man fishing from the rooty banks. When he spoke, his voice seemed born of the brown water, and I knew he was the voice of my people, the voice for my story. What I didn't know then was, because of avarice, greed, and even meekness, his voice would be extinguished and only nature's voice would prevail.

Edward Allen

ASHES NORTH

(from *GQ*)

R oy's two sons both cried on the phone when Bob finally
reached them from the lobby of a pizza restaurant whose
main dining area was filled with coin-operated cars and rocket
ships. Bob had been calling their house every few hours, not knowing when they would get back from their camping trip.

"So . . . where is he?" Jim asked, controlling himself, giving the
word *he* a kind of humiliated nonemphasis. His usually hale
foghorn of a voice trembled over the phone, as if he was afraid of
the answer.

Bob had to go ahead and tell his nephews that their father was
refrigerated and that the funeral home couldn't do anything with
the body until it had received written authorization from the next
of kin.

Refrigerated must be one of the less comforting funeral-home
euphemisms—though the people who devised that vocabulary
were probably right that to a grieving family the more exact word
frozen would sound a bit too industrial.

The receiver Bob was talking into had been sprayed with a
strawberry-scented disinfectant so strong that he didn't want to put
his mouth against it, so he had to speak louder than he really wanted
to, which made him feel even more conspicuous than usual, in the
midst of soft electronic music, still wearing the paisley tie and blue

cord jacket he had put on for this afternoon's discussion with the lawyers. In summer, around here, anything but shorts would be conspicuous.

The phone stood against the wall in a sort of corral where parents waited and their kids made loops in all directions, some with arms swept back like the wings of a jet. Where the corral narrowed to a sort of chute that led to the ordering counter, a tall college boy with a smile that never changed stamped every hand, carefully lifting even little babies' wrists, as the families moved through the turnstiles. From there they proceeded toward the kiddie-ride area, containing dozens of miniature Chitty Chitty Bang Bang cars and Harley-Davidsons, their headlights gently nodding up and down; or into the room beyond it, full of *Top Gun* and *Terminator* video games and a whole lineup of Skee-Ball games along one wall; or to the showroom, at the far end of the indoor space, where the human-sized figures of rabbits and chickens, plush as carnival prizes, swiveled back and forth and a precise electronic chorus of clown voices sang "Happy Birthday" cranked up into a hyperactive four-four fox-trot.

The worst thing about making this call was that Bob had to start talking business with these kids, or at least with the older one, right away, while they were still crying—or else he'd end up driving Roy's Oldsmobile around Fort Pierce for another week, waiting to get the last of his brother's loose ends tied up, having to sleep for another week on the slippery plastic air mattress he'd bought at Kmart after he had Roy's furniture taken away.

Retired people are instinctively supposed to love Florida, but whenever Bob got behind the wheel of that loose-springed station wagon, all he could think about was how great he'd feel on the day he got that wallowing boat headed north on I-95. Whenever he thought about it, his palms would start to itch on the steering wheel.

Maybe Dorothy hoped he would love it and would want them to move down. Every time she called him from home, she asked him how the weather was, even though he knew she watched the Weather Channel when he wasn't there.

"Not cold," he would say.

A man who had spent half his life as a salesman should have known better than to die without a will. Bob had tried diplomatically to bring it up with Roy in the hospital one night, during a commercial break.

"Do you have anything specific that you want me to say to Jim and Rich?" Bob had asked him, but Roy didn't even turn his face from the television.

"What, are you trying to get me in the ground already?" he said, and Bob let it drop.

Now he had to pick it up again. The funeral home wouldn't release or cremate the body until the next of kin had sent written authorization, along with a check for storage and cremation costs. As Bob explained this to Jim, he could hear his nephew's voice changing register, very quickly, from tears to anger, the way people have learned to do from watching those afternoon talk shows that were just becoming big in syndication the year Bob retired from the business.

"Let me get this straight," Jim said, and Bob could hear, along with the gathering anger, a family note, a harmonic of the same strong deal-closer's voice coming out. Near the phone, somebody's father had just put fifty cents into a game where kids threw beanbags into Bozo the Clown's mouth, and the distant "Happy Birthday" was drowned out by a circus march dizzy with trombones. "You say this so-called funeral home won't release the body until we pay them $235?"

"I don't like it, either," Bob said. "But without any written instructions, that's how they have to do it." This was as close as Bob wanted to come to getting into a discussion of the word *intestate*.

"So what you're saying is that they're holding my dad's body as a fucking hostage?"

With every beanbag throw, no matter how far off it was, the open space of Bozo's mouth boomed positive comments: "That's the spirit, partner!" or "Whoa, Nellie! Good try!"

"Jim, I can't stay down here and fight with these people. If you don't have the money, I'll pay it, but what I do need from you—"

"I'm not paying them, and you're not paying them." His voice was rising, a distorted buzz over the earpiece. "Nobody's paying them a goddamn cent! Do you fucking hear me?"

Bob moved the receiver a few inches from his ear. He could imagine Jim and his younger brother, Rich, on the other end of the line, up there in Pennsylvania, probably in the kitchen of some bungalow with dishes piled in the sink, both of them standing there red eyed—big, strapping right-wing kids whose father couldn't afford to send them to college and who couldn't get it together to go on their own any more than they could get it together to hop on a Skybudget Air flight for the whole three months that they knew their father was down here dying. The last time Bob had seen them, a year ago, when he came over to help Roy pack up the station wagon for Florida, the two boys had been working out so much on the Nautilus that they both looked as if they were wearing football shoulder pads under their T-shirts.

Jim's voice was out of control now, up to the pitch where people, especially fat people, stand up on-camera and point fingers at one another like pistols.

"If those people think they can extort money from people just because they're too far away to do anything about it, well, they can kiss my motherfucking—"

There was a slam and a crackle over the line, and then the sound clicked through a few switchings of empty channels until it lapsed back into a dial tone, just as Bozo's electronically synthesized drum-and-trombone music abruptly slammed shut mid-phrase during "A Hot Time in the Old Town Tonight." "Happy Birthday" had also stopped, from the other end of the restaurant, leaving the lobby bathed in a kind of endless chirp in the upper registers, a blend of all the children's voices together, not frantic but almost peaceful, like starlings up north when they gather in trees.

His brother had been dead for three days, which was long enough for Bob to start seeing potential jokes popping up in places where they didn't belong. Anybody who has worked in syndicated television or has had anything to do with cartoons knows that what was supposed to happen now was that the phone should ring again immediately, and Bob should pick it up, and he should hear the one word—"ass!"—before the phone was slammed down again.

But of course Jim and Rich didn't have the number. Bob accessed MCI again and called and got a busy signal. It was still busy when he tried two minutes later, and by this time he realized that Jim had broken the phone.

Bob was hungry, and the pizza smelled better and better the farther he got from the strawberry fragrance of the phone receiver, but this wasn't the kind of place where you'd want to eat. If you sat at a table without any kids, they'd think you were some kind of weirdo, and they'd be right. You'd have to put some kiddie-sized plates across from you, maybe with half-chewed pizza slices on them, and then people would think you were here with your children (or grandchildren, more likely; most of the parents, chunky and smooth in pleated shorts and bright collarless T-shirts, looked younger than Bob's daughters).

People would look at the remaining slices across from you and think your kids were away from the table, rolling Skee-Balls or hunched at the controls of the "Desert Storm" tank simulator— which would be like the old *Bob Newhart Show* episode where Elliot Carlin had no date for a banquet and draped a woman's sweater over the chair next to him, telling everybody the whole night that its owner was in the bathroom. Strange how references from the shows he'd been selling all these years to local television stations kept coming into play in the real things he was thinking about. Another sign that he had retired too early.

Roy and his family were the kind of people who would have liked this restaurant, if such places had existed in the years when he still had a house and a wife and was making enough money to have a little fun with it. Jimmie and Richie would have raced around from pachinko to helicopter to the interactive-video Kawasaki that actually leaned into the curves, and some kid at the next table would probably be swinging a long bridge of mozzarella between his mouth and hand like a jump rope—and Roy's big laugh would boom out through the game room, strong as Bozo's.

What a family. When they came to visit, Bob's daughters would hide their better toys from "the Destroyers." Roy was fascinated by comedy record albums, always bringing one or two new ones, which he played on Bob's hi-fi until it was so late at night that Roy was the only one laughing. Then Roy and Maude and the kids would all sleep late into the morning, as Bob's family tiptoed through breakfast.

Jim called the apartment that night. With all the furniture gone, the sound of the telephone resonated off the Sheetrock walls.

"I'm sorry I lost it like that, Uncle Bob," he said, so softly that Bob had to press the receiver against his ear. "The whole phone was just trashed. I'm sorry it took so long to get back to you."

Roy's little one-bedroom efficiency was bare, the cupboards sponged, the carpets steamed by a company Bob had called from a card that had come to Roy's mailbox the day he died. Bob had sold the furniture and the lamps, and even the big, splashy oil paintings of city skylines and yacht marinas, back to the same dealer Roy had bought them from. Bob sat on a metal folding chair under the fluorescent fixture of the kitchen nook, the only place with enough light now to read the paper.

They agreed on a tentative date for a memorial service up north and then moved on to settling the few details that Jim needed to take care of himself. He hardly sounded like the same person who had been shouting so loud on the phone a few hours ago.

Whenever Bob thought about his nephew, he still imagined the kid being twelve years old, he and Richie dashing across the garden Bob had just planted. He remembered one time in particular, when the grown-ups were on the porch having drinks and Jim's voice came bellowing out from the backyard through a megaphone made from rolled poster paper, so loud that the whole neighborhood could hear, "Now hear this! Now hear this! Uncle Bob's scarecrow is on fire!"

What does a man know about his brother? A big voice, a big handshake, bad luck. When the scrambling around to get furniture trucked away slowed down, Bob had ended up with a carload of things he knew nobody wanted, but he didn't dare take the responsibility for throwing them out. Whole boxes of monaural comedy albums going back to Shelley Berman. Pay stubs, Social Security statements, handwritten envelopes rubber-banded together, big, glossy folders from something called the Family Bargain Network, describing "Ten Building Blocks on the Horizon of Telemarketing Prosperity." Before Roy got sick, he'd had a part-time job, working out of the apartment, selling magazine subscriptions by phone. The entire sales pitch was printed out on three glossy pages: "Hi there! Could I speak to the lady of the house, please?" The stubs from the commission checks were scattered around the telephone desk, ranging from $30 to $48.19.

For the whole year he lived in Florida, even including the three months when he already knew he had cancer, Roy had also been answering personal ads from the back pages of supermarket tabloids. He put a classified advertisement of his own in the same newspaper that said Satan's face had appeared above the White House.

The letters that had come in, in careful, old grammar school cursive, said things like, "Hello, lonely stranger," and "Are you the person I'm looking for?" A few women had included professionally posed wallet-sized photographs, probably taken at Glamour Shots Senior, in which their white or frosted hair had been carefully spread out behind them on a satin pillow.

The only letter different from the rest was from a young blonde girl who had sent a nude Polaroid, her eyes red in the flash. Bob read a few sentences of her letter, until he came to the code word *generous*.

One of the last things Bob had to do—after he made sure that Jim was proceeding to ask around and find out where there was a fax machine from which he could send word to the funeral home—was to send some kind of acknowledgment to all the people who had written to Roy.

It made Bob feel like a bastard, but there were so many people to write to that he had no choice but to use a form letter.

Dear Friend:

I'm sorry to report to you that my brother, Roy Pollard, passed away in Fort Pierce, Florida, on June 25 after a brief illness.

He mentioned several times before he died how much he had been cheered by the kind and friendly mail he had received. Thank you for helping to brighten the last months of his life. In lieu of flowers or condolences, I know that my brother would appreciate contributions made in his name to the American Cancer Society.

Sincerely,
Robert L. Pollard

He took it to the twenty-four-hour Kinko's across from the apartment complex. Even after midnight, it wasn't easy getting across the street on foot. One carload of kids in an old Plymouth Fury were so amused to see a man actually trying to cross the five lanes of U.S. 1 that they whooped and honked and reached their hands out and pounded the doors of the car as they roared past.

When the envelopes were filled and addressed and stamped and sealed, Bob stood out on the balcony and watched the traffic and listened to the dry tire sound from all directions. After all the phone calls and the hours of carrying boxes down to the car, back and forth between the chill of the apartment and the blanket of heat outside, with his shirt soaked through, this was the first time in three days he'd had a chance just to stand and think about Roy being dead and not have to do something about it. The television was already packed in the back of the car, along with books and comedy records, so much weight pressing down the rear of the station wagon that when Bob had tried to drive it at night, people kept blinking their lights even though he had his low beams on.

The only thing he had forgotten to do was to clean up all the cigarette butts that were lying on the concrete balcony floor. Maybe the last cigarette Roy ever smoked was out here, when he already knew he was going into the hospital—but no, Bob remembered, he was still smoking even in the hospital. At that point, it didn't matter. He was so doped up that the cigarette kept falling out of his mouth, and Bob had to help him scramble after it in the rumpled bedsheets, while the voices of defense lawyers droned from a tiny color TV at the end of a long, jointed arm connected to the same bedside console where the buttons to call the nurses were located.

What does a man know about his brother? When Bob left the hospital that night to go back to the apartment, Roy looked at him and said, "Thanks." Bob thought he just meant thanks for finding the cigarette. But the phone in the apartment was already ringing by the time he got the door open, and Roy was dead.

People think about weird things. As Bob drove back to the hospital that night, the only thing he could bring himself to think about turned out to be another thought about television, which was a business that he was thinking more and more he should have stayed with for a few additional years at least, instead of ending up as a not quite old man talking shop to himself in traffic on the way to say good-bye to someone who would not be able to hear him because he was dead.

The main thing Bob couldn't stop thinking about, there in Roy's loose-springed car, was that Roy had been watching the same trial on his little television for twelve hours a day, and it was still only half over. In all his years in the syndication business, cataloging and summarizing episodes of *The Dick Van Dyke Show* and *Adam 12* for little stations that couldn't afford to buy the whole run, Bob had learned how important it is for a story always to have a beginning and an end; and that the upshot of a story, even *My Favorite Martian*, always has to affirm that we live in an orderly universe, where the vast majority of people are basically decent, where school bullies are reduced to tears in front of the class, and criminals, as if to affirm how hopeless it is to be a criminal in the first place, will try to escape in the last ten minutes by climbing up tall construction scaffolds that have already been surrounded by the police. And now Roy was cheated out of his right to see the story end with that $2,000 suit led away for the last time and all the heavy television watchers waving good-bye from their BarcaLoungers.

The Oldsmobile lost its power steering on I-95 in South Carolina, next to a billboard for a giant truck stop and tourist complex called South of the Border. A little figure named Pedro, whose head and sombrero extended a few feet above the main part of the sign, was saying, SENOR WANTS A COLD DREENK, I THEENK.

Bob drove along the shoulder at twenty miles an hour as the front end screeched and smoked and tractor-trailers, streamlined with plastic fairings, slammed past, jolting the Oldsmobile in a wave of displaced air.

From the South of the Border Service Center, he called the number on Roy's Keystone Motor Club booklet and got a girl on the line who spoke with a New York accent so rich and zaftig that Bob seemed to remember all at once how long he'd been away from the real world and how much he wanted to get that car moving north again.

Bob had always wondered what it is about being retired that pulls so many people south—maybe the same gravity that pulls the flesh of their faces down, into the heat and the flatness and the kids cruising around in boom-boom cars and the towns that blend into each other with nothing to mark the beginning of one and the end of another except a new name on the side of another windowless bank building. Dorothy talked about it sometimes, feeling him out on the subject, but whatever that geographical force was, it hadn't gotten to him yet.

"So, you're saying his address was in Flor-ida?" the girl said.

Each pay phone in this row of carrels opposite the fuel desk had in front of it a full ashtray the size of a cereal bowl. A yellow sheet

of paper taped in each carrel announced, RETURN LOADS AVAILABLE
TO THE WEST COAST. To his right, a picture window overlooked one
end of the parking lot, where Bob could see a trailer with steps
leading up to a door and a sign above the door announcing, FAM-
ILY MINISTRIES OF THE OPEN ROAD.

"You see, the problem is that Keystone is a regional organiza-
tion," she said, wrapping her mouth around the words so luxuri-
ously that if Bob had had more nerve he would have asked her
name, or at least come up with a few irrelevant questions just to
hear her talk a little longer.

"I understand."

"We just don't cover Flor-ida, or anything in the South. I'm
sor-ry."

Beside the center window, which looked out to where the big
slope-nosed trucks were fueling up, Bob could see an entire rotat-
ing rack of bumper stickers for sale, saying things like CLINTON
DOESN'T INHALE—HE SUCKS! and HONK IF YOU ALREADY KNOW
WHO MURDERED VINCE FOSTER.

All day the hiss of air-conditioning came down from a register
in the ceiling beside the bathroom door. Roy's ashes rested next to
the "Pedro's Hints for Guests" folder on the counter that ran the
length of the room. The ashes had come in a box much bigger than
Bob expected, about half the size of a shoebox, wrapped in brown
paper, bearing a label with Roy's name typed below the Memorial
Concepts logo.

It wasn't a bad room, for South of the Border. Out of curiosity,
he bought *TV Guide* in the convenience store and found out about
a local show called *Little Audrey and Friends,* with some of the
same King Features shorts that his company had done so well
reselling, back when nobody else in the business was interested.

He walked around the whole South of the Border complex,
from the reptile display to Pedro's Cantina to Senor Bang-Bang's
Fireworks Supermarket, where men and boys, dressed identically
in shorts and T-shirts, hurried in and out, with the gaudy explo-

sive shapes and colors protruding from the tops of brown shopping bags.

He wandered through the truck-stop parking lot, surrounded by the gargling roar of hundreds of idling diesel engines, an incredible sound, spreading out for a hundred acres, the earth alive. One of the companies, a big fleet called Covenant Transport, carried the same antiabortion message on the rear of every trailer. Bob wondered briefly what would happen if a driver there dared to say something about carrying a placard he might not agree with—but with all the combustion noise around it, the thought didn't last very long. Never had Bob had such a clear understanding of all the things meant and implied by the term *nonunion*.

The car came back so late Monday afternoon that he'd already checked in for another night. He walked around some more and went swimming while the pool wasn't yet busy and there were still only a few families checked in for the night, only a few kids stepping along the concrete on their heels, the way barefoot kids always walk around a pool.

At least it was good to hear real kids around. The motel before this one had been in Florence, South Carolina, which is apparently the place where people all over the south come for cheap dentures and bridgework. The sign in front of his Comfort Inn said, WELCOME DENTAL PATIENTS. A vending machine in the lobby sold nothing but painkillers: aspirin, buffered aspirin, acetaminophen, ibuprofen, and a locally popular anesthetic called Gumm-Eeze.

Even through the careful wrapping of brown paper, the ashes had started to give off a strange smell, hard and scratchy, like the upper notes of somebody's bad breath—unless it was the car, maybe an ashtray in back that he'd forgotten to clean out. It was the Fourth of July. He drove and drove, in the thick traffic, on three lanes of pavement that seemed to get whiter and whiter as the day got hotter and hotter.

What poem is that line from: "a little boy thinking long thoughts"? He'd read it somewhere, but he couldn't remember where. Now he was thinking his own long thoughts, thoughts about as far as you could get from whatever that poem was actually supposed to be about—sitting there, driving, with nothing else to do, the easiest job in the world, in the continuous machine of traffic, across a field of tiny tobacco seedlings, through the cooked pulpy sweetness of a paper-mill town.

Long thoughts. You can think one thought from the top of one rise to the top of the next, and another thought starting from the point where you first see the McDonald's arches on a pole hundreds of feet high and ending at the moment you get to it. What you learn from driving all day is that the longer you can think about something, the simpler it becomes. Really two thoughts, over and over, touching each other at different angles. What it's like to be alive, in a car, bored, tired—or in the hospital, trying to say thanks when there's so much poison in your blood that your face is a deep yellow and your brother doesn't know if you mean "Thanks for finding the cigarette" or "Thanks for being my brother." And then what it's like, or more accurately what it's not like, to be a bunch of stuff in a little box in the backseat for Jim and Rich to scatter in the surf at Wildwood, New Jersey, if they ever get around to it.

Thinking. Soon it began to get dark, and up ahead he saw the bursts of a municipal fireworks display starting. He watched it as he passed, the perfect spheres blooming in the late dusk, and a few miles later, some more going off. Something about the South is so friendly, even through car windows, that it doesn't matter that all the rotten things you know about it are true. To drive through those states is like visiting an entire nation where nobody ever gets cancer. It was nice to be able to see the fireworks shows one after another, sometimes the displays from two different towns at the same time, the far-off Christmas-bulb colors flashing over the black horizon of trees.

This was always Roy's favorite holiday. He and the boys would drive down to Delaware and come back with whole hundred-dollar assortments of rockets and flowerpots and buzz bombs and Roman candles and black cats and ladyfingers, all those dense and bright paper colors and shapes spread out on the porch under a floodlight. His kids always had cherry bombs and M-80s to set off under coffee cans, that old short Maxwell House shape that they don't make anymore, sending them high up into the trees in front of a house.

Bob passed a Howard Johnson Lodge with a VACANCY sign. He could have pulled in, but some fireworks were still going off in the distance, and he still had some things to keep thinking about. You get tired in a car, but it's hard to stop, so you go on, watching, driving, thinking. He was going to have to remember to wrap the ashes in a plastic bag if the smell got any worse, if that's where it was actually coming from.

He noticed for the first time that those bursts are prettier from far away, when you can't hear anybody saying *oooh* and *aaah,* just the spheres and the colors, and you don't have to think about how much television those families are watching on the nights where there aren't any fireworks, or what they are teaching their kids about angels during the designated half hour of every night when the television is supposed to be off.

He had planned to find a motel an hour ago, just to be sure he didn't get stuck with a hundred miles of NO VACANCY signs, but for now, the car was humming, those circles of lights were bursting out of nothing in the darkness, he didn't have to go to the bathroom—so he figured for tonight he'd just go and go and take a chance on a motel somewhere an hour or so to the north, after the fireworks displays had gone dark and everybody was back home watching television.

———

Edward Allen grew up in the Northeast and has taught in Tennessee, Oklahoma, California, and Poland. He currently teaches at the University of South Dakota. His short fiction has appeared in *The New Yorker* and *GQ* and has been anthologized in *The Best American Short Stories*. His two novels are *Straight Through the Night* and *Mustang Sally*.

*M*uch of the story of "Ashes North" was prompted by my father's description of the complications surrounding his brother's death in Florida fifteen years ago. What made the largest impression on me at first was the idea of the long meditation occasioned by a man driving north with his brother's ashes, with nothing to do behind the wheel but think and think.

The "fish out of water" idea, the idea of a thoroughgoing Northerner unwillingly immersed in various Southern locations, gave some vividness to the settings, I think. And moving the time frame close to the present allowed me to add some cultural textures that were fun to work with. My favorite image is of Bob, a sophisticated man in late middle age, trying at midnight to get to an all-night Kinko's, which lies on the other side of a busy Florida boulevard.

Ellen Douglas

JULIA AND NELLIE

(from *The Southern Review*)

Heaven and Earth have sworn that the truth shall remain forever hidden.

—I. B. Singer, "The Dead Fiddler"

To avoid confusion, I must tell you that although this "true" story will begin with an account by a real person, Adah Williams of Greenville, Mississippi, of the surreptitious blessing of a grave on a farm called The Forest in Adams County, Mississippi, Miss Adah will vanish from my story. Don't wait for her to reappear. Her presence, though essential to the story, is accidental. She would never have spoken to me of Dunbar Marshall's grave if we hadn't happened to spend two hours together one day in 1948, driving south from Greenville along Highway 61. And her curious tale set me wondering and asking questions about certain lives lived out in obscurity a long time ago.

It's her account of the blessing of the grave that now, in 1994, I recall most vividly, but entangled with that memory are tag ends of information I may have acquired then or some other time from someone else—fleeting memories of people I knew as a child, questions I asked years later that were answered or left unanswered—whole scenes that have mysteriously stayed with me. Of the people involved only two were still alive at that time, and they were very old. Now, of course, all are dead. That's why I put *true* in quotation marks. I can't honestly say I am telling the truth—not for sure—and there is no one left to correct me if I'm wrong.

But I know, or think I know, that Mr. Marshall lived for a while at Longwood (another house near Natchez) and died at The Forest. One verifiable fact is that he has a gravestone, dedicated to him by his wife, Fanny, in The Forest cemetery. Presumably he's under it.

Before you hear Miss Adah's story, let me tell you about Natchez and Longwood and The Forest. Think first not of Tara and hoop-skirts and ruthless Southern belles but rather of churches, bells ringing for Sunday services and Wednesday night prayer meetings, of ladies and gentlemen and children in worn but respectable Sunday clothes gathering to worship God and to find some order and joy in a difficult world. Think, too, of early-twentieth-century poverty, of making do in a Depression that began in the riverine South with—what? The end of the Civil War? The advent of railroads and the loss of the river as a highway? The feckless clear-cutting of that hilly land? The coming of the boll weevil in 1915? All of these. Sixty years ago when I was growing up, everyone I knew went to church, and almost everyone was poor. Not hungry. Not in rags (only the Negroes were in rags), but poor.

To me ours was never a doomish, a threatening poverty, but rather the comfortable limitations that may seem to a child to be—and be, at least for a while—security. In those days paint curled off my grandmothers' ceilings. Drapes had not been replaced in years. Scraps of newspaper folded into spills stood in a jar on the mantelpiece for use as matches, to light my aunt's cigarettes from the fire glowing in the coal grate. (Surely there was money for matches, wasn't there, if there was money for cigarettes? Or was the jar of spills evidence of Presbyterian thrift carried to its limits?) In any event, for us children, there were books (mostly very old ones, it's true) and someone always ready to read or tell a story. And in the country there were lakes to swim in, creeks to wade, ponds with ducks to be fed, and woods to explore.

Here, on the outskirts of the town of Natchez, is Longwood—a wildly extravagant Moorish castle of a mansion (Nutt's Folly, people called it) left unfinished in 1861 when war broke out. No one in the Nutt family ever again had the money (or perhaps the hubris, either) to finish it. Instead, they and subsequent descendants sold away or lost most of the land, lived on the finished ground floor, and left the top four floors (still littered with scaffolding, dried-up buckets of paint, canvas carpenters' aprons, ladders, and tools) to mice and owls and bats and children's explorations. I remember climbing among the rafters and floor joists and looking out from the windowed dome over abandoned fields and shaggy lawns, over thickets of gum and locust and pecan that I knew must once have been gardens, because in their seasons I could see unkillable spirea and daffodils and crape myrtles still blooming.

Here, too, is The Forest, another country place we occasionally visited—no more doomish or gloomish than Longwood. The main house—built by an ancestor named William Dunbar—had burned years before the Civil War, and the old carriage house had been converted into a long, low cottage with a gallery across the front (I seem to recall, though I haven't been there in more than fifty years). There, in the 1930s, my great-aunt Marian Davis lived with her husband, Jamie, whom she'd married in late middle age.

I remember we especially liked going to The Forest because Jamie and Marian had a donkey they would let us ride. Hard now to think of anything less exciting—I couldn't ever kick that passive beast into so much as a trot. But ride we did. The donkey existed: my sister has a snapshot of the two of us and a cousin sitting on him, our feet almost touching the ground. And then, when we tired of riding, while the grown-ups sat on the gallery in quiet and intimate conversation, we'd explore the ruin of the old house— nothing left but two or three crumbling columns and the half-buried foundation—and wander through the family graveyard close by.

The graveyard is the focus of Miss Adah's story.

We were driving south from Greenville, where we both lived, on a lush spring day in 1948, primroses and vetch awash along the ditch banks, bean and cotton rows whirling by, green spokes in the dark, flat disk of the Delta. Miss Adah, an elderly friend of my mother-in-law's, had caught a ride with me as far as Vicksburg, where she would visit cousins; I was going to Natchez to see my grandmothers, both in their late eighties, both lively still but undeniably fragile, moving toward death. We'd been exchanging tales of mutual friends and family connections—as Southern women are still wont to do when they begin to get acquainted.

"Natchez isn't a real town, is it?" she said. "Faulkner might have invented it."

Miss Adah was one of those gracious, self-confident women who used to be the products of regular army families. She sorted people out: officers, noncoms, privates, and foreigners. She'd seen the world and could cope with it. And she'd married a wealthy Delta planter and no doubt could cope with him, too.

"Well," I said, "the landscape. . . . The woods. The Spanish moss. All those movie-set pre-Civil War houses. But—I don't know—I see it differently. Longwood, for example. My father's family (he and his parents and his three brothers) lived at Longwood for a year or two when the boys were in high school. Before that they lived too far out in the country to go to school, and their mother taught them. But when they needed to learn geometry and trig and Latin to prepare for college, they rented the Longwood house. Near enough to town to ride their horses to school. Later my grandfather inherited a little money, and they bought a house in town."

"Lived there?" Miss Adah said. "At Longwood?"

"So in a way, for me," I went on, "there's nothing Faulknerian about it. I see that finished ground floor as a home, with my grandmother's furniture in it—the music box; the square piano; her little desk, littered with bills and letters to answer; her brown wicker rocker drawn up to the coal grate; the Bible on her sewing table, just as I remember it in the house in town."

"But Miss Julia Nutt—Dr. Haller Nutt's daughter—she always lived at Longwood," Miss Adah said.

"No, I think—let's see—I think she lived there sometimes. But I know my father and his brothers . . . She must have been living somewhere else when she rented Longwood to my grandfather. I seem to recall that sometimes she lived at The Forest. Maybe that's where she was when . . ."

"But that's impossible," she said. "There was a madwoman living at The Forest. A madwoman named Davis."

"Oh?" I said. "But . . ."

"Yes. I suppose she's dead now," she said. "A country woman, I think—*plain*—but I'm not sure. Maybe from an old family."

I'd been about to say, "but that was probably later." Now, though, I felt myself closing down. I wouldn't volunteer any more of my vaguely remembered family gossip. I'd listen instead, noncommittally, to what Miss Adah had to say about a madwoman named Davis, who was in fact my great-aunt, whom I knew well, and who in my view was not mad at all. Feisty, yes. Vigorous. Opinionated. But not mad.

"A patch over one eye. Fanny said she had a patch over one eye."

That was my great-aunt all right. She'd lost an eye to glaucoma in her early fifties.

"I suppose Miss Julia must have moved back to Longwood at some point," I said. "I don't know. It was all such a long time ago."

"Have you ever been out there?" Miss Adah said. "To The Forest, I mean."

"Yes. Mama and my grandmother used to take us out there sometimes when we were children."

"So you know that old Mr. Marshall (his wife, Fanny, was a distant cousin of mine) lived there for a while?"

I did have a vague memory of seeing an old gentleman sitting on the gallery—of knowing who he was because I'd seen him elsewhere—where?

"He's buried in The Forest cemetery," she said.

"Oh?"

"I believe (family gossip—somebody heard it from Fanny) she was abroad when Dunbar died. They'd been separated for some years, but they were always on friendly terms. Of course," Miss Adah said, "they were both Catholic, so there was never any question of a divorce."

My impulse now is to recall that I said, "Like Spencer Tracy," just to be catty. But I don't think the Spencer Tracy–Katharine Hepburn affair was common knowledge as early as 1948. I don't know what I said or if I said anything. I was probably silent, watching the ribbon of highway ahead and the orderly crop rows spinning by, thinking of that graveyard—untended, if my memory was accurate, surrounded by a foot-thick, six-foot-high brick wall with a wrought-iron gate. I could hear the creak of the gate's hinges when my sister and I struggled to push it open. Saplings had sprung up inside, and at one place the humped roots of a very old cherry-bark oak were tilting a gravestone.

"In any case," Miss Adah said, "the story is that when Fanny got home, she went down to see about a stone for his grave. No one down there, I suppose, who would have been responsible for that. His immediate family were all dead. And there might not have been anybody with money to spare for it, even if someone had wanted to. But Fanny had her own money—from her father's family. It was when she called on Dunbar's parish priest, to hear the details of the funeral, that she found out he'd been buried at The Forest, that . . ." A little shiver, as of revulsion, went over Miss Adah's shoulders. She too was Catholic, as I well knew. "No confession," she said. "No extreme unction. No mass. Not in consecrated ground."

"But why . . . ?" I said. "Why not in the Natchez cemetery?"

"Well, I suppose they'd have had to buy a grave space there," she said. "And he was a Dunbar descendant, after all. He had a perfect right to be buried in the Dunbar cemetery. I suppose this Davis woman decided that was the cheapest place to bury him. As I said, none of his family was alive except for Fanny, and she was in Europe—had been for years."

"Oh," I said, "I see," although I didn't.

"But what Fanny learned was that the burial service had been Presbyterian. No priest. No *nothing*."

"No nothing," I echoed, thinking to myself what Aunt Marian would say about calling a Presbyterian funeral *nothing*.

"Exactly. And when she went out to get permission to hold a memorial service—to bless the grave—she—the one-eyed lady—flew into a frenzy." Miss Adah broke off. "Do you know who she was?" she asked.

I was beginning to feel vaguely disloyal to my great-aunt. I didn't like hearing her called "this Davis woman," though I was perfectly sure she wouldn't give a damn what Miss Adah's husband or anyone else thought of what she'd done with Mr. Dunbar Marshall's remains. It was just that my silence was beginning to seem sneaky. Besides, since Miss Adah had Natchez connections, the truth would come out. She'd learn exactly who I was.

"As a matter of fact," I said, "the Miss Davis you're talking about is my great-aunt. I seem to have a vague recollection of seeing Mr. Marshall—everybody called him Cousin Dunny—at The Forest. But I didn't know he was buried out there, and I didn't know he had a wife. I never heard his funeral discussed. No reason why I should. He was just one of those people children see from time to time when they tag along with grown people."

One of those people, I was thinking, who die and disappear and whom you never hear mentioned again. And thinking, too, how lonely he must have been. No family. A Catholic among Presbyterians. No priest to hear his last confession.

"Mercy," Miss Adah said, "I hope I haven't offended you."

"No," I said. "I'm interested. After all, she does have a patch over her eye. And if she isn't a madwoman, she's certainly set in her ways."

"Well, I can't take it back, even if she's your aunt," Miss Adah said. "She flew into a frenzy. Told Fanny he'd had a perfectly good Presbyterian burial with a Presbyterian preacher and if that wasn't enough to get him into heaven, he'd just have to go the other way."

"Hmmm," I said. I could see Aunt M. running a hand through her short gray hair as if to make it stand on end, cocking her head to favor the sharp, ferocious good eye, and saying (firmly if not frenziedly) to anything she disapproved of, "NO."

"Fanny was humiliated," Miss Adah said. "Not just humiliated. Undone."

"I can imagine," I murmured.

"But not defeated," Miss Adah said. "Not defeated. Naturally she went back to the priest for advice, and—I'm vague on this. I think . . . he may have tried to persuade your aunt. I remember now. But your aunt was adamant. Immovable."

"Catholics have never had much luck persuading Presbyterians, have they?" I said. "Or vice versa." I was thinking of Foxe's *Book of Martyrs* on the shelf in my father's secretary, and of the note in my great-grandfather's family Bible regarding *his* grandfather, who "suffered much in the persecution of the church in the time of Mr. Erskine and Mr. Fisher's Secession."

"King Charles I," Miss Adah said. "Wasn't it you people who turned him over to Cromwell?"

"I never understood that," I said. "He wasn't really Catholic, was he? Just Anglo-Catholic. Church of England. Couldn't he just as well have become a Presbyterian? And then it wouldn't have happened."

"Oh, he was a good Catholic, all right. He wanted the whole country to go back to the Church. And you turned him over to Cromwell. To be murdered! And what about St. Thomas More?"

"Not guilty," I said. "Henry VIII."

"Of course," she said. "I apologize."

"But then there's Bloody Mary," I said. "You all have your share of villains." Yes. We were having this conversation about martyrs and persecutors in the Year of Our Lord 1948. "It's a toss-up whose ancestors were more bloodthirsty," I said, but all she said was, "Hmmm."

After a minute she went on. "Anyhow, Fanny took the priest and went out to The Forest. She thought they would slip in quietly and bless the grave and depart without saying anything to your aunt. But the gate—the main gate—was locked. Padlocked. Chained."

I saw Aunt Marian again, slight but wiry, spikes of iron-gray hair fairly vibrating, mouth drawn down, characteristically, in a knowing half-smile as she snapped the padlock through the links of chain.

The Forest cemetery now is just a few yards back from Highway 61, cheek by jowl with an oil-field equipment storage area littered with piles of drums and rusting pipes, the huge carcasses of flatbed trailers, pumping units with square heads and long necks like strange prehistoric birds. There are cylindrical oil tanks large enough to live in. One pumping unit cranes its neck over the brick wall that in my childhood loomed above my head. The tall central cenotaph is dwarfed by an abandoned storage tank pocked with rust.

In the 1930s, though, there was no four-lane Highway 61. You came to The Forest on old 61, graveled by then, but once a dirt track between shale bluffs, worn deep into the crumbling earth first by buffalo and the Natchez Indians and later by white settlers—by us. The scene Miss Adah described—Fanny and the priests coming back at night along that winding road, finding a place to conceal the cars while they did their work—has stuck in my mind for almost fifty years. For they did come back, toward midnight a couple of days later. It took Fanny that long to make the arrangements. They came in two cars of the period (a Model A probably, if it belonged to the diocese, as it must have, and a Buick or Cadillac, if Fanny was driving her own car). I can hear the loud put-put and rattle of the Model A, the smooth purr of the Cadillac. Fanny and two priests (Miss Adah said there were two), and a couple of acolytes. They followed the ancient road, turned off on a dirt track Fanny had scouted out the day before with the help of two black men who lived on an adjoining place. They parked. No one would have seen them. Like the road, the track was sunk deep between its shale banks. And who, in any case, would have been driving down old 61 at midnight? There, deep in the night, they met the two black men. The men lit their torches (*flambeaux*, Miss Adah called them—they were doubtless fat pine knots) and led the procession in, across a pasture at a point where the locust-post-and-barbed-wire fence was half down. All they had to do was push the leaning post lower and step over the strands of wire. They entered the woods then, Miss Adah said, and made their way to the cemetery.

"Can't you picture it?" she said. "Imagine! The deep woods. Spanish moss hanging low. Torches flaming! Censers smoking. . . ."

Really! I thought. Really!

They did whatever needed to be done to help Dunny begin his journey from hell through purgatory toward heaven, and then they left. Later, doubtless, masses would be said for his soul. Candles would be lit. Money would change hands from time to time over the years.

"So now," Miss Adah said—with considerable satisfaction, it seemed to me—"a piece of the Dunbar cemetery is Catholic."

It strikes me that there are going to be confusions and frustrations in this tale regarding kinship and identity. For those who, unlike most southerners (black and white), are not used to keeping lists of relatives in their heads, I append here for ready reference a partial list of characters:

Grandmother One—my maternal grandmother
Marian Davis—her sister-in-law, my great-aunt
Grandmother Two (Nellie)—my paternal grandmother
John—husband of Grandmother Two
Corinne—Grandmother Two's sister
Julia Nutt—friend of Grandmother Two
Dunbar Marshall, called Dunny—cousin to all these people
Fanny—Dunbar's wife

I couldn't wait to ask Grandmother One what she knew about this midnight invasion.

"I don't believe it," she said. "I just don't believe it. *She* was the madwoman—Fanny. If Marian had known she was doing that, she'd . . . God knows what she'd have done." (My grandmother often said *Oh, Lord* or *Lord knows,* but *God?* Only when she was really talking about God.) "God knows," she said again. And then, "Of course we all knew she'd come down here. That she wanted the grave blessed or consecrated, or whatever they do. Marian told me at the time. And then, afterwards, later, I knew she'd put a stone—a slab covering the entire grave. . . . Marian didn't object to that. Although . . . *Dedicated by his loving wife, Fanny?* It's clear what she meant to imply: You people buried him, but I had to come all the way back from Europe and buy a marker for his grave.

"But blessing—*consecrating*—the Dunbar cemetery? As if it needed it? And after forty years apart, with never a peep from her? Without the faintest indication that . . . Not, of course, that there was any reason for her to stay in touch with him." She shook her head and was quiet for a while, pressing her lips together now and again, as very old people do, as if biting off an invisible thread.

Now, in 1948, her lids drooped heavily over milky, almost sightless eyes. But when she was young, I knew from her wedding photograph, her gaze had been skeptical, ironic, compelling a response. "Look at this ridiculous getup," she seemed to say, gazing out of the picture. "What do you think of it?" Now, though, she saw only shapes, used her voice to draw you in. Sitting on her front porch, across the street from the cathedral, its red bulk rising from among squat live oaks, she'd listen for a familiar step, recognize her passing neighbors by their voices, call them in for a chat.

It was still true that nothing much escaped her.

Across the street a troop of children passed, followed by two sisters in dark blue habits, carried along by the white sails of their wimples, rosaries swinging from their belts. She heard the marching steps. "Children going to mass?"

"I reckon so," I said.

"Who knows why they separated in the first place," she said. "Fanny and Dunbar. But whatever the reason, they were separated. Even if they were not divorced. And as for that, my dear, the Catholics didn't have a corner on staying married and making your own discreet arrangements. I'd be the first to admit that. Nobody got divorced in those days. But Fanny and Dunbar were totally separated, totally. Two years after they married—they lived the whole time abroad, spent months on a European tour, and then settled in Italy, so we heard—two years later he came back here without a word to anyone about what had gone wrong. Not a word that I ever heard . . ."

"But if he wasn't a Catholic . . ."

"Oh, I suppose he must have converted when he married her. There wouldn't have been the possibility of marriage otherwise, given her family." She shrugged. "As you know, conversion would never be a matter of convenience in *our* family, but it must have been for him. He certainly, as far as I know, never went to mass once he escaped their clutches. And then! For her to come back here after he died and . . . !"

"But why should Aunt Marian care what Fanny did?" I said. "What difference did it make?"

"Ah, that's a puzzle, isn't it? Why? What difference did it make? Certainly it wasn't personal. Marian wasn't even living at The Forest when Dunny died, was she? Julia was in charge. She made the arrangements. But regardless of that, for Fanny to come back—to *imply* . . . As if Dunny had wanted confession and a Catholic burial, as if he'd called out for a priest when he was dying. You see? Fanny, after forty years of living a life of ease in Florence—yes, Italy. She stayed on after he came home, spent her life abroad."

"But why Miss Julia Nutt?" I said. "Why was she in charge? What was her connection with Mr. Marshall?"

"And how long had he been dead? At least a couple of years. Ridiculous! Did they think God had been hanging around waiting for the grave to be blessed before he could decide what to do with Dunny?" She laughed and shook her head. "Not that I have anything against the Catholics," she said. "I'm not like your father's family—so obsessed with being Presbyterians. Couldn't have lived across the street from the cathedral for eighty years and not had some fellow feeling for . . . But you can keep that under your hat when you're out at Nellie's." And then, "Poor old Dunny," she said. "For that matter, he probably needed all the blessing he could get."

Maybe she said that and maybe she didn't. I suppose it may just be that I have the memory now of wanting to sympathize with Dunny, consigned to the Catholic hell he hadn't thought of in decades, crushed under the slab set in place by the wife he hadn't seen for forty years.

"As for Julia's connection," my grandmother went on, "she was with him when he died. She buried him. If he'd wanted a priest, she'd have called one for him."

"Oh," I said. Now I began to remember. It was at The Forest that I had seen Miss Julia when I was a child, before Jamie and Aunt Marian lived there. She and "Cousin" Dunny, sitting on the long, screened gallery when my other grandmother had taken us to visit. Maybe that's where she was living when my father and his brothers lived at Longwood. But hadn't I seen her at Longwood, too?

"But why?" I said again. "What are you talking about?"

My grandmother's voice has almost left me now, imprinted though it was on my brain over and over again for almost half a lifetime. She couldn't carry a tune in a bucket, but there were lyric and dramatic qualities to her voice, a range in pitch when she was telling a story, an expressiveness. . . . Ah, she seemed to be saying, what I could tell you about this fascinating world! Ah, the perfidy of it! The high drama! The tragedy! And oh, how ridiculous we all are with our pretensions, how base with our betrayals. (Well, not us, usually, but sometimes even us.)

There she sits, Grandmother One, in a green-painted, rush-bottomed rocking chair. It's afternoon, and she's had her bath, carefully arranged her sparse white hair like a cap over her balding scalp and put on one of those thin, flower-sprigged voile dresses that old ladies used to wear in the spring and summer. Soon her daughters, my two aunts, will be home from work, bringing the day's gossip, but now she has plenty of time for me.

"Ah, Julia," she says. "What's the connection? Get me a cold biscuit, darling, and a glass of sherry, and I'll tell you. In the side-board. Lefthand door."

She nibbled at her biscuit, sipped her afternoon sherry, gave me a sidelong glance. "Julia *lived* out there with Dunny," she said. "They lived for some years at Longwood, and then, after she sold off the last of the farmland (or, I don't know, she may have lost it for taxes) and she still had a few cows, she rented part of The For-est—pastureland and house. She and Dunny and the cows moved there—Marian was living in town then."

"She and Dunny . . . ?"

"They were cousins, of course," my grandmother said. "And I think he looked after the cows."

Saying *cows* implied something modest indeed, something far less lucrative than *cattle*. Well, I thought, that was the sort of thing people did in rural Adams County—never mind that he'd been on the grand tour with his bride, settled in Florence (in a palazzo?). When he came back to Natchez, he helped Julia look after her cows. What to make of all this? God knows, as my grandmother would say in moments of stress.

"But you must have seen him when Nellie took you out to visit Julia. Didn't she take you out there sometimes when you were children?"

"Yes," I said. "I remember going there, and I remember her coming to call."

Here is Miss Julia coming to call on Grandmother Two. It's four o'clock on a summer afternoon in the late '20s.

Curious how one has precise and vivid memories stamped on the gray cells—of people one has known only as friends of grown-up relatives, with whom one may never have had the least personal connection. I remember, for example, a friend of my aunt's who wore extraordinary, brilliant spots of orange rouge, round as dol-lars, on her cheeks, applied over a base of powder white as a geisha's face in a Gilbert and Sullivan opera. I remember her dumpy figure, her guttural voice, the mole on her chin, even her white tennis dress, as precisely as if she were my mother and I'd begun to memorize her on the day of my birth.

And I remember Miss Julia Nutt just as vividly.

Here she is, coming to call on my grandmother. People still called, still left cards in those days. Ladies, even poverty-stricken ladies (and gentlemen, too), continued to call.

I can't remember how she arrived. Did she have a car? Did she drive it herself, or have a chauffeur? In this strange world and time—the late '20s in the South—one might have a chauffeur whom one paid five dollars a week and keep. I have the impression that very poor white people might not be able to pay their taxes, but they could afford chauffeurs and cooks. Is that possible? But . . . I don't know—I recall that there were also very, very poor white people who had no chauffeurs, no cars even, who drove into town in their buggies to "call" or to shop. These people, however, were looked upon as curiosities. Perhaps they were just eccentric—opposed to peonage and the combustion engine.

I see them—Julia and Nellie—in the wide hall of my grandmother's house. They are embracing, and then, together, arms about one another's waists, they're moving toward the horsehair sofa in the parlor, then sitting side by side, bending toward each other, talking. In this memory I would have been seven or eight years old, and they would have been in their sixties—very old ladies in my view, and probably in their own, though my grandmother would live another twenty-five years.

I hear the murmur of their voices. This grandmother's voice is softer, has a more limited range than the other's. She, too, is dressed in one of those flower-sprigged old-lady dresses—hers is always lavender and white, because she stays to the end of her life in semi-mourning for my grandfather, who at this point has been dead for five or six years. (Does anyone in the world besides me remember that lavender was the color for semi-mourning, put on after a year in black and two in black-and-white?)

I'm wandering. I want to tell about my memory of Miss Julia.

She's not in mourning. I'm sure she's not, though I don't recall her dress. I see instead the delicate band of ecru lace around her throat and the hint of lace at her wrists. She is erect, sturdy, high-bosomed, hawk-nosed, wattled—that's the detail that almost escaped me—her wattles half-concealed by the lace. Her softly wrinkled face is dusted, like that of my aunt's tennis friend, with white powder. No round spots of rouge on her cheeks, though. Just the faintest hint of a flush. (I suppose I must have noticed these cosmetic details because they were unusual. Neither my grandmothers nor my mother wore rouge or lipstick: my grandmothers because it was not done by women of their generation, my mother because, she said, my father didn't like makeup.)

I hear Julia's voice. Husky. Does she smoke? I believe she does. Yes. I see her fit a cigarette into a holder and light it. But mainly I remember that two-inch-wide band of ecru lace around her neck, and the lace, fragile as a cobweb, at her wrists.

I have no memory of eavesdropping on their conversation. I may have begun to listen, lost interest, and fallen into a reverie of my own contriving. In my other grandmother's house, conversations among grown people were dramatic. One listened. Drunken men staggered into her stories, flew into rages, tore up the very sheets on their beds or threw their shoes out the window. Gamecocks were killed by mistake and put into the Sunday gumbo. The levee broke and the cotton fields flooded. Grooms abandoned their brides at the altar. And there is this: stories happened to people you knew. I was left with the distinct impression that the roomer who shredded his sheets was frustrated because my grandmother, a young widow at the time, refused to marry him.

But this grandmother, Grandmother Two, inquired of her friend whether the cows were calving or whether the lespedeza had been planted. Had the late freeze ruined the plums and figs? Would there be a pecan crop from that fifty-acre grove in the bend of the creek? They were both farmers, after all: since my grandfather's death, Grandmother Two had supervised the operation of their farm. If these were the subjects of conversation, I would doubtless have lost interest.

I want to go back now to that afternoon's conversation with Grandmother One. I've gotten her a second glass of sherry and ferreted out the bourbon bottle to fix myself a drink.

"They were third cousins," she said. "Or fifth. I'm not sure. You're distantly related to Dunny, too, of course. But no connection with the Nutts. She and Dunny must have been cousins on the other side. But *distant* cousins. If they'd been first cousins, almost like brother and sister, you know, there would never have been any talk. No one would dream that *first* cousins could . . . could . . ." She broke off.

"Do you mean they were lovers?"

"That's what everybody thought. But who am I to say? Judge not that ye be not judged. They had separate quarters, of course. Or so people said. At both places. He had his own rooms. This is hearsay, my dear. We were never intimate. I'm . . . Well, of course it isn't exactly hearsay. I'm telling you what Marian observed at The Forest. But whatever the truth was, nobody called."

"What about you?" I said.

"We were never intimate," she said again. "But it was not an issue with me. You know. None of my business."

"But . . . *Nobody* called? You said Grandmother used to take us out there to see her. And she did. I remember."

"Oh, Nellie! I'm sure she never allowed a word spoken against Julia. Never."

And I was immediately sure of that, too. No word of censure was ever spoken against friend or kin in Nellie's house. No groom she knew would ever have left his bride at the altar. He'd sooner have had a heart attack and died. Not a year had passed since she had explained to me that a young cousin had not been to call for some months because he'd been on vacation in New Mexico. In fact, as Grandmother One had already told me, he and his lady friend had gotten drunk one evening in the cemetery—a lovely spot to share a drink, the loveliest cemetery in Mississippi—had stripped off their clothes to make love among the tombstones, and been arrested for committing a public nuisance. He'd lost his job. She'd lost all her tennis students. Grandmother Two said he didn't come back from his vacation bécause he had found such a tempting opening out there he couldn't refuse it. I've forgotten what became of the lady friend.

Is there any point in digging up these ancient scandals? Not only my grandmothers but those two insouciant lovers are long dead.

But they had to leave town. That's the point I'm making. They had to leave town because somebody caught them joyously fucking (and on his very own cemetery lot) in the middle of a beautiful, moonlit April night.

And Grandmother Two had to *not* know it happened.

Aside from that, what were the police doing harassing peaceful lovers in the middle of the night in the privacy of the cemetery?

Grandmother One was still thinking about Julia. "I'm not much of a caller," she said. "You know very well that I can't drive and never could afford a chauffeur. Here I sit on my front gallery in the six hundred block of Main Street, across from the cathedral, no distance from the Presbyterian church and the building and loan and Britton and Koontz Bank. Everybody eventually passes the house, and they're always welcome to come in and visit." She sipped her sherry, raised her head as blind people often do, seeming to listen for some faint signal, or to sniff the air. "The young men used to go out to see Julia and Dunny in the evenings quite often," she said. "They were always fond of the young men."

What to make of that?

"Your father's bachelor party," she said. She said nothing else for a few minutes.

I waited.

"Your father's bachelor party was held at Longwood. Even I took a dim view of that." She's speaking of the drunken brawl held for the groom on the eve of his wedding. She shrugged and smiled as if to say, "I didn't really." But instead she said, "I did."

The front gate creaked. "Ah," she said, "don't I hear the girls? Yes." The girls were my sixtyish aunts, coming home from their jobs as secretaries, one to the vice-president of a bank, the other in an insurance agency.

I was left to consider the implications of my father's bachelor party. There was no need for further questions. Grandmother One had made a clear statement. She had consigned Julia to the category of women who entertain men but not ladies. Shades of Belle Watling.

I haven't done justice to the stories Grandmother Two used to tell—or rather read aloud to us children. True, they were not about real people; there was never the baffling but fascinating glimpse into the crisis-plagued world of our grown-up family. But all the same, they rivaled in thrills the tale of the roomer who tore up his sheets and threw his shoes out the window.

Grandmother Two's characters were distant and mythical people, and her stories had shape—endings and, at least implicitly, morals. There was the Covenanter ancestor whose sister—when he fled her house, pursued by King Charles's troops—concealed under her voluminous skirts the League and the Covenant signed in the blood of the dissenters. There were the two children who wandered away from their lonely forest homestead and were murdered by Indians. And there was the gypsy boy picked up by a tornado from his family's caravan and dropped in the lap of a wilderness bandit from whom he was rescued by a pious country woman who promptly began to teach him his catechism. In one of these tales a stern father, crippled by gout, can't pursue his daughter and her forbidden lover when they flee like Lochinvar and his bride into the wild Mississippi night, moss blowing, limbs creaking, owls screaming in the darkness. But the storm pursues them— wind is precursor to downpour. Crossing the Homochitto River, the lovers are swept away in one of those flash floods that rush without warning out of the southern hills.

Sometimes the heroes and heroines are animals: a boy frog named Joe who repeatedly gets into trouble from which he is rescued by Mrs. Crow, a splendid elderly crow-lady in a bonnet and black shawl; a trickster rabbit escaped from the circus, shivering under the Chickasaw-rose hedge; a bear who has gnawed off his toe to escape a trap.

Vengeful Catholics. Stern fathers. Disobedient daughters. Murderous Indians. Animals escaping the devices of men who want to entrap and kill them. These were Grandmother Two's characters, and she thought about them, wrote down their stories, and read them to us on weekday afternoons after dinner or evenings at bedtime.

Sundays, after Sunday school and church and dinner (Grandmother carving the leg of lamb; dignified, officious Hampton, her chauffeur, now in his white waiter's jacket, handing the biscuits and rice and butter beans, tapioca pudding for dessert), story-reading was strictly from the Bible or *The Christian Observer.* Dominoes and checkers, croquet sets and packs of cards had vanished on Saturday night into closets and drawers. The Sunday funnies were put away to be read on Monday. If we were staying with Grandmother Two, Mother usually fled with us after dinner to Grandmother One, where you could read the funnies, play Parcheesi, and go to the Prentiss Club for an afternoon swim.

Those old Covenanters might seem to me as made-up as Bluebeard, but I was aware that their heavy hands still pressed down on my grandmother's shoulders.

Since I began a month or so ago thinking about Julia and Dunbar and Nellie, I have gone back to Natchez. I've gone to the cemeteries at The Forest and at Longwood. Julia, I've discovered, is indeed buried at Longwood, just a short walk into the woods from that astonishing five-storied octagonal mansion with its copper-colored dome and carved finial. She's surrounded by her kin—parents and cousins and the two nephews who inherited the house and sold it to buy food and clothes and whiskey.

She is visited now by thousands of callers: tourists who come from all over the world to see the house—widely advertised as a gem of Sloane architecture—and who wander in the woods and visit the cemetery and pay their respects to the dead.

I've looked at old photographs and gotten out boxes of letters. Photographs: in the one of Grandmother Two that I like best, she stands in the photographer's studio, trim and narrow-waisted in a formal riding habit and top hat, a tasseled crop in her gloved hands. The skirt of her habit (of course she rode sidesaddle) falls in graceful folds. The trim jacket is buttoned up to the barely visible starched collar of her blouse with eighteen fabric-covered buttons and fastened at the throat with what appears to be a silver brooch in the shape of a riding whip. Tendrils of dark, curly hair escape under the stiff brim of her hat. She is poised, self-possessed, gentle, a half-smile on her lovely, strong, intelligent young face. She can't be more than seventeen or eighteen. In another, she's a married woman seated at a spinet surrounded by her four sons, who gaze with uniform wide-eyed solemnity sideways toward the photographer. Nellie, her sad face in profile, her hair piled high and twisted into a French knot, looks at her sons. She wears a high-necked blouse in the style of the time, with long, cuffed, leg-o'-mutton sleeves. I can barely make out, propped on the lid of the spinet, a dim picture—it seems to be of a reclining child surrounded by flowers. On either end of the lid are small bronze figures—one a mounted Roman general, the other a woman carrying a water pitcher on her shoulder. I deduce from the apparent ages of the boys that this photograph must have been made not long after the death of Nellie's only daughter, Corinne, at the age of five.

I've also seen a photograph of Julia as a young woman, standing next to Nellie in a large group of tennis players who are disposed about a lawn, some standing, some sitting, in front of a columned house. She holds a racquet in one hand and looks directly into the camera. But her face is blurred. I can't make out either the features or the expression.

I have read the letters exchanged between Nellie and John Ayres, her husband-to-be, during their courtship and engagement, and later, after their marriage, when for periods of weeks or months he was working in a commission merchant's office in New Orleans and she was at home, either in town with her parents (this during the latter months of a pregnancy) or in the deep country on their farm.

Almost every one of the playful early letters refers to Julia: "My best friend," or "Julia sends her love and a saucy message which I won't relay," or "Julia's lieutenant is here." (Or is gone, or came to call.) Often in these letters she uses Julia or her sister Corinne as a surrogate for herself: "Corinne tells me to say that she longs to see you—hopes you'll soon return to our little town." Or "Julia sends you . . ." not just a saucy message, but sometimes even a kiss. "Julia," she writes, "isn't the kind of girl to be deeply distressed about any man, I reckon." Of herself in one of the early letters she writes, "I am a very cold woman and would not have you deceive yourself by thinking otherwise." "My dear Mr. Ayres," she addresses him in the courtship letters, and signs herself, "Your friend, Nellie Henderson." Later she writes "My dear Jack," but still signs herself, "Your friend."

Almost from the beginning he is direct, passionate. "My darling Nellie," he writes, "My own dear Nellie." And "You cannot imagine how much I love you," and "I would not have you believe me perfect nor rich. . . . You would be all I would have to live and work for." And (perhaps after the *cold woman* letter) "I love you too much to have you marry one you do not love and there is no sacrifice I would not make to save you from such an act."

The formal games of courtship continue into the engagement. She pretends, for example, not to know why he asks for her hand size. (Gloves, like candy and flowers, were acceptable gifts in those days from a man to a young lady.)

Suddenly, after more than three years (there is a period in the middle from which no letters remain; if he was in Natchez, maybe none were written), they are engaged and then married. "My dear Jack" becomes "My darling husband," "My dearest Jack" (this in a period when women customarily called their husbands *Mister*), and, to me even more moving, "My dear old man." One deduces that the cold woman has melted.

Julia is still a presence in these later letters. Nellie takes the babies and goes to Longwood to spend the day. But the correspondence centers now on planting time and harvest, on the chickens, the turkeys, the cows (Lillie Langtry, their soft-eyed Jersey, has calved), on the scarcity of money, on the children: "Richardson is asleep and Sister is rocking the baby." And, overwhelmingly, on her loneliness when he is away: "I long for the day when you'll never have to leave me again." About Julia's romances, her "beaus," Nellie falls silent. What happened to the lieutenant? Did she spurn him? Did he abandon her? Or was he, in fact, Dunbar Marshall? I don't know. But what happened eventually, as we know from Dunbar's tombstone as well as from ancient gossip, is that he married Fanny Bullitt.

What I didn't know—what neither Miss Adah nor Grandmother One told me, what I found out when I began just this year (1994) looking at old records and writing about these lives—is that not only were Julia and Dunbar "distant cousins," but Fannie and Julia were first cousins.

Now I am trying to fit this fact into my ancient romance. Did Fanny steal Julia's lover away? Is that the tragedy unrecorded in Nellie's letters?

As I gather the fragments of this story, I have a choice: I could invent—I am a novelist, after all, accustomed to inventing. I imagine that Fanny was yielding and soft and treacherous, that she feigned innocence and stupidity and helplessness. I could set her off against Julia, whom I remember so well as a sturdy, high-bosomed, hawk-nosed, deep-voiced old woman, and think of as the girl Nellie had called "not the kind . . . to be deeply distressed about any man, I reckon." The temptation is seductive. How deeply I would like to be able to tell you of Fanny's betrayal of her cousin, of Dunbar's escape from a hateful marriage, of her refusal to divorce him, of the climax: Julia's defiance of convention when she welcomes him to her house, her arms, her bed. And, finally, of how Fanny, after Dunny is dead, comes back to claim him, to put her name on his gravestone in a last, furious act of possession—how God and the Catholic church are mere excuses for the acting out of rage and jealousy and a rivalry begun, perhaps, when the two women were children. Julia was cleverer, more lovable, stronger, nobler, and Fanny . . . ! You see? I almost can't resist it.

But this is fiction—romantic nonsense. All I know is that Dunny left his wife, came back to Adams County, moved somehow into Julia's life, began "looking after her cows" and occupying quarters in her house. I have heard that no one called except Nellie and the young men. And I know that, in defiance of her church and his marriage vows, they committed themselves to each other and for a lifetime honored that commitment.

Yes, *her* church. Like Fanny, Julia was born a Catholic.

Later there are wills from which one can perhaps make reasonable deductions. There was Longwood—and the eventual disposal of Longwood must have been on a number of minds. It belonged to Julia, and its value as a curiosity, as a family property, as a tourist attraction (toward the end of her life when Natchez houses were beginning to be famous) would have been evident to the nieces and nephews who inherited it at her death and who later sold it. One of the nephews, I recall, was living there as a kind of caretaker and guide during my adolescence. One concludes, therefore, that Julia did not fall out with her family to the extent of disinheriting them. Perhaps, after all, they—the nephews in any case—were among "the young men" who continued to call.

Dunny left a will, too, as I discovered while nosing around the chancery clerk's office. His estate was modest, but not so modest as I had expected, thinking of him as the man who looked after Julia's cows— and her other needs. Some twenty thousand dollars in securities went to his daughter. Daughter? Where did she come from? No one had mentioned her. She and Fanny will remain shadows to the end of this story.

As I've observed, Dunbar is not mentioned in Julia's will. But surprisingly (to me), my great-aunt Marian and her husband are:

the will states that Marian and Jamie are honorable and trustworthy people, and they are appointed appraisers of the real property.

Nor is Julia mentioned in Dunbar's will. It is impossible for me to resist the supposition that the two of them talked to each other of their wills, that perhaps they decided together to let community and family finally have their due.

Here is another vivid memory from my childhood. It's summer, and as usual we are visiting Grandmother Two. I see myself sitting beside her in the backseat of her old black Buick. At this point, if I am a small child, the Buick is not very old. Grandmother Two didn't lose her husband's money until the failure of the Hibernia Bank early in the Great Depression. Thereafter her car got older and older. Hampton's chauffeur's uniform and the car's paint faded together from black to an acid, purplish green; but he managed to keep the car alive for years. In any case, Hampton is driving us to town. Now he has parked the car in front of the columned temple of Britton and Koontz Bank. He has opened the door and bowed Grandmother out. She is wearing her white-and-lavender, flower-sprigged summer dress and white cotton gloves and is carrying a little white crocheted drawstring pouch—her reticule. Then we are at home again. She must have cashed a check to pay Hampton, or Ida, the cook, or the vegetable man—or all three. For some reason money is about to change hands, and she must count it out and handle it.

We are in the bathroom now, and I am standing by the basin watching a process that takes place every time money comes into the house.

"Why?" I am asking.

She has removed her gloves. Her arms are bare to the elbows. She is bent seriously over the basin, but she turns toward me to answer my question, to tell me about germs and filth.

She is washing the money.

A few dimes and quarters and fifty-cent pieces lie glinting at the bottom of the basin. A number of bills (ones and fives, probably—

I'm sure I would have noticed tens, which were scarcer in those
days than hundreds would be now) float limply above the coins,
and Grandmother picks them up and soaps them and rubs them
together. She stirs the water, and the coins clink against each other.
She drains the basin. She rinses the coins and bills and lays them
on a towel to dry.

Grandmother Two is not crazy. She is a sane and gentle lady
who manages a farm (her husband and sister-in-law are dead now)
and a complex household consisting of her sister, her servants, and,
this summer day, three grandchildren and a pregnant daughter-in-
law. (I'm choosing for this memory the summer of my brother's
birth.) Dinner is served every day at one. Hampton puts on his
waiter's jacket and hands the cornbread, removes the plates, brings
in the dessert (tapioca pudding again). After dinner we may play
a game of casino, or Grandmother may read us one of her stories.
Or we may wind the music box that sits on the old square piano
and listen to "Humoresque." Or pretend that the scatter rugs in
the long, cool hall are pirate ships and mount an invasion of the
parlor. At four Hampton will close the downstairs shutters and
depart. Suppertime will come, and Grandmother and Mother will
make tomato sandwiches and cut us each a piece of Ida's delicious
sponge cake.

Nevertheless, it's true that she washes every coin and bill that
passes through her hands. Can money be washed clean? Can we
drive the moneychangers from the temple?

Has this anything to do with Julia? With the cousin who went
permanently vacationing in New Mexico?

Here is one of Grandmother Two's stories. This one she did not
write down. But she told it to us—and not only she but my
great-aunt, her sister Corinne. And since it was told in turn to my
older sister, my younger sister, my brother, and me, as we each got
old enough to hear and understand it, I heard it many times. It
seems to me now that it is the link between her written-down stories and a world in which every coin must be washed before it can
be touched.

In the early nineteenth century, Samuel Brooks and his wife Mary had two daughters (or family tradition says they did; I haven't checked the cemetery for their stones). Mr. Brooks was the first American mayor of Natchez, and another legend has it that in his Presbyterian zeal he closed down all the taverns and whore-houses and "gambling dens" of Natchez-Under-the-Hill (as noto-rious along the river in its time as the stews of London) and that the gamblers and pimps and prostitutes and riverboat men marched on his house to rout him out and force him to rescind his order, or else to kill him. One family myth (so bizarre that it may be true) is that a rock crashed through an upstairs window, and when Mrs. Brooks looked out and saw the mob, she began to scream. She screamed and screamed (rocks flying, presumably, windows shattering), until she burst a blood vessel in her throat and bled to death. Family tradition does not record whether Mr. Brooks rescinded his order.

Never mind about that. The story I want to tell is about the daughters, who, to make a long story short, were to attend their first ball as young ladies, escorted, as was customary in those days, by their parents.

I think of Tolstoy's joyous young heroines, doomed also to undergo great trials, of Katya and Natasha at their first balls; and I think of my own first evening wrap—a scarlet woolen cape with gold-braid frogs on the shoulders, a dramatic cape that swept the floor when I made my entrance at a dance.

So: gowns had been ordered—from Worth—from Paris! I seem to recall; but I must have made that up. The silks and braid, the vel-vets and peau de soie and moiré taffeta probably came up on a river-boat from New Orleans, and the seamstress, perhaps, was "French"—a mulatto slave woman. Or, who knows, Mrs. Brooks herself may have been skilled at needlework, as my own Grandmother One was.

The young ladies came down. I pictured them, as the tale was told, sweeping down the broad staircase in my grandmother's house in town, stairs that descended into a high-ceilinged parlor and airy open hallway. But they lived, in fact, in an earlier, Spanish-period house with low ceilings and narrow, enclosed stairs like a ship's companion.

Father and Mother awaited them in the drawing room, admired their gowns, had them turn round to be inspected on all sides. Mother adjusted the lace of a shawl, tucked in an errant curl. Did she know what was about to happen? Surely not.

And then the old man—the father, the Presbyterian elder, the sadist—folded his arms and addressed them. Was his voice gentle? His mien fatherly? "And now, young ladies," he said. "Go upstairs. Take off your ball gowns and go to bed. You must learn to bear disappointment."

One of those young ladies was Grandmother Two's grandmother. Who else could have passed along this story, made this comment on the character of Mr. Brooks—her father?

Here I think about the lives of women in that long-ago time when marriage was the only career open to ladies. I think of all those real and fictional nineteenth-century tyrannical fathers, and I begin to think of my grandmother's maiden sister and maiden sister-in-law, who for their own reasons used their own stratagems to avoid marriage—and stratagems they did have—or Corinne did, I know, because my father has told me about them.

These two women led busy, active, devout lives. One had her own money—half of the inheritance that enabled Grandfather to buy the house in town—and she helped him run the struggling farm, which belonged to them jointly. Often she stayed there alone, far out in the country, a mile from the nearest white family, when Grandfather was away and Grandmother Two was pregnant and staying in town with her parents. The other, Corinne, taught for a while (speech and elocution to young ladies, and of course Sunday school). She gardened and called and read. (By the time I came along, her favorite author was Edgar Rice Burroughs, her hero John Carter, Warlord of Mars.) She looked after her aging parents and helped her sister raise four boys, all of whom regarded her, I know, as a second mother.

I think about them—these women—and I think about my grandmother and the lovely letters addressed to *Dearest Jack,* to *My darling husband, My dear old man.*

And I think about the courage and passion of Julia Nutt.

What's essential, too, is to remember and understand, if we can, the depth and conviction and rootedness of Grandmother Two's piety and the virulence of ancestral hatred of the Catholic Church.

I see again, on the sewing table by her wicker rocker, her worn Bible, the gilt mostly gone from the page edges and from the letters stamped on its limp leather cover; and I remember how each morning she closed her bedroom door to read and pray. We were not allowed to disturb her then.

I recall the reading aloud of Bible stories on Sunday evening— stories of how Elisha called out the bears to eat the children who made fun of him; of how Jehovah drowned the armies of Pharaoh; of how, over and over again, the Israelites did evil in the sight of the Lord and were delivered into the hands of the Ammonites or the Moabites or the Philistines. And later how, when God relented, the Israelites fell on them (whoever they were) and slew them every one.

But Ruth, too, and Naomi. Ruth, who said, "Entreat me not to leave thee." I recall again the mention in the Henderson Bible of those long-dead dissenters who "suffered much in the persecution of the church. . . ."

And I remember my visit years ago to Scotland, remember seeing the wreckage, the devastation of ancient abbeys and churches, the statues of saints left noseless and sometimes headless and armless by the furious dissenters. I had gone earlier to Italy, had seen San Clemente and San Pietro in Vinculo and Santa Costanza and the duomos in Florence and Siena—the glittering mosaics, the carved pulpits, the great silver candelabra—and also the small, homely, pious men and women going about their tasks—sowing seed, plowing, baking, building—on the panels around the campanile in Florence.

And then, later, in Scotland, to see the awful noseless faces, the ruined abbey walls. . . . Ah, they were jagged stones in the middle of my life, even far as I believed myself to be from all those ancient passions.

Nellie was born a Henderson, a collateral descendant of Alexander Henderson, the Scottish divine who debated and prayed with Charles I for days, seeking his renunciation of the Catholic faith, and who, when he failed, turned the king over to Cromwell, "to be murdered," as Miss Adah said. Henderson, some church historians record, took to his bed afterward and never got up. Seven days later he died of grief. Others give a different account of his death.

For Nellie, the Covenanter has signed the League and the Covenant in his blood. His sister has concealed it on her person. The runaway lovers must drown. The straying children must be murdered. The young ladies must learn to bear disappointment.

I come now to Julia's death and burial and the mystery that surrounds them.

She lived only two years after Dunny: both died relatively young—in their early sixties. I think she must have moved back to Longwood when he died; that may be why I remember climbing among the joists and rafters there. Perhaps she gave up farming, since she no longer had him to help her with the cows. In any case, the snapshot of my sister and me on Jamie's donkey tells me that by the time I was ten or so, Jamie and Marian lived at The Forest. I was ten in 1931, the year after Dunny's death, the year before Julia's.

But it's the funerals that puzzle me—the role the Catholic and Presbyterian churches played, or didn't play, in both these deaths—the funerals, and Nellie's part in them.

Remember that Julia and Dunny—one born into the Catholic Church, the other a convert "for convenience" during his brief marriage—lived all their adult lives in what their church regarded as mortal sin.

Who decided to bury Dunny at The Forest? Surely it was Julia, not Marian. Who conducted the service? Not a priest, according to Miss Adah. Marian said he had had a Presbyterian funeral and if that was not good enough to get him into heaven, he could just go the other way. Did she say this out of loyalty to Julia and Dunny, out of knowledge of their private convictions? Or possibly—this has just occurred to me—she knew the history of his marriage and took genuine pleasure in foiling his wife, whom she believed to be the villain of the piece.

And then: *Presbyterian?* Where would Julia have found, in that rigid world, a Presbyterian minister willing to say his church's service over her fallen-away Catholic lover?

There are no answers to these questions, but they are enough to set the novelist off in half a dozen different directions.

Perhaps—can it be?—there was only Julia following his coffin to the dark, crumbling cemetery, only Julia standing by as the grave was filled. Or perhaps Nellie was with her. It may be that Nellie brought her worn Bible and read a psalm and said a prayer. It has struck me more than once, thinking about these lives, that Julia, out of deep knowledge of her friend's character, may, to shield her from distress, have concealed from Nellie the depth of hers and Dunny's indifference to what anybody's church said or believed or attempted to enforce in the community they lived at the edge of. She was never "the kind of girl to be deeply distressed about any man." Or about any church? Or community ostracism? Not those either, perhaps. But about her friend's concern for their souls? That may have been another matter.

Again I must resist making up their story.

Two years passed. Julia died. Her funeral was held in my grandmother's parlor. It was conducted by a priest. But of course (outside the church, in a Protestant house), no mass could be said.

How do I know this? I know it only because my mother chanced to tell me—years after my conversation with Grandmother One about the scandal of Julia and Dunny's life together. Such a funeral was strange enough for her to remark on it, to speculate about why, to suggest that Julia, because of her life, was denied burial from the cathedral. (We lived at the time in a small town in a neighboring state, and from what my mother said, neither she nor my father was privy to the arrangements or went to the funeral.) "That must have been the only time a priest ever entered your grandmother's house," she said.

A priest. Why did Nellie call in a priest? Is it believable even for a moment that after Dunny's death Julia went back into the Catholic Church, believable that she could call her whole life a sin and do penance for it? That would be one explanation, wouldn't it, for the priest? But such a thing is not believable, and for more than speculative reasons. If she had gone to confession, if she had been absolved, the lost lamb returned to the fold, she would have been buried from the cathedral with a proper mass.

"I've heard of cases like that in those days," a priest friend of mine said when I asked him to speculate about what might have happened. "If the dead woman was known to be an unrepentant sinner, and church burial was out of the question, some kind father might be willing to sneak in the back door and say a prayer over the body—wherever it was. No. It isn't surprising."

"What's surprising is who called him in," I said.

Why did Nellie call in a priest? Did honor somehow require it? Or could she find no one else, no one in her own or any other church to stand beside her and say a prayer at her friend's coffin.

I am sure now that I remember my grandmother and Julia—and Dunny, too—on the gallery at The Forest on a long, hot summer afternoon. I recall an embrace and then the two women in intimate, quiet conversation. I hear their soft voices, Julia's pitched a shade lower than my grandmother's, the voices, it seems now, of ghosts, alive only in my head and only for the time left to me to remember them. I remember the call and response of those voices as I might remember music—the oboe making room for the flute and then meditatively answering; and, like oboe and flute, they speak with deep emotion, but wordlessly.

Dunny sits a little apart from the women, dressed in shabby khaki pants and a collarless shirt. Is he perhaps smoking a pipe, having asked the ladies' permission? Hampton, I think, sits in the kitchen. I hear his deep, officious voice, condescending as a tuba. He too is in quiet conversation, with whoever presides over Julia's household.

The evening draws in. My sister and I come back from exploring the graveyard and the ruined foundation of the old house. I hear the locusts' stridulent, passionate calls rise and fall, as I have heard them all my life from the tree-shadowed galleries of the South.

Does it matter at all whether I recall or imagine this scene? There they are. I *know* they are there, the three of them together, making their mysterious music. I want to convey the quality of their lives, of their friendship, but I cannot. The secrets of a lifetime stand between me and them.

Instead I keep returning in my mind to one of the last times I spoke with Grandmother Two. She was ninety-four. Afterward I saw her only when she was very ill, dying. She walked with me— tottered—toward the front door to see me out. Jintzy, the black sitter who looked after her those last feeble years, alert to prevent a fall, hovered in the background. Grandmother steadied herself on my arm. I bent and kissed her crumpled tissue-paper cheek, told her I'd come again soon.

"You're married, aren't you?" she said anxiously. And then, "Of course. You were married *here*. I remember now."

"Yes," I said.

"All those camellias," she said. "I remember all those beautiful camellias."

"Yes. January. They were in full bloom."

She gripped my arm with a strong old claw. "Have lots of children, darling," she said. "Have lots of children."

We were indeed married in her house. I came down the stairs in an ivory satin gown and sweeping veil of peau de soie, as I had so often imagined those two unfortunate young ladies coming down for their first ball.

Lots of children? Grandmother was confused. I already had three sons.

But. . . . Perhaps she was going back to the joyous and difficult and tragic years when her own boys were growing up, when her daughter died. Perhaps she was still wondering and grieving for her sister Corinne's single life. Or perhaps she was thinking of Julia, who never had a child, could never have had a child.

When I saw her last, propped on a high hospital bed, dying of pneumonia—"the old man's friend," as people used to say—she was barely conscious, murmuring, whispering something I could not make out. Jintzy sat nodding, half-asleep, in a chair against the wall. Corinne sat in the brown wicker rocker with a Bible in her lap. She was reading aloud. All the time I stood by the bed she continued to read, or sometimes, lifting her ancient, ravaged, tear-streaked face, to repeat from memory: "Hear my prayer, O Lord, and let my cry come unto thee. Hide not thy face from me. . . ."

"Juh . . . juh . . . juh . . ." my grandmother was whispering. "Juh . . . juh . . . juh . . ." Hardly more than a breath.

". . . and my days are like a shadow that declineth; and I am withered like grass . . ."

Over and over again: "Juh . . . juh . . . juh . . ."

"So the heathen shall fear the name of the Lord. . . ."

Jack? Her darling Jack? Her dear old man? Or Julia?

But no, it was Jintzy for whom she called, when she finally spoke. "Jintzy," she said. "Jintzy, Jintzy, Jintzy, Jintzy."

For the rest she was silent still.

———————

Ellen Douglas lives in Jackson, Mississippi. She grew up in small towns in Louisiana, Arkansas, and Mississippi. She has received two NEA fellowships and an award from the Fellowship of Southern Writers for the body of her work. Her most recent novel, *Can't Quit You, Baby,* was published by Atheneum and is presently available in paperback from Viking Penguin. Earlier novels, *The Rock Cried Out, A Lifetime Burning,*

JULIA AND NELLIE

and *A Family's Affairs,* have been reissued by LSU Press. The University Press of Mississippi has reissued *Apostles of Light* and *Black Cloud, White Cloud.*

I am presently at work on a group of stories of which "Julia and Nellie" is one. The stories are about remembering and forgetting, seeing and ignoring, lying and truth-telling. Samuel Taylor Coleridge wrote that "friendship is a sheltering tree," and this was true for Julia and Nellie. This story is a tribute to their friendship, which triumphed over the circumstances of a limited and judgmental world and sustained them all their lives.

Elizabeth Gilbert

THE FINEST WIFE

(from *Story*)

When Rose was sixteen years old and five months pregnant, she won a beauty pageant in south Texas, based on her fine walk up a runway in a sweet, navy blue bathing suit. This was shortly before the war. She had been a skinny, knee-scratching kid only the summer earlier, but her pregnancy had delivered this sudden prize of a body. It was as though life was gestating in her thighs and ass and breasts, not in her belly. It might have seemed that she was carrying all the soft weights of motherhood spread even and perfect across her whole frame. Those parts of herself that she could not quite pack into the blue bathing suit spilled over exactly enough to emotionally disturb several of the judges and spectators. She was an uncontested champion beauty.

Rose's father, too, saw the pin-up shape that his daughter had taken, and five months too late, he started worrying about the maintenance of her graces. Soon after the pageant, her condition became obvious. Her father sent her to a facility in Oklahoma, where she stayed until she experienced four days of labor and the delivery of a stillborn son. Rose could not actually have any more children after that, but the lovely figure was hers to keep, and she ended up eventually married, once again on the basis of a fine walk in a sweet bathing suit.

But she didn't meet her husband until the war was over. In the meantime, she stayed in Oklahoma. She had developed a bit of a taste for certain types of tall, smiling local men in dark hats. Also, she had developed a taste for certain types of church-going men, and also for left-handed men, and for servicemen, fishermen, postmen, assemblymen, firemen, highwaymen, elevator repairmen, and the Mexican busboys at the restaurant where she worked (who reverently called her "La Rubia"—The Blond—as if she were a notorious bandit or a cardshark).

She married her husband because she loved him best. He was kind to waitresses and dogs, and was not in any way curious about her famous tastes. He was a big man, with a rump like the rump of a huge animal—muscled and hairy. He dialed telephones with pencil stubs because his fingers didn't fit the rotary holes. He smoked cigarettes that looked like shreds of toothpicks against the size of his mouth. He couldn't fall asleep without feeling Rose's own bottom pressed up warm against his belly. He held her like she was a puppy.

In the years after they got a television, they would watch evening game shows together on the couch, and Rose's husband would genuinely applaud the contestants who had won cars and boats. He was happy for them, and would clap with his big arms stretched out stiffly, the way a trained seal claps, and with all of a seal's delight.

They moved to Minnesota, eventually. Rose's husband bought a musky flock of sheep and a small, tight house. She was married to him for forty-three years, and then he died of a heart attack. He was quite older than her, and had lived a long time. Rose thought that he had passed the kind of life after which you should say, "Yes! That was a good one!" Her mourning was appreciative and fond.

When her husband was gone, the sheep became too much work, and she sold them off, a few at a time. And when the sheep were all gone—spread across several states as pets, yarn, dogfood, and mint-jellied chops—Rose became the driver of a local elementary school bus. She was damn near seventy years old.

* * *

Rose was no longer easy with names, but her eyes were good, and she was a careful driver, as she always had been. They gave her an excellent route of kindergartners. First, she would pick up the bus itself, at the station behind the gravel pits, over the double paths of train tracks. Then she would pick up the neighbor boy, who lived by the gas station near Rose's own house. Then she'd pick up the crying boy. Then she'd pick up the girl whose mother always dressed her in corduroy vests, then the boy who looked like Orson Welles, then the disgusted girl, then the humming boy, then the girl with all the Band-Aids. At the bridge by the Band-Aid girl's house, she would cross the river to the hill road. There, she'd pick up the black girl, the grateful-looking boy, the shoving boy, the other black girl, and the out-of-breath girl. Last stop was the absent boy.

Thirteen passengers. Twelve, if you didn't count the absent boy, as Rose tended not to.

But, on the particular morning that makes this story, the neighbor boy, the crying boy, and the corduroy vest girl were all absent. Rose thought, "Flu?" She kept on driving and found the Orson Welles boy and the disgusted girl and the humming boy absent, also, and she wondered, "Chicken pox?" After the bridge passed with no girl on it, and the whole hill road passed with no children near it, she thought with some humiliation, "Could today be Sunday?" She recalled, then, having seen no other bus drivers at the gravel pit station, nor any other school buses crossing the double paths of railroad tracks. She had not, in fact, noticed any other cars on the roads at all. Not that these were fast highways, but they were certainly used. And Rose thought lightly, "Armageddon?"

But she rode her route out to the end. It was a fine choice that she did, too, because there was someone at the bottom of the absent boy's driveway, after all. Two people, in fact, waiting for her. She stopped the bus, demonstrated the proper and legal flashing lights, cranked the door open, and let them in. They were two very old men, one short, one tall. It took them some trouble to get up the stairs.

"A ride for you gentlemen today?" she asked.

They sat in the seat just behind her own.

"It smells clean and decent in here, thank God," one of them said.

"I use a tub and tile cleaner," Rose answered. "Weekly."

The taller man said, "My sweet Rosie. You look terrific."

As a matter of fact, she did. She wore a hat and white gloves to work every day, as if she were driving those school children to church, or to some important picnic.

"You could be a first lady," the tall one went on. "You could have married a president."

She looked at him in the wide, easy reflection of her rearview mirror, and then gave a pretty little expression of surprise and recognition. She looked at the shorter man and made the expression again. And this is who they were: Tate Palinkus and Dane Ladd. Tate was the man who had knocked her up back in south Texas before the war. Dane had been an orderly whom she had often kissed and fondled during her recovery from childbirth, at the Oklahoma Institution for Unwed Mothers. Which was also before the war.

"Won't I be damned?" she said. "I sure never thought I'd see either of you two again. And right here in Minnesota. How nice."

Dane said, "Ain't this Tate Palinkus nothing but a Christless old bastard? He's just been telling me about getting you pregnant."

Tate said, "Rose, I did not know that you were pregnant at the time. I did not even hear about it until many years later, when I came around asking for you. That is the truth, Rose."

"Tate Palinkus," she said. "You big bugger."

Dane said, "Foolin' around on a fifteen-year-old girl. I guess that's about the worst thing I ever heard of."

"Dane Ladd," Rose smiled. "You big stinker."

"She was a hell of a pretty girl," Tate said, and Dane said, "You barely have to remind me of that."

Rose shifted her bus into a higher gear.

She said, "You two have surprised my face just about off my body."

"Don't lose that sweet face," Dane said. "Don't lose that sweet body."

They drove on. And, as it turned out, there was someone waiting at the end of the out-of-breath girl's driveway, leaning on the mailbox. Another very old man. Rose stopped and let him on.

"Precious," he called her, and he touched the brim of his hat. He was Jack Lance-Hainey, a deacon of the Presbyterian Church. He had once run an Oklahoma senatorial campaign. He used to take Rose out for picnics during the 1940s, with baskets full of his wife's real china and real silver. He had taught Rose how to climb on top of a man during sex, and how to pick up phones in hotel rooms and say, "This is Mrs. Lance-Hainey. Might you send me up a bottle of tonic for my terrible, terrible headache?"

Jack sat on the seat across the aisle from the other men, and put his hat beside him.

"Mr. Ladd," he nodded. "It's a beautiful morning."

"It is," Dane agreed. "What a fine country we live in."

"It is a fine country," Jack Lance-Hainey said, then added, "And good morning to you, Tate Palinkus, you fertile and lecherous old son-of-a-snake."

"I did not know she was pregnant at the time, Jack," Tate explained. "Not until years later. I would have happily married her."

And Rose said, under her breath, "Well, well, well . . . that *is* news, Mr. Palinkus."

Now she rode her abandoned bus route backward, and found it fully packed with all of her old lovers. She picked up every single one of them. At the house of the black girl, she picked up her Mississippi cousin Carl, who she had once met on an aunt's bed during a Thanksgiving gathering. By the shoving boy's mailbox, she found a small crowd of old men, waiting together. They were her postmen, out of uniform. They had once driven airy trucks and kept stacks of extra canvas bags in the back, for her to lay down on. She couldn't remember their names, but the other men on the bus seemed to know them well, and they greeted each other with professional politeness.

At the other black girl's house, she picked up two elderly veterans, who she remembered as enlisted men, their young scalps pink and shaved, their big ears tempting handles for tugging and guiding. The veterans sat behind Dane and Tate, and talked about the economy. One of them was missing an arm and one was missing a leg. The armless one punched Tate with his good arm and said, "You're just a lousy, no-good, knock-'em-up-and-leave'em old prick, aren't you?"

"He claims he didn't know that she was pregnant," Jack Lance-Hainey said, and the postmen all laughed in unison, in disbelief.

"I did not know she was pregnant at the time," Tate said patiently. "Not until years later."

"My God," Rose said. "I barely knew it myself."

"That baby got you that nice figure," Tate offered, and a shared murmur of endorsement at this thought passed throughout the bus.

At the grateful boy's house, she picked up a man so fat he had to reintroduce himself. He was her sister's first husband, he said, and Rose said, "Coach! You troublemaker!" He had been an elevator mechanic, who used to meet Rose in the shop at night to teach her how to trick shuffle a deck of cards and how to kiss with her eyes open.

"Those steps are lethal," he said, red-faced from the climb, and the one-legged veteran said, "Who you tellin', Coach?"

At the Band-Aid girl's house, she picked up the bartenders from three states whom she had fallen for, and at the humming boy's house, she picked up a highway patrolman she'd spent a night with in Oklahoma City, back when they were both young. He was with a shrimp fisherman and a man who used to drive fire engines. They let him on the bus first, because they thought he had rank.

"Ma'am," the highway patrolman called her, and smiled wide. Then he called Tate Palinkus a bad egg, a bad seed, a lowlife, a ruffian, and a dirtbag, for getting her pregnant, back when she was just a kid who didn't know a worthless son-of-a-bitch from a fruit bowl.

There was an Arizona circuit court judge waiting for her at the end of the disgusted girl's driveway, and he sat down with Jack Lance-Hainey in the front of the bus. He told Rose she still looked good enough to crawl up under his robe any day of the week.

She said, "Your honor, we are old people now."

He said, "You're a daisy, Rose."

She found Hank Spellman kicking rocks around the road in front of the Orson Welles boy's house. He got on the bus and the other men cheered, "Hank!" as if they were truly pleased to see him. Hank used to sell and install furnaces, and he had always been a popular man. He used to dance with Rose in her cellar, keeping time by tapping his hand on her hip. He used to slide his hands over her as they danced. He used to take big handfuls of her bottom and whisper to her, "If I'm ever missing and you need to find me, you can start looking for me right here on this ass."

Where the girl who always dressed in corduroy vests usually waited, there was a tall old man in a dark hat. He had been Rose's dentist. He'd had an indoor swimming pool and a maid, and the maid used to bring them towels and cocktails all night without comment. He carried a cane on the bus, and his glasses were as thick as slices of bread. He told Rose she was beautiful, and her figure was still a wonder.

Rose said, "Thank you very much. I've been lucky with my looks. The women in my family tend to age in one of two ways. Most of them either look like they smoked too many cigarettes or ate too many donuts."

"You look like you kissed too many boys," the elevator mechanic said.

"You could be a first lady," Dane said again, and Tate said thoughtfully, "You were my lady first."

There were four former Mexican busboys standing by the picket fence of the crying boy's house. They were old now, and identical, each one of them in a pressed white suit with handsome white hair and white mustaches.

"La Rubia," they called her in turn. Their English was no better than it had ever been, but the armless veteran had fought fascists in Spain, and he translated quite well.

This was the most crowded her bus had ever been. It was not a very large bus. It was just for kindergartners, and, to be honest, it was just for the morning class of kindergartners. Naturally, the bus company had given Rose an excellent route, but it was not such a strenuous one. She was generally finished by noon. She was damn near seventy, of course, and although she was certainly not a weak woman, not a senile woman, she did get tired. So they had only given her those thirteen children close to her own house. She was doing a wonderful job, a truly excellent job. Everyone agreed. She was a careful and polite driver. One of the better ones.

She rode her whole route that day, without seeing one of her children and without passing another car. She had decided, with some shame, that it might very well be Sunday. She had never made such a mistake before, and would not consider mentioning it to her old lovers, or they might think she was getting dim. So, she rode all the way to the very last stop, which was the house of the neighbor boy, who lived by the gas station near her own home. There was an old man waiting there, too, and he was a rather large man. He was actually her husband. The old men lovers, who seemed to know each other so beautifully, did not know Rose's husband at all. They were quiet and respectful as he got on the bus, and Rose cranked the door shut behind him and said, "Gentlemen? I'd like you to meet my husband."

And the look on her husband's face was the look of a man at a welcome surprise party. He leaned down to kiss her on the forehead, and he was the first of the men who had touched her that day. He said, "My sweet little puppy of a Rose." She kissed his cheek, which was musky, sheepy, and familiar.

She drove on. He stepped down the aisle of the bus that rocked like a boat, and he was the guest of honor. The old men lovers introduced themselves, and after each introduction, Rose's husband said, "Ah, yes, of course, how nice to meet you," keeping his left hand on his heart in wonder and pleasure. She watched in the wide, easy reflection of her rearview mirror, as they patted his back and grinned. The veterans saluted him, and the highway patrolman saluted him, and Jack Lance-Hainey kissed his hand. Tate Palinkus apologized for getting Rose pregnant when she was just a south Texas kid, and the white-haired Mexican busboys struggled with their English greetings. The circuit court judge said that he did not mind speaking for everyone by saying how simply delighted he was to congratulate Rose and her husband on their long and honest marriage.

Rose kept on driving. Soon, she was at the double paths of railroad tracks that came right before the gravel pit bus station. She stopped the small bus then, because she noticed that trains were coming from both directions. Her husband and her old men lovers pulled down the windows of the bus and leaned out like kindergartners, watching. The trains were painted bright like wooden children's toys, and stenciled on the sides of each boxcar in block letters were the freight contents: APPLES, BLANKETS, CANDY, DIAMONDS, EXPLOSIVES, FABRIC, GRAVY, HAIRCUTS—a continuing, alphabetical account of a life's ingredients.

They watched this for a long time. But those boxcars were moving slowly, and repeating themselves in new, foreign alphabets. So the old men lovers became bored, finally, and pulled up the windows of Rose's bus for some quietness. They rested and waited, stuck as they were before those two lazy trains. And Rose, who had been up early that morning, took the key out of the ignition, took off her hat and gloves, and went to sleep. Her husband sat in the stairwell of the bus, his big hand on her knee, warm as all mercy. The old men lovers talked about him among themselves, fascinated. They whispered low to each other, but she could hear some pieces of words. "Hush," she kept hearing them say, and "him" and "she" and "and." Murmured together, those pieces of words made a sound just like the whole word "husband." That's the word she was hearing, in any case, as she dozed on the bus, with all of her old men together and behind her and so pleased just to see her again.

––––––––––––

Elizabeth Gilbert's fiction has appeared in *Esquire, Ploughshares, The Mississippi Review, The Paris Review* and *GQ*. She received *The Paris Review*'s 1996 New Discovery Award for her story, "The Famous Torn and Restored Lit Cigarette Trick." Gilbert's first collection of short stories, *Pilgrims,* is forthcoming from Houghton Mifflin. Gilbert is also a staff writer at *Spin* magazine and is currently at work on a novel.

"*The Finest Wife*" began taking shape after a late-night phone call from an old friend who had just met his birth-mother for the first time. Like Rose, my friend's biological mother was a Texas teenager who had won a beauty pageant in the early months of a secret pregnancy. The story developed very easily from that point, and—as a true love story—it was a joy to write. I appreciate this story very much for its having been born so painlessly and for not giving me any trouble as it grew up.

At the time that I wrote "The Finest Wife," I was on the verge of getting married myself, and was nurturing some pretty warm feelings about husbands in general. And so it is that Rose's husband is such a good guy, such a comfort of a character.

The Mexican busboys are embellishments on a customer I used to know, back when I was a waitress in Philadelphia, who always called me "La Rubia." The happy Minnesota ending is a nod to my happy Minnesota mother. Everything else is made up.

Lucy Hochman

SIMPLER COMPONENTS

(from *Mid-American Review*)

I. BLOOD AND GUTS

Inside, my mother made a series of autumnal blunders, frying the pies, pouring boiled milk on the frozen pipes. I emptied my thoughts into a bucket a mile away, and scrambled around in the woods for tinder.

I blew on my supper and ate it while she mopped the kitchen with glue. I coaxed her into her snowsuit for the showdown. She was not normally so nervous, nor I so attentive. It was a bitch being quiet people. It doesn't matter what you do.

We trudged to our nearest neighbor's, balancing on the crusty snow or falling through. We bruised our shins and our noses ran. We were having problems with the neighbor. We wanted to fix it over hot toddies. Go away, we'd say, it's too hard, messy, eventually unkind. He wasn't home.

We took the tractor route back, animals crouched in the trees, and I thought I saw a piece of fire in a tree but it was a star. My mother's flashlight bounded ahead. Soon it found a carcass, the neighbor's old dog Muff, split down his belly from an impact, his ribs open like double doors. I knelt, wallowed, tried to replace the spilled innards. My mother put some in her jacket pockets.

This is why we stay in the woods. We suffer our respective natures with gumption. My mother concocts theatricality. Occurrences reply to my tidy life.

II. A REPRIMAND FOR AFFECTION

Old milk jug hands is trying to lace her boots again.

I let her work at it because I know she will grow tired and I know she will let me help her at the moment she finds it frustrating. Then she will go outside and feed animals all day.

"A barnacle has the largest penis-to-body ratio of any documented life-form," I tell her, because I like to keep her informed. It is difficult to do anything with milk jugs for hands. I cannot think what other point there might be to this experiment.

My mother says someone is going to slice the skin between her fingers. She says her brother did that to a frog and someone is going to do it to her, sooner or later.

She says my father lived first by the alphabet, announcing, berating, cajoling, and so on, then by numbers, one foot out of bed and then two, three minutes with the brushing of teeth, four items of clothing (socks, shirt, undies, slacks) then, as he grew older, according to one body part at a time.

"Finally one day I found he'd been trying to hang himself. I could tell by the ropes around his neck, and there he was, feet in the air, humping nothing, as usual." She is not cruel and not crazy. In fact, I am sure it is all metaphorically speaking.

III. LIFE IN A BOX

Convinced as I am of her ineptitude, I sit my mother on a kitchen chair and make her watch television while I soak and scrub her feet. First I have the water cold in case she has been near hypothermia. Then I add boiling water from the kettle and Epsom salts to draw swelling.

I scrub her feet with straw-bristled horse brushes and then pumice. I think she's been climbing the chimney again. I think the aged color her skin has taken is from soot, and I clean a whole layer away.

Onion and more onion beneath, seven layers of it are there; fat and springy with juice at her heel and the undersides of her big coarse toes, and transparent toward her arch and ankle.

She says, "My family was so full of money that they could turn entire seasons into verbs." "What do you want?" I say, defensive. "A cloned experience? This is okay," I say. "What we are. Everyone wants this. A good kitchen."

She decides she must get her feet out of the tub and make prints on the floor, and she does. She walks out a garden of footprints, even dunks her feet in the tub as they dry. She makes the garden with flowers, vegetables, and insects, and then she stamps out a box-frame around it, complete with wood-grain and diagonal joints at the corners.

Exasperated, I fix my eyes on a puddle and watch it disappear. Down it goes, into the plank floor, and up into the air. By the time it is gone, she has opened the oven door and is curled in front of it, sleeping.

The television hums and drums. I look at it in order to catch up with people and the way lives go. I look at the lives, other people's obsessions, their fruit canning companies and sexual fetishes, the consistencies or accumulating idiosyncrasies which define their characters, and I know what will happen in my life. I will fixate on a desire for my own box as I clean my mother's, and then I will receive a reprimand for my affection. Everyone will bump along our property lines and we will continue to be the everyone of whom I speak.

IV. OTHER PEOPLE'S OBSESSIONS

Having decided her personality, I turned my mother's routine actions into something I could understand. If she put down her fork and reached across the table for salt, I forgot the fork and the salt, and saw only the area of space cut by her motion. If she buttoned her shirt, I saw only her hands like dying spiders in the air.

In this way, my mother could seem to operate in pantomime, moving her hands and exaggerating her facial expressions as if searching for a right word which never surfaced. I took each silent gesture she made and isolated it. Then, I took each conjured notion to be a microcosm of a great profundity.

After all, some people collect pig icons, go bargain hunting, search for long lost brothers, study obscure bugs, or bury money.

We strapped ourselves into the truck and bumped toward the feed store. Here, on the edge of the state, people in trucks wave to other trucks for an instant reminder of community. When cows get out, we know whose they are. The neighbors get together because the Wilsons are out of town. We push the cows back off the road and seal the fence.

My mother was one of the children who rode luxury ocean liners from California to Hawaii to mark off the seasons, bunny hopping around the deck with libertines.

Years ago, I knew a skinhead named Uncle.

The older she grows, the more her body sneers at her. Moment to moment she must behave spinelessly, blindly, or spleenlessly, and many of her gestures are instigated by a desire to avoid pain.

"Go ahead and hate it, but don't let it stop you from doing what you love," I say, which is what Uncle said about heroin.

The feed store was an attachment to a convenience store. Besides feed, you could buy rawhide for your boots, beer and cigarettes, screwdrivers and crowbars, wire fencing, fluorescent ribbon, baseball caps, and down vests, and chewing gum, canned beans, and fresh onions.

My mother has taken to waving indiscriminately—at dogs, fences, trees, and the spaces between. "Everything has led to the place where you are," I say to make sense of it, which is a fact, and specifically not an affirmation of destiny.

V. THE EVERYONE OF WHOM WE SPEAK

Summer, and the squash is over our heads as it was when I was a child. The older we get, the higher the squash. We are fine gardeners. We eat and throw the scrapings in a heap outside and the next year . . . it goes to show.

We actually hold pieces of manure to the sun, imagining the lives represented there. It's all terribly warm, the huge leaves like stained glass, the yellow tiger spiders.

This is death: a cessation of spontaneous function, unresponsiveness to an isoelectronic electroencephalogram in the absence of hypothermia or intoxication by central nervous system depressance, or there's somatic death which is good as death, or neocortical death which is death, or there's a persistent vegetative state. I record none of this in protest. It's simply that everyone wants to know.

At night, we collect cabbage worms and put them in our jacket pockets, these little gray toes. Each clumsy attribute we employ while doing so should be recorded, but here, our knees, our bumpy backs, the cricks in our necks and hips, these should be enough for everyone.

Underground, eubacteria, prosthecate bacteria, budding bacteria, gliding bacteria, filamentous bacteria, spirochetes, rickettsiae, chlamydiae, mycoplasma, and blue-green algae float in the dirt with everything, breaking it into simpler components.

VI. A GOOD DAY

My mother is washing the dishes, and handily. She has let the horses out of their paddocks and they are grazing on the lawn, feeling this moment as hard as they can, because they are not often allowed to graze the yard.

My mother has also done the bills, found the misplaced two in her checkbook, and written a letter to the governor. All around, a smooth five-dollar wine, a well-risen cake, no lines at the grocery, a rare day, one so unrumpled it is a wonder there is time to notice how easy it has been to travel from one end of it to the other.

The sound of the water and the dishes, the way I have a cup of tea and am watching her wash without guilt that I'm not drying, the way I notice the silence more each time I hear a sound, all of this is a fine, fine state.

My mother is not herself after all, I think, and the thought lands immediately in the past, a car in the lane next to me, slamming its brakes. For the moment, I think I have ceased to summarize her.

I tell her how my day has been, now that I know hers.

I say, "Mother, I think I have ceased to summarize you," and knowing the correct responses, "have you, now?" "really?" and "good," she says, instead, "Your day *was* fine, now, wasn't it?"

I tell her how lovely the horses look in the yard, how their lips are frothy and green, how the old gelding is teaching the filly to scratch his withers for him, how I long to break through the wall in front of the sink and give her the window she's always wanted there.

The silence was fine—the lack of my voice or the voice of another—and I know that if I continue to speak, some recognition of difficulty will materialize, as if difficulty is produced from the interaction of my voice with the air it encounters.

It comes back to this condition. Sometimes I want to speak, and so I continue.

Lucy Hochman has lived in North Carolina for thirteen years. She attended Duke University and Brown University and has published stories in *Mid-American Review, North American Review,* and *Iowa Review.* Her work has been anthologized in *25 and Under: Fiction, Transgressions,* and *Chick-Lit 2.* She now teaches at Duke.

I keep lists of ideas, images, and words I'm thinking about, and sentences and scenes I've cut from stories but still like. When I'm not working well, I organize the lists according to what seems to go together. Usually, it's an exercise in figuring out what I seem to care about, as well as a form of busy-work—a way to trick myself into thinking I'm writing when I'm having trouble. This story is constructed almost entirely from those lists. I arranged the lines and wrote a few in between.

It's as autobiographical as I've ever been. The place is where I was living. The feelings toward the place and the mother are like what I was feeling. There wasn't any heat that winter and we kept having chimney fires. I wrote the story over six months (which is why, I suppose, the seasons changed) — a "space between" story in the sense that I worked on it between other stories, because that time in my life felt between other times and because the community is an in-between place, geographically and ideologically.

So the narrator is this one person living here, looking at the world. There's the vast one, and it's seeming desperate and inept. But then there's the world up close, the "neighbors," the garden, animals, all easy to see with simple specificity.

Gene Able

MARRYING AUNT SADIE

(from *Yemassee*)

G randpa was fond of turnip greens and kept a sharp eye on their preparation if he happened to be in the kitchen at the time. Had to be done just right, he avowed. But on this night he'd come in a little late and the turnips were already simmering. He'd been down in the Salkehatchie River Swamp fishing. He kicked off his boots on the breezeway—Grandma didn't like swamp mud tracked into her kitchen—and made straight to the stove. "Sadie, you didn't put sugar in these turnips, did you?" He aimed a scowl at her because he didn't trust her in the kitchen. Once he threw a whole batch of her biscuits out into the yard, then told Junie and me to gather them up and bury them because he didn't want the dogs choking on them.

"Daddy, I haven't been near those greens," Aunt Sadie said. She was jiggling little Nickolas on her lap in an effort to stop his whimpering.

Grandpa never sat at the table during dinner. He would heap food upon his plate straight out of the pots on the woodburning stove and, while eating and talking, would walk around the big room that was both kitchen and everyday dining room. The real dining room was the first room forward past the breezeway that connected the kitchen and a storeroom with the rest of the house. Houses were built like that back then because fires almost always started in kitchens, so even if the house could not be saved the family had a reasonable chance to get out alive. The dining room was the least-used room in the house, although it was opened up when there were big family doings and too many people to be fed at the kitchen table.

Like the time when Grandpa staked out the henhouse trying to catch a bandit fox. He loosed both barrels of his shotgun and killed the fox and five of Grandma's best laying hens. The next Sunday both the kitchen and dining room were filled with family and neighbors who came to sample Grandma's cooking and celebrate Grandpa's marksmanship. "Arie," great-uncle Josh said to Grandma, "seems like you'd been better off letting that fox have a hen now and then 'stead of letting Lige guard the henhouse." Grandpa joined in the laughter at his own expense and said if he wasn't such a good shot he probably would have maimed another seven or eight chickens. "I had to scatter 'em with the first shot and then shoot the fox," he said.

Grandpa strolled around the kitchen and tentatively tasted the greens out of the pot before scooping some onto his plate. "Who made this cornbread?" he said as he took a square off the platter on the table. "I helped," said Junie, who was nine, a year older than me. Her way of helping was that she got to stir the batter and put the pan in the oven.

Grandpa wanted to know where the boys were and Grandma told him she hadn't seen either of them since breakfast. "Doc is probably working over at the picture show since it's Friday night. No telling where Judge is. Off carousing, I reckon."

Doc and Judge were the only two Rowell sons at home. The older sons, Eli (named after Grandpa, whose real name was Elijah) and Brabham, were still in the Army. I barely remembered them since I was just a toddler when they went off to the war. Besides my mother, who was the oldest daughter, and Aunt Sadie, there was Aunt Annabel who was married to a well-respected grocer who was about fifteen years her elder. Grandpa had raised another family of five—he liked to say that the Lord said go out and replenish the earth, so he was doing his part—before he married Grandma. Except for Uncle Foster, who was the town magistrate, the rest of his first crop of children were scattered around the state.

Little Nickolas's whimpering was getting louder. "Sadie, take that baby in the other room and give him some tit," Grandpa said.

"Lige, hold your tongue! There's children at this table," Grandma said irritably.

"They know what tits are for," Grandpa replied. "A woman's tits ain't no different than them cow tits they see you pulling on all the time, 'cept there ain't but two on a woman." He always wanted to have the last word.

"He's been fed, Daddy," Aunt Sadie said. "He's just a little fussy. Soon as I finish my dinner I'll see if I can get him to sleep. And I don't appreciate being compared to old Brenda."

"Lige, I declare!" Grandma said. That ended the discussion. When Grandma *declared* that *was* the last word.

Aunt Sadie leaned over to my oldest sister, Quincie, and whispered just loud enough so everybody at the table could hear, "Maybe I ought to squirt some of my milk in his coffee in the morning since he thinks I'm a cow."

Quincie almost fell out of her chair and spit crumbs of food halfway across the table.

"Mind your manners, young lady," Grandma said, but she was having a hard time keeping a smile from pulling at the corners of her mouth.

Grandpa shoveled food into his mouth, smacking his lips over the fried squash and muttering about the grits being overcooked, probably because he was pretty sure Aunt Sadie was responsible for the latter. Grandpa had never forgiven Aunt Sadie for leaving home, going into the Women's Army Corps and staying in Washington for a year after the war ended while she went to school to learn how to be a legal secretary. What was worse, she came home with an infant child and no husband. No amount of interrogation could get her to reveal anything about the man who had fathered her child. Grandpa ranted and raved for weeks about finding out who the no-account was so he could send Judge off to track him down and beat the hide off him for abandoning his wife and child. Quincie said she heard Grandma saying to Aunt Sadie that Grandpa was afraid people were going to think Aunt Sadie was a loose woman. Quincie thought Grandma was trying to find out if Aunt Sadie really had a husband. Junie and I both wondered aloud how Aunt Sadie could have a baby without having a husband. Quincie, who was twelve and supposed herself to be somewhat sophisticated, just rolled her eyes at the heavens.

Grandpa walked around the table and stroked Junie on the head. "Mighty good cornbread," he said. He asked Quincie something about school, then walked past me without saying a word. I wondered if I was invisible or if he just didn't care for grandsons. The only time I recall him talking to me much, until after the incident with Aunt Sadie and Delaney Richards, was when he woke me up one night and got me to help him hide a batch of peach wine he had just run off. He had a tendency to get to nipping on the brew while he was bottling it and would forget which stumps and hollow trees in the wildwood, where Grandma never ventured because she was scared of snakes, he had stashed them.

I was not quite sure if Grandpa even knew who I was since he never called me anything but "boy." Once I was talking to him about my mother and wondering when she was going to come to Barnwell and take my sisters and me back to our home down in Jasper County. So I said, "You know? Ella Mae." Grandpa stared at me for a few seconds and replied: "Damn, boy, I know who your mama is."

I slept on a cot in a room I shared with Judge and Doc. I didn't mind because they were always telling entertaining stories, although I didn't understand the ones they told about girls they knew. Judge sometimes brought Chief home with him and let him sleep in the room with us. Chief was a big redbone hound who wandered around town square for a couple of weeks before the police department, where Judge worked as a part-time patrolman, adopted him. Grandma didn't like having him in the house, so somebody would have to get up before the crack of dawn when she first started stirring in the kitchen and put him out. That somebody was usually me. Sometimes Judge and Doc would wrestle one another over some point of disagreement that usually mystified me, and they were always playing pranks on one another. When Grandma got really peeved at Judge for staying out until the morning hours she would lock the doors. One time when she did that, Judge tried climbing into the bedroom window, but Doc, pretending he thought Judge was a house-breaker, kicked him in the chest with both feet and caused him to fall out of the window, which in that old house was quite a distance from the ground. Judge's cursing wakened Grandma and she gave him a piece of her mind for keeping indecent hours.

After she got little Nickolas tucked in, Aunt Sadie read an Uncle Remus story to Junie and me. Following the reading, Aunt Sadie would always have coffee with Grandma, then she would go check on Quincie and Junie, who slept in the same room, and then me. I anticipated those few moments when Aunt Sadie would come into my room, hug me and caress my cheeks with a cool hand. Then she would give me two kisses, one for my mother and one for herself. This night when she came in, she sat on the bed and talked with me for a while, just incidental things. I didn't want her to leave and was casting about for something to say that would detain her for a little longer. Finally, just as she was gathering herself to go, I blurted, "Aunt Sadie, I don't think your tits look like cow tits."

She smiled. "I don't think so either, Caleb, but your Grandma would take the broomstick to you and me both if she knew we were having a conversation about breasts, which is what they're called in polite society." She gave my head a pat and left. I went to sleep thinking about the time I saw Aunt Sadie remove the clothing from around a plump, white breast so Nickolas could attach his greedy mouth to the roseate nipple. I thought there wasn't much difference in the way Nickolas and Brenda's calf went after their dinner.

* * *

The next morning Aunt Annabel came in her husband's new 1947 Buick Roadmaster to pick up Grandma, Aunt Sadie, and the girls to go to the grocery store. Grandpa was working in the garden, and I wanted to stay because Doc, who drove a delivery route for the ice house in the daytime, said he would stop by and help me make a slingshot. I had found a blown-out innertube and the tongue of an old shoe and just needed a good Y-brace and a little expert assistance. I felt like it was going to be an exciting day, but I didn't know how exciting until Delaney Richards showed up.

I was sitting in the crook of the willow tree when he walked up into the yard. He was wearing an old Army field jacket and looked as if he had about two days worth of stubble on his cheeks. I guess he was handsome in a rough sort of way. He stopped under the tree and looked up at me. "Hey, boy," he said. "Is this the Rowell place?"

I said it was.

"Is Sadie Rowell here?"

I told him she had gone to the A&P with Grandma and Aunt Annabel, and, in anticipation of his next question, I didn't know when she'd be back. Then he started asking questions about Aunt Sadie, things like did she have a job and did she have a beau. I told him she didn't have either one because she had a little baby she had to look after. These questions were making me nervous, but then Grandpa came walking around the corner of the house with a hoe in his hand.

The stranger walked up to Grandpa and held out his hand. "Mr. Howell, I'm Delaney Richards," he said.

"Lige Rowell," Grandpa said and briefly shook the proffered hand. "What can I do for you, son?"

"Well, I was hoping to get to see Sadie, but the boy there says she's not at home."

Grandpa eyed Delaney Richards a little suspiciously. "How is it that you know my daughter, son?"

Delaney dropped his eyes as if he'd been caught at some mischief. Finally, he said. "Washington, sir. I knew Sadie in Washington. Right after the war. We were attached to the same unit for a while."

"You were in the WACs'?" Grandpa said.

Delaney laughed, a short chuckle. "No, sir. I was in the Fourth Army but I was attached to the Washington Garrison where Sadie worked in the judge adjutant's office."

"I got two boys in the Army," Grandpa said. "Eli's up at Fort Jackson. He was wounded at Pelipu. The other one, Brab, is still in the Philippines. I served with Teddy Roosevelt myself. Where did you see action?"

Delaney cleared his throat. "I didn't, sir. Never went overseas. I was a clerk typist. Same as Sadie."

I could tell Grandpa didn't like the sound of that, a man doing woman's work. Then I thought I saw a light come on in Grandpa's eyes. "Did you know Sadie's husband?"

Delaney was looking more uncomfortable by the minute. "No, sir," he said.

Grandpa was quiet for a moment. Then he gathered himself to his full height, which was considerable, and poked Delaney with the end of the hoe. "You the one that gave Sadie that baby, ain't you?"

Delaney said exactly the wrong thing next. He should have cut and run, but instead mumbled, "Yes, sir, that was me."

Grandpa made a looping swing with the hoe handle, which caught Delaney across the back and shoulders just as he was turning away from the blow. The hoe handle cracked on impact and Delaney went to his knees. Then he got up and charged Grandpa, knocking him down and crawling on top of him. I don't remember all of what happened next, but apparently I either fell or jumped out of the willow tree. Then I had one end of the busted hoe handle and was whacking Delaney Richards across the back with it while he was trying to choke Grandpa. I whacked on until two strong hands pulled me away. With all the fighting going on I wasn't aware that Doc had just pulled up in the ice truck. Judge was with him, and they subdued Delaney in short order. Judge gave him a bloody nose, then clamped some handcuffs on him. Grandpa was all right, just burning mad and rubbing at his neck. "This fellow is the one that ran out on Sadie," he told Judge and Doc.

I thought Judge was going to hit Delaney again, but Doc stopped him and asked Delaney if he had anything to say.

Delaney was pressing his bleeding nose against his shirt sleeve and breathing kind of funny. But presently he found his voice and said, "We wasn't married. We kind of rushed things and she got pregnant. I wanted to get married but she didn't. She's the one who left, not me. That's why I came down here, to see Sadie and try to get her to marry me."

Judge and Doc looked at Grandpa. "Daddy, did he tell you this story?" Judge said.

"No, he didn't," Grandpa said sharply. "I laid into him with the hoe handle after he told me he gave Sadie that baby. Then he jumped on me. There wasn't time for much conversation at that point."

"What are we going to do with him now?" asked Doc.

"You boys take him down to the jailhouse and lock him up."

"But, Daddy, you hit him first," Doc said.

"Hell with that," said Judge. "He was trespassing and assaulted Daddy. Besides what he did to Sadie." He glared at Delaney. "Around here we don't go in for that stuff." When I got older, I would laugh when I remembered Judge saying that and the stories he and Doc swapped about the girls they chased. I supposed it was all right to do what Delaney did as long as it was somebody else's sister. Doc and Judge both jilted their share of women.

Before they left, Doc came over and tousled my hair. "Way to go, tiger," he said with a grin. "You swing a mean hoe handle."

We didn't get around to making my slingshot that day.

Supper was a little strained that evening. Aunt Sadie stayed in her room, and Grandpa prowled around the kitchen with a mad look on his face. The house had been the site of a pitched battle between Grandpa and Aunt Sadie for most of the afternoon. Quincie and Junie and I were banished and told to go play. We went straight to our favorite listening post under the house by the chimney and eavesdropped. Grandpa harangued at Aunt Sadie for being a loose woman and asked her if it was true what Delaney said about her refusing to get married. She yelled back at Grandpa and told him the world wasn't the same as it was back in the dark ages when he grew up. "A woman doesn't have to marry a miserable man just because he makes her pregnant," she said. I asked Quincie what that word meant, seeing as how it was the second time in one day that I'd heard it. "It means making a baby," Quincie whispered, then told me to hush.

Grandpa called Aunt Sadie a name I had heard Doc and Judge use a couple of times and somehow knew it wasn't a flattering thing to call a woman. Aunt Sadie busted out crying and then Grandma took matters in hand. "Lige Rowell, you can be the biggest horse's ass the good Lord ever made," she said. I was shocked to hear my grandmother call anybody a horse's ass, especially Grandpa. "You treated all three of your daughters like little princesses until their hips and bosoms grew, and then you started acting like they were put on this earth to do your bidding. The Lord didn't make women to be slaves to the men in their family like you think. You didn't want these girls to ever grow up. That's what drove Ella Mae out of this house to get married at sixteen to a man she barely knew. Now she's getting a divorce, and it's as much your fault as anybody else's. I want you to get out of this house and leave Sadie alone. Go on, get out! Go down to the jailhouse and turn that man loose, tell him to go to Florida or go to hell, whichever is closest. And don't come back until suppertime."

Quincie's eyes were as big as sunflowers. "What's wrong?" Junie said. "What did Grandma mean about Mama getting whatever that was? Is she sick?"

Quincie scurried out from under the house and ran toward the garden. Then she came back to us, her face flushed and her eyes wet. "It means Mama and Daddy won't be married anymore," she said. "That's what divorce means."

I lay on my cot that night figuring that since Aunt Sadie didn't read us a story she wouldn't come to say goodnight. I thought about the times Mama and Daddy came to Barnwell to visit us, they just didn't come at the same time. Mama always said Daddy was away on a construction job, and I never doubted that. He was hardly ever home down in Gopher Hill, having worked on government projects all through the war and even after it ended. He came twice during the nine or ten months we had been living in Barnwell and both times said he was just passing through on his way to a job in Aiken or Cheraw or someplace upstate.

My eyelids had just started drooping when Aunt Sadie came in. She made me scoot over and lay down beside me. "Quite a day, huh Caleb?" she said. "You were some hero today."

"I was scared," I said. "And pretty mad, too."

"Brave, too," she said.

"Aunt Sadie? Why didn't you marry Delaney Richards?"

"Because he was no good," she said. "How'd he look to you?"

"Kind of like a bum."

She laughed and stroked my face. "Such an observant boy. Well, he was a bum, although I thought he was the cat's meow for a while. I made one mistake with him, and I didn't see any sense in making another one by marrying him."

"Then why is Grandpa so mad?"

"Didn't you hear Grandma? Because he's a horse's ass. He thinks because I'm not married and have a baby it will bring shame on the family. I don't blame him too much; that's just the way he is. He doesn't understand that it's wrong to marry someone you don't love, even if it means people will think and say bad things about you." She sighed. "I thought I could come home and stay here until Nickolas is weaned, then get a job in a law office and maybe meet a nice man and fall in love. You know—live happily ever after."

"Like Aunt Annabel?"

"Kind of like that. But somebody a little handsomer than your Uncle Martin."

"But not like Mama?"

She propped up on her elbow and gazed at me fondly. "Quincie told me what you all heard. Whether or not your mama and daddy love each other anymore doesn't mean they don't love their children. This is hard for them, too. Your mama didn't want you children to worry; that's why she didn't tell you about it. But you know what I'm going to do tomorrow?"

I shook my head.

"I'm going to write my sister, your mother, a letter and tell her to come up here and explain all this to you and Quincie and Junie."

My mother never did come up and explain anything about the divorce to my sisters and me. When she did come at the end of the summer, she brought a new husband, a man we had never seen or heard of before. But that's another story. I slept well that night after Aunt Sadie left and dreamed about marrying her myself when I grew up.

The next day Uncle Foster's long green Oldsmobile pulled up in the yard. Judge, Doc, and Delaney Richards got out of the car and followed him into the house. Then Grandpa came out and called for Quincie. All three of us appeared on the front porch in a matter of seconds—we had not been out of earshot all day. "You children come on into the living room. We got some family business and your Aunt Sadie wants you there," he said.

We exchanged puzzled glances and followed Grandpa inside. Aunt Sadie was sitting on the divan wearing her Sunday dress, Grandma and Aunt Annabel standing beside her. Judge and Doc were standing by the fireplace with Delaney Richards sandwiched between them like he was their prisoner. He was wearing a hang-dog look, a cheap suit that didn't fit him, and a bandage over his nose. "You children sit there on the divan by your aunt and don't say anything," Grandpa said. "Go ahead, Foster."

Uncle Foster cleared his throat and took some papers out of a big brown envelope. "This here is a marriage certificate," he said. My heart jumped into my throat. Aunt Sadie looked over and gave the girls and me a quick smile. Uncle Foster handed the paper to her, and she signed it. Then he took it to Delaney who did the same. "The date on this marriage certificate is April Second, Nineteen Forty-Six. It is witnessed by Ariel Creech Rowell and Elijah Collins Rowell," Uncle Foster said in his officious voice.

He pulled another set of papers out of the envelope. "This is a petition for divorce filed, it says here on May Seventeenth, Nineteen Forty-Seven on the grounds that the husband . . ."

"On the grounds of him being a no-good sonofabitch," Grandpa interrupted. "A shiftless womanizer who came down here pretending he was wanting to marry Sadie when all he really wanted was to get some money either from her or me."

"That's enough, Lige," Grandma said. "Let Foster get on with this."

"As I was saying," Uncle Foster continued, "on the grounds of desertion on the part of the husband since desertion and cruelty are the only grounds recognized in the state of South Carolina."

Uncle Foster passed around the petition papers for Aunt Sadie to sign and for Aunt Annabel and Doc to witness. He instructed them all that they were swearing and asserting that they had knowledge of the continuous period of a year's separation between the parties. Then he passed a divorce decree around to be signed by the principals. "This is a decree of divorcement that will be filed in the county courthouse today, July Seventeenth, Nineteen Forty-Seven. This marriage is now null and void." I didn't know what null and void meant, but I had been in possession of the definition of divorce for more than a day. My dream was still alive. Of course, only three years down the road I would meet a red-haired, green-eyed girl named Lacey Anne Jordan who would help me put my infatuation with Aunt Sadie in a waning light.

Uncle Foster fixed Delaney with a harsh look and handed him an envelope. "In here, Mr. Richards, is a bus ticket for Lake City,

Florida, and thirty-five dollars in cash. I have learned from the
Continental Timber Company, which has holdings in both South
Carolina and Florida, that there are jobs in the pulp industry in the
Lake City area. I recommend that you make application when you
arrive. A job will be available to you if you do. Judge here is going
to escort you to the Trailways bus station. If you're ever seen in
Winton County again, you will be arrested for disturbing the peace
because your mere presence in the county will greatly disturb the
peace of mind of this family."

Uncle Foster became my hero that day. Grandpa took the credit
for being the instigator of the whole scheme, but it had been
Uncle Foster who devised and refined the plan to save Aunt
Sadie's good name and the family's honor. When I think back on
that day I marvel that Uncle Foster, who was a magistrate and not
a lawyer or a judge, could bend the law to his own will and never
have it questioned. But that's the way the law worked in Winton
County. As for Grandpa, it must have really rankled him to have
to part with thirty-five dollars to get rid of Delaney Richards, but
he was so taken with the whole adventure that he never said a
word about it.

Grandma announced that dinner soon would be ready and that
we would all sit down in the dining room as soon as Judge
returned from his mission. Grandpa sat at the head of the table.
"Who made these biscuits?" he said early on in the meal.

"I did, Daddy," Aunt Sadie said with an impish smile, "and Junie
helped."

"Real fine biscuits," Grandpa said, and he actually looked at me
and winked, although I didn' t see him take another bite out of
that biscuit. Later in the afternoon he said to me, "Boy, I want you
to come down to the swamp and help me check my trot-lines."

So off we went down the road and through the cornfield and
along a trail into the Salkehatchie River Swamp. Grandpa told me
a story about the time he killed two rabbits with one shot. "They
were sittin' each on a different side of a sharp-edged rock," he said.
"I couldn't make up my mind which one to shoot, so I aimed at

the edge of the rock, fired off a round and split the bullet into two pieces that ricocheted and killed both rabbits."

It was the first of many excursions into the swamp that I would make with Grandpa, almost always coming back with two or three of Grandpa's slimy bounty draped over my shoulder. That afternoon as we were returning home with our catch, I screwed up my courage to say something that had been on my mind for a good while. "Grandpa? My name is Caleb."

Without altering his stride, Grandpa said, "Damn, boy, I know what your name is."

———————

Gene Able is a native of the South Carolina Low Country and works as a freelance writer and writing teacher. He is the author of three books of nonfiction and numerous short stories.

"*Marrying Aunt Sadie*" is based on a family mystery. Since my mother and my aunts begged ignorance of the particulars, I opted, after all the principals were deceased, to solve the mystery to my own liking. The setting is my maternal grandparents' home in Barnwell, South Carolina, where I spent the happiest year of my boyhood exploring and being enchanted by the considerable storytelling talents of my grandparents, aunts, and uncles.*

Brad Vice

MOJO FARMER

(from *The Georgia Review*)

Mr. Tibby watches the dark field for the creatures with shiny eyes that come to feed off the garden. From his bedroom window he looks over the shoulder of a naked scarecrow to the feathers of young corn waiting to shoot into stalks. Rooted loosely in the ground are tendrils of purple hull peas squirming with potential. Moonlight glints off pie tins hanging from the stick arms of his scarecrow. They hang still. Their strings point straight into the earth as if gravity were magnified by heat.

Even in the middle of a dry spell, Tibby keeps his garden clean as a family plot, tidy as death itself. In the cool of every morning he rises to make his field immaculate. In the gleam of sunrise he beheads violet morning glories and nut grass. He unearths coffee weed from under runners and shakes the precious dirt out of the roots so it is not wasted on the intruder. Gardening is ruthless work, making way for the struggle of young runners and tommy toe tomatoes.

Today Tibby rises especially early, since before work there is ritual. He pulls a large trunk, painted red and laced with rotting leather, from under the bed. He opens it and fingers the contents, feeling his way through the inventory. A Bible held together only by a rubber band holds four hundred and seventy-two dollars among the pages of Acts.

240

Tibby, tall and lean, now kneels on the warped floor of his small house. Item by item, he accounts for flowers pressed in between the pages of a tattered hymnal, delicate petals of rose and spider lily. A shortbread cookie tin holds a sewing kit with fifty-seven needles sunk into a fabric tomato pincushion and assorted patches and thread. There are hunting trophies: squirrels' tails, rabbits' feet, even a beaver pelt with the hot scent of mold. In a cigar box lies his father's yellowing ivory straight razor. An envelope holds his children's baby teeth. At the bottom of it all is a wedding-ring quilt, a patchwork of vibrant colors filled with interlocking circles. He unfolds it and removes a book of home recipes buried inside. Both were gifts from his mother. The quilt was a wedding present. The book came much later.

Finding all in order, Tibby selects a jar of dirty marbles—a collection he had started after the last of his nine children had departed for town—most of them found in the gravel road leading up to his mailbox. He tosses it carefully onto the mattress. From the cookie tin he selects a palm-sized sewing square and pins it to the left breast of his T-shirt with one of the needles. A spool lands on the bed next. He seals the trunk with a lock of braided hair and shoves it back under the bed.

He hugs the bedpost and pulls himself onto the bed. His legs are numb as a sausage. He has to spend a full ten minutes rubbing them, every nerve buzzing with the sting of blood. The fruit jar of marbles jiggles as he rises to his feet, still holding on to the post.

Across from the bed stands a pale-green chiffarobe with glass onion knobs. Tibby looks for himself in the mirror on its left door, but weak moonlight won't bring him into perspective. There is only the shimmy of his dark hands, never steady, in the corner of the pane. When the feeling returns to his legs, he opens the wardrobe. Inside are his wife's faded gingham dresses, hanging like unburied ghosts waiting in line for a chance to fly out. Tibby runs his hand down the hem of the one on the far left. The airy touch of cotton and the sweet decay of the rotting marigolds on the floor of the chiffarobe preserve Dell in his mind.

It is only when Tibby is in Dell's closet that he remembers having been young. He has opened the door often to touch her clothes. He imagines how each dress would look if Dell were inside it, how it would cling to her thighs in the summer and fold about the knee. Her legs had been delicate and strong, like those of a deer, or even a slim young mule. And like a well-loved mule she was happy in hard work. She was proud when her fingers brushed and braided her children's hair, and she was content in the smell of cornmeal and tea cakes that filled her kitchen. But she was also happy in the heat of the field, and never more so than when plucking horned green tobacco worms from growing tomato vines.

He sighs to think back further, to when Dell's dress made a mystery out of her legs. Tibby smiles to remember his fat mama laughing at him every time he came to supper, love-starved to the bone. With snuff under the blanket of her thick lower lip, she would chuckle like she had never wanted for anything. Mama had whispered in his ear, loud so his father could hear her, "Don't worry, baby, Mama's got a recipe for every little thing." Charming Dell was the best thing that ever happened to him.

Tibby holds the dress up to his neck and smooths it over his belly as if sizing it in the mirror. His stomach pokes through the fabric. He squeezes the sag of his left breast as if trying to separate it from his thin torso. His chest aches.

An hour later Tibby has prepared and eaten a breakfast of eggs, buttered toast, sorghum, and coffee. The buckled linoleum floor has been swept, and he washes the dishes with Dell's frayed apron on. Feeling the kitchen is squared away, he spreads newspaper out on the kitchen table, then walks through the living room and out of the house. There is still no hint of the sun. The stars are just pinholes in a dark curtain.

The nest of cats living under the house is restless. Country cats are feral and tame all at once. More than twenty of them live under his house, and many are in heat. They walk as if on piano wire.

They smell of blood and urine. Tibby keeps them all in petting condition. The ones with milk still in their teats are the most affectionate; the others walk coy circles around him as he discards scraps.

Tibby picks up a young tabby. Her eyes are wide and bright as a surprised possum's. He runs his finger over the cat's chin and down her back. He lifts her by the scruff of the neck, takes her into his arms. She lets him rest his palm on the top of her head, and Tibby firmly snaps her neck.

Careful not to break her ribs, he splits the cat open and removes every organ but the heart. Tibby takes her back into the house and lays her on the newsprint-covered table. From the refrigerator he removes a Tupperware bowl filled with chilled flowers and stuffs her ribcage with dandelions, pink hibiscus, and the navels of black-eyed Susan. He spices the corpse with gingerroot, rubs fresh dillweed into her heart. With fishing line he stitches her from belly to throat. Then, carefully, he places her in the space between his T-shirt and overalls. Tibby holds her still next to his belly with his left hand; he cradles the fruit jar of marbles with his right. Dell's cotton dress is flung over his shoulder. A spade is waiting for him as he makes his way to the garden.

Tibby's heart is a treasure map inked with the secret graves of young cats and the fragile bones of birds. Even an occasional possum or woodchuck has come to rest warmly under the bed of his garden. He steps politely over every unmarked tomb. Only the formless scarecrow made of mildewed hay and gunny sacks keeps watch in the glint of dangling tins.

Tibby gently removes the stuffed cat from his belly and places her in between the rows of young corn with his children's marbles. The earth is loose and dry, no more than sand and iron ore before a rain. He digs a hole. The bones of his hand tingle, the flesh on his fingers feels like gloves. His yellowing T-shirt and the red quilting patch over his left breast are soaked in sweat. When he closes his eyes, he feels the lids pulse like drum skins.

Tibby has a vision for this field. The tomatoes will crawl lively in their cages, producing huge roses of Big Boys and Whoppers well into August. Soon cabbages will thicken with elastic leaves, and greedy pea vines will lick every inch of available soil. Right here, the tongues of this young corn will shoot into green soldiers hiding gold and silver. The roots will twist into the spiced flesh of this cat, sucking the marrow from her ribs and holding her safe with a woody fist.

The sun rises behind Tibby. Soon the cat has a thick mound of red dirt on top of her. Tibby knows that when the rain seeps into the earth, it will find this garden rich.

He approaches the scarecrow. Lumpy bats of hay make up its stomach and torso. Tibby makes an incision into the canvas bosom of the make-believe man. He punches his fist inside the hole and digs out a handful of damp hay, then fills the void with his children's marbles. He removes the red square from his T-shirt and uses it to patch up the wound. Then he robes the scarecrow in the dress, slitting open the back of the dress and sewing it together around the newly sexed scarecrow. She has an air of secrecy, is mute as the tubers he pushes into the earth in March. Her lips are stitched shut.

Tibby kneels down and folds his hands to pray. He asks for the clouds to gather and the winds to blow up for a long slow rain. A good rain will wash away the telltale scent of the dead cat and make the pie tins titter. He hugs the scarecrow for support, finding it hard to rise. Slowly Tibby's hands walk up the scarecrow's body. Although the sun has not yet cleared the horizon, Tibby feels it bearing down on him. Despite this, he is sure the rain clouds will come, so he will return to the house and lie down—just as soon as he gets back the feeling in his legs.

Still embracing the scarecrow, Tibby whispers to the side of her stuffed head. He speaks to her of children and grandchildren, of holidays, seasons, and the happenings of the year. He tells her his dream for the garden. He leaves her to watch over it, confident she will frighten off any mangy strays that would dare to dig up her sweet-smelling cat.

Brad Vice attended the University of Alabama. He is currently enrolled
in the graduate writing program at the University of Tennessee, where he
is at work on a collection of stories.

*T*his is the story that fear wrote.

*I wrote "Mojo Farmer" in 1994, under the tutelage of visiting writer
Ted Solotaroff, when I was an undergrad at the University of Alabama.*

*Ted is something of an Old Testament prophet in the publishing business,
and looks like something of an Old Testament prophet in real life. He is tall
and dark, and sounds like an actor playing God when he talks. I dare say the
class was terrified of him.*

*But I really wasn't scared of him. I was too dumb to know who the hell he
was—I was petrified of the other students. I was just a lousy undergrad. The
other people in that class were working on book contracts and generally
preparing to spend the rest of their lives as professional writers.*

*I was so scared I couldn't even begin something new. I had already written
a poem about a farmer who buries birds to fertilize his garden. In the poem
were all these objects: the sewing squares, the marbles, the green chifforobe,
things that can be found in my grandparents' house on my family's cattle
farm in Lamar County. (The cat belongs to my fiancée.) They needed a
narrative to make them make sense together. The real job was finding a structure to support all these images. I worked day and night to find that story;
"Mojo Farmer" is the result.*

Beauvais McCaddon

THE HALF-PINT

(from *Quarterly West*)

Every afternoon when the compress whistle blew five o'clock during the summer months, Isabell Langley rolled out her push mower. On this hot July day, she had gotten out a pair of her daddy's old seersucker pants, one of his white cotton dress shirts, and his panama hat. She rolled up the bottom of the trousers and threaded the waist loops with a Countess Mara tie.

Prentiss ladies pulled up poison ivy and nursed along phlox seedlings, but Isabell was the only woman in town who mowed her own grass. Isabell wanted the town to think that she mowed out of eccentricity rather than need, and her dead father's clothes fit into her scheme nicely. As a child, she had wanted to wear mix-matched clothes to school, but her mother wouldn't let her outside unless she was properly dressed in a starched pinafore. After her mother died, Isabell had worn a 1910 batiste dress to church on Easter Sunday, and her gardening costume to her bridge club.

As Isabell rolled her mower from the tool shed into her backyard, she noticed Pearce Wallace sitting on his back stoop for the fourth day in a row. Pearce walked over to the iron fence that separated their two yards, leaned over and clamped his hands around the arrow finials. The fence had been rented in the 1950s by a movie company filming in nearby Benoit. Prentiss had turned out to watch the fence being dug up and then again to see it being put back. It had been a great source of disappointment to Isabell's mother, the town's gossip, that she had never found out how much rent money had been paid to the Wallaces.

"Do you know why the whistle blows a long, a short, and a long, and sounds like a riverboat?" Pearce asked.

"No," Isabell said, surprised that Pearce had spoken to her, the first time since his mother's funeral last year. Was this a riddle?

"First man to head up the Union Compress wanted the whistle to sound just like the *Kate Adams*," Pearce said.

"Oh," Isabell said, "Maybe Mother did mention it. You know, she and Daddy honeymooned on that boat. And, of course, she admired your house." Along the front of Pearce's white house were twelve windows, and around the roof line were sham smokestacks, surrounded by an elaborate wooden railing. On the very top of the house was a widow's walk where Isabell had often imagined herself leaning out, gazing across Prentiss, dressed as a riverboat pilot. Pearce's house was a replica of the *Kate Adams*.

"Excuse me," Isabell said, pushing the mower to a patch of clover where she had left off yesterday. "I really must get on this yard." She was intrigued by Pearce's sudden attention. Even when she went to the bank where Pearce worked, he would just nod at her.

"Cuz mows our yard," Pearce said.

"I like the exercise," Isabell laughed. She was surprised that she was flirting with Pearce. He was probably sixty, a good ten years older than she, and looked as if he had eaten one too many helpings of turnip greens and fatback. She liked his dark eyes though, and his hands were attractive, curled around the finials. She put her hands on her hips to emphasize her slim waist and tilted her head to one side. "Besides, you've got a whole city block over there."

"Thought maybe you'd want Cuz to come mow yours," Pearce said. "Do you ever take a drink?"

"Sometimes," Isabell answered. If she were invited to she would.

She and Ouida Green weren't included in with the bridge group who floated around the pool at the country club (they couldn't afford the fees) when the compress whistle blew, holding a bourbon and water instead of a hand of cards, discussing the civil rights workers' invasion. She wished very hard right then that Pearce would ask her over for a drink. But then, hadn't her mother said that she had never known Pearce or his mother to ever take a drink? And, Pearce had no tolerance for those who did drink and especially those who came to work on Monday morning with a hangover. She'd had it firsthand from a bank teller.

"Do you like to go riding around?" Pearce asked.

"Depends on where you're riding to," Isabell said.

"Supposing you don't mow tomorrow," Pearce said.

"Supposing I do?" Isabell questioned.

"Then you can't go riding with me," Pearce said.

At a quarter to five the next afternoon, Isabell put on a green cotton sundress and sandals, but no stockings. That morning she had gone to the Prentiss beauty parlor and had her hair fixed in a page boy, just as she did every week. Isabell's hair was dyed jet black, the same as her mother's, except for the Hedy Lamarr widow's peak. The beauty parlor operator had once cut off all her mother's long hair and it never grew back. Isabell's mother was forced to wear a switch on top of her head to cover her baldness.

Isabell walked to her sunporch and looked across the street. "Those people" her mother used to called them, not anybody her mother would associate with. The husband was getting out of his car and walling up the front sidewalk. Isabell imagined his wife putting out cheese and crackers, filling up the ice bucket, setting the Old Crow out in the kitchen. Drinks at five o'clock, a ritual in Prentiss that Isabell had been a part of growing up. Her parents took her when they dropped by friends at five o'clock for a drink. And even after Isabell had eaten up all the peanuts and crumbled up the last cracker and was ready to go home and eat supper and do her homework, her mother would say "just half a drink" and her daddy would add a little ice and a little whiskey and then they would reluctantly head home so her mother could heat up the supper the cook had left on the stove.

Isabell heard Pearce pull up in her driveway. Today she didn't have to envy the bridge club and the couple across the street, because she was a part of the five o'clock crowd too. Pearce's car was a '47 Plymouth coupé. If the Wallaces had as much money as her mother had always indicated, why was Pearce's car so old? When Isabell and Pearce drove out on the highway, the windows were down. There was no air conditioning. Isabell rolled her window up so her hair wouldn't blow.

"So," Pearce said. "I thought we'd ride over and look at the river." Pearce headed the Plymouth up Highway Number 1 towards Gunnison. Just north of Prentiss, he took the blacktop road to the cemetery. They passed through cotton fields, dotted here and there with a few people chopping cotton. "Don't see that much any more," Pearce said. "Cotton looks good, don't you think?"

"Yes," Isabell said. "It looks good." What, thought Isabell, constitutes good? She would have called it pretty. The white and pink cotton blossoms, the plants in neat rows. She didn't think she'd mind chopping cotton. Now that would really set people talking. But it was so unbearably hot—her bare legs were sticking to the seat—and out in the middle of the field it would be scorching. It appealed to her, though, catching the weeds with the corner of a hoe. Her mother's big hats she had saved would be perfectly fine, maybe the yellow straw with ribbons and violets.

They drove past the Prentiss cemetery, where her mother and father were buried. Below their names on the double marker, Isabell had had engraved "Mother" and "Daddy." She could see from the road that the grass was too high around their marble tombstone. She would call up the cemetery keeper and fuss. When it got cooler, she wanted to plant some little hollies that would have red berries by Christmas.

They drove up onto the levee on the gravel road and turned towards Terrene Landing. Pearce stopped the car just a few yards from the Mississippi. The Corps of Engineers had poured asphalt along the bank to keep it from caving in. A big barge was coming up the river from Greenville. Isabell opened her door to catch any breeze and Pearce opened his. A towboat with several barges in tow was moving very slowly in the distance.

Pearce pulled a half-pint of whiskey from up under his seat. He unscrewed the top. "Would you like a drink?" he asked. "Used to be whiskey boats on the river, blind tigers, until 1908. That's when Governor Noel shut them down. After that, my father bought whiskey over the levee, took it home, drank it in his parlor."

He passed her the bottle, wrapped in a brown paper bag. She touched his damp fingers and it seemed to her a forbidden pleasure.

Isabell took a swig out of the half-pint. She felt good in spite of the sweat rolling down her back. She felt good sitting in the car looking at the barge going up the Mississippi towards Memphis. She liked watching the light change, the beginning of a sunset reflected in the river. What would her mother have said? Isabell had never drunk out of a half-pint, much less with a man in a car. She took another swig. Isabell's mother once had harsh words for a sister-in-law who, in her mind, had disgraced the family when she walked down Main Street licking an ice cream cone. Isabell thought about all "those people" just over the levee in Prentiss, sitting around their living rooms, the ice melting in their drinks. This rendezvous was the kind of thing her mother had loved to talk about. She and Pearce would soon eclipse the freedom riders on the five o'clock circuit.

Pearce took another swig. "Engineers' revetments look good. River's low," he said and screwed the top on and put the bottle back up under the seat. He pointed to the marker which measured the depth of the river. He backed the car around. Even driving fifteen miles an hour, a trail of dust floated over the few houses near the landing. The houses looked pieced together with scrap lumber, the boards differing shades of gray. Some of the trim was painted pea green or bright blue. It had been years since Isabell had come to the river landing. There had been houseboat parties on the Fourth of July. Had the boat left from here? And who all was on the boat? Isabell remembered sitting by herself, hot and sticky, clutching the side rail, afraid of falling in the water while her mother and daddy sat happily with drinks on the upper deck.

When they came out of the Terrene road and were back on the levee, Pearce headed the coupé south toward Beulah. "I'm on the Levee Board," Pearce said.

"What are we going to do, look for cracks?" Isabell asked. She was joking and smiled but Pearce looked very serious. He drove cautiously over the cattle gap. There were pink primroses blooming all across the levee, a few white ones here and there. "Who do these cows belong to?" She thought another question would get Pearce to talking.

"Different farmers," Pearce answered. 'They rent from the Levee Board. I had a horse once named Steamboat. Used to graze on the levee." Pearce drove on for about two miles without talking. Then he stopped the car. "This is where the Beulah Big Boil happened," he said. "It was in 1912. I was eight years old."

"What was the Big Boil?" Isabell asked. It looked just like the rest of the levee, covered with grass and primroses. "All I know about is the flood of 1927. Mother and Daddy took all the furniture and put it up on the second story. Mother had an over-flow party and everybody came by boat."

Pearce took the half-pint from up under the seat and took another swig. His light blue shirt was wet under the arms. He raised his eyebrows. "You don't know about the Big Boil? First the river got high and started pushing against the levee. It found a weak spot. Might have been a rotten core or even a crayfish tunnel. The water got through and boiled up. That was the Big Boil."

Isabell watched dragonflies lighting on the hood of the car. She wasn't worried about crayfish or boils. She wanted Pearce to kiss her. She hadn't kissed a man since 1942. That was the year her husband had left to go to war, leaving her at home pregnant. She had gone to visit her husband's people in Sunflower County, near Quiver. They were country people and they were boiling water for a hog killing. Isabell heard screams, someone had been burned, and she went running across the big yard. But her feet got tangled up in barbed wire and she fell hard and lost the baby.

"If it was a clear stream that came through, it wasn't dangerous. But if it started churning up sand and silt, it was trouble," Pearce said. "Of course, the new levee . . ."

He's sorry, Isabell thought, that the new levee was ever built. He'd love a real disaster. It would probably raise his blood and he'd turn passionate. Pearce talked on about the new levee and how the Irish came to build it and how they would get drunk on Saturday night and shoot up the town. Around seven, when the half-pint was empty, Pearce took her home.

By five o'clock on the next Wednesday afternoon, Pearce had engaged Cuz to mow Isabell's grass. When Pearce picked her up, they drove out to a new spot, a big lake close to the levee. Pearce stopped the Plymouth near weeping willows. Through the green, Isabell could see the outline of an old houseboat.

"Do you know what a blue hole is?" asked Pearce.

"No," Isabell answered. It didn't look blue at all to her, but muddy with stobs poking through the chartreuse algae growing close in to the bank.

"The Blue Hole was made from water seeping through a crevasse in the levee, just like a boil, only it kept churning up land until it made a big lake. This hole is probably 90 feet deep all told," Pearce said. He took a swig out of the half-pint and handed it to Isabell. "It covers 83 acres." Then he turned and kissed her. Afterwards, she always thought of it as a whiskey kiss. It was neither long nor passionate. But something about the 83 acres or the 90 feet deep had stirred him.

Isabell liked being with Pearce. The whiskey kisses made her know how lonesome she had been. She had shut off, built a levee around herself. Ever since she had lost her baby. Her mother had brought her back to Prentiss and put her to bed and Dr. Dallas had given her a shot to make her sleep. But she felt as if she had never waked up. She and her husband divorced, Isabell took back her maiden name, and she never saw him after the War. Now, for the first time, she could feel a trickle of feeling coming through. It was no Big Boil yet, but it wasn't a clear stream either. It felt more like sand and silt being churned up.

In November, Pearce picked Isabell up early and drove them along the levee to Horn Lake. "Do you know what a horn lake is?" Pearce asked. "It's a lake made when the river changes its course and cuts off a piece of water."

"How far can you drive on the levee?" Isabell asked.

"All the way to Memphis," Pearce answered. He reached up under the seat and brought out, instead of the half-pint, a small velvet blue box, holding an emerald-cut diamond ring with sapphires on either side. "Will you marry me?" He handed the box to Isabell and then he reached up under the seat again and brought out the half-pint and took a swig.

Isabell knew she wasn't in love with Pearce and Pearce didn't love her near as much as he loved the river. She felt safe with him. It was comforting to sit close to a man, and give way to feelings now beginning to surface.

"Yes," Isabell said, admiring the ring on her finger. It was an expensive stone. She liked the idea of having money. She had been so miserly with her wants after nursing her parents through long illnesses. She thought later she and Pearce could drive all the way to Memphis on the levee in a brand new air-conditioned Cadillac and stay at the Peabody and go dancing on the Skyway. She could buy beautiful clothes at Lowenstein's. Maybe they would go to Europe and she could see famous gardens.

Pearce started the engine and shifted into first. Isabell dreamed on as they rode over the dusty levee road. And why did Pearce want to marry her? He was lonesome of course, living in that big steamboat place all by himself since his mother had died. Isabell would have Cuz busy all year, raking and planting hybrid lilies, restoring the steamboat yard to its former glory back before Mrs. Wallace went to bed with heart trouble.

The days were getting shorter and the dark caught the couple sooner than expected. Rounding the levee at Victoria Bend, Pearce was telling Isabell about the pits that bordered this section of the levee. "They are barrow pits, named for the wheelbarrows used to carry the dirt out of them to build the levee," Pearce said. "And don't ever let anyone tell you they are borrow pits. New folks around here that don't know any better call them borrow pits, for the dirt borrowed to make the levee." Pearce had raised his voice. "My father said never to let anyone dispute me on that point. In fact, you could pretty much divide the whole town into those who say 'barrow' and those who say 'borrow.'"

Isabell was trying to remember if her mother had ever talked about whether it was "borrow" or "barrow." Since Pearce thought it was so important, she'd have to remember which way it was supposed to be. Just as Pearce slowed down to drive over the cattle gap, he caught in the beam of his headlights a man carrying a shotgun.

"Good God, it's Mr. Whiteside. Doesn't he know who we are?" Pearce asked.

Keeping the gun pointed at the car, Mr. Whiteside walked slowly towards them.

When he saw it was Pearce, he began to apologize. "Mr. Wallace, I'm so sorry. Headlights blinded me. Never would have pointed a gun at you. Folks been stealing my cows."

"What's that?" Pearce asked.

"Well, sir," Mr. Whiteside said. "Sunday evening a man came knocking on my door, said his truck had a flat and he wanted to borrow a jack. I said I'd do one better and go help him. He said na, he didn't need no help. But it being Sunday and all, and me a good Methodist, I went with him. And it was just long about this same spot here that we come up on the truck broke down. And you know what?"

"What's that?" Pearce obliged by asking.

"Durn man had done loaded up his truck with my cows. He was

on his way to Memphis to sell 'em," Mr. Whiteside said. "They was probably freedom riders besides." And with that he turned and went on down the levee towards his farm.

Pearce cut the engine, but left the headlights shining. He reached up under the seat and pulled out the half-pint and drank what was left. "Never thought I'd come close to getting shot riding on the levee. And I'm not quite ready to die, yet. Come on," he said and they both got out of the car and walked over to the side of the levee nearest the river. Isabell looked to see if her new diamond would shine in the headlights.

"Let's see if I can hit the bottom of that barrow pit." Pearce threw the bottle as far as he could. "When the water gets high in those pits, they fill up with catfish, bull frogs, and sometimes even dead bodies."

They were married in the white wooden-frame Methodist Church in Prentiss a week before Christmas. Isabell wore a blue chiffon dress and carried a bouquet of white orchids. Isabell's daddy had been an only child, and her mother's brother and his wife had died childless, so there had been no relatives for Isabell in attendance. She invited her bridge club, most of whom were widows. Pearce's cousins from Risingsun in Leflore County came. It struck Isabell as odd that only a few guests were men.

"When my father was on the Levee Board," Pearce said, "they used to rent the *Kate Adams* and go up and down the river inspecting the levee. In 1927, the *Kate Adams* burned at its moorings." Pearce had booked them on the steamboat *The Delta Queen* for their honeymoon.

This night on the deck with Pearce, Isabell no longer felt alone. She wore the dark brown mink coat that Pearce had given her for a wedding present. She pushed tight against Pearce. With the river around and under them, Pearce kissed her long and hard. Smelling strong of whiskey, Pearce pulled her in close and held her. "This is more fun than any old Levee Board ever had," Isabell said and

Pearce smiled. It was good being with a man, Isabell thought. It was almost sweet.

After the honeymoon, they moved into Pearce's steamboat house and Isabell rented out her house. Pearce would fix a drink as soon as he got home from the bank at five o'clock.

Isabell couldn't get Pearce to Memphis, much less to Europe. He didn't seem to have the energy to go anywhere. Isabell drew up elaborate plans for the yard, but Pearce wasn't interested. She and Cuz had planted hundreds of daffodil bulbs, coming out from the steamboat house so that in bloom, rippling in the wind, they would look like waves churned up on the river. In the backyard, she put in forsythia and burning bush to remind her of sunsets.

"Why don't we go riding on the levee?" Isabell asked one afternoon, coming in from pulling Virginia creeper off the chimneys. She missed the rides and the half-pint. Pearce was sitting in front of the television, watching the news with a drink. The slant of the afternoon light caught Pearce's face, and Isabell saw tiny broken blood vessels crisscrossing his nose. Surely a few must have been there all along, but she noticed so many now.

"Why don't you fix yourself a drink?" Pearce asked. "Did I ever tell you about how my grandfather's plantation Jarnigan was lost?"

"No," Isabell called from the kitchen where she was pouring a bourbon and water. "The bridge club said today that the workers were right here in Prentiss now." Isabell had driven slowly through colored town when she took Cuz home, hoping she could spot one. She was curious as to what they would look like, what they would wear.

"The levee is like a fence," Pearce said. "The levee fences the river in. When a new levee had to be built in the old days, and a man's plantation was thrown outside the levee, he lost everything. He got no money for the land, nothing, just lost it all."

"Did you say Jarnigan Plantation was inside or outside the levee?" Isabell asked.

"I told you," Pearce said. "It was outside the levee and it caved into the river. Come on in here and sit down."

"Just a minute," Isabell said. "I've got to run upstairs a second." She took her drink and climbed up all the way to the widow's walk. At the top of the steamboat house, she loved thinking in the quiet of the afternoon, knowing that Pearce was below her, waiting for his supper. Why was Pearce no longer after her as he had been on the riverboat? Was the riding on the levee only reserved for their courting? Maybe she had let him down in some way. Had he really only wanted someone to drink with after his mother died? Isabell gazed out across the park, watching the red sunset, imagining the river red too. Her drink was gone, and she shook the ice in her glass. Would he like her better if she could understand what was inside and outside the levee?

A month later on a Wednesday, Isabell went to her bridge club at Ouida Green's house. She shuffled and dealt for a very old lady (it had been her mother's bridge club too) and stuck the cards in between her arthritic fingers.

"Just ask your cook," the arthritic lady was saying, "she'll tell you she has no interest in what the freedom riders are doing. She wants to go to her own church and I want to go to my church." The bridge club had been the source of all her mother's information: Bob Smith had changed his name to States Rights Smith; Dr. Dallas had offered to pay Doodle the barber extra if he wouldn't talk but instead Doodle had burst out at the end of the haircut and forfeited the dollar; the postmistress came home at noon and found her husband in bed with another man. Isabell told her mother she didn't like the gossip, but the details were compelling, glimpses into other lives, so close, yet for all intents and purposes, perfect strangers.

"Oh, Isabell," the arthritic lady twittered, "Marriage has done wonders. You never looked lovelier."

"I imagine the Wallace money has something to do with it," Ouida Green, who always said what she thought, chimed in from the next table.

Isabell wasn't sure about the Wallace money. It was nice that

Cuz took care of the yard and she wasn't so miserly with her wants anymore. But Pearce hadn't exactly bought her everything she wanted either. And she didn't have a cook to ask what she thought about the freedom riders. She pretended that she hadn't heard the remark, especially since it was Ouida's. She used to fill in for Ouida at her dress shop. Playing cards together made for a peculiar relationship. She had known of one particular feud that started over a three no-trump bid that should have been four hearts and carried over so long that one of the women had cut the other from her daughter's wedding list. The bridge club didn't know, nor would they ever guess, that Pearce was a secret drinker.

There was a loud knock at the backdoor. "Oh, bother," Ouida said. "Who in the devil is that?" Isabell smiled. Ouida could be crotchety.

"It's Cuz," Ouida said. "He wants you, Isabell, and he seems ready agitated."

Isabell put her cards face down on the table. Ouida Green's house was a shotgun, sharecropper's cabin that had been transplanted from a cotton field to town amongst big magnolias. It was like a doll's house, tiny and orderly. Isabell took a few steps to the backdoor where Cuz was standing outside on the steps. "Mr. Pearce done fell out in the yard," Cuz said. "He don't look right."

In fact, Pearce was already dead from a heart attack by the time Isabell got home. A week after the funeral, Pearce's lawyer called Isabell to tell her that Pearce had left her his life insurance policy, worth ten thousand dollars, and his old Plymouth. Everything else of the Wallace property and money was entailed to Pearce's Wallace relatives near Risingsun in Leflore county. Including the steamboat house. And why, Isabell wondered, had her mother not uncovered this startling bit of information?

Isabell climbed up the widow's walk. She was angry with Pearce for not telling her about the steamboat house being taken over by his distant relatives. She imagined it going to rack and ruin. His cousins would never move to Prentiss away from their business interests. Termites would eat the walls. The lovely old window panes would fall out. The railing that Isabell now leaned against would pull away, piece by piece. The chimneys would crumble away, brick by brick. She wanted to gather up Pearce's clothes and throw them out from the top of the house, and watch them land in little piles among the daffodils now blooming. But instead, she ran down the stairs and put on her long dark brown mink.

Isabell had not had a drink since Pearce died, because she didn't want to drink alone. But today she drove to the package store behind the jailhouse. She honked the horn and when the clerk came out she ordered a half-pint of whiskey. When he asked what brand, she realized she had never seen the label on the half-pints that Pearce had bought. "Whatever's cheap," Isabell said.

She drove Pearce's coupé past the cotton seed oil mill and past the cemetery where Pearce was now buried, not far from her mother and father. The road was dusty because of an unusually dry winter. She passed the place near where Pearce had thrown the half-pint into the barrow pit. She had read in the Memphis paper that morning that the skeleton of a civil rights worker had been found in one of the pits. Isabell was shocked over the murder but she knew Pearce would have only fumed because the paper called it "bar-pit," instead of "barrow" pit.

Isabell drove on until she came to a spur levee. She parked the coupé and got out, holding the liquor store package and pulling the mink tight. It was cold. She was surprised that she wasn't afraid to come by herself, wrapped in an expensive fur. She could hear Ouida Green saying she might get knocked in the head wandering around over here and that she should be home picking the daffodils to save them from the hard freeze expected that night.

She went down the spur levee, walking gingerly and sideways in her high heels, and went across a couple of acres of an old cotton field. She followed the path through the cypress trees and cottonwoods that Pearce had showed her, coming out on a high bluff overlooking the river. It was part of the old Jarnigan Plantation. Pearce had told her it was the highest bluff between Memphis and

Greenville, thought to be where De Soto had crossed the Mississippi. Ouida Green had since told her that it was the same bluff Emmett Till's captors had chosen to scare him on before driving him across the Delta to be cast into the bottom of another river for whistling at a white woman. Both events seemed equal, leveled in Isabell's mind as snippets of bridge club conversations, since her life seemed untouched by either.

Isabell walked to the very edge of the steep bank. A barge was making its way slowly up the river. The afternoon light was changing. She knew it would be a beautiful sunset, reflected across the water into Arkansas. Isabell held up her package and tore the paper sack off. It was a bottle of Four Roses. She took a swig out of the half-pint, but the whiskey did not make her feel good. How was it that Pearce had made her feel so safe? At the bottom of the river were many plantations, dirt from the levees that had given way, and someday, if the river shifted far enough, even Pearce himself.

Her face was cold and her feet ached. She wanted back that feeling that had come from drinking the half-pint with Pearce, riding along the levee and stopping at the Blue Hole. "Was all I got a diamond ring, a fur coat, and whiskey kisses?" Isabell asked aloud, as if in question to the lone man standing on the barge. She took a last swig out of the half-pint and threw it as far as she could into the river, intending to mark where it went down. But she didn't see when it was pulled under by the current. Isabell was distracted by the lone man. He had mistaken her gesture, and he waved back as the barge continued on past.

––––––––––

Beauvais McCaddon, a native Mississippian, attended DePauw University and was graduated from Millsaps College in 1966. She received her M.A. from Florida State University in 1995, and now lives in Florida. Her stories have appeared in *Quarterly West*, *The Virginia Quarterly Review*, *Sun Dog*, and *Micro Fiction*.

I was taken with my father's description of a courtship ritualized by rides
on the levee and a half-pint of whiskey. He was fascinated by levee lore,
and it was from him that I first got the idea of the levee as a fence.

My story grew from wanting to figure out such a peculiar ceremony.
Although Isabell and Pearce are imaginary, their romance encompasses bits
and pieces of my growing up in a Mississippi river town—the five o'clock cock-
tail hour, fishing at the Blue Hole, tales of high water.

The real Prentiss was an antebellum landing on the Mississippi. But the
once thriving town was eaten away by the river until it disappeared under
layers of silt. In May of 1956, I, along with hundreds of people in Bolivar
County, went to gaze at its foundations, brought back by shifting currents.
Before the historical remains were reclaimed by the river, most of the beautiful
old brick had been carted off to build patios and barbecue pits. In the
landscape of fiction, I can now resurrect Prentiss once again.

Rhian Margaret Ellis

EVERY BUILDING WANTS TO FALL

(from *Epoch*)

My father blew up buildings. You wouldn't guess it to look at him. He was small, with long, delicate fingers and the wispy fine hair you see on baby boys, and in his yellow hard hat he seemed overwhelmed and top-heavy, like a toadstool. He spoke so softly that if we were watching television while he talked, we had to turn down the sound and watch his mouth move. Nonetheless, he was famous for his demolitions. He blew up a five-building public housing project in St. Louis, a turn-of-the-century resort hotel in Atlanta, and a jail in Houston that could no longer keep its prisoners in, all without breaking so much as a window in the surrounding neighborhoods. He took pride in the gentleness of his destruction, and called it "bringing down," never "blowing up."

"Every building wants to fall," he told reporters who gathered at the sites. He believed it, too. Nothing moved him more than the sight of a building in collapse. He filmed each of his demolitions on a jumpy little super eight camera, but sometimes became too overwrought to hold it still. He'd lose focus, let the ground tilt upward, maybe catch a glimpse of billowing dust or a wayward, hurtling brick. He showed us these movies in the dining room of our house in New Orleans—a structure, he told us more than once, that was a mere two well-placed sticks of dynamite away from oblivion. With the shades pulled against the sun and my mother passing around a colander full of popcorn—a bribe to get me to humor my father—we watched building after building disintegrate on our plaster walls. Each warehouse or flophouse or abandoned orphanage seemed to take a last breath; you could see the walls swell outward just slightly before falling in, a movement so inevitable and deliberate they really did seem relieved to go down.

My mother never shared his enthusiasm for leveling. When she cried during the movies it was out of plain sadness; pity for the people who lived and worked in the buildings, never considering the impermanence of their walls. She didn't accompany him on jobs, and was satisfied to get postcards from all over the East Coast. Once he drew himself holding a little detonator next to a picture of the Empire State Building. DREAM COME TRUE!!! he scrawled across the sky, only half joking. He didn't have much business in New Orleans. The houses there are allowed to die lingering, natural deaths, shedding their bricks onto the sidewalk and slumping into the soggy earth. Every couple of years there'd be something in town to blow up, and I'd go with him to watch—a hotel so infested with roaches no one could stand to stay there, a gloomy graffitied high school, and once a beautiful old cathedral the police had to chase protesters away from, though the pews and altar had been taken out and the colored windows rescued. My father gave me an uncomfortable hard hat that matched his, and a pair of goggles that squashed my nose and made me breathe like a landed fish.

It was on the cathedral job, watching the gothic arches cave in on themselves through the scratched plastic of my goggles, that I first saw something go wrong. I was eleven, and had seen maybe a hundred buildings go down flawlessly. Someone leapt the yellow police barrier, sprinted across the street, and ran straight into the storm of rubble just as the middle transept began to implode. The thunder of falling rock hid the normal sounds of the world, so the sight of the little man running into the cathedral had a muffled, distant quality, like one of my father's movies. I thought of this and realized it was him at the same moment; I didn't recognize him at first without his hat.

My mother and I stayed in New Orleans another six weeks, just long enough to sell the house and give away our things. She had always been a nervous person—tall and thin, with huge, awkward gestures that knocked over glasses and flower vases—but she became increasingly restless indoors. She made excuses to go to the grocery store and spent whole afternoons pulling weeds in the yard. I came home from school one day to find her staring up at the house. The upper windows were streaked with pigeon droppings, the rain gutters dangled at absurd angles, the plaster was fuzzed with brown mold. Roof tiles from the last wind storm were scattered across the tiny square of lawn. She shook her head.

"I think your father was right," she said. "This house is beyond saving."

Soon, her discomfort spread to the city at large. She said she couldn't stand being surrounded by buildings she knew were aching to fall, bricks that strained free of their mortar. Every crack in a plaster wall sent a shock of worry to her heart. She even imagined that houses were lurching toward her when her back was turned, she said. It made her too jittery to eat, and she took up chewing gum.

But I liked the city. The streets were narrow enough so that walking down them, you felt like you were passing through two cupped hands. Trees grew out of cracks or hung overhead, and you could hear voices echoing in hidden courtyards. The walls you could touch from the sidewalk were always warm, and you knew that people were sleeping and eating and taking baths on the other side of them. Our own house was narrow and long, and in bed at night I sometimes imagined I was tucked into a deep drawer, among folded socks and sweaters. I didn't want to leave. Every time the real estate lady brought people to look at the house, I'd run out the back door and stomp angrily up and down the side-walk, planning the little fort I'd build in the alley, the garden I'd plant to feed myself.

The people who finally bought the house were a blond couple who had a tiny bald baby they carried around in a backpack. His name was Jocko, and his head bobbed over his mother's shoulder like a jack-in-the-box. I watched from the sweet olive tree in the back yard as the real estate lady showed them around, moving from room to room, window to window, my mother trailing several feet behind. The small white circle of Jocko's head infuriated me. I imagined pulling its little pink ears off, bloodying its little pug nose. I wanted to kick it across the yard like a soccer ball.

As I was thinking these things, watching the real estate lady and the little family pass by the round-topped window con their way up to the third story, I noticed that my mother had stayed behind. She had gone into the bathroom and shut the door; I saw the back of her head, the thin reddish hair pulled up in a bun. She leaned over the sink and washed her face, then dried herself on the towel that hung by the tub. She stood staring into space for a while before she turned and looked out the window.

She didn't know I was there, at first. I knew this because the expression on her face was one she'd never let me see: it was panic, pure, immovable fear, and it terrified me. Then my foot slipped, the branch shook, and her eyes swiveled up to mine.

We looked at each other for a long moment. It was as if my father—not this building—had been the house we both lived in, and now that the dust had cleared we could only stare at each other over the rubble, completely lost with each other.

I turned away from my mother, and climbed higher.

We went to live with my grandfather, a seventy-year-old doctor who lifted weights in his office and ran for an hour every day, wearing nothing but sneakers and a pair of red nylon shorts. He still lived in the town my mother was born in, Faberville, Louisiana. I had only been there once or twice, because my grandfather liked to visit us in the city, and I didn't remember it well. He brought me gifts whenever he came to New Orleans, things like apples or yo-yos, stuff you'd give to the neighbor child to make him stay out of your yard.

"Goodness, Noreen," he said to my mother when we got out of the car. "You're looking scrawny."

I felt her stiffen beside me. "Daddy . . ." she said warningly.

He stepped up to her and gave her a hug. He was wearing a pair of white corduroy shorts and no shirt, and he looked sweaty. White hair prickled his chest. I hoped he wouldn't hug me.

He shook his head. "I mean it. It's like squeezing a sack of tools." He gave me a quick nod and then said, "Well, I'm in the middle of cutting the weeds out back. Go in and get comfortable." Then he waved and was gone.

My mother sighed.

We unpacked the car and took our things inside. The house was low and brick, ranch-style, with air-conditioning and soft carpet in every room, even the kitchen. Unlike most houses in Louisiana it was built directly on the ground, on a cement pad instead of up on pillars. Everything was solid and cool. My mother sat down on the green leather sofa in the living room, and her mood seemed to brighten. "Anyone around here interested in ice cream?" she asked.

"I don't think so," I said.

She raised her eyebrows. "If I remember correctly," she said, "there's soft serve at the Chicken Hut around the corner."

"No, thank you," I told her.

She looked at me, then shrugged. My grandfather was right; she did look pretty skinny, all elbows and knees, and her hair was thinner than ever. The gold bobby pins had little to cling to. They glinted on her head like centipedes. "You know," she said, patting the armrest and looking around the room, "I never did like that old house. We should have been living in a place like this all along."

* * *

We settled in. My grandfather was nice enough. To my mother he communicated mainly in pithy sayings and health advice, and to me he made gestures—a tip of an invisible hat, a salute, two fingers held in a peace sign. The town itself wasn't much; two blocks of stores on either side of the train tracks, a short commercial strip outside of town with a movie theater and two or three burger places, and a large blue water tower looming over everything— the only tall thing in town.

After some argument I was enrolled in the local school. My grandfather wanted me to go to the private school in the next parish, but my mother balked; one school was as good as the next, she said, none of them taught you anything interesting. "Anyway," she added, "private schools are for ninnies," apparently forgetting I'd gone to one in New Orleans.

As it turned out, I was the only white child in the class, one of only half a dozen in the entire school. Although he probably would never have said so, I knew this was the reason my grandfather wanted me to go to St. Mary's. My mother, I was sure, neither knew nor cared. The teacher was a young white woman with big glasses who treated me with mild indifference; if anyone accused her of playing favorites, she'd remind us she disliked us all equally. At recess I jumped rope with the white girls from other classes. They were fat and scabby and smelled faintly of old underwear, and would get hysterical thinking up insulting names for black people. They weren't much fun, but no one else would have anything to do with me.

To my horror, my mother began dating almost immediately. The men were, I thought, wildly unsuitable for her: a pimply, chinless man who worked at the McDonald's, a huge Italian with a walruslike mustache and a white sports car, the guy who stocked produce at the Sunflower and couldn't possibly have been more than eignteen. She'd bring them home, sit them at the kitchen table, plunk a cup of tea and a plate of chocolate cookies in front of them, then sit with her chin in her hands as they talked. She seemed to pick the kind of man who didn't need much in the way of response—a few Reallys and Uh-huhs kept them going.

When she went out, my grandfather was left with baby-sitting duty. He took it seriously. He'd turn off the television and herd me out of my room then make me sit at the kitchen table with a stack of board games. We'd play a game or two of Parcheesi—or something else I could win at—before he brought out the backgammon. He tried several times to explain the rules.

The goal," he said, "is pure strategy."

And, "Never let your opponent get the jump on you."

He was mystified and hurt when I burst into frustrated tears, and I inevitably did.

"Now, now," he'd say, "it's just a game." He'd make my moves for me while I sat there sniffing and wiping my nose. "Anticipation is the key." He took an almost obscene delight in winning.

I took to hiding out in the bathroom. I'd excuse myself while he debated his move, and ten or fifteen minutes later he'd come looking for me.

"Hey," he'd yell through the bathroom door. "You alive in there?"

"I'm still using it!" I shouted back.

I'd hear him clicking the pieces as he played both sides, mumbling advice to himself.

Once I fell asleep on the bathroom floor, my head in the Sears catalog I'd brought in to look at while I waited out the backgammon. I woke up when one of my mother's dates bumped me with the door.

"Oh, hey," he said.

I thought, for a moment, that I was in my old bedroom in New Orleans.

"Dad," I said.

"Whoops, sorry," said the date. "You got the wrong guy."

I sat up, embarrassed.

"Um," he said. "I really have to go. You don't mind?"

I grabbed the catalog and ran out.

* * *

I made a friend. Her name was Phyllis and she sat next to me in the back of the class. She was tall and pretty, had beautiful hand-writing, and kept her hair in a stubby pigtail. Her front teeth were perfectly square, like Chiclets, and sat on her lower lip when she smiled. For the first week or so I didn't know why the other girls avoided her. She spent recess walking around the edge of the play-ground, dragging a stick along the chain-link fence.

Then one afternoon during math, Miss Olson took the flag off the wall and started slapping her desk with it, the fabric bunched in her fist.

"Listen!" she said. "I'm not talking to myself up here! Do you think I'm talking to myself?"

She whacked her desk so hard the stick that held the flag snapped in half, and the broken piece whirled up in the air. It landed in the trash can with a bang.

"Oops," she said.

Next to me, Phyllis let out a low cry. Then she threw her head back and fell out of her chair. On the floor, she began to shudder and thrash.

A girl named Tamitha jumped out of her desk and went to Phyl-lis, wrapping her arms around the girl's chest and pulling her head onto her lap. The fit lasted about a minute. When it was over, Tamitha laid Phyllis back on the floor and went to her desk. Phyl-lis lay there a while, blinking at the ceiling. There was a little trickle of spit at the corner of her mouth.

Miss Olson fished the broken stick out of the trash, set the crumpled flag on the bookshelf, and went back to teaching math. When Phyllis stood up, a little shakily, I noticed that some strands of hair had escaped her pigtail and were standing over her forehead like antennae, and that the back of her pink pants was wet. She went to the closet, took out a clean pair of pants and a plastic bag, and went out into the hall. When she came hack, her wet pants were in the bag and she clutched a handful of paper towels. She put the bag in her book sack and wiped the urine from the floor, then threw the towels in the trash and sat back down again.

My heart was beating so hard that it made me tremble. What I had witnessed was terrible and amazing. It made me think of the time I'd seen a cat get run over, then leap up and run away with its guts dragging along the ground. I wanted to touch Phyllis; I thought she was charmed.

Phyllis had more fits, one or two every week. A fire drill triggered one, the horn of a passing car set off another. Twice she fell to the ground at the noise of a slamming door, and once it was the sound of a whistle blown by a kindergartner at recess. Clapping was forbidden in our class; after movies and oral reports we cheered silently instead.

I became her friend through sheer persistence. Though she was nice enough—certainly not mean, anyway—she didn't seem eager for friends. I followed her around at recess and asked her questions.

"Do you watch TV?"

"No."

"Do you like movies?"

She shrugged.

"Do you like boys?"

She rolled her eyes. "Nuh-uh."

Phyllis didn't know how to jump rope, but she was willing to bounce a ball back and forth with me. One day I snuck a bag of potato chips out of our house and gave them to her.

"Thank you," she said, a little confused.

"Oh, sure," I said. "We have a lot."

She carried the puffy bag all during recess, afraid it would get stolen if she put it down. She couldn't play ball with her hands full, so we walked around the playground a while, then leaned against the school building.

"Hey," she said. "You want to come by my house?"

"O.K.," I said. Then, "Where is it?"

"It's far," said Phyllis. "You can take my bus tomorrow."

* * *

I decided against telling my mother. It was none of her business, and anyway, she was busy with her new date, Prentice, who seemed to be over all the time. He was short and bald, and had a loud voice and a glass eye. He called my mother 'Reen.

"Hey, 'Reen!" he'd shout across the kitchen at her. "How about that sandwich you mentioned?"

Or,

"'Reen! Where'd I leave my beer?"

He always seemed a little surprised when I came into the room, as if he'd forgotten I lived there too.

"Oh, hey there, kiddo," he'd yell. "What's cooking?"

"Nothing," I'd say.

I didn't know what my mother liked in him, unless it was his loudness, his lack of pretense. My grandfather called him A Solid Fellow.

"You know what you're getting with old Prentice," he said. "What you see is what you get, with him."

So, with a permission note I'd written myself in a careful imitation of my mother's backhand, I got onto Phyllis's bus. The children who rode this route seemed a slightly rougher crowd; a little dirtier, shiftier. I sat squeezed in between Phyllis and Tamitha, who, she said, was Phyllis's cousin. They lived next door to each other.

We took the highway out of Faberville, then turned on to a red dirt road that wound through pine woods. There were deep green ditches on either side of the road, and garbage—old appliances, tires, sofa cushions—scattered among the trees. The houses we stopped at were sad and dilapidated; some appeared to be tacked together out of flattened coffee cans, some had boarded-up windows and no doors. Old cars, chickens, dogs, and trash filled the yards. There were no lawns.

Phyllis's house was a trailer—blue metal with an addition made of planks. Chairs circled a smoking pile of trash in the yard, and a big spotted dog was twisting around on a rope tied to tree.

"He don't bite," said Phyllis. "Don't even bark. Barking dogs give me fits."

Several small children got off the bus with us, and two or three ran ahead of us into the trailer. Before we got there, though, a woman came out the door, a toddler dragging on her skirt.

"Who you got there?" she said to Phyllis.

"My friend," said Phyllis.

The toddler was waving what looked like a hard-boiled egg at the mother and saying, "Peel a egg! Peel a egg!" The mother picked the child up and took it inside.

"We should play out here," said Phyllis.

"What do you want to do?" I asked.

She shrugged.

We sat in the chairs and poked the trash fire with sticks, and Phyllis told me about everyone who lived in the trailer. She had three brothers, a sister, a mother, and her mother's boyfriend, a man named Paul who was turning white.

"Turning white?" I said.

She nodded seriously. "Whiter than you." Then she added, "I also got a dead sister. I'm the only one can see her."

I said, "You can't see her if she's dead."

"I can," said Phyllis. "I got power."

"Huh."

"It's true."

I didn't say anything. The fire was going out, so I bent down to blow on it. Ashes swirled up and got in my hair.

"Well," I said, "my father used to make movies."

She looked surprised. "He did?"

"Uh-huh."

I spent the next half hour describing, in careful detail, the plot of the last movie I'd seen—a spy thriller called *Double Duty* that my grandfather took me to. In it, a spy murders a woman by putting a poison snake in her purse. Phyllis listened carefully, then showed me a nest of snakes behind the trailer.

It was getting late. I asked her if I could use her phone to call my mother.

"Don't got a phone," she said.

The nearest telephone, it turned out, was at Tamitha's house. Phyllis held my hand as we walked there through the weeds.

My mother was surprised to hear from me.

"I thought you were in your room." she said.

"I'm at my friend's house," I told her, and tried to describe where it was.

There was a long pause. Then, "What are you doing out there?"

"I told you. I'm at my friends house."

'Well," she said.

Phyllis and I sat out by the road to wait for her. It had begun to get dark, and a thin mist floated over the ditch. Frogs cried from the trees.

Then, for no reason that I could tell, Phyllis had a fit. She struggled quietly in the grass for several seconds, and then I pulled her onto my lap, wrapping her arms around my chest as I'd seen Tamitha do. I held her loosely while she shuddered, her head bumping my stomach and her hands fluttering in the weeds.

I looked away.

When she woke up, I slid her off my legs and watched her blink up at trees.

"That trailer," I said after a while, "is about two sticks of dynamite away from oblivion."

Phyllis sat up and wiped her mouth. "Fell over last time it flooded," she said.

When I got into the car with my mother, I felt like I had forgotten how to talk. I wanted to say something about Phyllis — her fits, her brothers and sisters, her mother's boyfriend who was turning white. Though my tongue moved, nothing I said sounded right; it was as if I was speaking a language I hadn't heard in years. My mother didn't notice. She seemed preoccupied.

"I'm glad you have a friend." she said.

She chewed on her lower lip, fiddled with her hair in the rearview mirror as she drove. After a while she said, "You know, I think I'm going to marry Prentice."

I couldn't think of anything to say to this.

"I mean," she said, "he asked. He said he'd build me a house, one of those log cabins from a kit." She glanced at me, then looked back at the road. "You'd say yes, wouldn't you?"

We rattled down the dirt road, passing houses and trailers that were lit up inside. People were eating dinner. When we hit the highway everything got suddenly quiet; the tires made an electric hum on the grooved asphalt. It reminded me of the sound before a movie begins, the scratch of film threading through the machine.

She might help him build it, she said. It would take a long time, maybe a year. Until then, she could live with him in his apartment in Hammond, about twenty miles away.

"It's pretty small, the apartment, I mean," she said. "I guess what I'm saying is, you should probably stay here with your grandfather. Don't you think?"

"I don't know."

"You can visit any time you like," she said.

Over the next few weeks, I began to spend more and more time al Phyllis's house. After school and weekends, sometimes until dark, and I rode my bike so no one had to drive me. I got along well with Paul, the boyfriend—his face and arms were splotched with pale pink, and some of his hair was an odd, artificial blond— but Phyllis's mother didn't seem to like me much. She stayed in the house when I came over, and didn't invite me in.

I brought candy for Phyllis. My mother got it for me, paper sacks full, and even whole boxes of chocolate-covered cherries. She hadn't left yet, but she was getting ready; she had a new gold engagement ring and spent much of her time leafing through furniture catalogs. I stuffed the candy into baggies and put it in the pocket of my jacket, and took it out when Phyllis went into one of her quiet spells. She could go hours without saying anything more than "okay" and "all right."

But she was getting tired of my bribes, uncertain what she owed me. One afternoon I gave her a whole bag of suckers. She took out a green one and left the rest of the bag in the grass, without saying anything.

"You want to look for snakes?" I asked her.

She shook her head.

We kicked some rocks into the ditch, broke some twigs and threw them in too. I was thinking that I might go home when I heard a car coming up the road.

It was my mother driving by, very slowly, peering out the windshield. Prentice was in the passenger seat, and the back of the car was full of her things.

When she saw me she stopped. I thought she'd get out, and she might have, if I'd gone running toward her. But I didn't. I folded my arms and looked at the ground, looked at the grass. I heard the car start up again, and watched it bump gently over the ruts in the dirt road. I watched it go and didn't move.

"That your mama?" asked Phyllis.

I turned to her. The sun was brilliant. It shined on Phyllis's arms and forehead, and I realized how beautiful she was, and how tall. It enraged me.

"Fall!" I shouted.

To my shock, the green sucker flew from her mouth and she pitched to the ground. I watched as she thrashed in the dirt. When she got up again, there was a twig in her hair, a streak of blood on her lip, a wary smile on her face. Her hand shook.

"Fall!" I shouted again.

Rhian Margaret Ellis went to Oberlin College and the University of Montana. In between she taught elementary school in rural Louisiana. She recently won a Henfield Foundation/*Transatlantic Review* grant, and now lives in Missoula, Montana, where she edits *Teacup* magazine.

*T*here's a real family of demolitionists living somewhere in this country, and they do go from city to city imploding buildings. I saw them on television. It struck me that once you started doing that for a living, it would be awfully hard to stop. Watching big things fall is both fascinating and horrifying. Even seeing a tree fall over gives me goose bumps: it's hard to look at, but impossible not to.

Charles East

PAVANE FOR A DEAD PRINCESS

(from *The Southern Review*)

At an earlier time, at any one of a number of earlier times, Mrs. Miller would have resisted, but now, sitting here in her apartment overlooking the Gulf, it was as natural as . . . as, Mrs. Miller thinks, breathing. Her mind goes back to an evening years before in Memphis. One of her husband's business acquaintances, an architect, had taken them to see his elderly cousin—or perhaps it was a great-aunt, she couldn't remember. But she remembered the house, the fire in the grate, the cousin/great-aunt seated there on the sofa under the portrait done of her by a painter who had come down from the North—that was what she said—a painter who had come down from the North to paint her. The old lady must have been in her nineties.

Mrs. Miller herself was young then—she must have been in her forties that evening in Memphis. But age at that time meant so very little to her. She would have known only that the cousin/great-aunt was old and that the boy who came out of the back of the house to be introduced was making his home with her—this, Warren's friend told them. No, a boy to Mrs. Miller *now; then* he was a young man who looked to be in his thirties, though if there was one thing she had learned it was that looks could be deceiving. Age, she thought, was the least dependable of things—relative. He had not made much of an impression on her. He said very little—indeed seemed to hover just outside the fringes of the conversation. His name was Julian—for some reason, perhaps because it was not a name with which she was familiar, Mrs. Miller remembered it.

She did recall that at one point the old lady—Mrs. Holmes—had turned to the young man and asked him to play the piano for them. "Julian plays beautifully," she said. "Julian, be an angel and play for us."

Mrs. Miller thought the boy would as soon not have, but he went to the piano, lifted the key cover, and without getting out any music played a piece for them—a very short piece, she remembered, something that was familiar to her though she could never think of it, probably Ravel or Debussy. Mrs. Holmes looked pleased and glanced at them to see how they reacted. They all praised him for it and asked him to play more, but he modestly declined the invitation.

Mrs. Holmes seemed to have an almost unnatural vitality that Mrs. Miller had noticed in some women her age. She talked of working in her rose garden, and of her trips to North Carolina, where she said she enjoyed climbs to the mountaintops. But that was obviously some time in the past, for she also mentioned how distressing it had been to have to give up her car—driving her car. Warren's friend, the architect, had told them that she had a 1939 Packard. She had never driven in her husband's lifetime, she said. There was no need to. But once she learned, once she got behind the wheel of a car, "there was no going back"—she had gained her independence. That was her only reference to her late husband.

The young man sat there on the sofa by her and took in every word. Once he interrupted, or rather added the postscript that of course Mrs. Holmes had him to drive her wherever she wanted to go—a remark that clearly pleased the old lady. Altogether, Mrs. Miller thought, it was a curious evening.

Later, when Warren's friend was driving them back to their hotel, he made insinuating remarks about the boy. The old lady had adopted him. "At least," he said, "that's the story." The boy had shown up suddenly, or perhaps not so suddenly—Warren's friend admitted that it was months, sometimes years, between his own visits with her. One version had it that Julian was a cousin—a cousin on her mother's side, but so distant that no one else in the family had ever heard of him. There was even a story to the effect that she had married him, though not for the usual reasons, he told them with a sly laugh, but because she wanted the protection of the law that marriage would give her—give him—in matters of property.

Mrs. Miller remembered disliking Warren's friend for his insinuations and thinking there was very likely nothing to them. Her husband was less critical, but then he always had been. Warren wondered aloud about the house, what would become of it. It was one of those splendid late-Victorian residences with stained-glass windows and huge sliding oak doors that separated the rooms and a magnificent oak staircase. The reason, in fact, that Warren's friend had arranged for them to see it.

"Well, of course," he said, anticipating the question, "whatever he gets, I'd say he deserves it."

"What an awful man," she said to Warren when they got back to their room. "How on earth did you meet him?" Mrs. Miller was of an earlier school that believed the sheep and the goats—and those with and those without—should be separated. She despised above all else commonness.

Her husband was more tolerant. He had also been brought up in a society that believed in its own privileges, but he had been a banker long enough to know that the *withouts* sometimes become the *withs,* and that when they do, one should pay attention to them.

Mr. Miller laughed. "The way I figure it," he said, "is that Richard . . ."—Richard was the architect—". . . is that Richard was having regrets he hadn't been nicer to her."

Now, sitting here in her apartment overlooking the Gulf with night coming on, Mrs. Miller recalls another visit to Memphis.

She and Warren were passing through on their way to Nashville a few years later. On the spur of the moment they decided to leave the highway and drive through the old residential section of the city, past Baptist Hospital and the other landmarks they remembered from their earlier visit. But when they came to the street on which Mrs. Holmes had lived, they found only cleared ground where the house had stood. The home on the adjoining property, another of those Victorian mansions, was still there, but beyond it, to the end of the block, was a string of doctors' offices. Mrs. Miller felt a shudder run through her. Gone, just like that, she thought.

"What do you suppose ever happened to the boy?" Warren asked her.

She didn't answer, but her dislike of the architect who had accompanied them to the house returned instantly.

"Probably did well for himself," Warren said, and that was the end of the conversation. They drove back to the highway and continued on their way to Nashville.

Mrs. Miller remembers a summer much later, the summer after Warren died—ten years or more before Ellen died. Oh, Mrs. Miller thinks, to lose a child . . . there is nothing harder. She and Ellen had talked of taking a trip, perhaps to Pawley's Island, where Mrs. Miller and her mother had gone, or—closer to home—New Orleans. They'd decided on New Orleans. She recalls packing and Ellen getting out that red silk dress and that ridiculous straw hat, which wouldn't have gone at all with the lipstick she was wearing. It was a bad time for Ellen. She and George were having trouble—had been almost since the day they were married. But, Mrs. Miller thinks, it wasn't as if I didn't warn her. That was Ellen: she never listened to anybody.

But what a lovely girl, what a lovely, lovely girl, she thinks. Her father's eyes. When Warren looked at you, you couldn't deny him anything. But unfortunately, as so often happens, the daughter had inherited her father's disposition. No self-control. No self-discipline. Mrs. Miller could never understand it.

But the thought of that evening in Memphis reminded her of the trip she and Ellen made to New Orleans. They had driven down that summer after Warren died. She'd always liked New Orleans; it seemed to her such a civilized city while at the same time winking at the coarse and the common, for there was nothing, she thought, more common than Mardi Gras. Kings and queens in preposterous costumes throwing beads from floats. Crowds of people jostling one another. Not her idea of fun. It was the other New Orleans Mrs. Miller liked, the elegance of St. Charles Avenue, the moss-hung trees in the Garden District, even the dark green streetcars with their wicker seats and the bell that the motorman rang to clear the tracks ahead. And of course Galatoire's—she loved to dine at Galatoire's.

Ellen had a friend who lived in an apartment on the edge of the French Quarter, and one afternoon they rode the streetcar out St. Charles and wandered through the Garden District. You could do that then. Polly, Ellen's friend, asked if they would like to go into one of the houses. The old lady who owned the place had been a friend of Polly's grandmother. So Polly called and a visit was arranged, a time in late afternoon; the sun was still high in the sky at that time of the year in New Orleans.

They sat on the upstairs back gallery overlooking a garden fragrant with cape jasmine and hanging baskets of petunias and the other plants that grew there in those days. Mrs. Hays, for that was the old lady's name, was ageless, Mrs. Miller thought. She must have been in her eighties, but she could easily have passed for seventy-five or even seventy. She had lived all her life in New Orleans—had been born in one of the downstairs bedrooms in this very house, had been married in the double parlors. "And," she told them—Mrs. Miller remembers this distinctly—"I have left instructions that I am to be buried from the house. I've told them if they bury me from the funeral parlor I'll come back to haunt them." Mrs. Hays smiled, satisfied that *that* had settled *that*.

"But Aunt Lily," Polly said—Mrs. Hays was not her aunt except in the Southern manner of speaking—"you're going to outlive us all. You're going to be coming to our funerals."

Ellen nodded. Mrs. Miller nodded. The old lady smiled. She recognized the lie for what it was and was appreciative of it.

At that moment one of the shuttered doors down the gallery opened, and a young man came out and reminded Mrs. Hays that it was time for her medicine. Mrs. Miller noticed that he wore a white Palm Beach suit and carried a small tray on which she could see the pill—an ugly little red one—and a glass of water. Without a word Mrs. Hays took the pill, put it on the back of her tongue, and drank a swallow of the water. "Thank you, Louis," she said.

The young man did not respond but set the tray on a wicker table, pulled up a chair, sat down, and lit a cigarette, a gesture that offended Mrs. Miller. She'd never heard of a young man lighting a cigarette in the presence of ladies without asking their permission, and certainly not in New Orleans. Nor did he make any attempt to introduce himself.

But Mrs. Hays did not seem to notice. "Louis," she said, "is my eyes—my ears too. I don't know what I'd do without him."

The young man did not appear to have heard her. He stared down into the garden with an empty look that told Mrs. Miller his mind was probably somewhere other than in New Orleans. Then, as if suddenly aware they were looking at him, he turned back to Mrs. Hays and asked if she would like him to bring her a wrap; there was a breeze off the river that pulled at the ends of the old lady's white hair. Mrs. Miller thought she might be shivering.

"No, dear," the old lady said, and as if anticipating what might be going through their heads, she told them how good the young man had been to her. "And such good company. Knows all the gossip in New Orleans." And to him, "Louis, will you tell Camilla to serve the coffee?"

The young man got up, crushed out his cigarette on the tray, and disappeared inside the house.

There were so many questions Mrs. Miller would have liked to ask Mrs. Hays, but the opportunity did not present itself. Was Louis another of the servants? She imagined not. How long had he been there? What kind of life did he have beyond the cast-iron fence and the luxuriant garden? And of course Mrs. Miller—a bit older now, wiser—would have liked to know where he slept.

The last of these questions was answered when Ellen's friend said, "Aunt Lily, you don't mind, do you, if I take them through the house?"

"Why no," the old lady replied. "Go ahead. I'm just going to sit here. Polly, be sure to show them the clock."

It was a tall grandfather clock that stood at the head of the stairs. Mrs. Hays's grandfather had made it—or at least had built the case. Polly told them he had been a cabinetmaker.

Mrs. Hays's bedroom was at the front of the house and looked out onto the street. The bed was a graceful four-poster with a tester, probably mahogany or walnut, Mrs. Miller thought. No doubt a family heirloom. Clearly the smaller room adjoining was the one the young man occupied—his clothes, his shoes (among them, to Mrs. Miller's amazement, a pair of cowboy boots) were in the closet. In the bathroom she saw his comb and brush and razor on a small table by the lavatory. She had not really thought they shared a bedroom, but she was relieved to see they did not, and then annoyed with herself for having suspected that they might. She hoped Ellen's friend had not somehow read her thoughts.

"A charming house," Ellen said when they were seated again on the gallery.

"Yes," Mrs. Miller said, "perfectly lovely," and she commented on the clock, what a treasure it was. She had always made it a practice to tell people exactly what they wanted to hear. "And you were so sweet to let us see it, but we really must go now. . . . Ellen, get your things, we really must go now."

"Well," the old lady said, "I can't tell you how much I've enjoyed this. I seldom get out anymore, you know. Just Louis and me here, the two of us. But you must come again." And she raised her voice. "Louis . . ."

In that instant the young man reappeared from inside the house.

"Louis, would you show these ladies to the door?" she said.

As he was showing them the way down the stairs, Mrs. Miller noticed that he had taken off his tie and that his shirt was open at the neck. She was also aware that there was a sexual energy about him. She wondered if Ellen had felt it, or Ellen's friend, or if it was only she. At any rate, she was certain it was there.

In a letter written a few weeks after their return home, Polly told them of Mrs. Hays's death. She had simply slipped away in her sleep: *The way we would all want to go*, Polly wrote. Mrs. Hays had been buried from one of the St. Charles Avenue funeral homes. *Not what she wanted*, Polly wrote, *but her nieces preferred it. The story goes around that she left a nice sum of money to Louis and that the nieces plan to contest it. You remember Louis? I'm sure at the funeral poor Louis seemed quite broken up.*

Mrs. Miller shivers in the chill of the evening's last light. In a moment she will get up and turn on the lamp. She thinks of Warren. Dear, sweet Warren, that blue-eyed boy she loved so, wanted from the moment she saw him, loved in spite of all. Oh, Warren knew how to make you forgive him, how to make you overlook everything, except maybe the one thing, and that was what love was all about, wasn't it?

I've grown old, Mrs. Miller thinks. I've outlived my husband and my child, and nobody should do that. But I don't want to die either. Is that foolish of me?

She calls Ellen—calls out her name as if Ellen were there. It is the closest she has come in a very long time to venting her heart. She knows Ellen is dead and will not be coming back. And even if Ellen can hear her—and, Mrs. Miller thinks, who's to say she cannot?—how is she to know?

She waits. Through the double windows she sees lights on the water—a boat coming in from the Gulf. Then the lights pass from view, and she is looking into the dark again.

On the gallery that afternoon in New Orleans she saw something, the subtlest of gestures, a movement of a hand. The young man touched Mrs. Hays's arm, probably without intending to; the old lady instinctively pulled away—a movement so slight that in the bat of an eye Mrs. Miller might have missed it.

And again, another evening in another city, years later, she saw, or thought she saw, the same quick movement, that hesitation, that almost involuntary act of pulling back from something. It was in a hotel on the Gulf Coast: the old lady and the young man seated in the lobby, in those times when people—and the very best people—still sat in lobbies. The young man wore white shoes with his white suit, and he was quite attentive—fussed over the old lady, left her and went up in the elevator and came back with a shawl, helped her up and then offered her his arm, and they went into the dining room together. There was something else that she noticed: a girlishness, almost a flirtatiousness about the old lady that Mrs. Miller found unbecoming.

She herself was with a friend of her mother, then in her seventies, and the friend's unmarried daughter. The daughter was Mrs. Miller's age or older; she did a good deal of talking and had little to say—the curse of Southerners, Mrs. Miller thought. She was a Southerner herself, but she had lived too long in the North. She despised in them what she herself had never been: a bore, a chatterbox. She detested mindless conversation. But on and on the daughter rattled, at last coming back to the young man and the old lady, who were now seated at a table across the dining room from them. She wondered aloud if they were a couple, and if they were, how long they had been married, hinting somewhere in her chatter (Mrs. Miller's mind had wandered) that perhaps the marriage was not what it seemed. She had known one instance, she said, of a lady, traveling abroad, who had married a man forty or more years younger than she in order to bring him into the country.

Her mother lifted her eyebrows, exactly *why* Mrs. Miller could not be certain—probably raising the question of whether or not the marriage had been consummated. Mrs. Miller kept her thoughts to herself but was of the opinion that sex was the last thing that would interest a woman of eighty—wrong, as she was to discover, but she was then in her fifties.

The lady who had known her mother was not about to let the story go. She recalled an elderly cousin who had died soon after a young man showed up at her door one day. "Call it coincidence if you like," she said.

Mrs. Miller listened and said nothing. Life, she had learned from living it, was a series of mysteries.

Her mother's friend waited for a few moments before continuing. "There are angels of death," she said. "Oh, yes. I'm telling it as it was told to me. They come . . ." She looked in the direction of the other table. "Well, they are, as it was told to me, a sort of escort service."

The daughter laughed. "Mother!"

"Oh, it's true," her mother said. "I've seen it. I don't know how many times I've seen it."

So when the knock came Mrs. Miller was not surprised at all, but in the most peculiar of ways welcomed it. She got up and crossed the dark room, stopped to turn on the lamp by the sofa, made her way into the foyer.

The knock came again. Mrs. Miller stood at the door, not quite certain what she would do. Yet it occurred to her that she had been here before, stood at this same door, heart pounding as it was now, as if she were about to embark on the most extraordinary journey.

"Yes?" she called. "Yes?" This time louder.

Through the door she could hear a man's voice—she thought it was a man's—but she was unable to understand what he was saying.

Oh, Warren . . . Ellen, she thought, I know I'm getting ready to do something foolish, don't blame me.

Once, when she was a child and full of absurd fears, she had spent many of her nights dreaming. She had dreamed of falling from a great height. It was terrifying. She had wondered, in her dream, whether the fall would kill her, but always she had awakened before the fall ended. Or other nights, in the same dream, she had simply landed, feet first, safely on the ground, and after many of these she knew, even as she dreamed, that the fall would not hurt her. But the point was that it might, one night it might—there was always that possibility.

When the knock came again Mrs. Miller unlatched the chain and opened the door to him. As she did, something that she thought might be terror seized her. But almost in the same instant it passed.

His skin was pale, and he had a blush of red in his cheeks and long, sandy lashes. The bluest of eyes. The face, she thought, of an angel. He reminded her of a boy she had known once a thousand years ago at Pawley's Island. The boy's name was . . . well, she couldn't remember it now, in a little while it would come to her, but this boy did turn her mind back to him.

Then she saw that he was wearing a Mardi Gras costume. At least she thought it was a costume—he'd taken off his cap and mask and was holding them, but he was wearing a red devil's suit with a tail. He had a pitchfork in one hand.

"I think I've come to the wrong apartment," the young man said. "I'm looking for 204B—there's a party."

Mrs. Miller stood there for a moment and stared at him. "Oh?" she said. She was at the same time relieved and disappointed, but most of all puzzled. After she had caught her breath and gathered her wits she pointed him on his way—the party was in the next building, probably those girls with the three-legged cat and the friends who raced up and down the beach on their motorcycles. The last she saw of him he was dragging his red tail down the stairs.

Mrs. Miller laughed. When she had closed the door she sat down on the sofa and laughed again. She knew she ought to be embarrassed.

* * *

The angel of death never came for Mrs. Miller. It was the supreme disappointment of her life. No one came to escort her, or to look after her, or to light her cigarettes, or to listen to her stories, or to entertain her guests with a tune from Debussy. No, it was Ravel: "Pavane for a Dead Princess." Yes, Mrs. Miller thought, that was what it was—that was the piece the young man had played for them that evening in Memphis. It had been on the tip of her tongue all these years. But no young man came to do any of these things for her, and she was a part of no one's stories about how an old lady had brought a young man into her home, possibly (stories had a way of developing out of nothing at all) married him.

After a while Mrs. Miller grew tired of waiting and checked herself into a nursing home, where she died in her ninety-first year, deeply disillusioned but also wiser: she'd wasted too much time waiting, she'd spent too much time remembering Warren and Ellen and trying to figure out what she might have done differently. She'd been too critical of people. Common *is* as common *does,* her mother had told her, but she had missed the point. All those rules she'd memorized about what was the right thing and the wrong thing and what was common or not common really didn't matter. Didn't matter a damn, Mrs. Miller thought.

But she never discounted the stories—there *were* young men who came and took you out of this life, she was sure of it. Probably she had seen one—in Memphis and, unlikely place, New Orleans. For what else was Julian, driving Mrs. Holmes around Memphis in her 1939 Packard, and what else was Louis, with his white Palm Beach suit and the cowboy boots she'd seen sitting on the floor in his closet? It was just that one never came for her.

Toward the end, somewhere between four and five o'clock on a rainy spring morning when the nursing home was quiet, there was a knock at Mrs. Miller's door. She was at low ebb and tired of living, and she roused and told whoever it was to enter. But when the nurse on duty turned the knob and pushed her way into the room, Mrs. Miller was already dead.

Charles East is the author of *Distant Friends and Intimate Strangers,* the 1996 collection in which "Pavane for a Dead Princess" appears, and an earlier book of short fiction, *Where the Music Was.* He lives in Baton Rouge, Louisiana. A native of Mississippi and a former director of the Louisiana State University Press, he edits the Flannery O'Connor Award for Short Fiction series for the University of Georgia Press.

*P*avane for a Dead Princess" *grew out of a conversation I had with Eudora Welty one evening in 1985 at a celebration marking the 50th anniversary of* The Southern Review. *She and I were seated next to each other at dinner and were exchanging Mississippi stories — as Mississippians do. I recalled for her an occasion many years earlier when my wife and I were invited by the Greenville, Mississippi, literary light Ben Wasson to accompany him to a party at the home of one of the grandest of Greenville's grande dames. It was an evening that combined elements of Tennessee Williams and* Sunset Boulevard. *At some point soon after our arrival the lady brought over a young man who appeared to be in his twenties and introduced him to us. Her husband, I thought she said — an eyebrow-raiser, for the lady was then in her eighties. Had my wife and I heard her wrong? No, Ben said, when I got him aside to raise the question. And he filled us in on all the particulars, as only Ben could.*

Eudora liked the story, and had one of her own: another lady of some years, another young man who quite suddenly appeared on the scene.

A few days later I sat down and wrote the opening paragraph of a story about a woman who waits for the knock at her door that will announce the arrival of a young man who may or may not be the Angel of Death. But for years the story stopped there. Then in 1995 I got it out and picked up where I had left off. The young man in the Mardi Gras costume — a devil suit with tail — came to me on the third or fourth draft.

APPENDIX

A list of the magazines currently consulted for *New Stories from the South: The Year's Best, 1997,* with addresses, subscription rates, and editors.

Agni
Boston University Writing Program
236 Bay State Road
Boston, MA 02215
Semiannually, $14.95
Askold Melnyczak

Alabama Literary Review
253 Smith Hall
Troy State University
Troy, AL 36082
Annually, $5
Theron Montgomery, Editor-in-
    Chief

American Literary Review
University of N. Texas
P.O. Box 13827
Denton, TX 76203
Semiannually, $15
Fiction Editor

American Short Fiction
Parlin 14
Department of English
University of Austin
Austin, TX 78712-1164
Quarterly, $24
Laura Furman

The American Voice
Kentucky Foundation for
    Women, Inc.

332 W. Broadway, Suite 1215
Louisville, KY 40202
Triannually, $15
Frederick Smock, Editor
Sallie Bingham, Publisher

The Antioch Review
P.O. Box 148
Yellow Springs, OH 45387
Quarterly, $35
Robert S. Fogarty

Apalachee Quarterly
P.O. Box 10469
Tallahassee, FL 32302
Triannually, $15
Barbara Hamby

The Atlantic Monthly
745 Boylston Street
Boston, MA 02116
Monthly, $17.94
C. Michael Curtis

Black Warrior Review
University of Alabama
P.O. Box 862936
Tuscaloosa, AL 35486-0027
Semiannually, $14
Christopher Chambers

Boulevard
P.O. Box 30386

Philadelphia, PA 19103
Triannually, $12
Richard Burgin

Carolina Quarterly
Greenlaw Hall CB# 3520
University of North Carolina
Chapel Hill, NC 27599-3520
Triannually, $10
Fiction Editor

The Chariton Review
Truman State University
Kirksville, MO 63501
Semiannually, $9
Jim Barnes

The Chattahoochee Review
DeKalb College
2101 Womack Road
Dunwoody, GA 30338-4497
Quarterly, $16
Lamar York, Editor

Cimarron Review
205 Morrill Hall
Oklahoma State University
Stillwater, OK 74078-0135
Quarterly, $12
Fiction Editor

Columbia
404 Dodge Hall
Columbia University
New York, NY 10027
Semiannually, $15
Nick Schaffzin

Confrontation
English Department
C.W. Post of L.I.U.
Brookville, NY 11548
Semiannually, $20
Martin Tucker, Editor

Crazyhorse
Department of English
University of Arkansas at Little Rock
2801 South University
Little Rock, AR 72204
Semiannually, $10
Judy Troy, Fiction Editor

The Crescent Review
P.O. Box 15069
Chevy Chase, MD 20825-5069
Triannually, $21
J. Timothy Holland

Crucible
Barton College
College Station
Wilson, NC 27893
Semiannually, $12
Terrence L. Grimes

CutBank
Department of English
University of Montana
Missoula, MT 59812
Semiannually, $12
Fiction Editor

Double Dealer Redux
632 Pirate's Alley
New Orleans, LA 70116
Quarterly, $25
Rosemary James

DoubleTake Magazine
Center for Documentary Studies
1317 W. Pettigrew Street
Durham, NC 27705
Quarterly, $24
Robert Coles and Alex Harris

Epoch
251 Goldwin Smith Hall
Cornell University

Ithaca, NY 14853-3201
Triannually, $11
Michael Koch

Fiction
c/o English Department
City College of New York
New York, NY 10031
Triannually, $20
Mark J. Mirsky

Five Points
GSU
University Plaza
Department of English
Atlanta, GA 30303-3083
Triannually, $15
Fiction Editor

The Florida Review
Department of English
University of Central Florida
Orlando, FL 32816
Semiannually, $7
Russ Kesler

The Georgia Review
University of Georgia
Athens, GA 30602-9009
Quarterly, $18
Stanley W. Lindberg

The Gettysburg Review
Gettysburg College
Gettysburg, PA 17325-1491
Quarterly, $24
Peter Stitt

Glimmer Train
812 SW Washington Street, Suite 1205
Portland, OR 97205-3216
Quarterly, $29
Susan Burmeister-Brown and Linda
  Davis

GQ
Condé Nast Publications, Inc.
350 Madison Avenue
New York, NY 10017
Monthly, $20
Ilena Silverman

Granta
250 W. 57th Street
Suite 1316
New York, NY 10017
Quarterly, $34
Ian Jack

The Greensboro Review
Department of English
University of North Carolina
Greensboro, NC 27412
Semiannually, $8
Jim Clark

Gulf Coast
Department of English
University of Houston
4800 Calhoun Road
Houston, TX 77204-3012
Semiannually, $22
Fiction Editor

Gulf Stream
English Department
Florida International University
North Miami Campus
North Miami, FL 33181
Semiannually, $8
Lynne Barrett

Harper's Magazine
666 Broadway
New York, NY 10012
Monthly, $18
Lewis H. Lapham

Habersham Review
Piedmont College
Demorest, GA 30535-0010
Semiannually, $12
David L. Greene

High Plains Literary Review
180 Adams Street, Suite 250
Denver, CO 80206
Triannually, $20
Robert O. Greer, Jr.

Image
P.O. Box 674
Kennett Square, PA 19348
Quarterly, $30
Gregory Wolfe

Indiana Review
316 N. Jordan Avenue
Bloomington, IN 47405
Semiannually, $12
Fiction Editor

The Iowa Review
308 EPB
University of Iowa
Iowa City, IA 52242-1492
Triannually, $18
David Hamilton

The Journal
Ohio State University
Department of English
164 W. 17th Avenue
Columbus, OH 43210
Semiannually, $8
Kathy Fagan and Michelle Herman

Kalliope
Florida Community College
3939 Roosevelt Blvd.
Jacksonville, FL 32205
Triannually, $12.50
Mary Sue Koeppel

The Kenyon Review
Kenyon College
Gambier, OH 43022
Quarterly, $22
Fiction Editor

The Literary Review
Fairleigh Dickinson University
285 Madison Avenue
Madison, NJ 07940
Quarterly, $18
Walter Cummins

The Long Story
18 Eaton Street
Lawrence, MA 01843
Semiannually, $9
R. P. Burnham

Louisiana Literature
P.O. Box 792
Southeastern Louisiana University
Hammond, LA 70402
Semiannually, $10
David Hanson

Lynx Eve
c/o Scribblefest Literary Group
1880 Hill Drive
Los Angeles, CA 90041
Quarterly, $20
Pam McCully

Mid-American Review
106 Hanna Hall
Department of English
Bowling Green State University
Bowling Green, OH 43403
Semiannually, $12
Robert Early, Senior Editor

Mississippi Review
Center for Writers
University of Southern Mississippi
Box 5144

Hattiesburg, MS 39406-5144
Semiannually, $15
Frederick Barthelme

The Missouri Review
1507 Hillcrest Hall
University of Missouri
Columbia, MO 65211
Triannually, $19
Speer Morgan

The Nebraska Review
Writers Workshop
Fine Arts Building 212
University of Nebraska
   at Omaha
Omaha, NE 68182
Semiannually, $9.50
Art Homer

Negative Capability
62 Ridgelawn Drive East
Mobile, AL 36608
Triannually, $15
Sue Walker

New Delta Review
English Department
Louisiana State University
Baton Rouge, LA 70803-5001
Semiannually, $7
Erika Solberg

New England Review
Middlebury College
Middlebury, VT 05753
Quarterly, $23
David Huddle

The New Yorker
20 W. 43rd Street
New York, NY 10036
Weekly, $36
Bill Buford, Fiction Editor

The North American Review
University of Northern Iowa
Cedar Falls, IA 50614-0516
Six times a year, $22
Robley Wilson

North Carolina Literary Review
English Department
East Carolina University
Greenville, NC 27858-4353
Semiannually, $17
Alex Albright and Thomas E.
   Douglas

Northwest Review
369 PLC
University of Oregon
Eugene, OR 97403
Triannually, $20
John Witte

The Ohio Review
290-C Ellis Hall
Ohio University
Athens, OH 45701-2979
Semiannually, $16
Wayne Dodd

Ontario Review
9 Honey Brook Drive
Princeton, NJ 08540
Semiannually, $12
Raymond J. Smith

Other Voices
University of Illinois at Chicago
Department of English
   (M/C 162)
601 S. Morgan Street
Chicago, IL 60607-7120
Semiannually, $10
Fiction Editor

Oxford American
P.O. Drawer 1156

Oxford, MS 38655
Bimonthly, $24
Marc Smirnoff

The Paris Review
541 E. 72nd Street
New York, NY 10021
Quarterly, $34
George Plimpton

Parting Gifts
March Street Press
3413 Wilshire Drive
Greensboro, NC 27408
Semiannually, $8
Robert Bixby

Pembroke Magazine
Box 60
Pembroke State University
Pembroke, NC 28372
Annually, $5
Shelby Stephenson, Editor

Playboy
680 N. Lake Shore Drive
Chicago, IL 60611
Monthly, $29
Alice K. Turner, Fiction Editor

Ploughshares
Emerson College
100 Beacon Street
Boston, MA 02116-1596
Triannually, $19
Don Lee

Prairie Schooner
201 Andrews Hall
University of Nebraska
Lincoln, NE 68588-0334
Quarterly, $24
Hilda Raz

Puerto del Sol
Box 30001, Department 3E
New Mexico State University
Las Cruces, NM 88003-8001
Semiannually, $10
Kevin McIlvoy

Quarterly West
317 Olpin Union Hall
University of Utah
Salt Lake City, UT 84112
Semiannually, $11
M. L. Williams

River Styx
3207 Washington Avenue
St. Louis, MO 63103
Triannually, $20
Richard Newman

Salmagundi
Skidmore College
Saratoga Springs, NY 12866
Quarterly, $18
Robert Boyers

Santa Monica Review
Santa Monica College
1900 Pico Boulevard
Santa Monica, CA 90405
Semiannually, $12
Lee Montgomery

Shenandoah
Washington and Lee University
Troubadore Theater
2nd Floor
Lexington, VA 24450
Quarterly, $11
R. T. Smith

Snake Nation Review
110 #2 W. Force Street

Valdosta, GA 31601
Triannually, $20
Roberta George

The South Carolina Review
Department of English
Strode Tower Box 341503
Clemson University
Clemson, SC 29634-1503
Semiannually, $10
Frank Day

Southern Exposure
P.O. Box 531
Durham, NC 27702
Quarterly, $24
Pat Arnow, Editor

Southern Humanities Review
9088 Haley Center
Auburn University
Auburn, AL 36849
Quarterly, $15
Dan R. Latimer

The Southern Review
43 Allen Hall
Louisiana State University
Baton Rouge, LA 70803-5005
Quarterly, $20
James Olney

Sou'wester
Southern Illinois University at
    Edwardsville
Edwardsville, IL 62026-1438
Semiannually, $10
Fred W. Robbins

Southwest Review
Southern Methodist University
Dallas, TX 75275
Quarterly, $24
Willard Spiegelman

Story
1507 Dana Avenue
Cincinnati, OH 45207
Quarterly, $36.96
Lois Rosenthal

StoryQuarterly
P.O. Box 1416
Northbrook, IL 60065
Quarterly, $16
Diane Williams

Tampa Review
Box 19F
University of Tampa Press
401 W. Kennedy Boulevard
Tampa, FL 33606-1490
Semiannually, $10
Richard Mathews, Editor

The Threepenny Review
P.O. Box 9131
Berkeley, CA 94709
Quarterly, $16
Wendy Lesser

TriQuarterly
Northwestern University
2020 Ridge Avenue
Evanston, IL 60208
Triannually, $24
Reginald Gibbons

The Virginia Quarterly Review
One West Range
Charlottesville, VA 22903
Quarterly, $15
Staige D. Blackford

West Branch
Bucknell Hall
Bucknell University
Lewisburg, PA 17837
Semiannually, $7
Robert Love Taylor

Whetstone
Barrington Area Arts Council
P.O. Box 1266
Barrington, IL 60011
Annually, $7.25
Sandra Berris

William and Mary Review
College of William and Mary
P.O. Box 8795
Williamsburg, VA 23187
Annually, $5
Forrest Pritchard

Wind Magazine
P.O. Box 24548
Lexington, KY 40524
Semiannually, $10
Charlie G. Hughes

Yemassee
Department of English
University of South Carolina
Columbia, SC 29208
Semiannually, $15
Tracy Simmons Bitonti

ZYZZYVA
41 Sutter Street
Suite 1400
San Francisco, CA 94104-4903
Quarterly, $28
Howard Junker

PREVIOUS VOLUMES

Copies of previous volumes of *New Stories from the South* can be ordered through your local bookstore or by calling the Sales Department at Algonquin Books of Chapel Hill. Multiple copies for classroom adoptions are available at a special discount. For information, please call 919-967-0108.

New Stories from the South: The Year's Best, 1986

Max Apple, BRIDGING

Madison Smartt Bell, TRIPTYCH 2

Mary Ward Brown, TONGUES OF FLAME

Suzanne Brown, COMMUNION

James Lee Burke, THE CONVICT

Ron Carlson, AIR

Doug Crowell, SAYS VELMA

Leon V. Driskell, MARTHA JEAN

Elizabeth Harris, THE WORLD RECORD HOLDER

Mary Hood, SOMETHING GOOD FOR GINNIE

David Huddle, SUMMER OF THE MAGIC SHOW

Gloria Norris, HOLDING ON

Kurt Rheinheimer, UMPIRE

W. A. Smith, DELIVERY

Wallace Whatley, SOMETHING TO LOSE

Luke Whisnant, WALLWORK

Sylvia Wilkinson, CHICKEN SIMON

New Stories from the South: The Year's Best, 1987

James Gordon Bennett, DEPENDENTS

Robert Boswell, EDWARD AND JILL

Rosanne Coggeshall, PETER THE ROCK

John William Corrington, HEROIC MEASURES/VITAL SIGNS

Vicki Covington, MAGNOLIA

Andre Dubus, DRESSED LIKE SUMMER LEAVES

Mary Hood, AFTER MOORE

Trudy Lewis, VINCRISTINE

Lewis Nordan, SUGAR, THE EUNUCHS, AND BIG G.B.

Peggy Payne, THE PURE IN HEART

Bob Shacochis, WHERE PELHAM FELL

Lee Smith, LIFE ON THE MOON

Marly Swick, HEART

Robert Love Taylor, LADY OF SPAIN

Luke Whisnant, ACROSS FROM THE MOTOHEADS

New Stories from the South: The Year's Best, 1988

Ellen Akins, GEORGE BAILEY FISHING

Rick Bass, THE WATCH

Richard Bausch, THE MAN WHO KNEW BELLE STAR

Larry Brown, FACING THE MUSIC

Pam Durban, BELONGING

John Rolfe Gardiner, GAME FARM

Jim Hall, GAS

Charlotte Holmes, METROPOLITAN

Nanci Kincaid, LIKE THE OLD WOLF IN ALL THOSE WOLF STORIES

Barbara Kingsolver, ROSE-JOHNNY

Trudy Lewis, HALF MEASURES

Jill McCorkle, FIRST UNION BLUES

Mark Richard, HAPPINESS OF THE GARDEN VARIETY

Sunny Rogers, THE CRUMB

Annette Sanford, LIMITED ACCESS

Eve Shelnutt, VOICE

NEW STORIES FROM THE SOUTH: THE YEAR'S BEST, 1989

Rick Bass, WILD HORSES

Madison Smartt Bell, CUSTOMS OF THE COUNTRY

James Gordon Bennett, PACIFIC THEATER

Larry Brown, SAMARITANS

Mary Ward Brown, IT WASN'T ALL DANCING

Kelly Cherry, WHERE SHE WAS

David Huddle, PLAYING

Sandy Huss, COUPON FOR BLOOD

Frank Manley, THE RAIN OF TERROR

Bobbie Ann Mason, WISH

Lewis Nordan, A HANK OF HAIR, A PIECE OF BONE

Kurt Rheinheimer, HOMES

Mark Richard, STRAYS

Annette Sanford, SIX WHITE HORSES

Paula Sharp, HOT SPRINGS

NEW STORIES FROM THE SOUTH: THE YEAR'S BEST, 1990

Tom Bailey, CROW MAN

Rick Bass, THE HISTORY OF RODNEY

Richard Bausch, LETTER TO THE LADY OF THE HOUSE

Larry Brown, SLEEP

Moira Crone, JUST OUTSIDE THE B.T.

Clyde Edgerton, CHANGING NAMES

Greg Johnson, THE BOARDER

Nanci Kincaid, SPITTIN' IMAGE OF A BAPTIST BOY

Reginald McKnight, THE KIND OF LIGHT THAT SHINES ON TEXAS

Lewis Nordan, THE CELLAR OF RUNT CONROY

Lance Olsen, FAMILY

Mark Richard, FEAST OF THE EARTH, RANSOM OF THE CLAY

Ron Robinson, WHERE WE LAND

Bob Shacochis, LES FEMMES CREOLES

Molly Best Tinsley, ZOE

Donna Trussell, FISHBONE

NEW STORIES FROM THE SOUTH: THE YEAR'S BEST, 1991

Rick Bass, IN THE LOYAL MOUNTAINS

Thomas Phillips Brewer, BLACK CAT BONE

Larry Brown, BIG BAD LOVE

Robert Olen Butler, RELIC

Barbara Hudson, THE ARABESQUE

Elizabeth Hunnewell, A LIFE OR DEATH MATTER

Hilding Johnson, SOUTH OF KITTATINNY

Nanci Kincaid, THIS IS NOT THE PICTURE SHOW

New Stories from the South: The Year's Best, 1992

New Stories from the South: The Year's Best, 1993

Richard Bausch, EVENING

Pinckney Benedict, BOUNTY

Wendell Berry, A JONQUIL FOR MARY PENN

Robert Olen Butler, PREPARATION

Lee Merrill Byrd, MAJOR SIX POCKETS

Kevin Calder, NAME ME THIS RIVER

Tony Earley, CHARLOTTE

Paula K. Gover, WHITE BOYS AND RIVER GIRLS

David Huddle, TROUBLE AT THE HOME OFFICE

Barbara Hudson, SELLING WHISKERS

Elizabeth Hunnewell, FAMILY PLANNING

Dennis Loy Johnson, RESCUING ED

Edward P. Jones, MARIE

Wayne Karlin, PRISONERS

Dan Leone, SPINACH

Jill McCorkle, MAN WATCHER

Annette Sanford, HELENS AND ROSES

Peter Taylor, THE WAITING ROOM

New Stories from the South: The Year's Best, 1994

Frederick Barthelme, RETREAT

Richard Bausch, AREN'T YOU HAPPY FOR ME?

Ethan Canin, THE PALACE THIEF

Kathleen Cushman, LUXURY

Tony Earley, THE PROPHET FROM JUPITER

Pamela Erbe, SWEET TOOTH

Barry Hannah, NICODEMUS BLUFF

NEW STORIES FROM THE SOUTH: THE YEAR'S BEST, 1995

NEW STORIES FROM THE SOUTH: THE YEAR'S BEST, 1996

Robert Olen Butler, JEALOUS HUSBAND RETURNS IN FORM OF PARROT

Moira Crone, GAUGUIN

J. D. Dolan, MOOD MUSIC

Ellen Douglas, GRANT

William Faulkner, ROSE OF LEBANON

Kathy Flann, A HAPPY, SAFE THING

Tim Gautreaux, DIED AND GONE TO VEGAS

David Gilbert, COOL MOSS

Marcia Guthridge, THE HOST

Jill McCorkle, PARADISE

Robert Morgan, THE BALM OF GILEAD TREE

Tom Paine, GENERAL MARKMAN'S LAST STAND

Susan Perabo, SOME SAY THE WORLD

Annette Sanford, GOOSE GIRL

Lee Smith, THE HAPPY MEMORIES CLUB

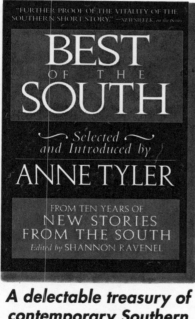